KIN

KEALAN PATRICK BURKE

Copyright © 2012 Kealan Patrick Burke

Cover Design by Elderlemon Design

All rights reserved.

ISBN: 1479110493
ISBN-13: 978-1479110490

DEDICATION

For Doogie, and the staff at The Delaware County 911 Center

OTHER BOOKS BY THIS AUTHOR

The Turtle Boy
The Hides
Vessels
Peregrine's Tale
Nemesis
Stage Whispers
Master of the Moors
Currency of Souls
Midlisters
Thirty Miles South of Dry County
Ravenous Ghosts
The Number 121 to Pennsylvania & Others
Theater Macabre
Jack & Jill
Dead of Winter
Dead Leaves
Digital Hell
You In?

(as editor)

Taverns of the Dead
Quietly Now
Brimstone Turnpike
Tales from the Gorezone

PRAISE FOR *KIN*

"If you're a fan of Jack Ketchum, Richard Laymon, or movies like *The Texas Chainsaw Massacre* and *Deliverance*, don't miss *Kin*. Burke's novel not only re-imagines the classic slasher tropes, but it invents new ones. This is a modern classic, and I cannot recommend it highly enough." - *Fearnet*

"If you took the moral quandaries about revenge, justice and violence against evil from Dennis Lehane's Patrick Kenzie novels, spread it over the sprawling cast of a Stephen King thriller, and mixed it with the Southern Gothic grotesques of Eudora Welty, you might end up with something like Kealan Patrick Burke's new novel, *Kin*." - *Litstack*

"From the first chapter I found myself comparing *Kin* to the absolute best work of Jack Ketchum, James White Wrath, and Richard Laymon. You might be thinking that I've listed an awful lot of great authors here and mentioned more than a few classics in this review and that there's no way this book could live up to that hype. You'd be wrong. *Kin* is not only the best novel I've read all year, it is one of the most horrifying ones I've ever read. I hope you give it a shot." – *Horror World*

"It's odd that an Irish transplant to the Northern US has written one of the best Southern Gothic novels in recent memory. I'll look forward to Burke's next work just as much as I hated to see this one end. I would highly recommend *Kin* to lovers of old fashioned horror fiction with a twist. If you're going to read just one noir cannibal revenge novel this year, *Kin* should fit the bill." - *Dark Discoveries*

"*This* is serious horror fiction that has set a high standard for future stories in this subgenre. Don't miss it." - *The Crow's Caw*

ONE

Elkwood, Alabama
July 15th, 2004

Everything is dead.

Naked, bloodied and stunned, the sun high in the cloudless sky and scalding her sweat-slicked skin, Claire Lambert nevertheless managed to note that the stunted, bone-white tree in the field to her right was the same one she'd commented on a few days, months, or years earlier, though what she might have said about it was a mystery now. She stopped walking—if indeed she'd been walking at all, for the sensation thus far was one of being still, spine bent, the road moving like a granite-studded conveyor belt beneath her torn and filthy feet—and squinted at the gnarled trunk, which looked like an emaciated mother with an elaborate wind-wracked headdress, twisted limbs curled protectively around its womb, knees bent, feet splayed and poking out from beneath the hem of a skirt that had been washed and worn a few times too often.

It fascinated Claire, and though she swayed as if she might fall on legs that had many miles ago ceased registering as anything but independent creatures burdened with her weight, she couldn't look away. Fire licked with cold tongues at her groin; the blood in her hair hardened, and whatever vile substance now lay in a gelid, solidifying lump in the hole which had once contained her right eye, ticked as if someone had replaced it with a watch to measure the time she had left. But still she looked, still she stared, as the merciless sun turned her scalp pink and cooked the flesh on her back. Sweat, cooler in the scant shade beneath her breasts, fell like tears. At length, she twitched, and her legs shuffled her toward the barbed wire fence that separated the field from the road. Cotton whispered in the breeze as her stomach met the wire, the barbs pressing deep into the skin; she felt nothing but an involuntary shiver. A startled bird exploded from the cotton with a cry that dragged her attention to its whickering form as it soared high, then lost itself in the blinding blanket of the sun. Claire lowered her head, licked dry, cracked lips with a sandpaper tongue and pushed again against the fence, unable to understand why her progress was being halted. Surely no one would begrudge her a conference with that tree, a taste of the maternal comfort she felt it might offer. Again she pushed, and again she was withheld. This time the barbs pierced her skin. Troubled, she took a half-step back, the black wire thrumming like a guitar string strummed by the breeze. A single drop of her blood welled from the iron tip of a barb and hung, suspended in time, refusing the sun, before it plummeted and colored crimson a finger of grass. Frowning, she looked slowly from the wire to the tree, as if the blame might lay with that withered woman, and tried to speak, to beg. A thin whistle was all that emerged from her parched throat—*Help me*—and she swallowed what felt like a handful of hot stones.

A sound.

She turned, reluctant to look away from the tree, but drawn by the only other noise she had heard thus far not immediately attributable to nature, or that soft voice inside her chanting incessantly and with tireless determination that everything was dead. A strand of her hair snagged on her lower lip, and stayed there, held in a fissure where the skin had split.

Raging white light thundered toward her. Of this she was only dimly aware, for between that light and where she stood swaying, was a man with no face or hands. No, that wasn't quite right. Daniel still had his hands, but they no longer had skin and looked impossibly dark and raw. This didn't concern her, for rarely had he held her anyway—a lapse in affection of which she had once upon a time hoped to disabuse him.

Why won't you hold my hand?

Because we're not kids anymore, babe.

But at the sight of that flayed skull, a tear, like the blood on the wire, defied the sun and spilled from her one good eye.

"We can hitch a ride," he told her, though his lips never moved. The raw ragged open wound of his face, topped by a nest of unruly brown hair, turned to nod at the glaring light behind him, which had grown closer still. The mirrored sun floated above shimmering metal, the wheels grinding up thick mustard-colored clouds.

She opened her mouth to respond, to tell her boyfriend that they really should wait for the others, but even had she possessed the voice to convey the words, a sudden bolt of dazzling pain tried to scissor her in half, forcing her to double over as she vomited into the dirt at her feet.

Everything is dead.

Her head swelled as she watched a dark red river flow from her mouth, turning dust to rust and spattering her ankles. The veins in her neck stuck out in thick cords, her ruined eye began to burn and throb, making it feel as if her brain was trying to force its way out of her, to distance itself farther from this confusing reality than she had thus far managed on her own.

Weakened, she dropped to her knees, felt the ground abrade the skin there. But there was no pain. Her flesh had become a thick heavy coat, and the many tears in the lining affected her not at all. Her palms slid into the dirt.

The sound of squealing might have been of old hinges in the doors of the earth opening to accept her; it might have been her own struggle to breathe against a torrent of vile regurgitated panic and grief, or it might have been the brakes on the car she'd seen coming because now a new voice, a strange voice, drifted down to her sunburned ears as a figure eclipsed the sun and a cool shadow was thrown like a blanket over her bare back.

"Jesus, Mary'n Joseph'n all the holy saints," it said. "What happened, Miss?"

It's them, she thought feebly. *One of them come to take me back. To hurt me again.* It was the same knowledge that had kept her going this far, the unmistakable feeling of being watched, stalked, hunted, meant to die but breathing still.

She shook her head to deny him. Opened her mouth to speak but only blood emerged, the river of sickness forcing her throat to swell. Still she tried to struggle, but when she raised her hands to protect herself, it happened only in her mind. Her limbs would not respond. The pair of dusty boots that had pressed into her field of vision moved away.

Good. Go. Leave me alone. You've done enough. Everything is dead. You killed them all.

"Christ, Pete, get me that 'ol dog blanket an' the flask. Move!"

At last the dizzying current ceased and she found strength enough to raise her head. The man was a wiry knot of shadow under a crooked hat, a scarecrow with a golden halo, trying to deceive her into thinking him salvation. Dread pounded at her chest, igniting further knots of pain that seemed to radiate from the core of her.

Another shadow sprouted from the man's shoulder, this one just as thin, but without a hat, just a fuzz of hair.

They're here to kill me.

"Oh God, lookit her eye."

"Shut your fool mouth, boy."

"What happ'ned to her? She ain't got no clothes on." The voice was filled with nervous excitement.

The hatless shadow was elbowed aside. The thin one flapped its arms until its chest became wings descending around Claire, swaddling her.

"Help me carry her."

She opened her mouth to moan at the sudden, terrible heat enveloping her and felt new warmth seep from between her legs. The dirt turned dark quickly.

"Pa she done wet hers—"

"*Now.*"

Before the arms could press their wings even tighter around her, Claire took a series of quick, dry, painful swallows, then drew in a breath that sounded like nails on a blackboard, and screamed for Daniel. But even as that tortured, awful noise poured out of her, and though she was surrounded by shadows that were lifting her up and carrying her back to Hell, she knew for the first time in her life that she was well and truly alone, and that no help was coming now, or ever.

TWO

 The smell of burned flesh, though only a figment of his imagination, made Luke's mouth water. He was hungry, his dinner having been interrupted not a full hour before by the sound of Matthew's keening from the woodshed. It had reminded him of that day when they were kids, when Luke had observed his younger brother trying to skin a deer they had taken down with a bow and arrow. Luke had known the excitement and desire to prove himself would lead Matt to make a mistake, and he'd been right. With a wide smile on his face, and sweat on his brow, Matt had held up the fistful of pelt he'd managed to free from the deer, his other hand still digging that Bowie knife into the carcass as he sought approval from Luke. *Told'ya I could.* Before Luke could satisfy him, the pelt slipped free of Matt's grip and the momentum made his other hand snap back. The blade cut a thin half-inch-deep groove through Matt's bare side, just below the ribs. Luke doubted it hurt very much, but it was enough to send his brother to his knees, hands grabbing fistfuls of hair as he vented his shame and disappointment in that irritating singsong keening sound—the same sound he'd used earlier today after the blonde woman drove a wooden spur through his chest.
 Anger made Luke forget himself and he rose from where he'd been crouching atop a grassy hillock. Up ahead, an old black man and his boy were helping his brother's attacker into the back of a flatbed truck. Helpless to do anything but watch, he'd been tracking the woman on this road, which few folk ever traveled, biding his time before he closed the distance and dragged the woman back to make her pay for what she'd done. Rage had made him abandon the traditional rules of running down the quarry and he'd stayed on the road, in full view of the woman. She hadn't seen him, and was moving slower than a crippled coon. Even if she had looked over her shoulder and spied through the heat haze his lean sinewy form

striding toward her, there was no chance she'd get away. She was bleeding a lot, and he didn't figure she'd get very far.

It should not have been a difficult task.

But damned if she hadn't kept on staggering away, her pace even despite her obvious disorientation. It was as if, instead of just floundering blindly through the woods, she'd been drawn to the road like an iron filing to a magnet. Still, he hadn't hurried. There was no need. He'd been confident despite the ache that throbbed steadily within him whenever it came back to him that Matt was hurt, and hurt bad.

But then Luke heard the truck, and noted the sound of the engine was not a safe, familiar one, and he'd quickly hopped the fence and ducked down in the grass, watching with queer, unfamiliar dread the red vehicle bearing down on the woman.

Claire, he remembered. One of the others had called her "Claire".

No one ever got away. Not for long. To let someone escape was an unthinkable, unimaginable mistake they had managed to avoid for as long as Luke had been alive. Papa-in-Gray had showed them how and what to hunt, and why it needed to be done, and they had executed his instructions flawlessly.

But today...

Today an implausible number of distractions had left Matt alone with the woman. Even so, she'd been tied to a stake, her hands and feet bound behind her, her mouth gagged. His brothers had already raped her and blinded her in one eye, cut off most of the toes on her right foot, and stabbed her repeatedly in the arms and legs. There should have been little life and even less fight in her, but yet somehow she'd managed to free herself and skewer Matt with the spur. She'd been gone damn near half an hour before Luke, oldest of his five brothers, heard Matt's pitiful mewling, and by then he'd all but bled out on the floor.

He knew it was not too late. He could still try to close the distance between himself and the truck before they got the woman settled and the engine running again, before they carried *Claire* out of their lives forever. If the two men he'd seen hefting her into the truck put up a fight, he'd deal with them. He had Matt's Bowie knife, plucked from his brother's hand with a vow to finish what the other had been denied the chance to do. Luke was quick. He could make it, and all their troubles would be over. All he needed to do was start running.

But then he heard the sound of the engine coughing, saw the dirty black plume of smoke puffing from the truck's exhaust, and knew it *was* too late. Slowly, he started moving toward the fence, and the road beyond. He wanted to scream at the top of his lungs, tear at his hair, rip at his skin, but instead he hopped the fence, and raced in the opposite direction, away from the truck, and back the way he'd come.

When he'd left home, Matt had been conscious. Breathing. Alive. That Joshua, Isaac and Aaron hadn't piled into the truck and come roaring down the road in pursuit of the woman told Luke that might no longer be the case.

Most telling of all, Luke realized, was that *he* hadn't thought to take the truck. He couldn't drive for shit, not with the way his fingers were arranged, but that was no excuse. Not now. He had always been an efficient hunter, and he knew the real reason his brothers weren't coming was because they assumed Luke would handle what needed to be handled. But for the first time ever, they were wrong. He had lost them their prey. And he knew what that would mean when he returned home. He would have to answer to Momma-In-Bed, and she would not be at all pleased. And the last time she'd been mad at him, she'd gotten Papa-In-Grey to bust the fingers on his left hand and set all but the thumb and the middle one wrong.

Dispirited and fearful, he slowed, and whispered a small prayer to God that she would go easy on him. But as the sun rose higher, became a blazing eye in the center of the cornflower blue sky, he knew two things at once.

God wasn't listening. Not to him. No more than Papa ever did.

And that today, there was every possibility that Momma-In-Bed would kill him.

* * *

"Stop starin'."

"Sorry, Pa."

"Watch the road."

Pete nodded and righted himself in the passenger seat. They had covered the girl with a tarp, which was all they had, but just now, through the small begrimed window at the back of the cab, Pete had seen that a corner of the tarp had come loose, flapping madly at the billowing dust the Chevy was kicking up and exposing the girl's right side, down to her hip. One small breast was visible and despite it being crisscrossed by cuts and scratches, the boy's breath had quickened, his heart beating faster and faster the longer he looked. He didn't even know if she'd been a pretty girl before whatever had happened to her. It was hard to tell because of her wounds, and the swelling, which made her face look like a beaten squash. He hoped she was, and that once she recovered—assuming she didn't die right there among the tools and empty chicken cages—that she might take the kind of interest in him he'd thus far been unable to excite in members of the fairer sex; maybe as a thank you for rescuing her.

Of course, it had really been his father who had plucked the wounded woman from the road, but Pete would be in no hurry to dissuade any misguided gratitude she might choose to throw his way in the first few days of her convalescence. And it wasn't like the old man hadn't needed his help.

"What do you think happ'ned to her?" he asked his father again.

"Animals."

Resisting the urge to glance back over his shoulder again, Pete focused on the road being sucked beneath the old Chevrolet's grille. "Never seen an animal do that to someone," he muttered. "D'you see her eye?"

"She's gonna be all right," his father told him, but he had the same look on his face he got on those days when the wind was high and the clouds above their farm were black and mean and boiling and ready to send whirling devils down to tear their place asunder. "You just sit quiet now. We'll bring her to the Doc's. He'll fix her up."

"Think he'll be able to save her?"

Instead of responding, the old man reached out a withered hand and jabbed at the radio. Low twangy music and his father's long low sigh infiltrated the silence. A moment later, the sickly sweet aroma of burning tobacco filled the cab as his father touched a flame to the tip of a crumpled hand-rolled cigarette. It was a smell that comforted Pete, a familiar scent that always seemed to drift through his skull and stroke some sense into the wild dog of his thoughts. He smiled slightly and went back to looking out the window.

He didn't care if the wounded girl wasn't pretty under all that blood and other stuff. He wasn't much to look at either and didn't think it fair to judge others by standards he didn't meet himself. And he'd had a bad heart since birth, which he figured maybe explained why he was always so quick to hope that whatever wounded bird he encountered would view him as her savior and love him accordingly. Repairing his flawed heart was not a job he would ever be able to do on his own, which, in a town like Elkwood—comprised mostly of hard-faced, hardworking men—meant his chances of dying young were better than average.

He wasn't afraid to die.

He was afraid to die alone.

At one time, Valerie Vaughn down at the grocery store had been the object of his fixation. She'd always been kind to him, and for a time, he might have loved her, until he summoned up the courage to confess as much and she'd folded in on herself like a deckchair with a bad leg, told him that was "nice" then went to great lengths to avoid ever having to talk to him again.

There were others, of course, all highly unlikely to ever give him the time of day, or stay around Elkwood long enough to see him as anything other than a not-so-bright farm boy with aspirations that didn't stretch farther than the town's borders.

Valerie had left, bound for Birmingham.

After that he'd quickly grown tired and discouraged by the amount of polite refusals or horrified rejections, the gleeful mockery and cruel teasing, and instead had taken his father's advice and focused on work at the farm.

And now they'd found an outsider—hurt, lost, and in desperate need of help. Help he could give her if she let him.

A nervous flutter in his stomach reminded him that all he was doing was setting himself up for more disappointment, more heartbreak, more blows to his fragile heart. *She's a stranger. She's prob'ly got a guy in some big city somewheres. She's prob'ly hitched. You're bein' a damn fool.*

As always, however, hope gave him the strength to ignore those warnings, and whatever reason or sense might have inveigled its way into them.

He smiled.

This one would stay.

He could feel it.

THREE

Luke knew there were three kinds of silence. There was the ordinary kind—when there was no one around to make a sound, like when he wandered down to the junkyard a half-mile from his home, where they flattened and crumpled up the cars they decided they had no use for, after flattening and crumpling up their owners. That was where he went for peace and quiet, to gather his thoughts, sometimes to pray.

Then there was the kind of silence you heard when it only *looked* like you were alone, when someone was watching you, hidden and holding their breath. That silence was different, heavier because it was unnatural, forced. And it never lasted long. Luke had long ago learned that no matter how clever, or scared they were, people were not good at staying quiet, even if it meant the difference between life and death. He had no idea how many of their victims might have gotten away, even for a little while, if they'd just held their breath a moment longer, or choked back a whimper or a sob, or watched where they were going.

The third kind of silence was when you were surrounded by people, all of them staring without seeming to breathe, none of them moving or saying a word because what they had to say was written in their eyes, and that message was not good. This was the worst kind of silence, the most dangerous kind.

This was the one Luke found himself faced with when he finally made it home.

A light rain had started as he'd crested the hill and started down the slope toward the house, as if God himself had chosen a side, and it wasn't Luke's. From his elevated position, he'd been able to see that the rain had not discouraged his brothers. Joshua, Isaac and Aaron were standing in a ragged semicircle in front of the house, facing him. Matt was a dark bundle lying in the mud before them, and there was no doubt that he was dead. He was on his back, shirt soaked with blood, eyes glassy and open, staring unblinkingly up at the rain coming down. Luke stopped a few feet away from him. "When?" he asked, as though it mattered. He was speaking merely to break the silence, which had already begun to coil like morning mist around him.

"Soon's you was gone," Aaron told him eventually, a hard edge to his voice. No grief at all, but plenty of swallowed pain. "Where's the girl at?"

Luke shook his head, unable to meet his brother's eyes. He did not want to see in them the disgust, the fear, and the relief that Aaron was not likely to suffer the same degree of punishment for letting the girl escape as he would. He almost expected his brothers to ask how she'd evaded him and where he thought she might have gone, but of course they didn't. It didn't matter now. Very soon they would have to uproot themselves and find someplace else to settle down, a task that, despite Momma-In-Bed's insistence that they not tie themselves to anything or indulge in luxuries they couldn't move at a moment's notice, would not be easy. It would mean a lot of hard work done quickly, all the time looking over their shoulders and listening for the sound of sirens. It would mean a new kind of silence for their family: an absolute absence of sound that might at any moment be broken by the enemy, by the Men of the World, as Papa called them, threatening the only world they knew.

"Momma-In-Bed wants to see you," Aaron said. "Tole me to tell you soon's you got back. 'Straight away,' she said. 'Don't even stop to make water. I want 'im in my room, soon as you see his face,' she said."

Luke finally looked up, and his younger brother's long narrow ashen face, made longer by the close cut of his dark hair, was grim. He couldn't tell if Aaron was getting any satisfaction from being the bearer of such a message, nor did he thank him for it, for they were not given to gratitude. Acknowledging it only risked opening themselves up to empathy for their victims, who were so often uncannily good at trying to evoke it from them.

"I'll go see her then," Luke answered, and took one last look at Matt, lying there looking perfectly at ease with his death, the picture of calm marred only by the small rusty-red puddles forming in the mud around his body, the deep dark puncture wound in his chest, and the scarlet rivulets meandering their way toward where Luke stood watching. "You boys go start the fire."

The twelve-year-old twins—Joshua, who could speak just fine but seldom did, and Isaac, who'd had his tongue cut out when he was nine years old for cussing at Papa-In-Grey—both nodded dutifully and hurried off toward the barn where they kept the stacks of old wood, a fragment of which the girl had used to end their brother's life. In the rain, they were going to need kerosene to get the fire to catch, so Luke mumbled instructions to this effect to Aaron and watched his brother lumber off, shoulders hunched, toward the small ramshackle shed with walls of badly rusted corrugated iron where they'd hung and skinned one of the girl's friends.

Then, with a shuddering sigh, he knelt briefly in a puddle of Matt's blood, and said a short prayer, intended not solely for the dear departed, but for himself too. He asked for forgiveness, and courage, but didn't wait to find out if either had been bestowed on him. Somehow he doubted it. Far too much had gone wrong for him to expect any mercy from God or anyone else.

Luke rose up and started up the steps into the house.

* * *

After what seemed like an eternity of waiting, Doc Wellman finally emerged from the bedroom he had once shared with his wife until her death in '92. Nowadays he slept on a tattered sofa in his living room, and always with the TV on and the volume turned low. He couldn't sleep without it. It was all he had for company. That, and the few patients willing to travel thirty miles outside of town to see him. He had witnessed much in his lifetime, not the least of which was the slow and painful decay of his wife in those endlessly long weeks before the cancer finally took her, but it was clear from the deathly pallor on his face as he stood before the old black man and his boy, that he had never seen anything quite like this.

Driven by equal parts excitement and impatience, Pete stood first, leaving his father sitting alone on the small wicker bench in the hall. "She alive?" the boy asked, searching but not finding the answer in the aged doctor's expression.

Wellman was so thin his limbs were like broom handles snapped over someone's knee, his chest a deflated accordion topped by a long face writhing with wrinkles in which small blue eyes, magnified by a pair of rimless spectacles, shone with surprising alertness. Those eyes looked troubled now as they found the boy's face. Pete had expected to be ignored, that whatever the doctor said would be directed toward his father, and so was pleasantly surprised to find the doctor addressing him directly. "Yes," he said in a quiet voice. "She is, but barely."

"Will she make it?" Pete persisted.

"I think so, though she's lost quite a bit of blood."

The boy let out a breath he hadn't realized he'd been holding.

"Who did this to her?" Wellman asked, frowning. "I can't imagine anyone..." He trailed off, and put a hand to his mouth as if censoring a line of thought that would yield answers he preferred not to hear.

"Animals," Pete's father said again, as if he'd been programmed to give that response whenever the question was put to him.

The doctor dropped his gaze from the boy to his father. "Not unless we got animals in this state can work a knife, Jack."

Pete looked to his father to see how this news had affected him. It hadn't, or if it did, he was doing a fine job of hiding the fact. In the dull gray light through the windows in the hall, all he saw on the old man's face were shadows.

"No," Wellman said, "Wasn't animals did this. Poor girl's been cut up something terrible. Beaten too. She's got a concussion, multiple fractures, and a couple of busted ribs. Whoever took a blade to her used it to take out one of her eyes and lop off a few of her fingers and toes. If it was an animal, the wounds would be ragged, Jack. No." He sounded as if he didn't believe it was possible or didn't want to believe it, but knew there was no other explanation. "Someone real angry wanted her to die, and die slow." He shook his head and touched a pair of trembling fingers to the small silver crucifix that hung around his neck. Then he sighed and stepped away from the boy. "Either one of you called the Sheriff?"

Pete shook his head. "I guess we wanted to get her here 'fore it was too late."

"Well that was the right thing to do, but we'd best give Hal a call now. Need to tell him he's got some kind of lunatic out there running around chopping up women." He started to move down the hall, but Jack stood and put a hand on his arm. Wellman looked at it like it was a strange species of exotic spider that had just dropped from the ceiling.

With a pained expression on his face, Pete's father leaned in close to the doctor and said in a low voice, "You can't. Not 'less you want more people in that room of yours tonight."

Puzzled, Wellman slowly withdrew his arm from the man's grip. "You know something I don't?"

Jack licked his lips and nodded slowly. "I do, but might be better if you didn't hear it." His gaze, which Pete was shocked to see was one of fear, dropped to the floor. "Now if you're sayin' that girl's gonna make it, I reckon me and Pete's done about all we can and we'll just head on home and leave her to you."

Wellman studied Jack's face. "What's going on?"

"Leave it, Doc. Please. It's the best thing to do."

"The hell it is, Jack. Someone's gonna be missing that girl and I don't know where to start. That's Sheriff's work right there, and how's he gonna help if he don't know about it?" He glanced at Pete and a funny look passed over his face. "You boys didn't have anything to do with this, did you?"

Pete felt as if he'd been punched. "Hell no, Doc. We found her just like that, honest we did. She was on the road, throwin' up blood. I reckon if we hadn't come along she'd be roadkill right now, or cooked in the sun. Me and Dad loaded her up and came right here, ain't that right?"

"That's right," Jack said, his gaze still directed at the floor as if something down there was of fierce interest to him. "This wasn't our doin'."

"But you know whose doing it was?"

Jack said nothing for a moment, then raised his head and looked hard at his son. "Go on out to the truck."

"But I want—"

"*Now*."

Pete knew it would be unwise to argue. He'd been on the receiving end of the back of his father's hand for less. But before he obeyed, he asked Wellman, "Can I come back'n see her?"

"If it's all right with your Pa."

"We'll see," Jack said, which Pete knew was as good as a "no", and stepped aside to indicate the boy needed to get moving.

"Thanks for patchin' her up," Pete said to the doctor.

The old man nodded. "Wouldn't have been a whole lot I could've done if you boys hadn't picked her up. You saved her life, I reckon."

"Will you tell her we was the ones brought her in?"

"Sure, son."

Reluctantly, the boy did as he was told, passing between the men and through an invisible cloud of their intermingled scents: sweat, tobacco, and disinfectant. Once clear of them, however, he took his time making his way to the door, pretending to admire the sparsely furnished interior of the doctor's house, hoping to hear just what it was his father knew, but they said nothing, obviously aware he was still within earshot. Aggravated by questions unanswered, he opened the front door and stepped out into the rain.

* * *

"You know I've got to report this, Jack."

"I know."

"Then you'd best give me a hell of a good reason why I shouldn't or that's exactly what I'm gonna do."

Jack was afraid. Good sense had abandoned him over the past few hours and all because he'd had the boy in the truck with him. If he'd just left Pete at home, he could have done what reason and common goddamn sense had suggested and just kept driving when he saw the girl in the road. Sure, the guilt would have weighed heavily on him later, but that was what whiskey was for, and it wouldn't be the first round of it he'd had to deal with. After sixty-one years of hard living, he'd gotten pretty good at sweeping things under the rug and stomping them down until they were easier to walk over than study. But he knew the boy wouldn't have let it go. He was too simple, too unaware that there was a great big gray area between right and wrong, especially when it meant putting yourself in harm's way. He had not yet been educated on the kind of monsters who preyed on Samaritans.

Jack had spotted the girl before Pete, but had kept his mouth shut, even tried to distract the boy so he might miss it, told him it looked like a storm if those thunderheads coming over the hills to the left of them were anything to go by. He should have known the boy would catch on. He rarely said two words to his son unless he had to— in all his years he'd never truly learned how—and certainly wasn't given to idle banter, so instead of looking out his window at the clouds, and away from the girl, Pete frowned and looked at his father instead. And from there, his eyes had drifted to the crumpled form at the side of the road. Even so, even when Pete had grabbed Jack's arm hard and pointed at the girl, he'd considered just stepping on the gas and telling the boy what he was telling the doctor now.

"It's just...trouble, Doc."

"What kind of trouble?"

Jack searched for a way to say what he wanted without saying too much, but his mind was a jumble of unfinished thoughts and burgeoning panic. It needed numbing. He ran a hand through his hair and looked beseechingly at Wellman. "You got somethin' to drink?"

The doctor nodded. "Come on into the kitchen."

FOUR

In the strained light of the ageing day, Pete inspected the rust-colored stains on his fingers, then held them out to the rain. It was strange to have her blood on his skin, something she would not have shared with him had the choice been hers. A secret she was not yet aware he'd been let in on, a part of her she might not yet know was missing. When they were wet enough, he withdrew his hands and rubbed them together, then wiped them on his jeans. It made him feel a little sad, almost disrespectful, as if her blood was of little consequence to him, like dirt he was anxious to be rid of. Nothing could be further from the truth. As he lingered before Doctor Wellman's door, still hoping to overhear something of the discussion inside, but thus far unable to make out much over the grumbling of distant thunder and the hiss of the rain, he wished he were inside. Not with the men and their whispering, but in the girl's room, if only so she would have someone there when she woke up. He hated the thought of her being alone, as she had been alone when they'd come upon her, as she must have felt when her attacker had done those horrible things to her. Alone, helpless, lost. It made his heart hurt to think of her that way.

Stepping out from the shelter of the porch, he narrowed his eyes against the rain and looked at the truck. It stared back, headlights dull, chrome fender long past gleaming.

Pete dug his hands into his pockets. *You don't even know her.* He exhaled through his nose. He wondered how long his father would be inside. He was a man of few words, so Pete guessed it wouldn't be long. Then again the way he'd looked in the hall, all wrapped up in himself, made it seem as if he had plenty to tell.

He glanced to his left, at the two windows at the front of the doctor's house. The window to the girl's room would be somewhere around back.

Leave her be.

Knowing he was probably making a mistake, and one that might get him in a world of hurt and trouble, he nevertheless ducked low and moved away from the truck, toward the corner of the house.

* * *

They sat facing each other at a small square table, which had once worn a lacy tablecloth, but was bare and scarred now. Since his wife's death, Wellman hadn't seen the need for those little touches that made ordinary things look pretty, not when the only thing he had ever considered pretty was buried in cold, uncaring earth. He offered Jack the bottle of Scotch and watched the man pour himself a half glass.

"Do you know who did this to her?" He accepted the bottle but did not take his eyes from Jack's face as he filled his cup.

"Not for sure, no," the other man said, before taking a draw from his glass that almost emptied it. "I mean...I didn't *see* 'em do it, or nothin', but..."

"Go on," Wellman urged when it seemed the man had snagged on his own thoughts.

Rain pattered at the window. The single bulb above them, hooded by a floral glass shade that was the room's sole concession to decorativeness only because the doctor couldn't for the life of him figure out how to remove it without breaking it, made their shadows long and blurry. It was not yet night, but plenty dark, almost as if Jack Lowell and his boy had brought it with them.

"You remember those kids that went missin' years back?"

Wellman nodded. "Backpackers. Couple of guys and their girls. I remember."

"Yeah. You remember the big fuss around here at that time. Kids were rich. Once their folks found out that Elkwood's where they'd last been seen alive, they came down here like an army, put the screws on the Sheriff pretty bad. Newsfolk and everythin'."

"That's right."

"I saw those kids." He joined his hands around the glass. There was dirt caked beneath his nails, his grubby fingertips touching.

Wellman sat back. "When?"

"Gave 'em a lift that day. Saw 'em all out there on the road, in that heat, sweatin' like a buncha hogs. Felt kinda bad for 'em, even though no one in their right mind should be out walkin' in that kinda heat. So I told 'em to pile in. Took 'em as far as the General Store, though it were closed. Even offered to take 'em farther if they wanted. They didn't. Heard one of 'em say the truck smelt like cowshit. 'Nother one said I was like somethin' outta *Deliverance*, whatever the hell that is."

"A movie," Wellman told him. "'About a bunch of hillbillies who hunt some city folk."

Jack considered this for a moment, then smiled, but only briefly. "Yeah. Anyways, I left 'em there, and they went missin' soon after."

"So you didn't see what happened?"

"No, but my place's only about twenty miles from the store. Only other house 'tween here and there is the Merrill's. Out there in the woods past the river." At the blank look on the doctor's face he said, "They don't come into town much. Keep to themselves. They have a junkyard. Hunt their own food. Buncha brothers, far's I know. Heard there used to be a sister too, but for all I know that might be just talk. Only one I ever seen in town is their old man, and he's a scary lookin' sumbitch. Has a way'a lookin' at you...like he's lookin' *inside* your skull or somethin'...readin' your thoughts or..." He trailed off, and drained the glass.

Wellman refilled it. "So you think they had something to do with those kids going astray?"

"I do."

"But...why? They could've gone anywhere. Might even have passed your place that day and you just didn't see them."

Jack raised his glass a little, tipped it in gratitude, and took a sip. Then he smacked his lips and stifled a belch. "I called the Sheriff a few weeks later when I heard those kids' folks was in town askin' questions. Told 'im what I thought, even though there weren't no good reason for thinkin' it other than a bad feelin' I got every time I passed that damn place. So McKindrey comes over, tells me he'll go out there and ask some questions. See if the Merrills know anythin'."

"And did they?"

"Dunno. He never went out there, or if he did, he pretended he didn't. But the night after I called him tellin' him what I knew, or thought I knew, I woke up to find Old Man Merrill standin' in my room with a big rusty lawnmower blade to my throat." He finished the drink, set the glass before the doctor, who filled it without hesitation and slid it back.

"Thought I was dreamin' 'bout Death itself, I swear. He was wearin' dark clothes: long coat, and one of them hats like the preachers used to wear." He raised his hand and made a twirling motion with one upraised finger in front of his face. "Big hat. Couldn't see his face. And he were tall. Least I think he was, but I guess anyone standin' in your room at night with a blade to your throat with only the moonlight showin' you he's there's gonna look tall, right?"

"Right," Wellman agreed, and noted the other man's hands had started to tremble.

"He says to me, and I'll never forget it: 'I don't want to kill a good, Godfearin' man like you even if you is just an old dirty nigger with a big mouth, but I won't hesitate to cut out your tongue if you keep spreadin' lies about my family.' He told me his boys never did nothin' they weren't forced to do to protect themselves and the family, and never would. Said they respected our boundaries and we should respect theirs."

Jack swallowed, eyes cloudy with the memory. He took a long drink of his whiskey, and it could have been water for all the effect it had on him. "I dunno what came over me, but I sat right up, despite that big ol' blade at my throat, and I told him to get the hell out of my house. He stepped away, and raised an arm that looked like it belonged to a scarecrow, and pointed at my bedroom door. I looked, saw a boy standin' there holding hands with Pete, who weren't more than a little kid himself at the time. He looked sleepy, standin' there in his underpants, wonderin' what was goin' on, and who this kid holdin' his hand was. And I couldn't tell him, couldn't say nothin' because that other kid, the Merrill kid, was holdin' a huntin' knife in his other hand and lookin' at me like he knew exactly how to use it, like he *wanted* to use it."

"Jesus..." Wellman said, and removed his spectacles so he could wipe a hand over his face. "Jesus."

"Merrill asked me if we had ourselves an understandin'." He shook his head slowly, and finished his drink. "I told him we did, and he left. Mussed up my boy's hair on the way out as if he were nothin' more than some 'ol kind uncle come to visit. I didn't sleep for weeks after that. Sat up with my shotgun and moved Pete's bed into the livin' room where I could watch over him."

"You tell the boy any of this?"

"Told him it were a dream. Didn't see the sense in scarin' 'im any worse."

"They shouldn't have gotten away with that, you know. No one should get away with that kind of thing. Not in this day and age."

Jack looked up from his drink. "I ain't never told no one what I just told you, Doc, but I'm tellin' it now because you wanted to know why I didn't want you callin' the Sheriff. Even if you do, he'll tell you he'll take a look, but he won't, 'cuz I reckon he's just as scared of 'em as I am. Maybe they paid him a visit one night, told him what they told me. But if *they* find out, it might be *you* they come see. You understand now?"

Wellman nodded slowly. He wasn't sure how much of Jack's story he should believe. It was madness what he'd been told, but then hadn't he witnessed firsthand the very worst kind of madness and desperation the world had to offer three years before when he'd been summoned to operate on Alice Niles, a fifteen-year-old girl who'd tried to burn her unborn baby out of herself with a blowtorch, believing it to be the spawn of Satan itself? That particularly frightening conviction had come courtesy of the girl's mother, Lynn, after she discovered her own husband was the baby's father.

What Jack had said scared him, even worse than the realization that had he not refused Alice Niles' anguished request to aid in the abortion, she might not have felt compelled to take the torch to it. This scared him more, because something had occurred to him that he wasn't sure he should say aloud for fear of terrifying Jack more than he already was. Assuming it hadn't already dawned on him.

What if they saw you, Jack? What if they saw you taking the girl?

* * *

She was sleeping, but it was not a peaceful sleep. Even over the rain that sizzled around him and the wind that had risen, even through the thick glass, Pete could hear her moaning low in her throat. One hand was flung over her brow; the other twitched spasmodically every few minutes. Doctor Wellman had washed her cuts and bandaged her eye, or rather the hole where her eye had once been, and put icepacks on her cheeks to help ease the swelling. She looked a little better now, but not much. She was still naked—he could tell by the shape of her, and the raised points of her nipples beneath the material, the sight of which caused something within him to stir—but the sheets were pulled up to her chin, as if she was cold. There were bloodstained cloths, swabs, and a kidney-shaped metal dish full of dark red water on a stand by the bed. Next to these, laid out on a blood-spotted white towel, a variety of steel instruments gleamed like shiny letters surrounded by wild crimson periods.

As Pete watched, consumed with the sudden urge to go back inside and bring her another blanket, she slowly turned her head toward him, as if following the flight path of a bird in a dream, and he almost ducked down beneath the sill for fear she'd wake and see him peering in at her like some kind of peeping tom. But he waited a moment, then straightened, his face pressed to the glass.

Who are you? he wondered, smiling slightly as he cocked his head to see better through the rivulets of rain streaming down the pane. *Where d'you come from?* He pressed his fingers to the glass, wishing it were her skin he was feeling beneath them, knowing her flesh would be infinitely warmer. He closed his eyes, confused by this yearning for someone he didn't even know, and not for the first time chided his foolishness. But the warmth inside him countered the uncertainty. She would wake, and she would need a friend, that was all there was to it. And if they forbade him his visits to see her, then he would sneak out. He had done it all the time for Valerie, even if she'd never learned that he'd been watching her, looking in on her from time to time like a guardian angel. On reflection, that had probably been for the best. She hadn't loved him anyway.

He wondered if it would be different this time.

The rain hammered the glass and needled the back of his head like nature's way of opposing such foolish thoughts, and he opened his eyes. The cold trickling down the nape of neck chilled him as he checked to make sure his father or Doctor Wellman hadn't suddenly appeared at the door.

The coast was clear.

Thunder made a sound like barrels tumbling down a stairs.

Pete turned back to the window, saw that the girl was awake, and watching him, and his mouth fell open.

A split second later, he was surprised when the girl did the same.

Then she screamed.

FIVE

"They'll come looking for her, you know. Someone will come looking for the girl. If not the cops, then her family, and even if by some miracle they don't, she's going to wake sooner or later and she'll want to go home."

Jack nodded his understanding and wiped tears from his eyes. "I know that. When she's able, you'd best just put her on a bus home. Though it might not be wise to keep her here longer than you need to. Take her to a hospital, soon. Tomorrow mornin'. Tell 'em you found her on the road and patched her up best you could. They'll get the cops involved and figure somethin' out for themselves."

Wellman finished his drink. "And you don't think it will all lead back here?"

"Doesn't matter if it does. We won't know nothin'."

"I will, Jack, and I'm a lousy liar."

"You won't know more than that you found her by the road. Half-truth's better than none, ain't it? And the girl'll be in good hands."

"Then what? Think they won't go poking around by themselves? And I'm only a doctor, not a surgeon. I can patch her up, but I can't give her what she needs."

Jack put his hands to the sides of his head and squeezed, as if hoping to compress the frustration. "Then drop her off somewhere. Drive into Mason City, leave her by the—"

A sudden terrifying shriek made them both jump. Jack's right hand flew out and knocked over his empty glass. It rolled toward the edge of the table but he caught it in time, then looked in desperation at the doctor, who rose and swallowed.

Overcome by panic, nerves frayed, "*Why?*" Wellman asked. "After all you've said, why did you *bring* her here?"

Jack stared dumbly. He had no ready answer, only unspoken apologies for an act he knew had endangered them all.

Pale-faced and trembling, Wellman hurried down the hall.

A moment later, Jack quickly and quietly stood and headed for the front door.

* * *

The face vanished from the window. It didn't matter. Whether or not she could see them, Claire knew they were close. She could smell their suffocating stink—a mixture of unwashed bodies, blood and engine oil. She screamed, and would not stop screaming, because despite what they had told her, despite what they had whispered lovingly into her ear, their noxious breath warm against her skin, *someone* would come. *Someone* would hear.

Casting a fearful glance at the window, empty now but for the rain, she felt a dazzling burst of panic and pain as she remembered being tied to the stake, remembered the feel of them taking turns as they violated her, tore her asunder, tried to reach the part of her she was keeping from them, the only part of her they still, after all their torturing, hadn't yet destroyed.

Her soul.

As if on cue, her ribs seemed to tighten, her lungs cutting off the breath required to carry the scream, and it died, became an airless croak that drained her. Searing pain chewed on her extremities, as if despite the warmth that lay upon her like an invisible lover, she was suffering from frostbite. Her body jerked of its own volition; her teeth clacked together hard enough to send a bolt of fresh, clear glassy pain to her temples. In her right eye, through which she could see nothing, a smoldering ember ignited anew, and she tried to scream again, as her hands—*wounded hands bandaged bleeding hands*—flew to the burning epicenter of her suffering and found no blood, no damage, only a soft, slightly damp gauze. She began to weep, and felt consciousness reel away from her, then back again, as if she were on a swing. Slowly, like fires lighting in the dark, other sites of pain registered across the terrain of her body, reaching toward the surface of her skin with flaming arms. Her back arched and she opened her mouth, but the scream she could hear in her ears stayed trapped in her throat. Her skin felt scalded.

Madness danced through her, offering itself up as an alternative to the unbearable suffering, and she grunted, pummeled by invisible fists of pain, and tried to listen.

Any minute now, that soothing velvet voice told her. *Any minute now they'll be back with their knives and their ropes and their filthy things, ready to do to you what they did to...to...*

She closed her eyes, opened them again. Darkness in one; light in the other. The room seemed to jump and jitter every time she tried to focus. The rataplan of the rain at the window was designed to distract her, to make her believe it was the dirty finger of one of *them*, eager to draw her attention, but she didn't look, didn't care. The pain was too much now, and even that didn't matter because pain meant she was alive, and alive meant they hadn't done to her what she'd seen them do to the others, to her friends, and she couldn't understand why they *hadn't* done the same to her, couldn't—

And then she did.

She hadn't let them.

She had escaped, survival instinct taking control of her, muddying her mind, narrowing her thoughts into one single inner cry of primal self-preservation.

Loosening rope burning her wrists. The dimwitted single-minded smile of her captor, as he tugged down his pants with trembling hands. Claire, arching her back away from the stake, spreading her legs, exposing herself more fully, watching his eyes drop to the raw wounded lips there. Come on, come take it you dirty fuck. *Her fingers fumbling, tips jabbed by the sharp point of a sliver of wood from the haphazardly stacked pile behind her and to the left. Reaching, weeping, gripping...*Come closer. *Swaying her hips despite the pain, the degradation, watching his fascination as he approached, his stubby cock springing free from his shorts, the tip glistening.* Come closer...*The memory of her friends, of what had been done to them, the black fire seizing her, the pain, the anguish, the horror...the rage.* Come on! *Then he was there, leering at her, hands outstretched to paw her breasts and her own hands were suddenly mercifully free, the rope falling to the floor. His mouth opening, eyes reluctantly leaving her body, frowning as he realized what that severed snake of rope on the floor meant, then a moan, low in his throat as she snatched the wood, swung it around and...*

She had fled them in a dream, and woken now to find that was all it had been, for wherever she was, it was no place she knew, no place she wanted to be. It was a bed, and had it been an earthen one she might have understood. But the sheets were clean where she hadn't bled on them. The room was tidy where there were no instruments and knives.

Knives.

Squinting, hissing through her teeth at the pain, she raised herself up on one elbow, and like a barrel full of rocks falling on its side, the pain seemed to tumble through her, settling in one half of her body, adding weight to the arm she was using to hold herself up. She took a series of short painful breaths as the light grew hazy and spun away from her, then she slowly, slowly opened her eye fully, willing it to focus on the small metal tray by the bed.

Knives. Lots of them, some still wet with her blood. The tools they'd used to fix her, sew her up so they could tear her stuffing out again.

She tried to smile but her lips felt like taut rubber, so she settled for a huffed laugh and the momentary surge of warmth that almost dulled the pain in her chest at the thought of what she was going to do with that knife—a scalpel, she noted.

Any minute now...

Yes, any minute now, they would barge into the room, those dirty seething bastards, but no matter how fast or how strong they were, they would not get her again.

They would not get a second chance to kill her.

Because she was going to do it for them.

SIX

As he approached the girl's room, Wellman heard the front door slam shut. Jack was gone, and that was good. His account had shaken Wellman, threatened to drain him of his resolve, imbuing in him the temptation to just drive the girl ten miles up the road and dump her somewhere, to avoid whatever her presence might call down upon him. But he was not going to do that, felt guilty for even thinking it. Once the girl was fit to be moved, he would put her in his car and drive her into Mason City, to one of the hospitals there, and once she was checked in, his next call would be to the police. The girl would have to be identified, her family told where to find her, so they could begin the long heartbreaking and arduous process of rebuilding their lives. He knew what that was like. He had been there himself. Hell, still *was* there, and he didn't envy them the journey.

What he didn't know was what would happen when he returned home after doing what he knew in his heart was the right thing. Would the Merrill clan be waiting for him? Would they simply demand to know what he'd done with the girl, or would they already know, having forced the information out of Jack? Surely, if they were indeed responsible for what had happened to the girl, wouldn't they now be too busy uprooting themselves and moving elsewhere in anticipation of a major manhunt once she was found?

He couldn't think about that now. He was old, and he was scared, and given too much consideration, the fear might consume him. All he knew was that he had watched a woman he had loved, still loved with all his heart, die in that room once and had never recovered from it, despite doing all he could to ease her suffering. He had prayed for Alice Niles's forgiveness the night he refused her request for help, and she had died too.

He would not idly stand by and watch another human being perish if it was within his power to prevent it.

The screaming stopped.

He hesitated at the door, listening. The silence in the wake of her scream seemed bottomless, and unsettling. After a moment, he gently gripped the handle of the door and eased it open.

"Miss?" he asked quietly, like a bellboy afraid of disturbing a guest, which was, now that he thought about it, not all that inaccurate, for until she decided whether or not to live or die, he was bound to serve her.

He stepped into the room.

She was awake.

Steel gleamed just above the covers.

Her body convulsed, just as he saw the scalpel in her hand, just as he noticed the fresh blood on the sheets.

Rain sprayed the glass as he hurried to her side.

She looked at him, frowned slightly, her face the same shade as the pillow beneath her bandaged head.

"My name is Doctor Wellman," he said, struggling to keep calm as he sat down on the bed and gripped her wrist. He was relieved to see that she had not had the strength to make more than a superficial cut, but it was bad enough. "I'm here to help you. You've been badly injured." A quick inspection of her other wrist revealed a deeper wound. It was from this the majority of the fresh blood had come. Still looking at the dreamy puzzled expression on her face, he reached blindly out and tugged open the nightstand drawer, fumbled inside until he found the bandages, and began to unwind them from the roll. As he wrapped her wounds, a flicker of pain passed briefly over her face.

"Am I dead?" she asked him in a whisper.

He summoned a smile. "You're going to be fine."

"I shouldn't be. Don't touch me." The struggle she put up was child-like, and not hard to restrain without causing her further discomfort. After a few moments, the strength left her.

"Hush now," Wellman soothed. "I'm a doctor. I'm not here to hurt you. I want to help you."

"Are they here?"

"Who?"

"Those men. They took the skin from Danny's hands. And his face. They pulled it off like it was a Halloween mask." Her breathing caught. Her face contorted into a grimace as a tear welled in her uncovered eye. "They hurt me. All my friends are gone. Everything is dead. Make it quick."

His smile faltered. "Honey, I'm not one of them. Listen to me now." He gently stroked her hair. "I'm a friend."

"All my friends are dead."

"How many were with you?"

She didn't reply. At length, she seemed to drift off to sleep, but whispered, "I have to die now. If I don't do it, they will and I can't let them." Her eyelid fluttered. Wellman did not panic. She wasn't going to die. He knew that. Her pulse, though weak, was constant. Her breathing was fine, her pupil no longer dilated. Unconsciousness was probably her only solace from the pain and the horror, and he permitted her the escape. While she slept, he wrapped her wrists and injected her with a dose of morphine in the hope that it would ease her dreams and numb the pain, at least for a little while. Then he set the tray with the instruments against the far wall, pulled a chair close to the bed, and listened to the rising wind trying to drown out the sound of her peaceful breathing.

He would wait a while for the bleeding to cease, before he sewed her up again.

Until then, he would pray.

And when he was done, he would take the girl to his car and head for Mason City.

We'll get you home, he promised.

SEVEN

Her room was in darkness.

Luke stood by the door, fists clenched so she wouldn't see them trembling, because even in the dark he knew it would not escape her attention. The room smelled of sweat and bodily fluids, but he did not mind. It was his mother's perfume to him, and ordinarily soothing.

But not this evening.

Now he craved the smell of cooking meat and kerosene, of wood smoke and sizzling fat that would soon permeate the air outside as his brothers burned the bodies. It was a ritual he had been a part of for so long he had ceased to appreciate it. But he appreciated it now, would rather be drawing that pungent mixture of aromas into his nostrils than the smell of shit and piss and vomit that hung in the air in the small squalid room his mother called her own.

From the wide bed, shoved into the corner farthest from the window, where the darkness was thickest, he heard the sound of her moving, just slightly, maybe raising her head to look at him, to peer at him through the muddy gloom. The bedsprings did not so much creak, as whimper.

"Momma?"

"Boy," she responded in her bubbling voice, as if she was forever gargling.

"Momma I—"

"Come 'ere."

He pretended he hadn't heard because it was safer by the door, and that in turn made him feel guilty because he knew if he stayed here she would not rise up and come get him. She couldn't. In over two years she hadn't left that bed, not once, and in daylight, when the clouds covered the sun and the flies obscured the window, it was hard to tell where Momma ended and the bed began. It was all darkness, with lumps of paler matter here and there.

That bed, like the woman in it, dominated the room. Papa-In-Gray had told them in the same reverential tone he used to begin their prayers every night before supper, that their Momma was a saint, a suffering martyr not yet found by the grave. *Wires'n springs'n flesh'n fat*, he told them, like it was the opening line of some long forgotten nursery rhyme. There was no Momma anymore, he said, not the way they remembered her. Now she was a mass of suppurating bedsores, fused to the mattress where old wounds had healed and the torn flesh and pus had hardened to form a kind of second skin around the material and bedsprings beneath. The mattress, once plump and soft, had been worn down by her weight to almost nothing, a wafer thin slice bent in the middle, pungent, soggy and stained by the fluids that had soaked down from her corpulent body over the years. The boys took turns washing and tending to her wound, grooming her, scooping out the large quantities of fecal matter that gathered between her enormous thighs, then giving the remaining stain a cursory, half-hearted scrub before leaving her to wallow in the vestiges of her own waste.

She complained endlessly, spoke to herself day and night, sometimes sang little songs in a voice barely above a whisper, and was quiet only when they brought her food.

Waves of stink rolled from the crooked sagging bed. He had long ago stopped suggesting that they let some air into the room. He didn't even know if the windows would still open. Some kind of putrid brown grease had started climbing the foggy panes, like corrupted spirits risen from the heaps of dead flies, and had gathered in the cracks like glue.

But God, how he loved her, despite the fear she instilled in him, and despite all she had done to make him sorry for his sins. He loved her more than life itself, quietly believed that he loved her most of all, more than his brothers did, though he would never say so. He believed himself the favorite, even when she challenged that belief by hurting him.

"You hear me boy?" she said, and he licked his lips, felt his tongue rasp against the lack of moisture there, and when he drew it back in, he tasted something foul, something he had tugged from the air into his mouth.

"I hear you Momma," he said, and took a few steps closer to the bed. Beneath his boots, the floorboards creaked and breathed miniature puffs of dust into the air. *Shouldn't be no dust*, he thought, staring down at the dissipating clouds. *Floor's well-traveled*. And it was, but like the intricate but drooping black cobwebs that hung like dreamcatchers from every corner of the room, he knew this room held onto every particle of skin that fell or rose from his Momma's body, then waited until dark to begin fashioning them into elaborate constructs to convince the world that time was passing faster than it really was, hastening his Momma toward her death. Trying to make her believe she'd been forgotten. Which of course was Momma's only true fear. That they would abandon her. That one day she'd wake and find herself calling out to an empty house, listening to the echoes of her voice coming back to her with nothing to obstruct it. Listening to her frantic cries slithering out into the woods to get lost among the trees, to be heard by the deer, the squirrels, the jays, and ultimately, the coyotes, who would sense her panic and follow it to the source. Then, as she had told her sons a thousand times, the coyotes would eat her, and scatter her bones across the land so her spirit would never find peace.

"Sit," she commanded, and he squinted down at the bed to be sure when he obeyed he didn't end up pinning a flap of flesh from her arm beneath him. He sat and the bed hardly moved, but the stench from the damp mattress and the body upon it was strong enough to make his eyes water. Whenever Aaron and the others came to see Momma-In-Bed, they wore bandannas tied across their lower faces, but Luke refused to show such disrespect, and wondered why she let them get away with it.

In the gloom, Luke could only make out her eyes, small dark circles in a doughy face almost indistinguishable from the pillow.

"Girl got away, Momma. She tricked Matt'n kilt him. Then she got loose. Didn't think she'd get far, not the way we had her cut up, but she did. Got to the road and someone picked her up."

There was silence so deep that Luke, perched precariously on the hard metal edge of the bed, feared he might fall headlong into it and be devoured. Then Momma began to sing, a low growl that was not in the least bit melodic, and chilled him to the core of his being. The song had only a few notes as far as he could tell, but the way she sang them reminded him of the sound a fire truck made when it flew by, the way the song changed, grew lower and lower as it got farther away. He swallowed and his throat clicked. As if it had been a signal, Momma stopped singing.

"Someone picked her up," she repeated. Then, "You 'member what happ'ned to yer pizzle, son?"

He felt his face redden and was glad she couldn't see it, but couldn't prevent his head from lowering, his shoulders from tightening at the mention of that horrible day he had tried so hard to forget but never would, not as long as he had to see the mangled thing that emerged from his pants every time he had to make water.

"I 'member."

"You 'member why it happ'ned?"

Again, he nodded, but felt his throat constrict.

"Tell me." He flinched as her hand, almost the size of his Papa's hat, but white as fresh snow, found his knee. After a moment, he felt the damp from her moist skin seeping through his jeans. "Tell your poor Mama what happ'ned."

"It—" he began, then tensed as her clammy fingers tightened on his knee. "It were my thirteenth birthday. You threw us a big party, with cake'n balloons'n streamers. You got the place lookin' real nice, and Papa were home. I 'member he even took off his hat for a spell."

"That's right," whispered Momma, lost in a memory she clearly enjoyed. "Go on now."

"Me'n Aaron rode the horses through the woods that evenin'. Susanna were on the back of my colt, hangin' on to me fer dear life. We kept goin' faster'n faster, and 'fore we knew it, we was racing, Aaron and me. Racin' like the wind, and Susanna screamin', but a good kinda screamin' like she was enjoyin' herself."

"She liked the horses, and loved you boys, didn't she Luke?"

"Yes Ma'am."

"Tell me how much she loved you, Luke."

The memory to this point was a good one. It had been, as far as Luke could recall, the most beautiful day of his life. The sun had been shining through the leaves, cooking the red clay so it was spongy under the horses' hooves and flew in their wake. The air was warm, the sweat cooling on their faces as they flew through the woods, laughin' and screamin' at the top of their lungs, mimicking loons as bugs smacked into their faces and leaves caught in their hair. He remembered Susanna's grip, her skin warm and slippery against his belly, her breasts soft against his back as he angled the colt toward the creek, then down the embankment. The horse, more machine than animal, like a series of cogs, pistons and hydraulics beneath a black tarp, muscles rolling fluidly, didn't pause as the soft earth changed to rock and water. Instead it plowed straight through, head low, snorting as the cold spray soaked the children. Luke had never had such fun in his life, and he delighted in the look on Aaron's face as he rode his mare a few paces behind. His brother was red from the exertion of trying to keep up, eyes wide from a mixture of fear at the breakneck pace and excitement that they dared go so fast.

"We came to a clearin'," Luke said, his voice low. The stench of death and sickness abruptly filled his nose and tickled his throat, making him want to gag, but he resisted, and turned away, discreetly sucking in air that was not much cleaner. If he vomited, he knew he'd be no better than his brothers with their insulting bandannas. So he took small short breaths, cleared his throat, spat a sour wad of phlegm on the floor and continued. "The Lowell Creek clearin' where Papa used to hunt rabbits, 'fore they was all gone."

"Beautiful place in the summertime," his mother said.

"Sure was."

"Was?" she asked with mock surprise. "Ain't no more?"

"We rested there for a spell," he said, joining his hands and secretly chiding himself for the uncharitable thought that had just come over him. He had wished, just for a second, that his mother would take her hand off his knee. The weight of it was cold, and unpleasant, as if while dampening his flesh with hers, she was, at the same time, leaching something vital from him. He could almost feel it leaving.

"We rested there some," he repeated, trying to regain the thread of his thoughts. "Played around for a couple of hours, till the sun started goin' down. Aaron got bored. Wanted to go home, and Aaron, you know, he don't like bein' bored. Gets riled up real easy that way. So he started teasin' Susanna somethin' fierce when she says she don't wanna go home yet, callin' her names, peggin' sticks at her. He even threw a dead possum he'd found that had all its guts hangin' out. That was all she wrote right there. Poor Suze had all its insides stuck in her hair, maggots on her dress, and she went crazy. Damn near chased Aaron all the way home and ten miles farther." He smiled, just a little. Then it faded as Momma shifted a little in her bed, those dark eyes gleaming like beetles in the moonlight.

"He stayed home; I stayed at the creek, feet up on a rock, in no hurry to go nowhere, not on my birthday, which the way I saw it, was the best damn day of my life so far. The horses was with me, and they seemed pretty satisfied too, standin' in the shade as the sun went down. I might even have dozed some."

"And where was Susanna?"

Momma-in-Bed knew the answer to that already. She'd heard this story a thousand times, but her eagerness to hear it again never waned. She was prodding him, impatient to get to the important part, the part where everything went wrong.

"Somewhere in the woods," Luke said somberly. "I thought she'd gone home after gettin' bored of chasin' Aaron."

"But she weren't home."

"No."

"Where was she?"

"She were there, with me, only I didn't know it 'till she stepped out from the trees and called my name."

"Your sister had such pretty dresses, didn't she Luke?"

"Yes Momma."

"Made most of them myself. What dress was she wearin' that day, Luke? I forget."

"A pink one."

"Of course, you got a good head for mem'ries, boy. And what was she wearin' when she stepped out and called your name?"

Luke answered, quietly. "Nothin'."

"I can't hear you."

"Nothin' Momma. She weren't wearin' nothin'."

"That must've surprised you."

"It did."

"Say again?"

"It did, Momma. I didn't know why she did that. Thought she might've been skinny-dippin' in the creek like she done sometimes, maybe cleanin' the possum guts off, and Aaron had stoled her clothes, or somethin' because she were all wet."

"Go on..." Momma urged.

"I asked her what were she doin' without no clothes on, and she said it was too damn hot and her dress were ruined and she'd taken a dip to wash off. I told her if anyone came along'n seen her, there'd be trouble. She said no one was gonna bother us, and then she came over to where I was layin' and started openin' up my belt. I told her to stop, was she crazy or somethin' and she wouldn't. She just kept tearin' at my clothes till she had my..." He swallowed again, the words lodged in his throat.

"Your what?"

"My pizzle, Momma. She had it in her mouth, and I couldn't make her stop."

"You couldn't stop because you didn't want to. Your Jezebel sister had her lips on your dirty thing and you liked it, didn't you?"

Luke nodded. Truth was, and he'd never denied it because lying was something of which he seemed completely incapable, he *had* enjoyed it, and enjoyed it a great deal, despite knowing that he and his sister, who was older, but only by a year, were doing something that went against nature, and worse, against God himself. But he had been unable to stop the queer, frightening, but unstoppable current of sensation that her lips evoked as she sucked on him. It had felt as if she were drawing out all the bad things, all the fears, worries, and the pain he'd carried within him since he'd first come to understand the world into which he'd been deposited. And when his seed erupted, he felt as if dynamite had detonated in his balls and would blow him to little bloody pieces. He lay there panting as the incredible, terrifying sensation ebbed away and his member slackened. Then he stared, open-mouthed, as his sister stood and spat, then walked away toward the creek. He'd followed a moment later, intending to ask her what had just happened, and why. He was hurt, a little angry, but more confused, and it seemed to steal a little bit of the color from the world, darkening it with a mystery he needed solved. He found Susanna washing herself in the cool clear water, her back turned to him, her hair wet, but before he had the chance to put to her the burning question, she spoke first:

"I love you, Luke," she said softly, sadly. "And I'm leavin'. I know you won't come with me, that you can't, but I gotta go, gotta get out. I'm not supposed to be here. There's a big world out there for people like me. Yours is here, with Momma and Papa. I wanted to kiss you on the mouth back there, but I reckon that should be kept for my husband. What we did…Lorraine Chadwick at school told me she saw her mother do it to her boyfriend and he seemed to enjoy it all right. Said it was a secret kiss, and now we got a secret all our own." She shrugged, cupped water in both hands and washed out her mouth as if she'd just eaten a bug. "I guess I were curious, and…maybe I didn't know stuff like snot was gonna come out…but I ain't sorry none…. It's your birthday'n all, and I know I love you Luke. Maybe even enough to kiss you on the lips, but like I said, I reckon I gotta keep somethin' for my husband."

"The seed of incest is the devil's milk," his mother said. "And it poisons everythin' it touches." Her playful tone was now gone completely, replaced by bitterness and shame. "Your Papa stood a few feet away watchin' the whole wicked thing. You were lucky he didn't kill the both of you that day, right there and then. Maybe he should've."

Luke had nothing to say. If Susanna hadn't sinned with him that day, he would still have skin on his privates, and maybe his sister would still be here. Of course, for a long time, he'd borne his punishment well, consoled by the knowledge that she had made it out, was on her way to a new and better life somewhere, where no one would ever find her. He fantasized about growing up and finding her, or maybe not even waiting that long. Maybe someday he would end up possessed of the same wanderlust, the same certainty that life was better Out There, and he'd travel the same path, his beloved sister waiting for him at the end of it. He knew he wouldn't care if she were married when that time came. He didn't want her for a wife. He loved her as a sister, and as the best friend he'd ever known. And he had always envied how much different she was from the rest of the family. She was independent, headstrong, and defiant, all traits Luke admired greatly, but never dared try to learn.

"Tell me what became of her, Luke."

For two years he had thought Susanna gone. It had cheered him and brightened his darkest hours, of which there had been many. He wondered what she looked like, whether she was rich or poor, still in the South or elsewhere. He dreamed of her voice, and waited for her to write him with details of her adventures.

It was another summer before he found her old blue suitcase half-buried in the barren field behind the acre of corn. It was the same one he'd seen tucked beneath her arm as her shoeless feet carried her up the dirt path and away from the house, bound for town, and the strange unfamiliar lands beyond. Inside that suitcase were her meager possessions: two dresses, a pair of socks with holes in the heels, two pairs of underwear, a cold roast beef sandwich wrapped in waxpaper, a small hunk of cheese, a notebook and a small stubby pencil, and a small pink purse with a brass clip in which she carried ten whole dollars to start her on her way.

All of these things were still inside the suitcase when he'd yanked it free of the dark red earth that day years later. Also inside were Susanna's small yellow comb, a rusted switchblade, a doll with a cracked face, and Susanna's badly decomposed head.

"Tell me about the note."

Someone had shoved a rolled up piece of notepaper into his sister's right eye socket. With trembling hands, and hardly able to see through the sparkling film of tears, a sob caught in his aching throat, Luke had withdrawn the scroll and turned his back on his sister's remains to read it.

"Two pieces from Leviticus," he told his mother now, his tone grave.

"You 'member them words?"

There was no way he'd ever forget them. They were branded in his brain, a signpost on the border of a part of his mind he seldom ventured into. "'None of you shall approach any who is near of kin to him to uncover their nakedness: I am the LORD.'" He took a breath, slowly released it. "'The nakedness of thy sister, the daughter of thy father or daughter of thy mother, whether she be born at home or born abroad, even their nakedness thou shalt not uncover.'"

"Amen," said his mother, serenely and he could tell from her voice she was smiling. "It was his message to you, son."

She had said that more than once before, and still he wasn't sure whether she meant that his father, or God, had written it for his benefit. At the time, and the years had only bolstered the conviction, he'd considered it a warning. A lesson, meant to scare away whatever latent strains of rebellion might have been subconsciously forming inside him in the wake of his sister's desertion. He remembered the anguish, the suffering, somehow infinitely worse than the day Papa-in-Gray had strapped him to a chair in Momma's room and used his razor on Luke's privates. The pain had been excruciating, but it was pain of a different kind. In the fallow field the day he'd stumbled on his sister's final destination, he had sat with Susanna's rotted head cradled in his arms as the wind chased shreds of the sundered scroll away across the field, and he had felt as if her death had shoved him into a new world, a terrible place where no one could be trusted and the ground could swallow you and your dreams. And if the ground didn't get you, the coyotes would, or Papa would see to you with his blade and carve the sin from your soul, the skin from your skull.

"Why did I ask you 'bout this today?" Momma asked.

Luke shrugged, his mood darkened by the memory of his sister.

"'Cause you poisoned your sister," she answered for him. "And for that she had to be dealt with. Don't you understand that if we'd let her go, she'd've been corrupted even further by Men of the World, and they'd've sent her back to us once they'd filled her with their wicked venom, and through her they'd've corrupted *us*, destroyed *us*, Luke." Her hand left his knee, and found his fingers, enveloping his warm skin in a cold damp cocoon of flesh. "We're the last of the old clans, boy. We stay together. We hunt and we kill Men of the World. We devour their flesh so they cannot devour us. We hold them off and resist their attempts to convert us to sinful ways. We protect each other in the name of God Al*mighty*, and punish those who trespass, destroy those who would destroy us. We are the *beloved*, Luke, and once the light has been shown to those who are not of the faith, they must embrace it or be destroyed. All your life you have understood this.

"Today, you were lazy, and foolish. You let one of *them* get away. You sucked out her venom and showed her the light, but now she's Out There again, with the light in her eyes and our fate in her hands. They'll send her back again someday, Luke, and by then it'll be too late. She will not come alone, and their numbers'll be too great for us to survive. They'll kill us and scatter our bones so our spirits cannot rest. Our work'll be over, and it'll all have been for nothin'. You and me, and all our kin'll be left in the dark, far away from God's grace."

Luke was afraid. He believed her, knew she did not lie. And if the girl—Claire—came back with others, with Men of the World, he knew it would mean the end of everything. And it would be his fault.

"What do I do, Momma?"

"Talk to Papa. He knows the townfolk. He'll know who owned that truck. Then you find 'em, and you'll find the girl. Once you do, take her heart and bring it back to me. Burn the rest. We'll share her meat, and save ourselves from Purgatory. But you ain't got much time to waste now. You best move."

Luke stood. But Momma's grip tightened around his hand. She tugged him close. The stench was overwhelming, and he shut his mouth, hoping she couldn't hear him gagging. "You find her, or we'll take what's left of your pizzle and eat it with grits for breakfast, you understand?"

He nodded, and held his breath until she released him. Then he turned and headed for the door. As his hand gripped the moist, grimy knob, her voice once more stopped him.

"Keep the skin," she demanded.

"What, Momma?"

"My boy. My Matthew. Tell your brothers to eat whatever needs eatin', to take what they need, but they need to keep the skin for me. Winter's comin' and I need all the heat I can get."

Though Luke couldn't imagine his mother ever being cold beneath the heaps of her own slippery rotting flesh, "Yes Momma," he said, and opened the door to the rain and smoke and the aroma of cooking meat.

EIGHT

There would be no prayer. Not yet. Momma-In-Bed had made it clear that there was not enough time to indulge in giving thanks, not when Hell itself might already be gathering on the horizon. He'd been with her for what had felt like hours, a long slow walk through the sluggish waters of unpleasant times. And because of that inner sense of more time lost than they could afford to lose, the sense of urgency increased. Every minute that passed him by was more distance between him and their quarry, and closing the distance between him and whatever Momma-in-Bed would do if the girl was not retrieved.

Luke ducked his head as he stepped off the porch into the gloaming. The fire cast reddish yellow light, the flames sizzling in the rain and casting shadows on his brother's faces as they looked at him, but he didn't spare them a glance before moving off toward the wood shed. Still, he found it harder to ignore the smacking of lips, the clicking of teeth, the greedy swallows, the tearing of meat from bones, and the murmurs of appreciation as they sat around the smoldering corpse of their brother. It was even harder to resist the smell the breeze carried to him before whipping it away into the trees behind him, where animals with dark eyes would pause and look up, curious but not nearly enough to follow the scent to its source. Even the carnivorous creatures that existed in the premature twilight beyond the trees—among them, the coyotes Momma-in-Bed feared so much—knew the small series of cabins in the woods were best avoided, for they had seen few of their fellow scavengers return from there, and so their curiosity abated quickly and they wandered on.

Luke was hungry, his stomach hollow and aching, and he was as eager as the rest of them to feed on the meat, to savor both the taste and the feeling of their dead brother's strength settling in his own body, Matt's unspoken thoughts, dreams, and ambitions, however simple, weaving themselves into his own brain. But the flesh would keep, he told himself, as he sighed and felt his worn boots sinking into the moist earth. He knew the importance of the task that lay ahead. If they failed this time, if the girl had already found her way to a haven they could not reach, then there would be more than the authorities to worry about. Momma-In-Bed had threatened him, but it had been merely a formality, and not a true promise. What she would do to him, maybe to all of them, if the girl was not returned, would be much worse than simply skinning his pizzle with a rusty knife. She loved him, as he loved her, but that would not be enough to save his life if he didn't make things right, no more than it had saved poor Susanna when she'd defied them.

Teeth clenched to force back the emotions that always tried to insinuate their way into the forefront of his mind whenever he remembered his lost sister, Luke climbed the small rise where the bare earth narrowed to a single trail that wound unsteadily through a short stretch of wild untended grass. The woodshed was narrow, and old, the wood bleached by the sun so it was a mottled white, with patches of gray. In the rapidly fading light, it looked leprous, with yellow light around the edges. The door bent outward at the bottom like a well-turned page, and as he approached, that splintered corner scraped dirt and the door swung wide with a sound like rocks tumbling down a hollow pipe.

Luke stopped in his tracks.

Though not a large man, Papa-In-Gray cut an imposing figure. In daylight, his skin was the same shade as the door that was now swinging away from him. In town, he was respected, but it was respect borne of fear. At home, among his kin, things were not much different. Now, in the gloom, beneath his angular, inverted triangle of a face, the chin topped with a peppering of silver stubble, Papa wore a dirty brown apron, which Luke himself had made for him from the skin of one of the men they had caught the summer before. Strands of blue nylon rope had been looped through holes at the top corners of the apron, the holes ringed by steel washers to stop the rope from sawing through, keeping the rough rectangle in place, and also, as was the case now, to conceal the wearer's nakedness.

Grim-faced, Papa raised his right hand. In it, he held the head of one of the youths—the one the girl had called 'Stu', which the family had found amusing since they figured this was most likely going to be the way he ended up. His blonde hair, though matted with filth now, still managed to retain a healthy look death had denied the rest of his body. The tanned handsome face of which Luke had found himself mildly envious, was no longer so handsome, slackened now by the pain that had ushered it into death. The eyes were closed, pale brows arched, the thick-lipped mouth open slightly, as if starting a sentence that would forever remain unspoken. Papa-in-Gray very rarely did a sloppy job with the carcasses and this one was no different. The machete had made a good straight cut through the boy's neck, and no bone or flesh protruded from the wound.

"A good'un," Papa said now, in his gravelly voice. "Who took the girl?"

Luke couldn't meet his gaze as he spoke, so instead he stared at the ground. "Big red truck came and picked 'er off the road. Two niggers—one old, one young it looked like. They made off with her. Headin' east."

Behind his father, Luke glimpsed the rest of the boy's naked body, splayed out on the worktable in the shed underneath a single bare light bulb. His hands and feet were gone, and his chest had been opened and excavated, the organs collected in a rusty bucket on the floor. As Luke tried to get a better look, Papa surprised him by tossing the severed head in his direction. Caught off guard, it hit Luke in the chest and he was knocked back a step. With a grunt, he staggered, feet splayed, and quickly righted himself, grabbing with his crooked fingers a handful of the boy's hair just seconds before it hit the ground, a development he knew would not have impressed his father.

As if anything ever would.

Exhaling heavily, Luke straightened and clutched the head to his chest. Papa-in-Gray nodded, but it was not a gesture of satisfaction, rather confirmation that his disdain for Luke was justified, and no one would ever convince him otherwise.

"Take it," the old man said, wiping bloodstained hands on the apron. The flesh seemed to soak it in. "We're bringin' it with us. Tell the others to get themselves a piece of those kids each'n load 'em up."

Though Luke wasn't sure why they were bringing along pieces of the dead kids, he knew better than to question Papa's instructions.

"All right," he said, and waited.

"Tell Aaron bring the truck 'round, and make sure all you boys got yer knives." He looked over Luke's shoulder. "Get movin'."

Luke started to say something, but Papa turned his back on him, and in two short steps was back inside the shed, the door swinging shut behind him.

As he stood there, the rain still pattering on his shoulders, the severed head gripped firmly by its hair, Luke felt overcome by bitterness toward the old man, who, ever since that day in the clearing with Susanna, had shown no affection, or respect toward him, not even a little. Worse, the old bastard had never once sat him down to explain why he'd done what he'd done to his sister, why they couldn't have just let her go, or maybe tried to talk some sense into her. No, he'd left that task to Momma-in-Bed, and he suspected, at the back of his mind, that all she'd done was make excuses because she wasn't rightly sure herself, no matter what she'd said about the poison in his seed. Neither one of his parents had grieved for her.

Luke turned away, and looked from the head to the semicircle of bodies huddled around the fire—his brothers, still eating, Matt's skin draped like an animal hide across a battered old workhorse between them and the four ramshackle sheds they used for the Men of the World. Luke hadn't given them the order to keep the skin for Momma. They had known, most likely because one or more of them had been listening at the window when Momma said it, and they'd worked quickly. For one brief moment, a flame ignited inside him, hot enough to make tears of shame and hurt blur his vision. He imagined them crouched down beneath that dirt-smeared glass, their heads bowed as they listened to the story of cold-blooded murder, his part in it, and the warning he was given. They would have heard the fear in his voice that only surfaced when Momma or Papa threatened him. They would have heard it all, and hurried to deny him the one command he could use to reinstate his authority over them. Then they'd watched him—he had felt their stares on his back as sure as the rain—through the smoke and heat from their meal, as he'd picked his way toward Papa's shed. And they would have known he would find even less warmth up there, a fact confirmed by their father's sudden tossing of the severed head, done, Luke guessed, to entertain his other, more faithful sons. In fumbling it, Luke had given them all exactly what they'd wanted.

As he approached them now, he forced a crooked smile. They looked up expectantly, blood and fat smeared across their faces.

"You been cryin'?" Aaron asked tonelessly.

Luke shook his head. *Not crying*, he wanted to say. *Just 'memberin' how much I hate that kin-killin' son of a bitch*. But he would never say such a thing, no matter how true it might be. To say it aloud would be to condemn himself, for he had no doubt that as soon as the words left his mouth, Papa would hear them. And a blade would cut those words in the same swing that took Luke's head off at the shoulders. His brothers would mourn him without weeping, devour his flesh without hesitation, and promptly forget he'd ever existed, like they seem to have done with Susanna and now Matt, their gentle brother, who would be remembered only for today, and only when the taste of him rolled back up their throats. So instead he took a deep breath, watched as Joshua and Isaac stared curiously at the head in their brother's hands, and delivered the instructions his father had given to him.

Immediately the boys moved into action, scrambling toward the sheds, propelled by the excitement of another hunt so soon, leaving Luke alone to stare at the gnawed remains of his brother, the smoke burning his eyes, the smell taunting his belly.

To anyone watching, the small shake of his head would appear to be a gesture of sympathy, or regret.

But it was none of these things.

It was anger, pain.
And envy.

* * *

"Pa?"

The old man sat in a chair by the fire, chin on his chest as if asleep, but his eyes were open and watching the door, one hand on the stock of the rifle he'd set across his lap, the other on the neck of a bottle of rye whiskey.

Pete, right ear still ringing from the blow his father had dealt him when he'd caught the boy looking in the injured girl's window, wasn't sure if he should head upstairs to bed, apologize again, or just keep his mouth shut. But he wanted to hear his Pa speak, because since they'd come home, the old man hadn't said a word. This in itself was nothing unusual, but something about the silence tonight was different. It unnerved Pete, thrummed through his stomach until he thought he was going to be sick. Even the crickets and bullfrogs seemed to sing with less enthusiasm, the birds sounding tired and wary, as if eager to warn the old man and his boy of something bearing down on them, but unable to find a song they would understand. Night had come fast too, the unseen sun sinking down behind the trees at the edge of the property, sending out a low cold and steady breeze like a ripple after a rock has been dropped in a pond. Quietly, Pete moved to the table and took a seat, his arms folded on the chipped wood among the remains of a hastily thrown together rice and corn dinner, which Pete had cooked, and had seemed to have been alone in enjoying. From here he had a clear view of his father, whose sharp profile was silhouetted by the flickering flames, but should the old man erupt into a sudden violent rage, the table was between them, and would afford the boy protection, however briefly.

"Pa?"

Slowly, so slowly Pete imagined his neck should have creaked like an old door, his father turned his head to look at him. His eyes were like smoked glass, a cold fire flickering beyond them.

"You hush up now," Pa said. "Need to listen."

"For what?"

His father sighed, but didn't reply, then went back to looking at the door with such intensity that Pete found himself checking it himself for something he might have missed all these years—a word, maybe, or a carving or engraving, something that might justify his father's scrutiny.

"You scared'a somethin'?" he asked then after giving up on the door and focusing instead on his father's taut, aged face.

He didn't understand a whole lot about his old man, but figured himself a pretty good judge when it came to moods. Anger was the easiest one of course, given that it was, more often than not, a whole lot of blustering, heavy breathing and cussing, followed by a couple of open-handed smacks across the head if the fault was Pete's, and a couple of kicks in the ass if it wasn't. Sorrow was a tougher one, but over the years Pete had learned to recognize that too. He reckoned his Pa had never really gotten over Louise—who Pete considered his second Ma—leaving him, and the boy thought he understood that. Sometimes late at night when he lay in bed, Pete would watch the stars, untainted by city light and sparkling like shattered glass in the moonlight, and go over the constellations in his mind, summoning the memory of her, imagining her there beside him, listing off all the names. Sometimes he imagined so hard he could almost feel her there, could smell that scent which had always brought to mind images of spring flowers and clean laundry as she sat next to him on the bed, her fingers stroking his hair, her other hand on his wrist. *There's Cassiopeia*, she would whisper in his ear, *looks just like a double-u, see it? And there's Orion, and those three stars right there, that's his belt. Up'n the corner, see that one look's red?* And he would nod and wait for an answer that wasn't coming, because she hadn't stayed around long enough to offer it, and so there his imagination would falter and the loneliness would rush in like cold water through holes in a sinking ship. But there were always dreams, and in dreams she never left him, was still here cooking mouth-watering food for them, singing with that beautiful voice of hers, and messing around with Pa, who would scowl and look irritated but only because he was struggling not to smile.

It had been a long time since Pete had seen his Pa smile about anything, and he often wondered how much of that was his fault. He knew because he wasn't all that smart, he wasn't likely to ever get the kind of job that could give his Pa and him a better life. He wasn't ever going to be mayor or President or an astronaut like his second Ma had told him he could. She'd said he could be anything he wanted, just like she aimed someday to be a famous singer, but he knew that wasn't true now, and Pa knew it too, even said as much when he'd had a few days drinking under his belt and didn't seem to know what he was saying, or that he was saying it out loud. *Coulda been somethin' boy. Coulda been a real man, but you ain't never gonna amount to nothin' more than a farmboy with cowshit on your shoes and straw in your head, standin' at that door waitin' for somethin' better to come along that ain't never comin'. Not for you, boy, and sure as hell not for me.* Pete would listen carefully to his father's words, and feel the pain that came with them, but told himself Pa was only saying those things out of disappointment and anger, and because it was better to throw mean words at the boy than at his own reflection in the mirror. Pa had wanted a better life too, but as soon as second Ma walked out, bound for Detroit with some man Pete had only seen once, and that by accident, the old man had given up hoping for a future. He had given up, period. The woman he'd loved had left him here with a son that wasn't of his own blood, a dying farm, and plenty of time to sit and drink and wonder why she'd given up on them.

"I reckon I am," his father said, in such a low voice that Pete had to strain to hear it, and even then he had to struggle to remember the question his father was answering. His thoughts had set him adrift from their conversation and now he had to search quickly for the thread. He found it as he watched the old man raise the bottle of whiskey and study the remaining dregs.

Pa was afraid, and as it was a state Pete seldom, if ever, saw in him, it had the effect of galvanizing his own discomfort. He stood, shoving the chair back with his knees, and came around the table to stand beside his father. "What's wrong?" he asked.

The old man lowered the bottle, but kept his eyes on it as he spoke. "I don't reckon I did much of a job by you," he said. "Don't reckon I could even if I tried. My own Pa wasn't much of a man neither, and never treated me right, though I don't expect that's much of an excuse."

Hearing his father talk of such things disturbed Pete more than the odd silence and the sudden sense that their house had shrunk around them, but he shrugged and forced a smile.

"S'okay, Pa. Don't nobody know the right way to do everythin'."

His father considered this. "Maybe that's true, but there ain't no excuse for not tryin'."

"You did try," Pete told him. "You looked after me pretty good. I ain't wantin' for nothin'."

A small bitter smile twisted his father's lips. "You wantin' for plenty, boy. Some of that I can't do nothin' about. Some, I reckon I could've fixed."

Pete frowned. "Well...it ain't too late, Pa. We got time."

At that, the weak smile vanished from his father's face. His eyes widened as he glanced from the bottle back to the door. "That's the trouble, son. I got a feelin' we don't."

* * *

He had promised himself he wouldn't scare the boy, but after a good deal of thought and a great deal of whiskey, Jack had realized there was no way around it. If the Merrill clan were coming, better Pete know, so he would at least have the chance to run. He set the now empty bottle down between his chair and the fire, and let his hands rest on the polished walnut stock of the rifle. He'd kept the weapon in pretty good shape all these years, better shape than anything else, his son included. Jack was truly sorry for that and he'd meant what he'd told the boy. There was so much else he wanted to say too before time ran out, but no matter what way he came at it, the words wouldn't come. Even now, with the hounds of hell thundering a path to their door, he couldn't tell his boy he loved him. And maybe that was because he didn't. There was no doubt that he cared for Pete, and worried after him constantly, but years of disappointment, self-loathing, and resentment for the child he secretly held accountable for the only two women he'd ever loved abandoning him, didn't allow those seeds to blossom into a full flower of adoration. In truth, he'd never wanted a kid, and had been doing just fine avoiding the whole problem until he'd met Annabelle, who been nurturing one in her womb. Even so, he'd figured he'd adapt just fine to the role of parent, even if she ended up doing most of the raising. But then she went and died on him soon as that child drew its first breath. For almost fifteen years he wallowed in self-pity and thoughts of up-and-leaving, reasoning that someone would find the kid and take him in, and to hell with whatever they thought of him for deserting it. He was no monster, and it would have been a bald-faced lie if he'd ever claimed he hadn't taken a shine to the kid. But though on paper it would always say Jack Lowell was a father, he knew in his heart he wasn't equipped to be one. Someday, he'd known, that kid would wake up and be alone. It would kill him to do it, but staying would be worse for them both.

Then he spotted Louise Daltry in town, being guided around Jo's Diner in preparation for her first day's work. Aside from waylaid vacationers, or guys from the forestry department, strangers were rare in Elkwood, so the arrival of Ms. Daltry, come all the way from Mobile and an abusive husband, was the talk of the place that whole summer. But from the moment Jack set eyes on her caramel-colored skin, high cheekbones, swept-back hair and soft lips, all of which were presided over by a pair of golden-brown eyes that paralyzed him whenever they strayed to his booth, he knew he'd never be concerned with her past. Only her future interested him, and in particular, whether or not she'd ever in a million years consider sharing it with him.

He smiled, just a little, and rubbed a calloused thumb over the rifle's trigger guard.

"Who's comin', Pa?"

We're moths in a killin' jar, he thought as he tried to summon a smile of reassurance for the boy that felt more like an expression of pain. *Just like your Momma said.*

The best day he could remember in his sixty-odd unremarkable years started as the worst. He'd been hungover, his head stuffed with cotton. The sour taste in his mouth had resisted his attempts to wash it away with toothpaste, then coffee, and finally a breakfast of toast, egg, bacon and grits down at Jo's. Even the presence of Louise, dressed as she was in an immaculate white blouse and blue jeans, looking as beautiful as he'd ever seen her, her skin radiant in the same morning light that skewered his eyes through the slats in the blinds of the diner's plate glass window, couldn't raise his spirits. He'd argued with the boy the night before, over what he couldn't remember, but he remembered striking him, and more than once, so on that day, while the smells of fat and bacon on the griddle turned his stomach and the whiskey hammered his brain, guilt gnawed at his guts.

"Someone went a few rounds with a bottle and lost," Louise had said, surprising him out of his self-pity and he'd looked up to see her sitting across from him, arms crossed on the table, head cocked slightly, a small smile on her lips.

He'd nodded and given her the usual perfunctory responses, and when he'd forced himself to look at her, he was struck, not only by her beauty, but by the sense that she was peering past his facade, into the dark turbulent sea of his guilt, as if she recognized it because she'd swam in those waters more than once herself.

"Wanna talk about it?" she asked, and though he'd thanked her and shook his head—*I ain't much of a talker*—she hadn't left, or taken those incredible eyes of hers off him, and at last he began to speak, slowly at first, then with more ease, until that darkness flowed out of him in a torrent he feared might wash her away and out of his life forever.

"The boy ain't yours?" she asked when he was done.

"He were already in the oven when I met my wife," he told her. "She never told me who the daddy was, and I guess it didn't matter. He was long gone when I showed up."

"Where's she at now?"

"Dead. She died givin' birth to 'im."

"I'm sorry."

"Yeah, me too."

That day had broken down some barrier between Jack and Louise he hadn't realized existed. It had been more than just the protective bubble that surrounds each and every man and woman when in the company of people they have no reason to trust. He got the feeling Louise had seen something in him he hadn't known was there, something that appealed to her. Though in hindsight, he thought maybe *suited* her might be a better way of putting it.

"Pa, say somethin'..."

She'd loved him for a time, and they'd been happy, but if he was honest with himself now, he could admit that he knew from the moment she stepped foot into this house, and their lives, that she wasn't going to stay. It wasn't because she didn't love them. She just wasn't a homebody. After eleven years of living with a man who'd beaten her senseless with whatever object was close at hand whenever she dared sass him, she wasn't willing to be owned again, or tied down to relationships that were just waiting to go sour. In walking out on that sonofabitch, she'd found her freedom, and though he'd sensed her restlessness right from the start, had known she would never stay, Jack had allowed himself to ignore the reality of it until it smacked him right in the face two years after the day she'd moved in.

We're moths in a killin' jar, Jack, she'd said to him when he'd come downstairs to find her with a single suitcase at the open front door, an unfamiliar car with a tall handsome black man at the wheel, engine idling, waiting for her. *You leave that lid screwed on tight, we're gonna die sooner'r later. Best just to set us loose while we still know how to fly.* Then, without another word, she'd kissed him and walked out the door, leaving him with an eternity to think of all the things he should have said but didn't.

Now he turned and looked at the boy who was not his blood, the boy he wanted to love but couldn't.

Then he looked down at the rifle.

Set us loose while we still know how to fly.

"Somethin' we gotta do, son," he said, and slowly rose from his chair.

NINE

Deep night came and with it long shadows that crept inexorably toward the Lowell farm.

The Merrill clan was among them.

Aaron had parked the truck at the foot of the hill and killed the engine then joined his father and Luke in walking the long straight path up the rise to where the Lowell farm sat brooding in the dark. The twins stayed in the truck, along with the body parts they had wrapped in plastic, surveying the night for signs that the old farmer and his boy were fleeing, or that there were flickering lights burning the bellies of the clouds on the horizon, foretelling of trouble's advance on them if it turned out they were too late.

Luke said a silent prayer that they weren't.

He carefully scanned the wide open areas to their right, where nothing sprouted from the dead earth, and listened to the hissing of the corn in the field to their left. Those sibilant whispers seemed like voices, but he had heard such things enough to tell the difference should a human voice be among them.

Making no attempt to be quiet, Papa-in-Gray, now dressed in a frock-like gray coat—which the kids acknowledged as his preacher garb, for he had told them once he believed himself a messenger, despite his failure to be inducted into a legitimate order—led Luke and Aaron to the door, the fluttering light within assuring them that someone was home, even though the truck Luke had seen earlier was nowhere in sight. Its absence worried him. Where were they if not home? With the Sheriff? The doctor? Luke let his eyes fall to the blade gripped in his father's right hand, the tip of the ivory handle a pale smudge in the dim light. As a child, he had watched his father sharpening that curved six-inch blade, had marveled at the craftsmanship, but had feared it also, and with good cause. Some years later it would be the instrument they would use on his genitals.

Papa-in-Gray stopped by the door, then turned his head and slowly stepped toward the window.

"He there?" Aaron asked.

Their father leaned his face close to the dusty glass, his shadow sprawling over his sons. His nose brushed the window.

"Papa?" Aaron asked, the nervous excitement in his voice infectious. The air grew taut between them; the temporary reprieve the rain had brought banished now. It was balmy, humid, their clothes stuck to their skin, and with the heat came short tempers.

The old man seemed to stiffen, his shadow flinching as if eager to be free of the tension that held its host in thrall. Luke felt something twist inside him. Something was wrong. Even if instinct had failed him, it was compensated for by the sudden rage radiating from his father's body. Whatever he had seen in there had not agreed with him.

Luke swallowed. Was the house empty? Were they too late?

His father turned to look at him. At the same time, Aaron moved to take Papa's place at the window. He drew in a breath. Luke did not hear him release it.

"What is it?" Luke asked. Now that Papa's back was to the window, the warm light spilling out around him, his face was in shadow. Yet Luke could still feel his eyes on him, cold black things that reminded him of Momma's glare from her foul bed in the dark. If there had ever been any question of Papa's feelings toward him, there wasn't one now. Pure unbridled hate contaminated the air between them and Luke would not have been at all surprised had tendrils erupted from the old man's body and enveloped him, drawing Luke into his father's body where he would burn in the fires of contempt. He squirmed in the glare, until Aaron stepped between them, quietly walked to the door, tested the handle, and opened it. New light carved the dark.

"C'mon," Aaron said, and disappeared inside.

For a moment longer, Luke's father pinned him with that raging and yet unseen look. Then he stepped close, his breath foul in his son's face, and brought the knife up between them, the point pressed to Luke's belly. When Luke tried to back up, Papa's free hand clamped down on his shoulder.

"You best start prayin' for salvation," his father said, his eyes black holes. He dug the knife tip a little deeper, until it broke through Luke's shirt and pricked the skin. "If'n you don't get it, you gonna feel this blade in your asshole 'fore I cut you wide open and let your brothers feed on your still steamin' insides. You hear me?"

The blade pierced the skin and the sting of it forced Luke to take an involuntary step back. This time his father didn't stop him. Instead he straightened, sheathed the blade beneath the folds of his coat in a leather scabbard at his hip, and headed inside the house.

Luke stood there for a moment, staring at the open doorway, trembling. A circle of heat drew his attention down to his shirt, where a spot of blood was growing at his belly.

He put the knife away, Luke thought, his mind a confusion of emotions. *There's no one inside.* Darkness that was not of the night edged into the corners of his vision. It was tinged with red. At length, when it became clear he was not going to be summoned inside, he followed, entering the warmth of the house and shutting the door behind him. Instantly, he saw he was wrong. There was someone here.

"Take a good look," Papa sneered, and stepped aside. Beside him, Aaron watched Luke for a reaction, his face impassive.

Luke, head pounding, studied the man sitting in the chair by the fireplace. It was the farmer, Jack Lowell, the black man he had seen, with his son, loading the girl into their truck. Lowell was of no use to them now. A rifle lay on the floor, muzzle pointing toward the fire. The air smelled of gunpowder and singed hair. The old man's head was lowered, as if he'd fallen asleep, but the angle allowed all gathered to see the gaping hole in the back of his skull through which the bullet and brains had exited and painted the wall and window behind them in gray and red. Blood had pooled around the chair, the old man's checkered shirt soaked with it.

As Luke watched, heartsick, Papa dropped to his haunches by the chair and dipped his fingertips into the blood on the floor, brought it up to his nose, then rubbed it, as if testing the consistency of paint. Then he rose and looked at Aaron. "Still warm," he said. "Ain't been dead long."

Luke felt himself being wrenched in two different directions at once. Part of him wanted to take his knife and cut the dead man to ribbons, punishment the farmer would never feel, but might sate Luke's frustration. Another part of him wanted to turn tail and run, to get away from his father and the deepening sense of danger, to see how far he could get before they took him down. He did not want to be here, did not want to think about what they were going to do to him, and yet fear held him in place as surely as Papa's blade had done.

He wasn't going anywhere. They wouldn't let him. *God* wouldn't let him.

Aaron sheathed his own blade, shoulders slumping in disappointment. He looked up at Papa. "What now?"

Papa continued to study the blood on the tips of his fingers. "Luke said there was a boy, didn't you?"

"Yes sir."

"Find him."

* * *

In the last days of Abby Wellman's tortured life, her husband decided to kill her. He reasoned that the cancer was going to do it anyway, and in a decidedly less merciful fashion than he could with a needle and some morphine. As the only doctor within a thirty-mile radius, and being more or less a recluse since his wife had fallen ill, he doubted anyone would find her passing suspicious, or feel compelled to study too closely the means by which she'd found her eternal rest. If medical questions in Elkwood were raised, Wellman was the only one called upon to answer them, so unless someone went to the trouble of bringing an outsider in to confirm his story, there was nothing to stop him from going through with it.

And yet he hadn't. Instead, he'd watched his beloved suffer, knowing it wasn't right and desperate to save her. The morphine he administered was always the correct dosage, never too much despite how easy it would have been to increase it. He could even have told himself later that he hadn't been paying attention, or was an innocent victim of subconscious mutiny, but nothing stuck. Every day he let his wife writhe in pain because he couldn't take her life.

"It hurts..."

Presently, as he looked down at the young battered and broken girl in the same bed in which his wife had once said those exact words to him, the same look of pleading in her eyes, he wondered if it would be better to show her the kind of mercy he hadn't shown his wife. If the girl died, it wouldn't matter if the Merrills came. He would let them take the corpse if they so desired. Once the life was gone from the body, what remained would no longer be his concern. And with her dead, they would have no reason to hurt him, as long as he kept his mouth shut.

He shook his head and drew the fresh blankets up around the girl. He had disinfected her wounds, then stitched them, but it was not within his means to give her the attention she so desperately needed. The damage to her eye was serious, as were the severed digits on her fingers and toes, but other than cleaning them, and applying pressure bandages and tourniquets above the amputations, he was out of his league. There was a good chance that if he didn't get her to a hospital soon, she would die.

She was awake, however, and apparently lucid, though given the trauma she'd endured, he didn't know how much of it was genuine and not just a reaction to the painkillers. What he did know for certain was that the girl looking at him now was not the same one Jack Lowell and his boy had brought to him. She was still pale, and dazed looking, but her pupil had returned to its normal size and her trembling was not nearly as severe.

Slowly, he sat back in his chair. "How're you feeling?" he asked.

"Hurts," she replied, in the small voice of a child who has just scraped her knee. It was so heartbreakingly sincere, Wellman found himself wondering if she had receded into madness to protect herself from the pain.

"I know, but we'll take care of you."

She blinked. "Where am I?"

"My home, in Elkwood."

"Elkwood?"

"Alabama. My name's Doctor Wellman." He offered her a warm smile, but resisted the urge to lay a hand on her, no matter how paternal the gesture was intended to be. After all she'd gone through, physical contact outside of the necessary medical ministrations might not be wise.

"Claire," she told him. "Claire Lambert."

"How did you end up here, Claire? I'm just guessing you're not from Alabama."

"Ohio." She winced as the pain fluttered within her. "Columbus, Ohio."

"You're a long way from home."

"I know. Can you call my Mom?"

"Of course," he said, but didn't think it the wisest idea. If he did, who was to say her family wouldn't pile on the next flight down and be here right when the Merrill clan decided to pay a visit? As bad as leaving Claire at the hospital and driving away was going to make him feel, putting the rest of her family in jeopardy was not something he was willing to have on his conscience. But having her contact information would help the doctors in Grayson identify her and they could take it from there. This in turn triggered the notion that although Sheriff McKindrey might be useless, the State Police might prove more helpful. But would they make it here in time to counter the tide of violence that must surely be bearing down on them? He resolved at least to try. But for now, he could only concentrate on one thing at a time, and so fetched a pen and some paper and jotted down the girl's address and phone number as she gave them to him.

"They tried to kill me," she said afterward. "They killed my friends."

"Who did?" Immediately, he regretted the question. The less he knew about all of this the better. But how was he supposed to play dumb when the victim of the atrocity had become his patient, and after Jack Lowell had told him his terrible story? "Never mind," he added. "We can talk about this later. Most important thing now is that you get some sleep and concentrate on feeling b—"

He stopped. A rumbling sound registered from outside the house. It was coming closer. Wellman watched as bright white light spilled in through the window, washed over the ceiling of the room before crawling down the walls, then sweeping across them to the door and vanishing into the corner. *Headlights*. The rumbling sound stopped. He listened for footsteps and after a moment was rewarded with the sound of boots crunching gravel. Approaching the house.

"You just relax now," he told the girl, alarmed at the quaver in his voice. "I'll be back in just a moment." He tried to think of something more to say, but his brain was scrambled, his thoughts lost in a fog of panic. He hurried from the room, bound for the kitchen and the cabinet where he kept his liquor, glasses, and an old tin box. Inside that box was a gun he hadn't used in over twenty years, an old military issue Colt .45 a veteran had given him instead of payment one winter when it was clear the diagnosis he'd been given was a terminal one. Wellman hadn't wanted the gun, but the look on the patient's face had told him it was less an offer than the last command the retired Colonel was ever going to give, and therefore needed to be obeyed. The doctor had accepted the gift, stashed it in an old filing cabinet, and for over ten years had managed to keep its existence a secret from his wife until he retired and forgot the gun was in a box full of medical forms. To his surprise, Abby hadn't demanded he get rid of it, but requested it be kept somewhere out of sight for the duration. He hadn't thought of it again since shutting it up in its little tin box, but he was forced to think of it now.

It felt heavier than he remembered as he removed it and checked the magazine, which had been kept apart from the weapon at Abby's insistence. She didn't want that tin box tumbling down some night and blowing holes in the kitchen, or *them*. With five bullets still nestled in the clip, he slid the magazine home and cocked the hammer.

The footsteps stopped.

Wellman glanced toward the sound, or rather the complete absence of it, and held his breath.

Someone knocked on the door.

TEN

"He ain't here," Aaron said, and Luke felt his guts plummet even though he had reached the same conclusion almost as soon as he saw the dead man downstairs.

"Wait a minute, we ain't checked the barns yet," he protested.

"*I* did," Aaron told him. "Nothing but a bony 'ol horse and a pig or two. Papa's out there now, inspectin' 'em, seein' if they're worth comin' back for."

They were in what might once have been a large bedroom, but was bare now aside from a small table in the corner, upon which stood a fancy looking but dusty lamp without a bulb. Next to that was a chiffarobe. Both boys had viewed it as an ideal hiding place for the kid they were searching for, but all they found was a few old moth-eaten shirts and one faded dress. A window looked down onto the yard below and faced the large red barn, the interior of which was cloaked in shadow. Security lights glared in at Luke as he tried to make out his father's lithe form. But for now, there was nothing to be seen.

Behind him, Aaron stood tossing his knife in the air. Luke could hear the swish of the blade as it sliced up, then downward, the fall intercepted by his brother's sure grip. He wished he'd stop. The sound of that blade only heightened his anxiety. But then he thought of something and turned, his shadow robbing the blade of its gleam.

"Papa said see if they're worth comin' back for?" he asked, and watched Aaron's head bob in the gloom. "Why come back? Why not just take 'em now?"

Aaron shrugged, and concentrated on the gyrations of his blade. "Papa said we ain't goin' home yet."

"Where *are* we goin?"

"He says that girl weren't gonna last much longer, shape she was in, so if she ain't here, then someone took her to get fixed up."

Luke was almost afraid to hope. "That old doctor out on the edge'a town."

Aaron grinned. "Yep."

Luke felt a smile flutter over his lips.

His brother snatched his blade from the air, sheathed it and headed for the door. As he passed Luke, he said, "I hope she's there."

"Me too," Luke agreed.

"Cuz if she ain't...if she's in some hospital somewheres, you're as good as dead."

* * *

Wellman was exhausted. The fear and adrenaline had drained him, and now all he wanted was to close his eyes and sleep like the dead. Twenty minutes had passed since the knock on the door, since he'd felt the kind of terror that threatened to disable him, leave him prone on the floor, victim of a heart that had taken pity on him and shut down, spiriting him away from whatever horrors lay ahead.

Now as he opened the front door and slowly eased himself down to sit on the stoop, the night air muggy and suffocating, he felt like a shadow of himself, the sad result of a life only half-lived. His bones creaked and popped painfully as he settled himself, ass on the wood, legs outstretched, heels dug into the dirt and scattered gravel of the driveway. In one hand he held the bottle he had shared with Jack Lowell, who he figured was most certainly dead now, or as good as. In the other hand, he held the small picture of himself and Abby, thirty years younger and beaming, not yet educated in the ways of suffering and death, their faces unlined, eyes not yet dulled by pain and the realization that there is no control, no dictating of how destiny will unfold, no real choices. Everything is preplanned, a fact that might not upset humankind as much if they were let in on the secret, if they were offered tantalizing glimpses of what the future holds. But no such previews exist, and so man flails blindly through the dark, hoping to avoid the holes through which he has watched so many of his fellow man fall.

The Colt was a cold unyielding lump against his spine, held in place by a waistband three sizes bigger than the one the younger, happier version of himself was wearing in the picture. Those forgotten youths, bursting with love and high on the promises they intended to fulfill together, as one, forever and ever amen, smiled up at him, attempting to convince him that happiness did exist, while at the same time torturing him with the truth that he would never know it again.

A droning sound echoed in the distance, bouncing against the hills and passing through the longleaf pines like gossip among old women.

The fear coiled inside him, but he was too weary to swim against its current, instead choosing to focus on the smiles from that handsome couple and their sepia world, as if wishing enough might enable him to travel back in time, to that place.

Headlights appeared on the horizon, twin moons punched in the canvas of night. The car was coming fast.

Wellman brought the open whiskey bottle to his lips, took a mouthful, swished it around to burn away the taste of bile, and swallowed. Then slowly, he rose and stepped outside. He monitored his breathing, regulating it in an attempt to steady his nerves. Then he reached behind him and untucked his shirt, letting it fall loose over the gun. In his left hand he still held the picture, the frame slick in his sweat-moistened grip. *Give me strength, honey*, he thought as he brought the picture up to his lips and kissed the dusty glass.

Then lowered it.

Give me strength.

* * *

Luke's head felt like a honeybee's nest. Ill-formed thoughts and paranoid suspicions bounced around his skull like smoke-addled drones protecting their queen. His palms were soaked with sweat, his brow beaded with perspiration, and not for the first time in his life, he cursed his lack of education. Papa-in-Gray had yanked his children out of what passed for a school in Elkwood as soon as Momma fell ill and was re-christened to suit her new permanent quarters. At the time, Luke hadn't cared one whit about being taken away from that low-slung series of prefabricated shelters. They'd been too cold in winter, too damn warm in summer, and the other kids had treated them like they'd fallen off the back of a circus wagon that had passed through town. Since then however, there had been occasions and developments in his life that had made him regret not picking up his schooling, even if it was restricted to their home, and even if Papa taught them. But Papa, though plenty sly, wasn't all that smart himself. He could trap a deer, a fox, or a man a thousand different ways, but when it came to things like numbers, or geography, he just scowled and spat and threw a fit to cover his ignorance.

Luke wished for smarts, especially now when he knew without a doubt they would help him sort out his thoughts, align them into some kind of orderly formation so they could be inspected, studied, and understood. So he could use them to engineer his escape.

But brains couldn't save him now. The window of opportunity had slammed shut ten minutes ago when they'd left the Lowell farm burning behind them. Papa had set the lone horse free, but it hadn't moved from its dark stable, so he'd left it there, figuring if it stuck around and burned, it was probably too dumb to be of much use to anyone anyway. And as stringy as the old mare looked, they wouldn't be losing much of a meal even if it wised up and took off. The pigs were a different story. Lowell had kept them plump, but even if he hadn't, swine are resourceful sonsabitches and will eat each other before they'll die of starvation. A thin pig was about as common as balls on a scarecrow. With Aaron and Luke's help, Papa had cornered the animals and deftly cut their throats. They were now bagged in burlap sacks and bleeding out in the bed of the truck as it reached the bottom of the hill and swung around a short hairpin bend. Doctor Wellman's place, old as the Lowell farm, but a lot less neglected, was dead ahead, waiting at the end of a long ribbon of gravel.

"Someone's there," Aaron said, unnecessarily, for they could all see the man standing before the open door of the house, silhouetted against the golden light from within. He had something in both hands. Luke guessed one of them might be a small thin book. The other item caught the light from the house and mangled it, making the bottle seem like it held aggravated fireflies.

"Looks like he's aimin' for a fight," Aaron said, and Luke looked at him, caught the relish on his brother's face. Ordinarily he'd have shared his sibling's excitement at the thought of what was going to happen here, but not tonight.

"Looks like he's aimin' to die," Papa mumbled, as the headlights washed over the old man, forcing him to squint and raise the hand holding the bottle to shield himself from the glare. Papa eased the truck to a halt, but kept the lights blazing. Then he killed the engine, and sat for a moment, staring out at the doctor.

Luke could feel his heart roaring. Could feel where his bare elbows touched his brother's. Aaron was trembling too, but for different reasons.

From the small space between the front seats and the cab window, the twins were electric balls of energy, their impatience making the truck rock slightly. Joshua's fingers were clamped on the back of Luke's seat. He could hear his younger brother's rapid breathing in his ear.

"What're we waitin' for?" Aaron asked, sounding just a little annoyed.

Around them, the night was uncannily quiet.

Wellman stood bathed in the stark glow of the lights.

"Search the house," Papa said at last, still watching the doctor, as if he knew more than any of them possibly could just from the look in the old man's eyes.

Luke moved, much too slow for Aaron's liking, and barely had the door open before his brother scrambled over him, knife drawn. The doctor may as well have been a cigar store Indian guarding a store full of free candy for all the attention Aaron paid to him as he hurried into the house.

"Go," Papa grunted, and Luke flinched, then obeyed.

The twins slid over the seats and followed.

Luke took his time, and heard the truck door slam shut as Papa stepped from the vehicle and drew abreast of him. The doctor looked on as the twins shoved past him, their feet thundering against the wooden floor as they disappeared inside. Then silence fell, and to Luke, it may as well have been an axe descending on his neck. His brothers knew better than to waste time. If they'd found the girl there would have been whoops and cries of delight, their way of letting the others know the chase was over, the day—and Luke's life—saved.

But now the quiet that held the night by the throat had infiltrated the house. The only sound was Wellman's unsteady breathing.

Papa did not look at Luke as they stopped in front of the old man, and Luke was thankful. He could not bear to see what remained of his increasingly dwindling hope being swallowed by the cold in his father's eyes.

"Where is she?" Papa said, and slowly withdrew his handmade blade from the lining of his preacher's coat.

Wellman was trembling, and as they watched, he slowly dropped to his haunches and set on the ground what Luke now realized was not a book at all but a picture. He straightened and tossed the bottle into the darkness.

"Bring that here," Papa said, nodding pointedly at the picture. Luke moved forward but Wellman shot an arm out, his palm mere inches from the boy's chest. Luke looked from the splayed fingers to the doctor's eyes, and what he saw there was not fear, or anger, but pleading. It was a look he knew well.

"Don't," Wellman said quietly. "Leave it alone."

From inside the house came the sound of something heavy falling then smashing against the floor, but Wellman's eyes stayed fixed on Luke.

"I said bring it *here*," Papa commanded, and Luke bent to retrieve the picture. He had just managed to get his fingers around the edge of the frame, the gravel biting into his knuckles, and was starting to rise, when the old man's bony knee loomed large in his vision. He lurched to the side just in time to avoid having his nose broken but caught the blow in the cheek before he rolled and got to his feet, face throbbing.

The old man was breathing heavily, shoulders forward, head low, as if he was waiting for retaliation. Behind his spectacles, his eyes burned with cold fire.

Papa laughed.

Luke, one hand massaging his cheek, didn't find anything humorous in what had just occurred. Their prey fought, punched, kicked, scratched, and bit all the time. It was nothing new. But the prey was always young, and strong, sometimes stronger than all of the brothers combined, so when they fought back it became a welcome challenge, an accepted part of the process. Sometimes they laughed about it later. But this was a sad old man who looked like he could be snapped like a twig. The twins wouldn't have trouble subduing him, and yet he'd taken advantage of Luke's distracted mind, just as the girl had used her sexuality against poor dimwitted Matt. But Papa had not laughed at that. No, because it had cost Matt his life, and he had loved Matt. He'd laughed at the sight of the doctor driving his knee into Luke's face because he didn't care. Because he was going to take Luke's life *himself*. Anything that happened between now and the moment he took his blade to his son's throat meant nothing in the larger scheme of things. If the girl were found, they'd take care of her. If she eluded them, they'd pack up and move. But either way, Luke wasn't leaving Elkwood. At least, not with all his parts intact.

"You're not takin' Abby," Wellman said in a low growl. "You don't have no right."

Luke drew his glare away from Papa to reappraise the old man. *Old, weak*, he thought, *and crazy as a goddamn loon*. Why else would he be talking about a dumb old picture as if it was his wife they'd tried to steal from him? Far as Luke knew, Wellman's wife was cold in the grave, but it didn't seem as if the old doctor had been let in on the secret. Either that or he'd somehow managed to forget it. *Crazy's a shithouse rat*, he thought. *No wonder Papa found it funny*. But justified or not, Luke felt the resentment colonizing him, and he took a step back from the doctor. To Papa it might have seemed as if the boy was doing nothing more than turning the show over to him, but for Luke it was an act of defiance, denying his father the opportunity to laugh at another thwarted effort to retrieve the doctor's beloved picture. The humiliation ended here. Over the years Luke had said goodbye to whatever dignity he had come into the world swaddled in, but if nothing else he still had a sense of pride, the latter instilled in him by the same man responsible for the erosion of the former.

Off to the right of the house was Wellman's old, green Volkswagen Beetle. Luke made for it, watched by the doctor, who made no move to stop him as the boy used his knife to jimmy open the hood, cut the cables and wrench out the plugs. Then he bent low, and slashed the tires. If by some miracle the old man managed to make a run for the car, he wouldn't get very far now. Luke stood, brushed dirt from his knees and rejoined his father.

Aaron appeared at the front door, face grim. In his hand he held a bloodstained ghost. With a flick of a wrist he tossed the sheet out into the night. It settled at the doctor's feet.

"She were here all right," Aaron told them. "But she ain't now."

Something else was knocked over inside the house—the twins, having their fun, high on adrenaline and compensating for the absence of their intended victim.

Papa-in-Gray stepped close to the old man. Aaron remained in the doorway, the gleam of excitement returned to his eyes now that he was watching his father at work.

"I'm gonna ask you one more time, Doc, and then I reckon I'm gonna have to start cutting itty-bitty pieces of you off until you tell what needs to be told."

Wellman backed away, toward the side of the house opposite the disabled Volkswagen where the darkness was heaviest. From there he had all of them in his sights. He stopped, swallowed. "She was here for a time. I didn't know what had happened to her. The man who brought her here—"

"Lowell," Papa told him, and Wellman's shoulders dropped a notch, the light in his eyes dimming. "We took his head as a souvenir. Wanna see it?"

Wellman paled, and shook his head. "No...I don't. I—"

"Clock's tickin'," Papa said.

"They brought her here, but I didn't know she was...yours. I thought she'd been in an accident or something. Jack didn't know nothing either. I did what I could for her, but she was too badly off...needed more help than I could give, so..."

Papa closed the distance between them. "So?"

The old man seemed rooted to the spot with fear. "So I sent her on her way."

Papa smiled. It was a predatory look and though Luke wasn't sure if the doctor knew it, it was also the telltale sign that the man's time had just run out. "With Lowell's 'lil nigger pup, right?"

Wellman said nothing.

Aaron let loose a frustrated sigh and stepped out into the yard but not before leaning back and calling out to the twins that it was time to go.

This was where it was all going to end, Luke realized. They had wasted too much time at home, with Momma's little speech, then Papa's display with the severed head for the boys' amusement, then again at the farmer's house, fucking around with the animals when he could have been in the truck, trying to make it here before the Lowell kid took off with the girl. If he hadn't known any better, Luke might have thought Papa had delayed on purpose, might have come to the conclusion that his father didn't give a rat's ass about the girl and had done all this simply to get rid of the family's one remaining rotten egg. To dispose of the kid he didn't love. After all, why punish Luke for a mistake Matt had made? None of this would have happened if that simple-minded fool hadn't fallen for the girl's tricks.

The more he thought about it, the more he felt a terrible, repulsive affinity for the people they had hunted and killed over the years. For the first time in his life, he felt the sensation of the trap closing in on him, the jagged teeth descending to rend his flesh and snap the bone.

He was no longer kin.

He was prey.

His father's voice jarred him from his thoughts. "Aaron."

"Pa?"

"Scalp him."

For one dazzlingly horrific moment, Luke thought his father meant him, that the execution of the mutinous plan had already begun, but then he saw the doctor back away as Aaron moved in on him, knife held with the point aimed skyward, and he let out a small inaudible sigh of relief.

"Make it fast, boy. We've got some catchin' up to do." Papa turned and headed for the truck, apparently uninterested in the torture that was about to be visited upon the old doctor.

He had one hand on the door when Aaron said, "Uh, Pa..."

Luke was surprised to see that all trace of fear had vanished from the old man's face, as if it had simply been a well-rehearsed act to fool them into assuming him an easy target. But as it turned out, *they* were the targets now, for in the old man's trembling hand was a gun, the muzzle looking as cold as the crooked grin on the face of the man aiming it at Aaron's face.

ELEVEN

Wellman had never been so afraid. His bladder felt explosively full, the valve responsible for keeping his urine inside jerking spasmodically every few seconds, threatening to release the dam if he didn't remove the hand of terror that kept squeezing it. His knee ached fiercely from its collision with the boy's cheek. But his concerns were not on his bodily functions at that moment. His perspective had whittled itself down until it was snugly focused on the tableau contained within the field of the Merrill patriarch's headlights.

They had destroyed his car, but that didn't matter. He hadn't entertained any notions of fleeing. In fact, though they didn't yet know it, in disabling the old Bug they'd inadvertently aided him in his cause.

The boy with the knife—Aaron—didn't move, but there was no fear on his face, only hatred, dark eyes ablaze with contempt.

"You better put that down now," he said, tilting his head slightly to spit.

Wellman waved the gun. "Back up."

The boy ignored him and looked to his father, who still stood by the truck smiling as if eagerly awaiting the punch line of a joke, and asked, "What're we gonna do, Pa?"

"Same's we always do," the man said.

The other boy, the one who had crippled the Volkswagen and whose face Wellman had caught with his knee, stared at him. Lurking beneath the grime and sweat and practiced callousness, the doctor thought he detected, not the anger he'd expected, but embarrassment, and perhaps the slightest trace of doubt.

"Why are you doing this?" he asked the boy now, the gun still trained on Aaron. "Why do you want to hurt folks who've never done anything to you?"

Luke, who seemed startled to be addressed directly, opened his mouth as if to respond then shut it just as quickly and frowned, his eyes moving from Wellman to the ground, then up again to his father, who answered for him.

"Because some people're born to die, Doc," he said and at last started to move. Wellman felt a surge of panic, his gaze flitting from the glaring Aaron to his father, uncertain now which one of them represented the bigger threat.

"You s-stay where you are," he stammered.

Papa-in-Gray kept coming, his strange dusty frock-like coat brushing his heels and kicking up dust.

"You think you was born to die, Doc?"

Breathing hard, Wellman slowly shook his head. "Nobody's born just to die."

Papa smiled. He was now less than ten feet away, his narrowed eyes catching the golden glow from the open doorway, making them gleam with odd light beneath the wide brim of his hat. "You really believe that?"

"Yes."

Finally, Papa stopped moving, just outside the reach of the truck's headlights, but he was close enough now that if Wellman stretched out a hand, he could have brushed the man's chest.

"You think me and my boys was born to die?"

Wellman considered this, but knew he couldn't give the response that immediately suggested itself. *Goddamn right. All you rotten bastards deserve to die for what you've done.* Instead he shook his head. "No. I guess you don't."

"Then tell me somethin'," Papa asked, chin raised slightly in the manner of a shortsighted man appraising a gem. "If'n you really believe what you're sayin'...and with you bein' a man respects life and all...tell me why we should be afraid of you when you're holdin' a gun you ain't gonna use?"

Wellman started to speak, to tell the man to back the hell up and enough with his goddamn talk, but the words died in his throat when he saw Papa's grin widen at something slightly to the right, something in the dark over the doctor's shoulder. Too late Wellman turned and saw one of the twins standing behind him, stepping forth from where he'd been concealed by the dense shadows at the side of the house. He had time only to see the impossible mask of utter loathing on the begrimed face and the dull shine on the blade in his hand before the child lunged forward and buried the knife deep into Wellman's thigh.

Pain exploded in his leg. The blade made a horrible sucking sound as the child jerked it free. Blood spurted outward, painting the boy's face, and Wellman staggered, his free hand clamping down on the wound. His back hit the wall of the house and he struggled to remain standing even as waves of agony washed over him. The blood continued to fount, jetting from between his fingers, and "oh," was all he could say as the strength started to leave him. Still, he kept the gun in his hand, the sweat beneath his finger on the trigger guard cold, but even though the temptation to turn that weapon on himself and end this now was greater than ever, he knew there was no need. Despite the unbearable pain, which felt to him as if someone had ripped wide the wound and were tugging on the nerves and muscles in his leg, he was aware of what had been done to him, and what he still needed to do before he bled to death. He willed himself to raise the gun, even as he slid down the wall. The figures in the yard had gathered around him, one of them laughing. Standing with the headlights behind them, they looked like devils come from Hell itself.

So much blood, Wellman thought, as he watched it continue to spurt from between his fingers in time with the beating of his heart. *Little bastard got the femoral artery, most likely. Gives me about five minutes, if I'm lucky.* But he had been given no reason thus far to think himself lucky, and so he shook his head to clear it of the clouds that were already starting to gather behind his eyes, and summoned every ounce of strength he had left to keep his head from nodding forward and pitching him into a darkness from which he was not likely to return.

"You got 'im good Isaac," Papa said, though he didn't sound entirely pleased. "But this ain't how I wanted it."

Wellman wasn't sure what that meant. Had they been bluffing? Had they meant to just scare him into telling them what they wanted to know, or to warn him as they had Jack Lowell all those years ago when he'd stuck his nose in where it wasn't wanted? No, there was no bluff here. Perhaps if he hadn't seen the faces of those boys, the cold malevolence in their eyes, he could have told himself that this had all just been some kind of terrible mistake, a rash move perhaps from a boy too young, or too simple, to know what he was doing. But he had seen them, had felt the threat saturating the air the moment they'd arrived. These people had come to kill him, just as they had butchered those poor kids and God only knew how many before them, just as they would murder Claire if he told them where she was.

"You can end this," he said weakly, his gaze directed at the tallest shadow now dropping to a crouch before him. "Hit the road, clear out of town and never look back. You've got time." He let out a long low breath. Part of him seemed to escape with it. The pain was maddening, a raging itch deep inside his leg he would have to tear himself asunder to reach. His heart ached as it strained to compensate for the amount of blood he was losing. He could smell himself in the air, the urine and feces as his bodily functions gradually started to relax and void themselves, giving up before the rest of him. He could smell *them* too, their foul breath, the old sweat, the dirt and filth. These were not the scents he imagined would herald his death, but on some level he supposed it was apt. Abby's death had been no more elegant.

"Ain't about time, Doc," said Papa-in-Gray.

"Then what is it about?"

They were closer now, or maybe that was just his own failing vision playing tricks on him, but the light penetrating their semi-circle seemed thinner, as did the air allowed to infiltrate the group. It was getting harder to breathe.

"We're gonna get that bitch girl, then come back," Pa continued. "And we're gonna make it look like you kilt yourself, though that leg wound won't help us none."

One of the smaller shadows swallowed audibly and looked away.

"Then we're gonna put your body right back in that house'a yours, get you all comfortable, maybe with that pretty picture of your wife. Make it look all peaceful."

Wellman was fading fast, the ground beneath him warmed by his own life's blood, the flesh above it growing steadily colder.

"Why's he smilin'?" one of the boys asked.

"I expect he's acceptin' his fate."

Get this one last thing done, Wellman told himself, but his own thoughts sounded distant, a voice heard calling from beyond the hills. Then: "One last...thing," he said aloud. It was not until he drew in a sudden breath and forced his eyes wide that he realized they'd been shut. His vision wavered, the figures around him blurry and indistinct as if seen through billowing sheets of plastic. He clenched his teeth, and willed his hand to bring the gun up. Miraculously, for it felt as if it existed independently of him, it obeyed, though the gun seemed to have increased in weight and size.

"Well lookit that," Pa said, and chuckled.

"Best step back, Pa."

The man's tone darkened. "And you best watch who you're advisin', Aaron."

Wellman gasped as a bolt of pain shot through him. For a moment he thought he'd been stabbed again, but realized as it ebbed away that it was merely an involuntary spasm, his body protesting the systematic shutdown of its component parts.

Papa-In-Gray's face was mere inches from his own.

Wellman straightened his arm and aimed the gun point blank at the man's right eye.

Knives found his throat. The twins, he suspected, on either side of him, their hands small as they brushed his chin.

"Easy boys. He ain't shootin' nobody."

"But Pa—"

"Get in the truck."

Wellman drew back the hammer. The ratcheting click sounded impossibly loud. The only sound in the world. The boys tensed.

"You heard me, now get movin' dammit," Papa commanded.

Wellman felt their reluctance as they moved away, heard their footsteps crunching gravel, the truck doors opening and closing again. Then it was just silence, one shadow, and the gun.

"You change your mind, old man?" Papa asked. "Fixin' to go out a hero?"

Wellman's eyes were starting to close, the shades on his evening coming down to usher in endless night. He jerked himself back to consciousness and muttered a curse.

"Go ahead," Pa told him, leaning in so the gun was pressed beneath his eye. "Pull the trigger. God might forgive you for doin' what you thought was right while the pain had you addled. And I ain't scared none. You might say I'm awful curious about what's waitin' for me up there."

"Let her go. *Please*. She never hurt you."

"She kilt my boy's what she did to me."

"She was... Just...let her go. She's suffered enough."

"Only reason you gotta stake in this is 'cuz you got in the way, ol' man. What happens to her ain't none of your concern. Shouldn't've wasted your time on her."

"You'll burn in Hell," Wellman whispered, his breath whistling from his mouth. Shuddering, he put as much pressure on the gun as he could muster, digging it into the flesh beneath the other man's eye. "You'll burn for what you've done. And someday... someone will stop you."

"Oh?"

"People like you..." He grunted as another bolt of pain shot through him. "Monsters like you...don't last long. Someone will put an end to this."

Pa sounded as if he was smiling, but his face was nothing but darkness. "But not you?"

"No." Wellman drew a breath he was afraid would be his last. He was wracked with pain, every muscle contracting, making it an effort to breathe, to think, to see..."No," he said. "Not me."

With the last of his strength, he swung his hand to the left and pulled the trigger. Pa jerked back with a grunt, one hand clamped over his ear as he spun away. The gun kicked in the doctor's hand, sending a shock of pain up his arm and he almost dropped it. But he brought the weapon up one last time, tightened his quivering grip, and pulled the trigger again, and again, even after he could no longer see, and the sound of the bullets leaving the gun was a distant echo.

* * *

The truck bucked and dropped low on the right side, the headlights tilting, sliding away from their father and the dying doctor before coming to a halt at a crooked angle. The windshield shattered, scattering glass, and from the back seat Joshua gasped as a bullet sheared off a piece of his right ear and punched a small hole in the rear window, starring but not breaking it.

"That son of a *bitch*," Aaron roared, jerking on the door handle. "He got the goddamn *tire*." Then he was out and running, door swinging wide, the knife held at his side in a fist so white it could have been sculpted from limestone.

"You all right?" Luke asked quietly, his eyes on the mirror and his younger brother's pained expression.

Joshua nodded, one hand cupping his bloody ear.

Isaac shoved the newly vacated driver seat forward and filed out with Joshua at his heels. They slammed the door hard behind them as if they had sensed Luke wasn't going to follow.

They were right.

Instead he sat still, and watched, absently picking fragments of glass from his hair and brushing them from his clothes. The cuts on his face stung where the shrapnel from the windshield had punctured the skin, but he was only barely aware of them. The tender area on his left cheek hurt more, even though the pain was no more potent than the nicks made by the glass. Shame made his face fill with blood and throb with the impotency of anger. He should have lashed back at the old man, snapped his bones and torn his flesh. There had been time. But he had just stood there in shock, overwhelmed by the dawning of what this new development would mean to his family.

The old man caught Luke a good one, he imagined them muttering to each other as they grinned up at their father, who would shake his head in disappointment. *Should've seen that comin' a mile away. Boy's gettin' slower'n a dog in the summertime. And y'all know what needs to be done when a dog ain't no good no more don'tcha?*

Panic lodged in his throat at the image of them turning as one to look at him wherever he stood waiting for their verdict.

We do, Pa.

Doubt delayed him, one clammy hand slippery against the door handle. These people were all he had. They were all he knew, and maybe at the back of it all he was getting too far ahead of himself. There was no doubt that Pa had no time for him, but would he go so far as to end his life? Over this?

Out in the yard, Pa was rising. Like Joshua, who stood by his side, nudging the doctor with his foot, he had one hand over his ear. Luke had seen the doctor move the gun away from his father's face and pull the trigger, shooting out the tire, and while Aaron had cursed and ducked, Luke had stayed where he was, watching until the moment the windshield exploded, hoping against hope that one of those bullets would tear through his brain, curing it of confusion and fear once and for all, or that the doctor would save at least one round for Papa.

It was a terrible thought and one he couldn't help but feel guilty for, and yet up until Pa had risen just a moment ago, proving he was still alive, Luke had prayed the man was dead and out of their lives forever. Now he watched as Aaron plucked the gun from the doctor's hand and checked the chamber. "Ain't got but one bullet left," he told their father.

One bullet, Luke thought. *F'only he'd used it. F'only Aaron'd use it now.* But his brother would never do such a thing. Aaron would forever be loyal to their father, whether out of fear or respect was unknown, and it hardly mattered. Aaron had watched Susanna die. Despite his apparent concern back at the Lowell farm, he would not intervene should Pa decided to kill Luke. It would be their father's will, and that will was as good as God's own for them. They served and did not question, and it was something Luke, despite his own years of faithful service, had never understood. If not for Momma-In-Bed's words, he might never have comprehended why they did the things they did, and the confusion and inner conflict of emotions that had manifested itself in those days after his sister's death might have driven him mad, or forced him to run away to escape them.

A farmer shoots the crows and sprays the bugs to protect his crop, don't he? Momma had once told him. *Shoots wild dogs and foxes and them sonofabitchin' coyotes to keep 'em from eatin' his chickens'n killin' his herd, don't he? Well, that's what we do. We're a rare breed, all of us, and what's outside there in the world would love nothin' better to destroy us because of what we believe in, because of our closeness to the Almighty God. To kill us outta jealousy because they ain't never gettin' so close to Him. They're the predators, Luke. They're the skulkin' dogs creepin' up on us, tryin' to snatch you from my bosom, from God's grace, like they did with your poor sister, fillin' her head with sick thoughts and vile dreams, corruptin' her till she was so diseased she went crazy and had to be put to sleep. Don't let them do that to you, boy. Let your Papa show you how to protect yourself, and your kin.*

"Luke," Pa called. "Get your ass out here."

It was too late. He could run, but they'd run him down. He could beg and they would ignore him.

He was going to die. Right here. Right now.

The warm breeze through the glassless window flowed over him, and still he did not move.

One by one, their heads turned to look at him. It was the scene from his worst imaginings come to life.

Y'all know what needs to be done when a dog ain't no good no more don'tcha?
We do, Pa.

His father spat. Wiped his mouth on his sleeve. "You hear me boy?" He was holding the doctor's gun. The gun with a single bullet left with which to end a life. *His* life.

Trembling uncontrollably, Luke let his hand slip from the door handle.

"Maybe he got shot," Aaron said. Then louder, "Luke, you shot?"

Papa stared for a moment, waiting for a reply, then started to walk toward the truck. "He better be goddamn shot," Luke heard him say.

He had seen their victims piss themselves many times over the years, had even seen the old doctor do it tonight, but had never really understood the kind of fear that could make that happen, make a person forget their dignity, and reduce them to the level of scared little children. But as he watched the lithe shape of his father striding toward him, that gun gleaming in the light from the truck, the understanding finally came to him, manifesting itself as a sudden wet warmth at his crotch. And as if everything that had been holding him back had been flushed out in that hot stream, galvanizing him into action, Luke choked back a sob and quickly scooted over into the driver seat.

"Pa?" Aaron called, in a worried voice.

Their father said nothing, but stopped walking. "Whatcha doin' son?"

Son. It was the first time Luke had heard the man call him anything but "boy" in years, but whatever power Pa wanted it to have over him was diluted by the fact that affection didn't suit him, and never had. His father was trying to stall him.

With clumsy hands he reached down, praying that his fingers wouldn't find only air down there in the dark beneath the steering wheel, the keys tucked securely in Aaron's pocket. A slight jingle of metal and he allowed himself a breath, then quickly straightened in his seat and turned the key. The engine rumbled to life.

He looked up, out into the night, into his father's face.

The eyes looking back at him almost sucked the soul from his body, leaving him a withered empty shell with his hands clamped on the wheel.

"Don't you fucking *dare*," his father said, and his right arm rose, knuckles tight on the trigger of the doctor's gun. Behind him, the boys were frozen, pale faces making them ghosts in the headlights.

Time seemed to stretch, as if those dark tendrils Luke had feared earlier had finally burst from Papa's eyes and mouth, and were anchoring the truck in place, crystallizing the breath in Luke's lungs before it had a chance to reach his mouth.

When they were kids, Aaron had once surprised a backpacker who had stumbled upon the body of her friend. Before she had a chance to scream, he burst forth from the trees and wrenched her head around, breaking her neck. For Luke, who had been crouching on a branch above the scene, it was the first time he had heard the sound, and the memory of it had never left him. He'd heard it a hundred times since, but that first time had stayed with him because it had sounded like the hinges opening on a forbidden door, a door to a new and terrifying world he was preparing to enter.

This was the sound the gun in his father's hand made as he slowly cocked the hammer.

"Was it the old man?" Pa called to him over the sound of the engine. "He say somethin' that tripped the switch? Make you feel bad? Get you thinkin' about your poor 'ol cocksuckin' sister? Get you all choked up, wonderin' if what we're doin' ain't right?"

Luke cleared his throat, watched the exhaust fumes tumble out around his father's feet.

"Maybe it was that *pic*-ture," Pa said, mockingly. "You got a hankerin' for some wrinkled 'ol cunt, that it?"

"Luke," Aaron cried out, his voice unsteady. "What you doin'?"

"Fixin' to run," Pa answered. "Ain't that it? He's ready to turn his back on us. On *God*."

Luke's heart thumped so hard against his ribs he figured they could all hear it, even over the engine. His breath shuddered out of him, as he slowly brought his hand down to the gearshift and jerked it out of neutral, keeping his foot planted firmly on the brake. The vehicle rocked. The engine started to choke, and for one heart-stopping moment, Luke thought it was going to stall. But it coughed once and ran steady.

"You ain't gettin' far boy."

Luke knew he was right. But then, he hadn't far to go.

"Now why'nt you just cut that engine and step out here where we can talk face to face?"

His father's eyes refused the light, but Luke leaned forward a little to peer into them for a moment. He had transcended fear now, the adrenaline in his veins burning through him, lapping at his brain, trying to force him over the border of that place he had kept away from all his life—the place where the truth, and his sister, were buried.

He pressed his other foot down on the gas, the other still on the brake. The engine whined, the sound deafening. The smoke from the exhaust rose like fog around the truck. When his father spoke, he did not hear the words, but understood the message on the lips that formed them.

"You ain't leavin' here alive."

The faint trace of a smile faded from Papa's face as if he too realized what was going to happen, what *had* to happen if he expected to maintain control of his children. Unlike the doctor, his grip was dead steady, the black hole of the muzzle targeting a point somewhere in the trembling oval of his son's face.

From the light side of that secret place in his mind, Luke heard his sister whisper to him, and could almost smell her perfume assailing his senses. *We was wrong, Luke. What he taught us was always wrong, and* we *are the sinners.*

Swallowing back the tears, "Who said I was leavin'?" Luke said, and took his foot off the brake. The truck lurched forward, closing the distance between him and his father in a heartbeat. Just long enough for a whispered prayer, a plea for forgiveness, for Luke to shut his eyes, the image of Papa-In-Gray's livid face made chalk-white by the lights branded onto his retinas as he pulled the trigger.

TWELVE

"You like to sing?" Pete asked, drumming his fingers on the steering wheel to some imaginary tune. "My Pa don't. Second Ma—I call her that because she weren't my birth Ma—was a great singer, and even my first Momma weren't too bad, but Pa can't carry a tune for *nothin'*. I ain't so bad myself, though I always forget the words, so I don't much like to sing. Prefer to hum. Don't need the words to hum." He smiled broadly, and wished he didn't have to watch the road, but every time he stared into the mirror at the girl lying swaddled in blankets in back, he heard Doctor Wellman's no-nonsense voice warning him, *And don't you keep leering at that girl like you're doing now, you hear me? You're not going to do her much good if you run yourselves right into a semi.* So he limited himself to short glances and resisted the urge to pull over for a while, just to sit in the peace and quiet and listen to the girl's breathing, just so the false breeze of their passage didn't keep creeping in the window and stealing away the smell of her. But the cranky old doctor had warned him about delaying too, said the girl mightn't make it if he dawdled, so he kept the truck moving steady through the night, the high beams picking nothing out of the dark but gray ribbon and yellow stitching, and the occasional mashed up bit of roadkill.

He couldn't believe his luck.

He'd fully expected an earful from his father, especially after the old man had grabbed him and all but flung him into the truck after catching him spying on the girl. Then he'd watched him get drunker and drunker, which was never a good thing, and guessed things were going to get even worse. But to his surprise, his father had told him he was sorry for what he'd done, for the way he'd been to him over the years, and that he wanted to make things right while there was still time. Pete had listened, not entirely sure he wasn't dreaming it all, but when his old man stood, put his arms around him and gave him a stiff awkward hug, he'd known it was happening for real. A change had come upon his father, as sudden and unexpected as snow in summer. Pete had stayed quiet, afraid if he opened his mouth he'd say something dumb enough to undo whatever had brought about the transformation. Instead he'd just sat by his father, and basked in the kind of attention and affection he'd only ever seen between other kids and their daddies, and had given up expecting for himself. He liked it a whole lot, so much so that, as overjoyed as he was to be entrusted with the girl, he couldn't wait to get home again.

But for now it was just Pete, the road, and the girl, and he was plenty proud of that.

Go to Doc Wellman's, his father had told him, a strange look in his eyes. *He'll know what to do. And tell him I'm sorry.*

Pete hadn't really understood what there was to be sorry about. They had, after all, done the sensible thing. But he didn't want to ruin his father's newfound kindness toward him, so he'd wordlessly accepted the task and hightailed it over to the doctor's house. There he'd found Wellman a little nervous, as if he was expecting a tornado to come down and pull away everything he owned. He'd hustled Pete and the girl into the truck, hardly saying anything at all, except to give Pete some stern instructions.

Here's her address. Listen to me carefully. You give that to the orderlies so they'll know who to contact. Now get moving, and don't stop for a goddamn thing, Pete. Not a thing, you hear me? She might die if you do.

At the memory of those words, Pete checked the speedometer and figured it wouldn't hurt to pick up the pace a bit. Wellman had told him it would take him the better part of an hour to reach the hospital. They'd only been on the road for half that, and the last thing Pete wanted was for the girl to die. They'd say it was his fault, that he hadn't driven faster, and his father would go back to being angry all the time again.

Pete had his own reasons for wanting the girl to survive. He wanted to hear her voice, to hear her say his name. When they'd loaded her into the truck, she'd been asleep, and still hadn't woken up. He wished she would, if only just for a few minutes. So he talked to her, keeping his voice low, hoping she might grab onto his words like a drowning man might grab a tossed rope. He wanted her to see who had carried her away from whatever bad things had happened to her in Elkwood. He wanted her to see her rescuer and know his face so she would know who to look for when she was able.

It was not until later, when the road widened and split into four lanes, the sulfuric radiance of the sodium lights jaundicing the horizon, the stars erased from the sky and pulled down to form the glittering lights of the Mason City skyline, that the girl spoke. Slack-jawed by the sheer size of the sparkling canvas overlaid on a horizon he seldom saw uncloaked, Pete at first didn't realize he was hearing a voice other than his own in the confines of the truck's cab, but when at last he registered her soft whisper, he jerked in his seat and almost lost control of the vehicle. Forcing himself to be calm, he eased the truck back into the correct lane, held his breath, stomach jittering madly, and raised his gaze to the mirror.

She was looking straight at him.

Instantly, all moisture evaporated from his lips, and a strangled croak emerged from his throat. He had to remind himself to watch the road, but as hard as it had been before, it was next to impossible now that she was awake. He swallowed with an audible click. Hoped she didn't scream like she had the last time she'd seen him.

"Hello Ma'am," he said.

"Who are you?" she replied, and for the first time in his life, Pete had to think about the answer.

"Uh...I'm Pete. Pete Lowell. I'm a friend."

Her voice was soft, so soft he had to strain to hear her over the droning of the tires, the hum of the engine. "Where are you taking me Pete?"

She said my name. The butterflies in his stomach caught fire, lighting him from the inside out.

"Hospital. You know...to get you fixed up and back to wherever you come to Elkwood from. Doctor Wellman told me to take you. Hope that's all right." He smiled, forgetting she probably couldn't see it in the mirror. "We all want for you to get better."

She stared for a moment, then her one uncovered eye drifted shut. She was silent for so long he thought she'd gone back to sleep, but then he heard her whisper, "I don't like to sing either."

Pete nodded, his smile threatening to split his face in two, and felt something like sheer, uncontaminated happiness settle like a warm blanket over his soul.

"I live in Columbus," she said. "You know where that is?"

"No," he said, and wished he did, if only to seem worldlier than he knew himself to be.

"Ohio," she said. "When I'm all better, I want you...to come see me. So I can thank you."

Pete didn't think he'd ever felt such elation. What had previously only seemed like unattainable fantasies were rapidly evolving into possibilities, and he vowed to explore as many of them as she saw fit to allow him.

Her voice was growing softer, and he felt a pang of sadness that it might be the end of their talk. "Will you come?"

"Yes Ma'am," he said, grinning toothily. "I swear I will."

He went back to watching the road.

PART TWO

THIRTEEN

For an eternity she lives in a world of dreams, and there is no pain. She is vaguely aware of figures dressed in white constantly shifting in and out of the twilit world between waking and sleeping, but most of the time she does not fear them. Their presence soothes her, represents a reprieve from the pain. Sometimes there are voices but when she tries to focus on the speaker, she sees only blurry shapes sitting on her bed, figures cut from the daylight pouring in through the large veiled window. They tell her things about her body, about her progress, but the words mean nothing. Sometimes there are others, voices she knows, familiar voices that make her heart ache as they weep beside her, and hold her. She does not like to be held, feels her skin crawl as their hands alight on her tender flesh, but she knows they do not mean to harm her, and so she says nothing, even as she withdraws a little more inside her shell. For a long time she says nothing. For a long time she lives inside her head, crouched in the dark peering out at the light, at the endless parade of unclear faces, not yet ready to accept them but glad they are there.

She does not want to be alone.

Alone, the nightmares come unbidden. The men put their dirty hands on her naked body; crush her beneath their weight. She smells their sweat, a stench she will remember for the rest of her life, feels the piercing pain in her groin as they roughly enter her—no romance, no desire—just rape, taking what they want, what they have no right to take, delighting in her objection, relishing the violation over and over again, stealing a little piece of her every time. Then their smiles as they step back to appraise her, crooked yellow teeth gleaming, eyes like polished stones, studying her, taking in every bead of sweat, every hair, every part of her bare battered body. In their hands they hold dirty blades as they turn away like magicians waiting to spring a surprise on the audience. Though she has transcended pain of the physical kind, she wishes for death, for sleep, for escape. Most of all, she yearns for the chance to turn back time, to contest Daniel's decision to shun the highway in favor of a merry jaunt through the backwoods. But she'd been outvoted, and a little drunk, a little high, and so had kept her mouth shut as they headed off down the narrow path marked by a signpost that told them they were three miles from a town called Elkwood.

* * *

This is where the nightmare began in real life, and in the realm of turbulent sleep, it does not deviate from the script, though sometimes the scenes are rearranged at the hands of a deranged editor.

The four of them, toting backpacks, a colorful bunch: Daniel in a gray Old Navy T-shirt, knee-length jean shorts with frayed hems and sandals; Stu in an appropriately loud lemon T-shirt and red and green floral-patterned Bermuda shorts, his shades hanging around his neck, a NY Mets cap pulled backwards on his head; Katy, more conservative in a khaki "skort" and a lime green polo shirt marred by slight sweat stains beneath the armpits, her dark hair tied back in a ponytail, one thick lock of it following the curve of her cheek; and Claire, wearing denim shorts and a white cutoff shirt that displays her toned stomach and the belly-button piercing she'd had done before they left Columbus. She remembers that ring most of all— a silver circlet running through a small fake diamond—because it was the first thing the men ripped from her body.

Her mind skips to this scene:

She is still dressed, but tied to the stake. She screams against the oil-stained gag as the man she will later attack with the wooden spur laughs through his teeth and pulls the ring from her navel, then holds it up to show her. There is a little speck of her skin still attached. And as he brings it close, she recalls the courage it took to get it done, and the complete absence of that same courage every time she thought of having to show it to her mother.

Then back to the carefree wanderers: Daniel and Stu walking ahead on the shaded road, trading memories of the last drunken night in Sandestin and chuckling while the canopies of oak leaves allowed golden pools of sun to warm their backs, Katy and Claire following, Katy strangely quiet. Bug spray doesn't dissuade the clouds of mosquitos that hang around them like stars around the moon.

Are you worried? Claire asks her friend when the guys are far enough ahead of them.

About what?

I don't know. You're not saying much.

Katy shrugs, smiles just a little. Just thinking. About us.

You and me? Or...

Yeah, *Katy replies.* Or.

He seems to be all right, *Claire tells her, with a nod in Stu's direction.* You don't think so?

Another shrug. Seems to be is exactly the point. He hasn't said a thing. Not a damn thing.

Maybe that's for the best. Maybe it's his way of letting you know it's over and done with, water under the bridge.

Katy looks at her then. If you cheated on Danny, you think you'd take him being quiet as forgiveness?

In the dream, before Claire gets a chance to answer, a disembodied hand appears before Katy, dirt under its nails, grime covering the skin, as it drives a rusted metal spike upward, penetrating the soft skin underneath her friend's chin. Blood spurts, Katy's eyes widen in horror, but she keeps talking, keeps trying to explain why she did what she did, why she betrayed her boyfriend with someone she had no feelings for, but the words keep getting harder and harder to get out as the spike appears inside her mouth, still traveling upward, puncturing her tongue and driving it toward the roof of her mouth. And now Katy is speaking as if she has never learned the right way to do it, as if she's been deaf since birth and will never be sure if the words are produced the right way. I...hink...I wanhed...to...hurt him...buh I hon't knowww why...*Then, as the spike continues its passage through her skull, Katy's eyes roll and bulge, begin to leak blood.*

Claire screams.

Ahead of her, in the middle of the road, Daniel and Stu turn, but the movement is not theirs. They are tied to stakes driven deep into the crumbling asphalt, their hands bound behind them, and when they turn, it is at the behest of the wind, as if they are little more than extravagant weathervanes. They are both naked. The skin has been removed from Daniel's face; Stu's head is gone, severed at the neck. And yet, somehow they continue to speak, permitted by the skewed logic of dreams to say what they once said in life.

We should have just driven, *Stu says.* Why the fuck would anyone want to walk in this heat?

You're missing the point, man, *Daniel tells him.* Everybody drives everywhere. Unless you're willing to spend a fortune on some goddamn guided trail in the Rockies, your options are limited. We got where we needed to go, had our fun, now it's time to get back to nature, see things as people used to see them. It could be our last summer together, so why not draw it out a little?

You're a fruit, you know that?

Maybe, but you'll thank me later. We're going to see things no tourist ever sees.

Claire looks away. The light fades. She is no longer on the road, but back in the woodshed that smells of waste matter, of blood and decay and sweat and oil. There is a window in the wall to her left that she does not recall ever seeing. Through the dirty glass Daniel stands there, once more dressed, his face returned to him but wearing a somber expression as he looks in her direction.

And, I'm losing him, *she thinks, as she thought earlier that day.* Things are changing. We both feel it. I'm losing him.

She opens her mouth to call out to him, to plead with him to save her, to save them both, but her words are obliterated by the filthy probing fingers that have found their way inside, forcing her to look away from the window and into the face of her nightmare.

Here she wakes, the smell of blood and dirt clinging to her, and she thrashes against it, against the arms that appear to hold her down, to tell her that everything will be okay, that she's safe now.

But she isn't, and she knows it. The killers may be gone, but they have planted something inside her with their fingers, their tongues, and their cocks. She feels it all the time now and it's getting worse, drawing nourishment from her, waiting until she relaxes, believes those who are telling her there is nothing left to fear before it claws its way out of her to prove them wrong.

* * *

"Claire?"
"Yes."
"Can you hear me?"
"Yes."
"Do you know where you are?"
"Hospital."
"That's right. You know why?"

She nodded, slowly, but still refused to turn her myopic gaze on the man sitting in a chair to the left of the bed. With him came an air of importance, authority. *Police*, she suspected.

"Can you look at me, Claire?"

She ignored him.

"My name is Sheriff Todd. Marshall Todd. I'm with the state police."

"Hi Sheriff Todd Marshall Todd," she said, and the policeman laughed, but it was practiced laughter, a preprogrammed response, the slush left behind by the icebreaker. His voice sounded gritty, worn, and she guessed he wasn't a young man.

"Let's just keep it to Marshall then, okay?"

He was trying to be friendly with her, keeping his tone light, but behind it she could sense his impatience to unburden himself of something. Perhaps he wasn't sure how much she knew, how much of the horror she had seen before she got away. And she wondered how much she could stand to hear. She knew a considerable amount of time had passed. It had felt like years, but the last time she'd been fully awake, the kindly patrician doctor had told her it had been over nine weeks. Countless times over that long stretch of terrible nights and days marked by pain, she'd imagined a convoy of police cruisers cars kicking up dirt, overseen by black helicopters, doors being thrust open, voices shouting as men wearing mirrored shades ran toward a sagging house, guns drawn. She imagined the media helicopters whirling above the organized calamity, flashing lights and camera lights as dirty men in overalls were led out in handcuffs squinting up, then out at a crowd of men and women who were eager to be at them for different reasons. Some just wanted the scoop; others to see the face of pure evil for themselves; and then there were those among them, the quieter ones, who wanted nothing more than ten minutes alone in a dark room with these depraved monsters.

And none of it would bring her friends back.

"How are you feelin'?" Marshall asked.

"Tired. Sore."

"Doctor Newell says you might be able to check out by the weekend. I'll bet you're anxious to be home with your family again."

"Yes," she replied, but wasn't entirely sure that was true. She dreaded the thought of what awaited her outside of this place—the reserves of energy she would be required to draw upon to satisfy the concern and curiosity of her well-wishers, the ill-concealed looks of resentment and accusation she expected to see in the eyes of the her friends' parents, the ones who had no child to welcome home. She was safe from the men now, for however long, their power over her limited to dreams and the occasional waking nightmare, but little could protect her from the maelstrom of emotions that would come crashing down upon her as soon as she stepped foot outside this place. The mere thought of it exhausted her, made her want to cry.

"Well," the Sheriff said. "Your Mom and sister are eager to see you. They've been stayin' in a motel close by, checkin' in on you often as they can."

Claire exhaled. She recalled their visits, how relieved she had been to see her mother and Kara, the agony reflected in their faces, the uncertainty of not knowing for sure how much she had suffered, and unprepared to accept any of it. But she was alive, and in their eyes had glimmered the joy of that simple undeniable truth. She was *alive*, back with them, when so many others had perished.

"Is there anythin' you need?"

"I'm fine."

"Okay. I just wanted to have a little talk with you today, check on your progress, make sure you ain't wantin' for nothin'."

She nodded slightly, her bandages chafing against the pillow. "Thank you."

"And I wanted to let you know that the man who did this to you and your friends is dead. Not how we'd have wished for it to go, but I'm guessin' he's facin' justice of another kind now."

She started to respond, then stopped. Surely she'd misheard. *The man who did this...*

"What did you say?" she asked, and finally looked directly at him. She saw she'd been right; he was old, his hat resting on his lap, held there by thin wrinkled fingers. He had a generous head of gray hair, which the hat had all but tempered flat against his skull, and kind brown eyes, which seemed designed for sympathy. His face was lean, and deep wrinkles ran from the corners of his mouth down past his chin.

He leaned forward a little. "How much do you remember?"

She stared at him for a long moment, then licked her lips. "I remember what happened, what they did to us. I remember getting away, but not much more." Her eye widened as a fragment of memory returned, though she wasn't sure how reliable it might be. "There was a guy, about my age, maybe a little younger, a black kid. His name was..." She struggled to pluck the memory from the swamp her mind had become. "Pete. That was it. I was in the truck with him."

Marshall nodded. "Pete, that's right. Pete Lowell."

"Is he here?"

"'Fraid not. He took off soon's he brought you in and saw you were in good hands. We sent a patrol car out to bring him back, but turned up nothin'. We found his house burned up though, and his daddy..." He waved a hand. "We can talk about all that some other time."

Claire planted her hands on the mattress and started to ease herself into a sitting position. Immediately her body became a combat zone, the pain exploding in various parts of her, a stern reminder that she was not yet fit enough to be attempting such hasty and ambitious movements. She squinted against the discomfort and when next she looked, Marshall was at her side, strong hands beneath her armpits, pulling her up as she dug her heels into the bed and pushed to assist him. "Easy. Hold on now," he said, and arranged the pillows so that she could lay back. She did, out of breath, her body humming with the exertion. Her joints were stiff and stubborn, her skin taut like dried leather. She was perspiring and when she raised her left hand to wipe her brow, she saw the source of at least some of the pain. It was missing two fingers—the pinky and the ring finger, and where they'd been nothing remained but twin half-inch nubs of smooth flesh. Staring in a kind of grim disassociated fashion, she withdrew her right hand from beneath the covers, and released a breath, relieved to see that aside from some angry looking pink scars, possibly self-inflicted during her escape, it was not mutilated. She raised her watery gaze to the Sheriff, who wore the expression of a man suddenly very much aware of the limitations of his job.

"You're gonna be fine. All kinds of surgery nowadays can fix you right up good as new," he said softly, but it was a weak effort at consolation and they both knew it. It wouldn't matter if they found her fingers, or her eye lying in a ditch somewhere, remarkably preserved, and sewed them back. It wouldn't matter if between now and her time of discharge they discovered a cure for rape, a way to give a sexually abused woman back her dignity, and in Claire's case, her virginity, the fact was that the violence had been done, its impact irreversible, and some vital part of her had been destroyed in the process, a part of her she hadn't known existed until it was stolen. Her friends were dead and gone, brutally tugged from life. Nothing they could do for Claire would repair that horrifying reality, or fill that dark gaping rent in her world and the worlds of their families.

Dark spots speckled her vision and she had to take a moment to steady herself, to anchor her consciousness. When at last her vision settled, she said to the Sheriff, "You said 'the man who did this is dead'. Who were you talking about?"

"Garrett Wellman."

Claire shook her head and frowned. "Doctor Wellman?"

"He was the town doctor, yes, or as near as they had to one. Some of the folks in Elkwood said he always seemed real nice, but started keepin' to himself after his wife passed on. Cancer. She didn't go quietly they say, and after her funeral, Wellman all but shut himself up in his house just outside of town. Took to drinkin' hard. No one knew what he got up to out there all by himself. Looks like it weren't anythin' good."

"Sheriff—"

"When we got there, he'd burned the place down around himself."

"Sheriff, listen to me. More than one man attacked us. There were at least three, and they were young, the oldest about eighteen, maybe, and the youngest not more than eleven or twelve. You've got this all wrong. Wellman *helped* me."

He smiled uncertainly. "We found remains, Claire. Your friends. In Wellman's basement. And he had access to all kind of—"

Claire stopped listening. She felt that old familiar panic rising in her chest. If there had been some kind of mistake, if the authorities were pinning this on the wrong man as it seemed they had, it meant the real murderers were still out there and the police weren't even looking for them.

But maybe they'll be looking for me.

Suddenly, the room began to tilt, the dark spots returning, bigger now, like black holes in her vision. Shadows pooled in the corners of the room and began to reach toward the ceiling, dimming the light. Nausea whirled through her. "Oh God..."

"Claire?" Marshall put out a hand to her.

Imagination gave it a knife.

"Oh G—" She turned away from him and vomited over the side of the bed.

FOURTEEN

"Goddamn it, Ty. Keep your hands to yourself."

The three workmen in the booth grinned at the fourth, an overweight black man in a padded check shirt and worn navy baseball cap with an M embroidered in the middle. Beneath it, Ty Rogers's broad face settled into one of apology though his large yellow teeth were bared in a grin as he raised his sap-stained hands in a gesture of placation.

"Not my fault, Louise. You keep shaking that fine ass in our faces every time you walk away."

Louise tucked the pencil she'd used to jot down the men's orders into the breast pocket of her pink and white striped shirt and folded her arms.

"Wouldn't mind being that pencil," another of the men muttered and his coworkers sniggered.

Louise, more tired than offended, glared at each of them in turn, until only Ty was looking at her directly.

"Maybe I should give your wife a call," she said, and at his nonchalant shrug, addressed the rest of them. "All of your wives. I'm sure they'd be real interested to hear what you boys get up to on your lunch break."

Ty pouted. It made her want to slap him.

"Aw c'mon now, girl. We were just playing witcha. You should be flattered. I mean, look at the rest of the girls in here." He nodded pointedly toward the counter where the other waitresses, Yvonne and Marcia, hugely overweight and looking forever unhappy about it, scowled over steaming plates of homemade fries, hash, eggs and sausage. In the warming light above the stainless steel counter, they looked like operatic villains.

"Flattered? I should punch you in your fat head," Louise told him and the men erupted into laughter. But Ty's smile faded, just a little. It was enough for Louise to see that she'd gotten to him, hit him where he didn't like to be hit, especially not in front of his friends. Though she'd seen him in here almost every day over the past month, had weathered his innuendo, crude passes, and vulgarity and thought him a pig, she hadn't been afforded this intimate glimpse of the man he most likely was at home. Dirty, abusive. Worse than a pig, she thought. A pig with a violent streak. She was more than familiar with the type.

"Talk like that," he said, "I should put you over my knee."

"With knees like yours, you could put me and everyone else in here on 'em and there'd still be room for a grand piano."

Ty's smile didn't drop any further, but it was frozen in place, as if the muscles responsible for relaxing it had gone into arrest.

"Got an awful smart mouth on you," he said coldly.

"And you got awfully twitchy hands. Keep 'em to yourself from now on you won't have to listen to my smart mouth or any other." She gave him a final withering look, then went to put in their order. Behind her she sensed the man's icy stare, but it wasn't hard to ignore. He could glare and grumble all he wanted and it would never bother her. She had bigger problems, and as The Overrail Diner was her sole solace from a life gone bad, not to mention her only source of income, she was more than willing to deal with whatever took place within its plate glass walls and acoustic-tile ceilings.

She reached the counter, ripped the order free and slid it across to Marcia, who snatched it up and deposited it behind her in the little square hole in the wall separating the business area from the kitchen.

"He giving you trouble?" Marcia asked, though Louise knew she'd seen and heard it all from behind the counter.

"It's no big deal. Pinched my ass, is all. Isn't the first time; won't be the last. I dealt with it."

Marcia glanced over her shoulder. "Way he's looking at you, you might want to watch your back."

Louise leaned against the counter and sighed. "Don't worry about it. Guy got his feelings hurt. He'll get over it."

"Probably," Marcia said, in a tone that said she wasn't convinced. "But be careful is all I'm saying. That's a big bull to have on your tail. And he isn't used to having the girls in here do anything but flirt with him, or at least take it a little better than you did."

Louise found the thought of that nauseating. She was about to say as much when Chet, the cook, appeared at the hatch and cried out in his irritating nasally voice, "Order up!"

Marcia waggled her eyebrows in an "I'm just saying" gesture before she turned and grabbed the two plates Chet had set there. A pair of mushroom omelets threaded steam as the waitress beamed her way down to the booth by the front door.

Outside, the snow had robbed the streets of color, reducing them to a monochrome depiction of quiet streets and tall silent buildings framed by a lead-colored sky. Dirty slush had gathered by the curbs, and what little life moved through that drab watercolor did so wrapped up tight in warm clothing, heads bowed to watch booted feet traversing treacherous ice-limned sidewalks.

This is not my world, Louise thought, but felt a pang of frustration when it came to her that though she'd had that same thought innumerable times over the years, she had yet to find a place that was. She was adrift and always had been, in a sea of other people's unhappiness, seemingly incapable of finding that single tributary that would lead her away to the place she sought and couldn't name, or even imagine to any encouraging degree. *Elsewhere*, she decided. *Anywhere but here.* But how often had she thought that too? And every single time, she'd picked up her life and moved, buoyed by the promise of light at the end of the tunnel, gold at the end of the rainbow, only to find herself in the same situation again and again and again. Stuck, miserable, and as good as alone, with a view of the future that never extended beyond the next paycheck.

Tomorrow, she decided, repeating the mantra that kept her from losing her mind. *Tomorrow it'll be better.*

Chet hailed her and she moved around the counter to pick up the order. There were four plates, each loaded with enough cholesterol to kill a horse, and that was before the men doctored their fries with catsup, salt and vinegar, and whatever else they could find to smother the taste. The smell of the food made her stomach turn. She stuffed some knives and forks in napkins, then expertly balanced the plates in both hands and headed for Ty's table.

"Damn that smells good," one of the men said, and rubbed his hands briskly together. "I'm starving here." And while the other men nodded their thanks, or smiled at her in appreciation, hunger bringing back the manners their Mommas had taught them, Ty, his face close to hers as she set the plates down, continued to stare. If he was indeed as pissed as Marcia had seemed to think he was, there was nothing to stop him making it known now through violence. She was all but presenting herself to him, and he could do plenty of damage by the time anyone realized what was happening.

"Somethin' you want to say to me, Ty?" she asked quietly, as she set down the napkin swaddled knives and forks.

"Just looking at that bruise around your eye," he said, his voice equally calm. His tone threw her a little. It was almost one of concern, as if he was preparing to make a conciliatory speech on behalf of his fellow swine.

"What about it?" she asked, and felt her cheeks redden, suddenly self-conscious.

"How'd you get it?"

"That ain't none of your business."

"Well," he said, leaning closer. She could smell cigarettes on his breath. "You should tell your man that his fists aren't doing the trick. You still haven't got no respect."

She felt her face grow hot, and the eyes of the men on her, waiting for a reaction. They said not a word, forks held close to their mouths, still loaded with food as they absorbed what had just occurred. A line had been crossed they would never have crossed themselves it seemed, but perhaps out of fear, they weren't about to point that out to their boss, who showed not the slightest sign that he regretted what he'd said. Louise straightened slowly and brushed absently at some imaginary wrinkles in her skirt. She looked from Ty, and the satisfied smile on his thick rubbery lips, to the cutlery she'd just set down before him, the tips of the knife and fork catching the fluorescent light, and she knew she was going to kill him. The awareness came without fear, or anxiety, or concern for the future she would be denying herself by plunging that knife into his throat. There was no future to squander. There was only now.

"Now get me some A1 sauce for my meat, okay?" Ty said sweetly around his victorious sneer.

She saw herself doing it. Though the fantasy seemed to last forever, she knew the moment itself would not. It would be quick. *Pick up the knife, drive it forward into his throat, step back to avoid the worst of the blood.*

"You hear me?"

Then sit down with a cup of coffee and wait for the cops to come write your future for you, takin' the choice out of your hands for good.

There had been many men in Louise's life. Too many, she sometimes thought, and yet still not enough to balance out the investment she had put into them. From Louisiana to Alabama to West Virginia and now Michigan, the path to her present could be found by following the trail of shattered dreams, empty promises, buckled pride and heartache. She'd been the sole burlesque performer in a theater filled with dead-eyed men.

And though she had never unlocked her most secret desires for the hulk sitting before her now, his eyes were just as lifeless, reflecting only inward, studying the desires and dreams of the self, incapable of recognizing those of others.

Her hand found the knife. Ty glanced down.

"What do you think you're going to do with that?"

"Is there a problem here?" a voice said, and Louise jerked, her hand splaying, releasing the knife. She felt her muscles relax, even as some other part of her tensed in disappointment. The invisible strings that had been tugging at her heart, her mind, and her arms, encouraging her to cut loose from them in the same swoop that would see the knifepoint piercing the sagging black flesh beneath Ty's double chin, released her. She had to struggle not to collapse from the recession of that furious impulse.

"I said is there a problem here?"

Louise glanced to her right, into the face of Robbie Way, her manager. He was at least ten years her junior and seemed condemned to use his authority to compensate for his lack of good looks, charm, and physique. His skin was pale and supple, slack around the dull gray eyes, and speckled with angry red pimples around the chin and nose. Now those eyes were narrowed, and fixed on Louise.

"There ain't no trouble."

"What?"

"I said there ain't no trouble here."

Robbie turned his attention to the men at the table. All but Ty had resumed eating. The manager watched them for a moment, then sidled up to the big man. "Everything all right, sir?"

Louise felt her guts coil.

Ty, armed with his most winning smile, nodded once and held up a flaccid cheeseburger seething with grease. "Sure is," he said, beaming. "We were just asking Miss Daltry here if she could get us some A1 sauce. Not sure she heard me properly though. It's what I get for eating with my mouth full, I guess." He chuckled, and Robbie smiled. Nobody seemed compelled to point out that the burger was untouched, and that there was no food in Ty's mouth.

"I'll take care of that for you right away," Robbie said, and turned, his thin fingers squeezing Louise's arm as he led her away from the table toward the counter. "What's going on?"

"Nothin'," she replied, sourly.

"Didn't look like nothing." They reached the counter and he plucked a bottle of A-1 from beside the cash register, then looked squarely at her. "This can't keep happening, you know."

"I know."

"No...I don't think you do. This isn't some sleazy bar where you get to back-talk the customers for ogling you, or get up in their faces because they were staring at your tits. This is a *restaurant*, Louise. We serve food. We get kids and old folks in here. Last thing we need is for the place to be in the newspaper because a waitress decked a regular. Case you haven't noticed, we're not exactly roping them in as it is."

Louise felt like a child, but couldn't summon the will to raise her head and look the manager in the eye, opting instead to just stare at the floor, and the still-wet boot prints from whomever had come in last.

"Problem is," Robbie went on, "Half the guys we get in here only come to look at you anyway. We all know the food is crap, and Elmo's Pizza is only two blocks from here, but have you seen the waitresses over there?" He shuddered. "They've got some kind of faux Italian thing going on, which would be fine if their ancestors didn't all hail from Montreal."

She smiled at that, and nodded. Robbie chose to take it as an encouraging sign. "You're a good looking woman, Louise. You gotta expect to have to take some shit from these guys, and learn to let it go right over your head. It's the only way you're going to last in this business."

Louise sighed and offered him the smile of understanding she knew he was waiting for. Unfortunately, Robbie was another dreamless wonder. He assumed anyone who worked under him entertained the same grand notions of one day opening up a restaurant of their very own as he did. Somewhere along the crooked road of his life, the young man before her had considered his options and found but a single route still open to him. He'd hurried down that road, his mind fixated on the one thing that would allow him to retain his pride, and had done so with such veracity that it had brainwashed him, consumed him, and now anything beyond that single well-trodden path seemed incomprehensible, perhaps even threatening to him because it was a facet of life of which he would never get a taste. Louise imagined his apartment dark, damp and empty, with Robbie in the bathroom, still dressed in his trademark white shirt, red tie and black pants with the razor sharp creases, practicing the many expressions of authority and stern speeches he needed to excel at his job.

It was this summation of his character in Louise's mind that negated his words to her now. Everything he told her was trite, pulled straight from *The Idiot's Guide to Diner Management* or some other textbook dedicated to showing you what you already knew but needed to see in writing.

"Thank you," she said, and exhaled heavily.

"You're welcome," Robbie replied, obviously pleased with himself. "Now bring this bottle down to that gentleman's table." He slid the A-1 into her palm and watched her carefully.

"Okay." She started to turn, then paused and looked back into his expectant face. "Can I take a five minute smoke break after that?"

Robbie frowned, shirked back his shirtsleeve and checked his watch, then sighed. "Five minutes. But do it around back. I don't need smoke blasting in on people while they're eating every time someone opens those doors."

Louise nodded and headed away. As she approached Ty's table, the large man looked up, mouth stuffed with cheeseburger, a smear of cheese on his lower lip.

Dead eyes, she thought.

"About time, sugar tits," he mumbled around his food and reached out a hand for the bottle.

Breathing hard with anticipation, she grabbed his wrist with her left hand and quickly yanked it aside.

The men froze.

Ty's eyes bugged. "The hell you think you're d——?"

"Hey!" Robbie called, and she heard his perfectly polished shoes slapping the tiles.

"Sorry," she said, aware it would not be clear to whom she'd been speaking as she swung the sauce bottle into the side of Ty's head.

* * *

Later, she would wonder if it was possible that her thoughts had somehow summoned him, pulled his likeness from the ether, a mixture of memory and yearning designed to torment her further.

But he was real.

She took the long way home after spending three hours in a cafe, nursing a cup of scalding hot coffee and feeling sorry for herself until it was close to the time she'd normally be clocking out at the Overrail.

She felt no satisfaction from what she'd done to Ty Rogers, though she didn't regret it. The son of a bitch had it coming, and God alone knew how many battered women in the man's life she had struck a very literal blow for today. And yet she felt nothing but emptiness. Ty had been a victim by proxy, a piñata for all the pent-up anger, frustration, and self-hatred that had been gathering within her over the past few months.

As she turned the corner on East Pleasant Avenue, the hair prickled on the nape of her neck. She tugged up the collar of her fur-lined parka and shivered. It was cold, the sidewalks like polished glass, the wind dragging its ragged nails across her cheeks.

What the hell had she been thinking coming to Detroit?

It was a silly question of course, one she would have been better not asking herself again, for the answer never failed to further darken her thoughts.

She had come here because of Wayne, whom she'd loved, whom she feared she still loved, despite realizing long ago that every second word that spilled from his mouth was a lie, his promises glass birds destined to shatter sooner or later against the cold hard surface of reality. And the worst truth of all, the black knot in her heart that she couldn't unravel, was that for this life, for this misery, she had abandoned with hardly a second thought a man and a child who had truly loved her, dumped them for a yellow brick road that had led her straight into a wasteland. She'd shut the door and driven away without looking back at the sad weathered man and his simple-minded boy, who would never understand the lure of her dreams, the hunger for ambition that drove her. Into Wayne's car and out of their lives, headed for a recording studio in Detroit, where Wayne's cousin Red was as eager as he to make her a star.

700 miles later, she'd realized her mistake.

There was the cold, a development she had anticipated but which still came as a shock to her system. Even so, her spirits held. She was prepared to make sacrifices for the sake of her career, and if singing her heart out in an icy room while the whole world got buried under six foot of snow outside was what it took, then so be it.

But there was no studio, and for all she knew never had been.

According to Red, he'd been forced to sell his studio a month before when the bank threatened to take his house for failure to make mortgage payments. From the look of the man—shifty eyes, shiny red leisure suit, hair in cornrows, smile so full of gold it made her wonder why he hadn't sold them instead of the studio to save his house—they'd been had. Wayne would tell her later that he thought Red had a drug problem, that he was a habitual user and a compulsive liar. Three months of ever-worsening misery would pass before Louise would lose her cool enough to tell him that maybe he and Red had the latter attribute in common.

And Wayne would stun her, figuratively and literally, by responding with his fists, breaking her nose and two of her teeth in the process. It was the first time he'd hit her, and wouldn't be the last.

And still she wouldn't leave him. She couldn't. Despite his infrequent bursts of violence, she was drawn to him by the other part of him, the part that held her in bed at night and sang songs in her ear, the part that told her everything was going to be all right and that she should never doubt that he loved her. The tender side of him that promised someday everything would work out, that he never meant to hurt her. *It's just that sometimes you shoot your mouth off a little, that's all...*

She supposed that today she had proven how hot-headed she herself could be. After all, didn't what she had done to Ty for his ill-chosen remarks make her no better or worse than Wayne?

He was her anchor. That was it. Her anchor in a hurricane, the tether that kept her from being swept away in an ugly wind that might destroy her in a maelstrom of loneliness, of isolation and fear, a fear that was infinitely worse than her fear of him when his moods turned black.

He was all she had left.

Wayne, and the dreams that stubbornly refused to leave her be.

Dreams, hope, and her memories of better times.

Wincing against the bitter sting of the cold, she pictured Jack and his son standing at the door to their rundown old farmhouse, the red dust swirling about their feet then rising behind the tires of Wayne's car to obscure them from view, leaving nothing but dark crooked smudges amid that cloud, over which the eave of the sagging roof cut a red triangle from the clear blue sky.

She blinked away tears, and stepped over a mound of slush to cross the street. Her apartment was close now, and a dull pang of unease passed through her. Wayne would not take too well the news of her being fired, and though Louise had no doubt she could pick up something else soon, he would be sure to make a production out of it, as if berating her was a ritual he had a religious obligation to fulfill. But she knew his tirade would be nothing more than a means of avoiding reality yet again. She had lost her job; he'd never had one, and probably figured if he gave her a hard enough time about getting fired, she wouldn't think to point out his own insufficient contributions to their survival. He smoked too much, drank too much, and frequently vanished on late night walks she had long ago ceased believing were as benign as he made them out to be.

Sighing heavily, she told herself that at least Ty hadn't pressed charges today, a development that had surprised her until she realized having her arrested might mean word would spread about what had precipitated the drama between them, and he would be understandably leery about such details hitting the streets where his wife might hear it. It was about the only positive she could find in another dismal day.

Someone was standing outside the apartment.

For a moment, she thought it might be Wayne, but as she drew closer, she saw that the body was too thin and a little too short. Only the jacket he wore looked the same. The man stood there, staring up at the windows on the second floor, alternating between stamping his feet on the sidewalk and blowing into his cupped and ungloved hands. She felt sorry for him being out here so ill-equipped for the harsh cold, but had no notion of stopping to tell him so or to offer him charity, which in this part of the city, was most likely what he wanted. The streets were too dangerous here, and if he wasn't a bum hoping for a handout then chances were he was waiting for some unlucky sucker to rob.

Louise surreptitiously reached for her purse and unzipped it. Inside was the can of Mace Marcia at the Overrail had given her on her first day, after Louise told her she wasn't driving home, but walking. *Girl*, Marcia had said, with a disapproving shake of her head, *Around here, no one walks anywhere unless they're carrying a gun.* The threat was worse at night, which was why Louise had requested the day shift, but in winter, when the light faded early, there was little difference.

As she approached her building, stepping off the curb to avoid having to pass too close to the man, he stopped his bouncing and turned. His lower face was hidden by a threadbare black scarf, a wool cap pulled down almost to his eyes.

She saw that he was young, the visible part of his face unlined by the wringer through which all young men were passed as the dark secrets of life were eventually revealed to them.

Louise ducked her head and moved past him.

He mumbled something to her.

"Sorry," she said, nerves jangling, and quickened her pace. It was not a question, but an apology that she could not stop to listen. She hadn't been able to make out the words, but it had sounded like he'd said "Wanna sleep." Trying hard not to think too much about what such a cryptic message might mean, she trotted up the steps of the building and quickly snatched her key from the jumbled guts of purse, her hands trembling from the day's ardor as she drove it into the lock and turned. When the man spoke again, his voice was clearer and this time his words made her freeze, every hair on her body standing on end.

You're dreamin'.

Eventually, she turned.

The man—the *boy*—had pulled down his scarf to reveal an uncertain, yet hopeful grin, and with him came a tsunami of emotion that crashed down on Louise, sucking the air from her lungs.

"Oh God."

Her past approached her in small careful steps, wreathed in the smells of dust and leaves and forgotten warmth, but it was only a memory, as she feared was the boy standing before her.

It had to be a memory. Or a ghost.

His eyes were wide, and alive, as he came to her. "Mom...it's me."

FIFTEEN

Finch was there when they brought her home, though he tried not to let himself be seen.

The Lambert House was modest but attractive. A white-tract home with brown decorative shutters and dormer windows, it was set just far enough apart from its neighbors to avoid looking like part of a subdivision, which is exactly what it was—just one of thirty-nine buildings of similar design. The house was relatively new, had not yet conceded defeat to Ohio's scorching summers or freezing winters. The roof looked pristine, the windows polished, the lines straight, the angles sharp. The lawn was neatly tended. But Finch knew that if there were any validity to the claim that houses absorbed the emotions of their owners, the Lambert home would soon begin to sag. The windows would darken even in sunlight, spots of dirt would speckle the siding, the bones beneath the skin of the house would weaken, and cracks would appear. There would be too much hurt and misery for the house to remain standing proud.

He watched as a gray SUV slowed and turned into the driveway. The windows were tinted, so he couldn't see the passengers, only a darker version of a sky pregnant with rain, but he knew the car, had seen it many times before. It had spent its fair share of time in his own driveway over the years.

There were no reporters at the house. They had kept vigil there like hippies at a folk festival since the day the news broke about the murders, but as soon as the murderer was named and his death announced, they started to lose interest. Killers were always popular in the news, particularly one this savage, but dead ones weren't worth the hassle, not when the space could be filled by the latest atrocity in the Middle East. Even at the height of the frenzy, coverage of the Alabama murders had paled in comparison to that of beheaded engineers and assassinated politicians in Iraq. Now, the farther away from the epicenter of the massacre you went, the further into the paper you had to look to find mention of what had happened in Elkwood. It was a different world these days, Finch realized. Since 9/11, society's gaze had shifted outward in search of blame, to places unseen and seldom heard of except in grainy pictures on the news. Everyone was looking for the boogeyman. The worries of a nation were with their soldiers, no longer on their own stoops. And every day there was more cause for grief as word was sent home of another casualty. The internal corruption and strife of America went unnoticed, its troubles measured only by the amount of bodies and flag-draped coffins.

Finch sighed, shifted in the car seat and lit a cigarette. The smoke filled the Buick and he waved a hand through it.

He had been there, at the core of the unrest in Iraq, and had seen Hell firsthand. It had infiltrated him, possessed him, destroyed him, and they'd sent him home, promising he would be fine. But he hadn't. He'd taken Hell home with him. The army, the government, some faceless son of a bitch in an expensive suit chomping on a cigar a thousand miles away from the conflict, had put him there and hadn't been able to exorcise it from him when he'd returned. Despite the pride and strength he'd always claimed were his biggest assets, his turmoil was so great he'd sought assistance, but a series of stops at the VA center and hospital in Columbus yielded little help. He was put on a six-month waiting list and told to sit tight. And in that time, he read the papers and watched the news, and saw his fellow marines die of neglect, turned away by the very administration that had made so many promises. *Die over there, or die at home*, seemed to be the consensus, and in that respect, they held true to their word. Finch turned to alcohol, and briefly to drugs, but they only fed the horror inside him, fortified it, allowing his demons a legitimate stage from which to torment him. More marines had died. He quit watching the news, quit listening to the world.

Until it took his brother from him.

Danny.

The last he'd seen his face had been on the main evening news, his gangly arm thrown over the shoulders of his girlfriend Claire. Now he was dead, hacked to pieces by an insane doctor.

But of course, that wasn't true. Not if Claire was to be believed, and why shouldn't she be? Who else alive could tell the world the truth about what had happened down there in that dirty little town? Except, they refused to believe what she'd told them because they had already celebrated the end of their grisly case weeks before Claire was even conscious, buried it in the same pit with the remains of the old doctor, who they knew without a shadow of a doubt had, despite having no previous history of violence, gone berserk and hacked up a load of kids. Backs had been slapped, folders had been tossed into filing cabinets, and sudsy beers had been tossed back while they grinned at each other, dug into steaks and thick fries smothered in ketchup, before going home to their wives and girlfriends, maybe to sleep after a hard day's work, maybe to make love to put the proper end to a case they hoped someday to tell their grandchildren about.

The Sheriff who'd seen to Claire in Birmingham, a man by the name of Marshall Todd, had called Finch's mother to offer his condolences for the umpteenth time, to let them know Claire's release was imminent, and that they might do well to prepare for all kinds of questions from left-field. The girl's story, he informed them, ran contrary to what they knew to be true. He suspected she was out of it from the painkillers, was misremembering things as people do in the aftermath of such a terrible trauma. All it would take to inspire a story like that, he said, would be repressed memories and a shifting of the wrong ones. She could be remembering the scenes but superimposing things over them that hadn't been there at all. He could understood completely how a woman forced to endure such an awful ordeal, crazy with pain, disorientated from the abuse she'd taken, would see phantoms where there had been none. *Even so*, he'd conceded, *if it turns out Wellman had an accomplice, we'll look into it, but the important thing to keep in mind is that the main figure at the center of this atrocity is dead, and I hope that brings you some little peace of mind.*

Finch shook his head as rain beaded the glass and the SUV squeaked slightly to a stop close to the front door of the house.

It hadn't brought them peace of mind, and, standing in the kitchen, trembling, his mother had yelled at the Sheriff, questioning his foolishness in thinking it might when her son was dead.

The driver side door of the SUV opened and Claire's mother got out. A high school teacher at least two decades his senior, he nevertheless recalled fantasizing about her during those halcyon days back when everybody lived forever, and happiness was daydreaming about taking your teacher over the desk during detention, or asking a girl out and having her look at you like she thought you'd never ask. It was a basketball victory, a smoke behind the bleachers, a Friday night cruising with your friends, sipping beer outside Wal-Mart until the cops came, the smell of the air, electric with possibility.

Then the war had come, and he'd taken it home with him, only to find a worse one waiting.

He shuddered the smoke from his lungs and squeezed his eyes shut for a moment, then raised his head.

Mrs. Lambert didn't look nearly so appealing now. Her face was wan and pale, her eyes liquid smudges peering out at a world she no longer took for granted, or trusted. Her long curly brown hair was in disarray, her clothes shabby and wrinkled from a long drive.

The year Finch graduated, Mrs. Lambert retired from Hayes High School after coming home one night to find her husband dead on the kitchen floor in a puddle of milk after his heart gave out while he was getting a drink. Surviving him had aged her considerably. Finch suspected what had happened to Claire would push her further to the grave than time alone could ever manage.

He watched Mrs. Lambert move to the side door of the SUV and, with visible effort, wrench it open. She looked like a scarecrow trying to throw wide a barn door. At the same time, the front passenger door slammed shut, and Kara emerged, looking like a younger but just as harried version of her mother. Finch felt something akin to excitement in his stomach, but it was immediately quelled by the memory of what had happened between them, how she had managed to move on with her life and he had gone to war to forget his, only to have bullets compound the fear that wherever he turned, he'd still be punished.

Unlike her mother's, Kara's hair had been cut short. Finch didn't approve of the style, but figured that would hardly send her world careening out of orbit if she somehow got wind of it. Besides, when they'd been together, she'd had her hair long to suit him. The new cut was to suit someone else, or maybe just herself, as whenever he saw her around town she was alone, and not looking at all put out by it.

It made him ache to see her.

Now she joined her mother and reached in, pausing a moment to look around, probably to ensure no cameras were rolling. Finch guessed that the hospital might have leaked news of Claire's discharge to the media, but the date would have been intentionally inaccurate, allowing the Lamberts to get Claire home a few days before the vultures descended. The reporters would figure it out, of course, but by then there'd be little they could do, assuming they'd care.

Kara's gaze settled on his Buick, where he'd parked it facing out of a driveway two houses down on the opposite side of the road. He had to resist the urge to duck and felt his insides squirm the longer she watched him. She would recognize the car of course; he'd had it since their dating days, had driven her to Niagara Falls in it, made love to her in the back seat one drunken summer night then laughed about the immaturity of it, and the rearview mirror still held the memory of her standing at her front door six months later after she told him he scared her, that she couldn't tolerate his moods or his temper any longer.

A pair of emaciated arms reached out from the darkness inside the SUV and Finch rolled his window down, just a little. The breeze snatched the smoke from the car, dragging it out into the rain.

Claire stepped out into the dim daylight and raised her face to the clouds, as if challenging God to throw his next unpleasant trial at her. She looked frail. Had Finch not known who she was, he might have thought her an elderly woman, some long-lost grandmother come to visit her relatives.

They raped her.

Slowly, one hand clamped on her mother's arm, Kara's hand on her back for support lest she should fall, they guided her toward the house and the shelter of the eave.

They cut out her eye.

Claire took the steps on her own, but paused at the top, as if the three stone steps had been enough to exhaust her.

They cut off her fingers.

Finch tossed his cigarette out the window. In the rearview, he was startled to see an old man in a check shirt and dungarees emerge from the house that belonged to the driveway and squint at the Buick as he started toward it. "Hey!"

Finch started the engine. He wasn't going to think of this as a missed opportunity. After all, he'd had no intention of approaching the Lamberts. He'd only wanted to see Claire, to get as accurate a picture as he could of what they had done to her, so he could add it to the bloodstained collage he was developing in his own private darkroom.

They killed Danny.

He pulled out of the driveway and the old man slowed, then stopped as Finch turned out onto the road. He sped up, driving in the direction of the Lambert house but not stopping, the windshield wipers laboring to clear the glass of the strengthening rain. As he passed by, he looked and saw that Claire and her mother had already gone inside. Kara followed, but turned as she shut the door, and hesitated.

She saw him. There was no way she couldn't have. But her expression remained the same.

Again, his stomach jumped.

Then she was gone.

Finch hit the gas.

Not today, he thought. *Not now.*

He would return, and when he did it would not be to offer his sympathy, or to torture himself by looking into the eyes of the only woman he'd ever loved.

It would be to see Claire.

SIXTEEN

Louise prayed he wasn't home, but of course, considering the way the day had gone thus far, she wasn't at all surprised when that prayer went unanswered. Upon entering the apartment, she found Wayne asleep on the sofa in front of the television, his bare feet propped up on the battered pine coffee table. A cigarette he'd set in the ashtray had burned itself out, a long worm of ash dipping down into a sea of its crumpled comrades. The apartment reeked of stale sweat and spoiled milk. Louise sighed and tossed her purse on the floor, inches from where Wayne dozed, his head to the side, a thin string of drool dangling from his jaw. He awoke at the sound, and yawned, then frowned and made as if to go back to sleep.

"Wayne."

Sluggishly, he opened his eyes and straightened, squinting, struggling to make out who was standing before him.

"Hey," he mumbled. A smile turned into another yawn and he stretched, sat up and reached for pack of cigarettes, but froze, his hand still in the air as he registered another presence in the room. "Who's here?" He rose unsteadily, shaking himself alert. Louise thought she detected fear lurking in his eyes. *What are you afraid of?* she wondered, casting her mind back to all those nights when he'd jumped at sounds outside the apartment or on the street below, sounds she hadn't even heard. His nocturnal walks did little to reassure her that he was not up to something. Lately, the caution she had initially interpreted from him as protectiveness had become something dangerously close to paranoia, and it worried her. She liked to assume he did nothing while she was at work. He had all day to himself but was always right there in his spot in front of the TV when she left and when she returned, so it was easy to pretend he hadn't done much else. Now, she wondered.

But such concerns would have to wait.

She stepped aside, allowing Wayne to see the teenager who'd been standing between her and the door.

Wayne frowned. "Who the hell are you?"

Pete smiled and snatched off his wool cap, as if it might make recognition easier. The boy's eyes were wide, desperate.

"Pete," he answered. "Lowell."

Still confused, Wayne looked to Louise.

"Jack Lowell's boy," she told him.

Recognition did not come. "Jack Lowell?"

"The man I was with before you. Back in Elkwood. The farmer. This is his boy."

Wayne's features softened. "Ah shit, *right*. I remember. Christ, you got *tall*."

Pete's smile held, but he looked uncomfortable.

"Well, come on in. Sit down. You look chilled to the bone, son."

"Cold out there," Pete told him, but waited for Louise to extend the invitation.

"Go on, sit," she urged. "How about I make us some coffee? You drink coffee Pete?"

"You got any hot chocolate?"

"Sure." She headed into the small kitchen, which was little bigger than a walk-in closet, the room further constricted by the cupboards and small table on one side, the sink on the other. As she set about making the drinks, she noticed how hard her hands were shaking. She clenched them and closed her eyes. It was going to be all right. It was. Pete's arrival was an omen that there was still some hope for the future. Maybe he was just visiting; maybe he was here for money—in which case he would leave disappointed—or maybe he was here to stay, his father finally having given up on him. As Louise retrieved the container of hot chocolate from the cupboard, and rinsed out a chipped mug and a spoon from the sink, she realized that Pete might very well be part of a life she wanted after all, a life she hadn't realized she'd yearned for until she'd walked out and left it to be erased by the dust from Wayne's tires. Perhaps the boy was part of a grander picture she could not yet see, a picture that did not have Detroit as its background.

Listening to the shy monotone muttering of the boy as he answered Wayne's cheerful queries, she tried not to think about what she had to tell Wayne later. Aside from everything else, Pete's presence had bought her some time. Time to work out in her mind what she was going to tell him, if anything. Time to try to grasp those elusive threads and weave a better story in which she was the victim, not the villain.

But isn't that the truth? she asked herself, and realized that she was no longer thinking about the diner and what had happened there.

With a deep breath, she hurriedly brushed her hair away from her face and took the hot chocolate and coffee into the living room. It was a mess, but Pete didn't seem to notice. She supposed he wouldn't. The farm had hardly been well maintained, inside or out.

"So," she said, handing him the mug. "How on earth did you find me?"

Wayne took the coffee from her without looking away from the boy. "And what made you think of lookin' for her now?"

This was going to be Louise's next question, and she wished Wayne had let her ask it. She would have put it to the boy with less suspicion in her tone.

Pete looked from Wayne to Louise, then down into his hot chocolate. An expression of deep sadness came over his face and Louise felt her chest grow tight. *Somethin's happened.* The boy confirmed this a moment later when, eyes still lowered, one gloved finger running circles around the top of the cup, he said, "My Pa's dead."

Louise gasped, a hand to her mouth, though in truth the shock was less potent than she pretended. Something about the boy's posture once she'd recognized him outside the apartment had suggested loneliness, and his face when he removed the scarf seemed thinner than she remembered it, the light in his eyes dimmer than before.

"What happened?"

Knowing how close Pete had been to his father, despite the man's utter inability to express any kind of love for the boy, she fully expected to watch him crumble, to see the tears flow as his face constricted into a mask of pain.

What she saw instead surprised her.

There was grief, and pain, but presiding over them all, was anger.

"They kilt him. The Doctor too."

Wayne's eyes widened. "*Shiiit.* I think I seen that on the news."

Louise turned to look at him. "And you didn't tell me?"

He shrugged. "It was half over and I was drunk when I switched it on. Didn't get no names. All I remember thinkin' is: 'Damn, Louise used to live somewhere around there.'"

"We've talked about the farm, Wayne, don't give me that shit. I must have mentioned Pete and his daddy a hundred times. Why didn't you tell me?"

Wayne's face darkened. "I said I didn't hear the goddamn names, all right?"

Not now, she cautioned herself. *The kid doesn't need this, and I don't either.* She returned her attention to Pete who seemed to be preparing to withdraw into himself. She scooted close and put her hand on his wrist.

"Who killed them, Pete?"

"We found a girl, in the road. She was messed up pretty bad."

"Messed up how?" Wayne asked.

"Beaten. Cut up. She were naked, all covered in blood. Me and Pa...we stopped to pick her up, brung her to the doctor's house to get her fixed up." There was no emotion in his voice now, as if this was a story he had grown weary of telling. "Pa told the doc it'd be better if he didn't ask any kinda questions about it all. I didn't understand that. Not then. I was worried about the girl. We went home, left her with the doc. But then my Pa...he got his rifle out and sat there like he were waitin' for the devil to kick down the door, and he...he told me I needed to get in the truck and go to the doc's house again, even though we'd just come from there. He said the doc would tell me what to do. So I went, and when I got there the doc said to me I needed to bring the girl to the hospital 'cuz she was in real trouble."

"Who was the girl?" Louise asked. "Did you know her?"

Pete raised his head, shook it once. "Her name was Claire. She were pretty like you wouldn't believe. Least I guessed she was. It was hard to tell because of all the blood and they had cut out one of her eyes."

Wayne frowned. "Jesus."

"You took her to the hospital?" Louise asked. "Why didn't your Pa go with you?"

"He stayed home," Pete said. "And he shot himself. Don't know why, but I guess he were too afraid of what was comin' to want to be there when it did."

Louise buried her face in her hands. "Oh God."

"I didn't know, or I'd never have left him. Maybe if I was smarter I'd have known, but I ain't, so I didn't. I just drove the girl outta town to the hospital." Something like a smile turned up the corners of his mouth. "She were real nice, though. The girl. We talked some on the way. Just a little because she was tired. But I liked her. Wished I could have stayed with her a while." He dipped his head, sipped at his drink, and his smile grew. "This is real good. I always liked your hot chocolate."

Louise's vision blurred with tears, her throat tightening as she struggled to keep her composure. *It's not fair*, she told herself. *Not fair that I left them. Not fair that he died.* And when a grimmer thought followed, *What if I had stayed with them? Wouldn't I have died there too?* The answer was: *Maybe you should have. Maybe that was where your true path ended and now you're wanderin' blindly ten miles farther along the same road 'cept now you know for sure it ain't goin' nowhere.*

"You tell the cops what happened?" Wayne asked, his interest apparently sincere.

Pete frowned. "When?"

"When you got the girl to the hospital?"

The boy shook his head. "I didn't want to answer no questions. I was afraid, so...so I just got the girl inside and let the hospital men take her away. One of them asked me my name and I told him, but then he told me to wait and I ran. Maybe I shouldn't've."

"You were scared," Louise said.

"Sure was," Pete agreed. "More scared than I've ever been in my life. I drove home pretty fast. But when I got there, the house were burnin' and weren't no one tryin' to put it out. I tried to do it myself but couldn't." A single tear welled in his left eye. "I told myself Pa got hisself out. Told myself a piece of burnin' wood had tumbled out of the fireplace and Pa had tried to put out the flames, but then run when it got the better of him. Told myself he was out there somewhere in the dark past the fire, waitin' for me, and I just couldn't see him. So I looked." He drew the back of his glove across his nose and blinked, freeing the tear to run down his cheek. "That's when I found all the blood. In the barn. It was burnin', but only the roof. I went inside, to see if Pa was in there maybe tryin' to free the animals—" He glanced at Louise. "That's what I'd have done." Then he lowered his head again. "They was gone, but there was a whole lotta blood in there, all over the place, great big puddles on the floor and splashed up the walls like it had come outta a hose. There were plastic there too, bits and pieces of it, like someone might've wrapped up the pigs before cuttin' on 'em."

"Are you sure your Pa didn't—"

"No. He wouldn't've. They was all we had left in the world, 'sides each other."

Louise moved close, put her arm around him and let her chin rest against his head. "Why would anyone take the pigs?" she asked quietly, and felt him shrug against her.

"Horse was gone too. Cora."

"Cora?"

"That was the mare's name. Good horse too. But she weren't hurt. I found her on my way into town after I gave up tryin' to find Pa."

"What did you do?" Wayne asked, his elbows braced on his knees, fists propping up his chin like a child watching Saturday morning cartoons.

"Rode 'er to Sheriff McKindrey's, but he weren't there. The lady at his office said he was down at The Red Man Tavern, so I went there. The Sheriff was pretty drunk, but when I mentioned the fire, whole buncha folks ran out and got in their cars and went out to the farm. They got the fire out pretty quick and found my Pa in there, all burned up."

"How do you know it wasn't just an accident?"

"Heard a few of the men talkin' to the Sheriff. They said they found some canisters of kerosene that we always kept in the barn. They were inside the house. Said they thought someone set the fire."

Wayne scratched his chin. "Maybe...and I know this ain't gonna be easy to hear, but..."

Louise shot him a glare. "Don't."

Wayne shrugged, but said no more.

"S'all right," Pete said softly. "I know what you was gonna say, but Pa didn't burn himself up. Not unless him and the doc had the same idea at the same time, cuz the doc's place was all burnt up too."

"Yeah," Wayne chimed in. "That's what I saw on the news. They found all those pieces of bodies there. Doctor went mad or somethin', didn't he?"

Louise spoke before Pete could answer. "Who do you think hurt all those people, Pete? Who do you think did this to your Pa?"

"It weren't the doc," he said. "It weren't him, no matter what they're sayin'. He wanted to help that girl real bad and when he sent us away, I could see he was afraid of somethin', just like my daddy was. They were waitin' for bad folk to come."

Louise kissed his head, suddenly reminded of the nights she'd spent in this same pose with the boy while they looked at the stars, and that one night in particular as they watched one fall from the sky when he asked her, "Are you gonna leave us too?" She'd been unable to reply, unable to lie to him, and so had distracted him with talk of the Heavens. Then she *had* left him, and now his world had been obliterated, leaving him in the company, however temporary, of a woman he had to believe didn't care.

"How did you find me?" she asked in a whisper, unsure whether the question was a rhetorical one.

"They had your address at Jo's Diner. Said you called them with it so they could send you a paycheck they owed you or somethin'. After the funeral, the Sheriff organized a collection and they gave me some money. I used some of it to take the bus here."

"So you've still got some left?" Wayne asked.

Louise stared at him. It wasn't clear whether he was asking because he didn't think they could afford to keep the boy for long, or because he planned to relieve the child of his money. Again she was struck by the unpleasant feeling that he was hiding something from her, that his paranoia might have its roots in something very real, and very troubling.

"Some," Pete said. "Not much."

"Well," Louise said with a sigh, "We need to get you cleaned up, fed and bedded down if you're going to be stayin' with us for a while."

She stood.

Pete frowned up at her. "I don't want to stay with you," he said, and Wayne couldn't restrain a small sigh of relief.

Louise raised her eyebrows. "I don't understand. I thought that's why you were here."

"No," said the boy. "I came here to tell you what happened to daddy, because I know he loved you and would want you to know."

"Well, I'm glad you did. I'm glad—"

Pete set his hot chocolate down and rose. Wayne was right. The boy had grown. He was now as tall as Louise. When she'd left him, he'd barely been up to her shoulders.

"And I came to tell you," he said, his face impassive, a queer light in his eyes. His hands had begun to tremble and she reached out to hold them in her own. His skin was cold. "That I aim to find those folks and make 'em sorry for what they done."

SEVENTEEN

It was a Tuesday night, and McClellan's Bar was mercifully free of the rowdy crowds it entertained on the weekends. There were no businessmen with their ties slung back over their shoulders, shirts unbuttoned as they spoke to each other in roars; no manicured women in short dresses trying not to look desperate as they eyed the men who appeared drunkest, and wealthiest; no underage teens balancing false courage with crippling nerves as they waited to be asked for their fake I.D's; no couples canoodling in the red leather booths beneath veils of smoke, their hands touching as they preserved a blissful moment sure to be destroyed out there in the world where uncontaminated love was a thing of fairytale and film; no loud music as young men and women fed the jukebox in the corner by the restrooms; no girls dancing on tables, cheered on by their equally inebriated girlfriends; no aggravated men looking to start a fight with the first guy unfortunate enough to nudge against them while pushing through the crowd.

Tonight there was only the tired-looking barman polishing glasses that were already clean, a lone woman with long, tousled yellow-gray hair smoking a cigarette and staring at her own unhappy reflection in the mirror behind the bar, and Finch, who sat at the far end of the long narrow counter, away from the door but facing it, so he could see whoever entered. Kara had thought this habit—his refusal to sit with his back to any door in any establishment—a dangerously paranoid one, the behavior of a criminal, or a mafia soldier. He had never disagreed, or tried to explain it, but was glad that they had already broken up by the time he returned from Iraq, because it was much worse now. He had never admitted to her that his caution had been an affected thing, taken from some gangster movie he'd seen once in which one of the characters had professed an unwillingness to sit with his back to the door because one of his friends had been 'clipped' that way. Finch had liked that movie, though he couldn't remember much about it now, and so had secretly justified his wariness as good sense in a world full of unseen danger. Nowadays, the paranoia he'd feigned had mutated, become real. Nowadays he sat facing the door because he was afraid something dangerous might at any moment explode through it.

A woman in an abaya perhaps, a scared smile on her face as her hands moved to her waist, to the wires...

Elbows on the bar, he brought his hands to his face and scrubbed away the memory of blood and smoke. He could still smell it on his skin, all of it mingled with the scent of fear that forever clung to him. And when finally he lowered them, he sensed the woman at the other end of the bar watching him, and there was a presence to his right, standing unsteadily between Finch and the door.

"Whassup?" said the man, and smiled. He had short blonde hair, a tanned youthful face, and was obviously drunk, his eyes bloodshot, Abercrombie & Fitch clothes slightly wrinkled, his shirt untucked. Finch figured him for a sole survivor of a bachelor party, or an escapee from a frat house where the celebrations had been defused, leaving this guy to seek out any excuse to perpetuate his immaturity. An oddly feminine hand with delicate fingers was braced on the bar, and seemed to be the only thing delaying his inevitable appointment with the floor.

Finch nodded, and went back to his drink. There was only the woman in the bar with them, and given the lack of aesthetic appeal she would have in Frat Boy's eyes, he expected more shallow conversation to come. He was not disappointed.

"You look pissed off," the guy said. "Lighten up, man!" He brushed a hand against Finch's elbow. "S'early!"

Finch ignored him.

The barman materialized. "What can I get ya?" he asked the wobbling man.

"You got Sambuca?"

"No."

Finch noticed with amusement the bottle of Sambuca on the shelf behind the barman.

"Shit then, I'll have a beer. Make it cold though, okay, man?" He laughed at this, and turned to Finch. "Three fridges in the goddamn place, and not one cold beer. Ended up drinking vodka instead. *Vodka.* Russian pisswater, my friend."

Again, Finch said nothing, hoping it would be enough to carry a message through the drunken padding in the other man's brain that he was in no mood for company, at least of this kind. But instead, the guy moved close enough that Finch could smell his breath. He'd heard it said that vodka, once ingested, didn't give off a smell, a quality that, along with gin, made it the yuppie drink of choice, but he could smell it on this guy, which pretty much confirmed his theory that saying liquor of any kind didn't come with its own stench was akin to claiming no one would know you pissed yourself if you were wearing rubber trousers.

"You in the war or something?" he asked now, and surprised at his perceptiveness, Finch looked at him.

"Yeah. I was."

"Figured."

"What gave it away?" he asked.

The other man shrugged. "You're not the first guy I've seen tonight that got himself all messed up over there. The other guy didn't even have legs. Said he got them blown off in..." He struggled to recall the name, but gave up with a wave of his hand. "Over there."

Finch bridled. "What do you mean 'messed up'?"

The barman reappeared and slid a Budweiser before Frat Boy. There were still flecks of ice on the bottle. He nodded approvingly and dropped a ten on the counter.

"Besides," he continued, ignoring Finch's question and the tone with which it had been delivered. "My older bro was there."

"In Iraq?"

"Yep."

Finch pictured the type: Rebellious, conscientious rich kid, eager to prove he was worth more than *Forbes* would estimate in two decades time, eager to show his loveless father that he was his own man and not afraid to step outside the protective bubble his family's wealth afforded him. A casualty of wealth would become a casualty of war, one way or another.

"Can't understand it myself," Frat Boy went on. "No need for him to do that shit, know what I'm sayin'. Plenty other guys out there fighting the good fight. No offense."

"None taken," Finch lied. His perception of how indifferent and selfish society could be had been heightened by his time away from it. The kids coming up these days, and most of their parents, had no idea what the world was waiting to do to their children, no concept of the depth of evil that permeated the world ready to corrupt the naive.

The door squeaked open, and a tall, well-built black man entered. He was dressed in a red OSU sweatshirt, navy sweatpants and sneakers, and though he didn't look big enough to play football, he was too large to be mistaken for a basketball player. His head was shaved, and the gold stud in his ear glinted in the light. In his right hand he held a large manila envelope.

"Huh," Frat Boy said. "Lookit Billy Badass."

Finch grinned. While the wariness in the guy's tone undoubtedly stemmed from his stereotypical view of men bigger than him, it might have cowed him further to know he was right. The man at the door's name wasn't Billy, but "Badass" was right on the money.

Finch leaned back in his seat, so Frat Boy wasn't shielding him from view. The black man spotted him immediately and his lips spread in a winning smile, exposing large perfectly straight white teeth. He jabbed a finger at the booths lining the wall opposite the bar and Finch nodded.

"Friend of yours?" Frat Boy sounded disappointed.

"Yep."

"Huh."

Finch grabbed his beer, and headed for the booth halfway down. It was far enough from the door and Frat Boy to give them a little privacy, unless of course the guy decided to invite himself into the conversation. Finch hoped he wouldn't. It might force Billy Badass to live up to the name he had just been given—a name he might have liked, as it was infinitely better than his unwieldy real name, which was Chester "Beau" Beaumont.

"Orange juice if you got any," Beau told the barman and turned his back on him, leaning against the bar as he appraised Finch, who had just slid into the booth. "Slummin', are we?"

"Hey, I like this place."

"Wasn't talkin' 'bout the place, man." He looked pointedly up the bar at Frat Boy, who quickly looked away and started muttering to his beer.

"Just one of those kids in the middle of a transitional period," Finch said. "Going from idiot to asshole, though someday he'll probably end up owning half the city."

"He's welcome to it," Beau said, and nodded his thanks to the barman, took his drink and joined Finch in the booth. "I swear," he continued, as he settled himself and set the large envelope between them. "Every time I walk these streets I think we made some kinda bet with God and lost. I was down this way over the weekend and you know what I saw?"

Finch shook his head.

"Two guys in the alley, up by that clothes store with the funny name?"

"Deetos?"

"Yeah. Reminds me of chips. Well, here were these two guys right? One's down on his knees with the other guy's dick in his mouth. Nothin' funny 'bout that if that's your thing, but get this...the guy gettin' lubed is slappin' the other guy in the side of his head. *Hard*. Over and over again. Now, maybe I'm gettin' old or somethin', but if I got some babe workin' me down there, I ain't doin' shit to break her concentration, know m'sayin'?"

Finch grinned. "Yeah."

"Damn, I don't know if it's some shit I missed in all those porno's growin' up but I can't understand it. And hey, let's just say for argument's sake I'm the one doin' the lubin. *Strictly* for argument's sake, right?"

"Right."

"Well, I ain't lettin' the guy *privileged* enough to have me down there in the first place smack on my skull. One time is all it'd take and I'd have that motherfucker mulched."

Though enjoying the camaraderie and Beau's banter, Finch was eager to get down to business. He looked down at the envelope. "That what you got in there? Pictures of the one time you experimented?"

Beau smiled. "Naw. Any mother took pictures of my dick, they'd need a tapestry, not a camera."

Finch nodded. "I'm sure there's a whole wall in the Metropolitan reserved for it."

Beau slid the envelope to him. "I figure everythin' you need is in there. Sorry it took so long. Hard to find shit out if no one talkin'. You may as well be askin' what happened to a white supremacist in Compton."

Fingers trembling slightly, and aware that Beau's eyes were on him, Finch turned the envelope over. It wasn't sealed. He opened it and withdrew a sheaf of paper.

The barman, apparently bored of listening to Frat Boy complaining and the inaudible conversation from their booth, ducked down behind the bar. A moment later, soft bluesy music rose up and danced with the smoke.

"Looks like a lot of info," Finch said, examining the papers. He nodded appreciatively. "Hell of a lot more than I was able to find on my own."

"Yeah, there's some readin', but I don't think you gonna find everythin' you need to know. Lot more about the victims than the villains. Got names for them, but no faces and that was hard enough. They're like ghosts, man."

"Well, thanks. I know what you're risking here."

Beau looked around the bar. "I ain't riskin' nothin'. I'm a good liar if it comes to it. You, on the other hand, lookin' to get into a whole world of hurt if you're plannin' any Charles Bronson shit."

"My gun's a lot smaller."

"Yeah, and Chuck was a whole lot better lookin' but you get what I'm sayin' right?"

"Sure, and it's duly noted, but I can look after myself."

Beau gave a rueful shake of his head. "Wish I had a dollar for every time some dumb white boy said that to me. I'd be drivin' a Cutlass Supreme with Lexani alloys by now instead of a piece a' shit Toyota." He leaned forward. "And if I remember correctly, you were damn glad to have my ass coverin' yours back in the desert."

Finch didn't look at him. "I can handle it."

"Not what I'm sayin'."

"Then what are you saying?"

"I'm saying ain't no man tough enough to fight a war on his own, especially if it's a personal one and he's outnumbered. You need my help, you ask."

"I did ask." Finch tapped a forefinger on the stack of paper.

"Don't play dumb with me, man. This ain't the first time I been sittin' across from a guy who looked ready to jump headfirst into Hell without an asbestos swimsuit. I knew when I was puttin' that file together what you were gonna use it for. Think I'm dumb? And I also knew what would happen if I gave it to you."

"But you gave it to me anyway."

"Wouldn't have if I didn't think you'd just find some other guy to dig it up for you, or go and dig it up yourself. Might have taken a while longer, but the end result would've been the same. Besides, like I always said, we look out for each other, and I guess I should be grateful you trusted me with this." He sighed. "Though somethin' tells me you callin' me up has less to do with trust and more to do with convenience."

Finch shrugged. "Told you in the desert if you went through with the crazy idea of trying to become a P.I. I'd drum up some work for you."

"Yeah, but I didn't think it'd be this kinda work. Work that could get your ass killed. Shit, if I'd known you had a death wish, I'd have let you die over there and saved us all a lot of trouble."

It was a joke, and both men knew it, but nevertheless Finch had to suppress the memory it evoked.

"You get your license yet?" he asked.

"Workin' on it."

"Should be a cinch. You were always nosy."

"I prefer to call it curiosity. You know what though? I thought it'd be just a case of applyin' like you do for a fishin' license or some shit. Turns out I gotta take classes man. Get myself a diploma. Can you see me tied to a desk listening to some uptight sonofabitch tellin' me what I already know?"

Finch couldn't. Beau had a real problem with authority, as evidenced by the amount of sergeants whose blood pressure had suffered an astronomical rise while he'd served under them. "Well, I'll wait to read these files before I give you my professional opinion on whether or not it's wise to pursue it."

"Yeah, sure. I'll try to contain myself until then. 'Course, chances are you'll be in itty bitty pieces and not worth the price of the bag they stuff you in and all my anxiety will be for nothin'."

"Thanks for the vote of confidence."

Beau laced his fingers together, all trace of humor gone from his voice now. "You gettin' a clear enough picture here? This ain't your fight, man."

Finch appraised him. "They killed my little brother."

Beau unclasped his large hands and joined them again around the glass of OJ, then brought it to his lips. After a small sip, he lowered it and studied Finch.

"I know they did, and I'm sorry as hell, but—"

"Save it."

"It's true."

"I know it's true, but I don't want to hear it. Not from you." Finch sighed heavily, his fingers caressing the flap of the now empty envelope. "It's not about bringing him back."

"Then what is it about? You even know? This here's a little more than punchin' out the bullies who been pickin' on your brother, man. You go down there with your head all muddied up, you ain't comin' back in one piece. Or if you do come back alive, you got blood on your hands and you're lookin' at hard time. Life, man."

"If I get caught."

Beau shook his head. "Prison ain't the only kinda life sentence. You know that well as I do."

At the bar, Frat Boy began to argue with himself. The barman told him to keep it down. The gray-haired woman chuckled. Finch decided to use to distraction. "You want a drink?"

Beau nodded at his OJ. "Got one."

"I meant a real drink."

"Naw. I ain't touched it since I got back. Don't need any help gettin' fucked up these days. Nice way to change the subject though."

"There isn't a whole lot to talk about."

"You're shittin' me, right?"

Finch met his stare. "You know how it goes, Beau. If by some miracle someone decides to look into this, to entertain the possibility that they were wrong about the doctor, and they find out they pinned it on the wrong guy, what happens next?"

"They go after the right guys, and if they catch 'em, they go to jail for a very long time."

"Exactly: *if* they catch them. And say they do, say they go to jail, those bastards will probably end up with better lives than they have now. Three square meals a day, rest and exercise, TV—"

"Man, you ain't never been in one of those shitholes, have you?"

"That's not the point—"

Again Beau cut him off. "Sure it is. Some of the joints we got over here make Abu Ghraib look like the Waldorf Astoria. A bunch of murderin' rednecks ain't gonna have any kind of peace in no jail, man, not after what they did."

"It's not enough," Finch said.

"So what if you kill these motherfuckers and it still ain't enough. What then?"

"It won't come to that."

Beau sat back and sighed. "Whole lotta folks said that same thing before they went to the desert, Finch. All of us said it, and if we weren't sayin' it we were thinkin' it. 'Not gonna happen to me, man.' Remember?"

Finch glanced at the bar to avoid the weight of the other man's gaze. When at last he looked back, Beau had drained his drink and was rising.

"Danny was a good kid," Beau told him. "A real good kid. Had his head screwed on right."

Finch nodded his agreement.

Beau stepped out, and took one last look around the bar. "Do yourself a favor though, and don't use him as an excuse to let loose some of that hate the desert put into you. We saw some real cruel shit over there, and what's happened here ain't a whole lot better, but you in danger of dyin' or spendin' the rest of your life behind bars or lookin' for targets if you go through with it."

Finch started to protest, but Beau raised a hand to silence him.

"I put some other stuff in that file you might want to take a look out before you go headin' off playin' Rambo. Read it. See what you think. It ain't subtle, but hey...you know me. I'll be down at Rita's on Third this Sunday after eight. It's my cousin Kevin's 21st birthday. We're throwin' a little shindig. You ain't invited because if I see you there I'll know you're gonna see this thing through to the end."

"And if I can't resist the urge to gatecrash?"

"Then I guess because it's you and I don't want to be lookin' at your ass cut up on the main evenin' news, I'll help you, whatever you need. But just so you know: I'll be hopin' for a night of family and friends, not vigilantes. Catch you later."

He walked away, and all faces present turned to watch him go. The gray-haired woman offered him a smile and he returned it, then eased himself out into the street. The door swung shut behind him.

On some level, Finch knew Beau was right, about everything. There were risks here he hadn't considered, repercussions he couldn't yet see. But none of it mattered. Reason had no hand in what was going to happen. Rage dictated it all, and no amount of good sense or logical argument was going to change his plans.

"See you Sunday," he said quietly and turned his attention back to the file.

EIGHTEEN

"Claire, there's someone here to see you."

Sitting with her back against the headboard, legs folded beneath her, Claire looked up from the photo album. Her face was damp from tears and now she rubbed at it as her mother watched from the doorway.

"I can tell him to go away if you're not up to it."

Claire shook her head. It had been almost two weeks since she'd seen anyone outside of Kara and her mother, and as much as she loved them for what they were trying to do, she was beginning to feel suffocated by their constant worry. They were treating her as if she'd turned to fragile glass, as if the slightest touch might shatter her. She knew it was silly and selfish to expect anything different from them, or anyone else after what she'd gone through, and yet she yearned for normality, no matter how forced, longed to come downstairs and not have them look at her like a wounded dog that had just limped into the house. In their faces she saw empathy and a reflection of her own pain. In their eyes, she saw a victim, and nothing more.

"Who is it?"

"Ted Craddick."

Claire's breathing slowed. Her yearning to see a face outside of her family's own faded a little upon hearing the name of her dead friend's father. She had spent the past hour or so torturing herself by looking through her photo albums at countless pictures not marred by awareness of death, nothing but sunshine and smiles, eyes bright with the promise of the future. There had even been a few of Ted, his bald head catching the summer sun as he stood on the porch of the house he'd shared with his son and Stu's younger sister Sally, arms around them both, all of them grinning, Sally somewhat self-consciously as she tried to draw her lips down enough to conceal her new braces. In another, Daniel and Stu mugged for the camera, Claire and Katy looking on in faux disapproval. In the background, Ted had his forefingers in his mouth, stretching his lips wide in a comical grimace, his tongue lolling. There were others, but already Claire couldn't recall which of them she'd seen him in. Ted Craddick had always been a peripheral figure in her life. She had spoken to him occasionally, but it had never graduated beyond idle conversation and pleasantries.

Hi Mr. Craddick.

Hi Claire. Stu's upstairs with Katy. And please, call me Ted.

Okay...Ted. Thanks.

Of course she had never called him "Ted" outside of those few occasions when he requested she do so, and even then it had felt awkward.

"Tell him come up," she told her mother, who lingered, uncertain.

"Are you sure?"

She nodded.

"He'll have questions."

"I know," Claire replied. "Tell him come up."

With a final dubious glance, her mother disappeared from the doorway. Claire listened to her heels clacking on the stairsteps, heard the reverent mutter of voices, then the front door closing. While she waited, Claire shut the photo album and slid it beneath her pillow. Her joints still ached in protest with every move, but it was not enough to bother her. It was what they represented that bothered her. Every twinge, every dull throb of discomfort jerked loose another unpleasant memory, and made her skin crawl at the thought of what she had endured.

Stop it, she told herself. *You can't think like that. You can't. Not if you ever want to get better.*

Better. She almost laughed at the thought, but was interrupted by movement in the doorway. It was her mother again, moving as if sound itself might harm her daughter.

"Claire?"

Her mother stepped aside, and Ted Craddick entered the room. Claire felt a jolt. She had expected a lesser version of the man in the pictures, but nothing like this. It was as if she was seeing his reflection, leached of color in a dark window. His clothes looked two sizes too large for his sagging frame, the gut that had always forced his shirts to stretch to accommodate it now gone, his jeans hanging loose on his hips. The smiling face from the photographs was drawn down like a theater mask of sadness, his green eyes lost in puffy sockets. The man carried about him an air of desperation, as if he had come here not for consolation, or empathy, but to be told that there had been a terrible mistake, and that only Claire could confirm it. He looked like he wanted to be told Stu was alive and well and due home at any second, that it had all been a misunderstanding.

"Hi Mr. Craddick," Claire said, sliding from the bed and coming to him. They hugged awkwardly, death and mutual suffering not enough to force a connection where there had never been one. His body felt like a live wire, humming beneath the skin. She released him and stepped back, then gestured for him to join her on the bed, where she sat, hands folded in her lap. He eased himself down with some effort and tried to smile. It was a wretched thing to behold.

"Thanks for agreeing to see me," he said.

"I'm sorry about what happened," Claire told him. "I'm sorry about Stu. He was one of my best friends, and I miss him."

Ted nodded slowly, and looked up. Claire's mother offered him a weak smile and then moved away from the door, leaving them alone. Claire didn't hear her descending the stairs, and knew she was still out there on the landing, listening.

"I'm glad you're okay," Ted said, staring down at his hands. "When the news first broke, we thought all of you..." He frowned. "Why did they do this?"

"I don't know," Claire said truthfully. She had asked herself that same question many times over the past few weeks, and no answers had presented themselves.

"I mean...you were just kids. Why would anyone want to hurt you like that?"

"We were in the wrong place," Claire said softly. "We crossed the wrong people." 'Crossed' wasn't exactly the right word though and it felt wrong to say it. They hadn't crossed anyone. They'd been minding their own business when Stu and Daniel had stopped walking, their eyes on the woods that ran along the road on both sides. Someone had been moving in there, a ragged looking shape, moving closer as they watched. *If this guy's got no teeth and a banjo, I'm running. Try to keep up*, Stu had joked.

Stu, shut up, Katy had told him, with just the slightest quaver in her voice, and then all of them had frozen as the sound of laughter cut through the trees, not from the shape before them, but from somewhere in the woods behind them.

Stu, a man's voice had said mockingly.

They turned as one, and there were children there, grubby, mean-looking kids standing in the road behind them.

Hey there, Katy had said, trying to be her usual pleasant self.

One of the children, the closest one to her, answered by carving an arc through the air with a wickedly sharp looking blade they hadn't realized up until that moment he'd been holding. Katy had said, "Oh," and looked down at herself. A wide slit had opened in her right leg just above the knee, dark blood already pooling in the wound. Before the attack had fully registered, a spike was driven through her skull.

Claire shook off the memory, aware that Ted was looking at her.

"My sister," Ted said, pausing a moment to swallow. "She's in the hospital."

"Is she okay?"

He shook his head. "She and Stu were real close. Up until a few years ago, y'know, until Stu got too cool for it, they used to go horse riding together. She has a little ranch up in Delaware. When she heard what had happened, she shut herself up in her house. I dropped by yesterday and found the back door open. She was upstairs, out cold, an empty bottle of Scotch and a pill bottle beside her. She'd tried to kill herself."

"Oh God, I'm so sorry." *A stone dropped in a pond*, Claire thought, *forever making ripples*. And it would never stop. There was no bank for it to break against. Instead, like a shockwave, it would continue on until there was no one left to feel it.

"She's a good girl, Yvonne," Ted told her, picking at a patch of raw sore-looking skin under his thumbnail. "She loved Stu."

"Is she going to be all right?"

"Doctors say she'll be fine. I'm thinking maybe I should get her and Sally away for a while. Maybe take them on a cruise."

"That'd be nice."

"Yeah."

Claire smiled, but wondered if Ted knew the distraction didn't exist that was powerful enough to stop them from feeling what they'd lost. She guessed he did, that he was grasping at straws in an effort not to cave in on himself, and lose all he had left in the process. His eyes were red-rimmed from crying.

"How is Sally?"

He shrugged. "Holding up, best as she can I suppose. Worst thing is, she keeps coming to me to tell her everything's going to be all right, or to make sense for her of what happened, and I can't seem to find the words. Everything sounds...forced, as if I'm lying to her. But I'm not, you know? I just don't know what to say."

Claire did know. It was exactly what she was doing now with the father of her dead friend.

"There isn't much you can say," she said. "I still, even with everything that's happened, have trouble believing it."

Ted looked at her for so long she had to resist the urge to stand and busy herself with anything that would get her out from under his gaze. At length, he sighed. "I'm sorry for what they did to you."

In that moment Claire knew how Sally Craddick had felt, seeking comfort from her father only to suspect his words were empty. There was no emotion in his voice, and she wondered just how much this man hated her for coming back alive when his son had died a horrible death.

His hand found hers and his skin was cold. "Tell me," he said.

She looked at him, trying to read his will in the lines on his sallow face.

"Tell me how he died. Tell me what they did to my boy."

Images passed through Claire's mind, some of them taken from the photographs, others from the equally vivid vault of memory. She saw Stu standing on a jetty with Katy, him in black swim trunks, her in a cute peach-colored bikini, both of them wearing sunglasses as they posed, their skin beaded with water, hair wet from swimming. Then Stu drunk at the bar at the hotel in Sandestin, chatting up the barmaid, who looked completely uninterested, Katy sitting at a table with Claire and Daniel, all of them watching. *Think I should tell her he has a tiny dick?* Katy had said, and they'd laughed, but after several shots of tequila, she hadn't been able to disguise the hurt in her voice. *Thank Christ for college next year,* she'd added, raising her glass. *No more men with the maturity of a dragonfly.* Daniel had frowned at her, puzzled by the analogy, then laughed so hard he'd almost choked on his beer. They all had, the sound of it enough to draw Stu back from the bar. *What's the joke?* he'd asked, prepared to join in if he deemed it worthy. But then Katy's smile had vanished as she'd looked away and told him, *You are.*

"He tried to protect us," Claire told Stu's father. "He tried to fight them off."

This was a lie, but a necessary one. The truth would almost certainly destroy him.

"That's my boy," Ted said with pride, his eyes watering.

Claire smiled. *He ran,* she thought. *He ran and left us there. Left Katy dead. Left Daniel and me to fight them on our own. He ran, and he might have made it if one of them hadn't been waiting for him in the woods.*

"Did he...was it quick?"

"I don't know. They took us to different rooms, sheds, away from each other." *But I saw them dragging him in, and couldn't see his face for all the blood.*

Ted nodded gravely. "He was a brave boy, my son. I taught him to be a fighter. Told him he'd need to be, the way this world has gone."

Claire squeezed his hand. "He did all he could for us."

"Have you spoken to the other parents?"

"No. Not yet." The thought of it turned her stomach, and after this encounter, she decided she might not.

"They'll want to see you. They'll want to know what you know about what happened."

"Of course." But she knew none of them would want to know that, not ever. Not if they wanted the truth. She could not give them the peace they sought unless she lied to them as she had lied to Ted, because the end, what she'd seen of it, had not been pretty, or dignified or heroic, and that wasn't what they wanted to hear. The deaths of their children had been horrendous, violent, and messy.

"Did he say anything?" Ted asked.

"What?"

"Stu. Did he say anything before...?" He shook his head. A tear ran down his unshaven cheek.

"He was happy," she said. "He was with Katy, and they were in love."

This sounded utterly false, but Ted smiled slightly. "Good. That's good. I liked Katy. She was a nice girl."

"Yes she was." Claire felt her throat constrict as the memories assailed her. How many times had Katy sat on this very bed with her, discussing their ambitions, their fears, laughing like idiots over something that might not have been that funny until Katy let loose her strange oddly manlike laugh, which would set Claire off every time she heard it? She recalled the night Katy had slept in the bed with her, wracked by sobs as she confessed that she had missed her period and was deathly afraid she was pregnant. *If I am*, she'd moaned, *it won't be Stu's. We haven't slept together in over four months.* Claire had held her, told her it would be all right, and it had been. Katy wasn't pregnant. Six months later she would say those same words as she held her on the road to Elkwood, her friend's blood pooling around her. Except it hadn't been all right, not then, and now Katy was dead, her body cut up into pieces and scattered in poor Doctor Wellman's basement.

"I think I need to move," Ted said. "I think I need to get out of this town."

Claire said nothing. Had Stu died at home, moving away from the scene and the awful memories they conjured up might not be such a bad idea. But Stu had been murdered miles away from there, in some place he'd never been before, a place Ted Craddick had never, and likely never would, see with his own eyes. The worst of the pain would be inside Ted's own mind, and there was no moving away from that. The agony would follow him no matter where he went.

Abruptly he rose, releasing her hand. "I'm glad you're okay," he said again. "And I'm sorry about what happened to you, and my boy, and your friends. It's not right." He lowered his gaze to the floor. "It's not right what happened to you." His winced as if the tears that were now flowing freely scalded him. Then his face relaxed and he tried to smile. "He never said anything but good things about you," he told her and Claire guessed maybe that was Ted's own untruth. She and Stu had had their share of run-ins, the unavoidable result of personalities too dissimilar to ever fully jibe. They'd both been stubborn, unwilling to back down, a stalemate seldom helped by Claire's protectiveness toward Katy, who Stu had frequently hurt, whether he meant to or not.

"I loved him," she told his father. "They were my life."

She half-expected him to say, "A life you still have," and spit on the floor as he stormed out, but instead he nodded, and put a hand on the door. He was almost in the hall before he turned, looking more troubled than she'd yet seen him. "Has Danny's brother been to see you?"

"No."

"He will," Ted told her. "He's calling on all the parents, and he mentioned wanting to see you too."

"Why?"

A curious look passed over the man's face. It was almost relief. "It's better if he explains it to you himself."

Any further questions she might have asked died in her mouth as he exited the room. She heard him talking to her mother as she escorted him downstairs, then he was gone, and once more the house was quiet.

* * *

In the photo album, beside a picture of Daniel in his football uniform, was a scrap of yellow notepaper riddled with creases. On it was written his cell phone number and beneath that, his barely legible scrawl tangled into the words "*Call Me!*"

Claire smiled and ran a finger over the clear plastic sheet holding it in place beside the photograph. In her old life, the happy, unthreatening one she'd known before the men had taken it from her, she'd been a packrat. There were no empty spaces in her room, and her closet was filled with old boxes, each of them containing memories and keepsakes from her years spent wandering through the minefield of teenage life. There were rolled up posters of football games, victories made memorable by the mischief perpetrated later beyond the sidelines. There were ticket stubs and receipts, kept to remind her of special moments with old boyfriends, most of whom she still cared for in some small way, but seldom thought about anymore. Pennants and flyers, old high school and even middle school notebooks, branded with scribbles of trivial significance now, but which had had monumental import back then; love letters from nervous young boys on the threshold of puberty; report cards which had earned her $50 a piece from her father, allowing her to save up and be the first of her group of friends to own a car; the police report of the drunk-driving incident that had seen that car totaled; video cassettes of long gone birthdays and Christmases her mother had wanted to throw away after her father died, too pained by the memory of his prominent role in them; brochures from vacations with her family, getaways with Daniel and her friends; the audio CD Daniel had given her of love songs for Valentine's day. She hadn't cared for most of the songs, but had appreciated the sentiment.

And of course, there were the photo albums.

She looked at the slip of paper bearing Daniel's cell phone number and felt a tightening in her throat.

Then she thought of Muriel Hynes, and though her face was hard to recall, Claire remembered she'd been a mousy, shy girl with glasses, lank brown hair, and a prominent overbite. She remembered feeling sorry for the girl, then being ashamed that she had. It was not her place to pity anyone, and by doing so was subconsciously assuming herself on a higher position on the social ladder. But as wrong as it felt to think it, she realized it was true. Claire had always been popular, blessed (and often cursed) with long blonde hair, generous breasts, and a trim figure. It had made her passage through high school much easier for the most part, despite the disdain her appearance and the company she kept instilled in the other cliques. The Goths had viewed her as a stuck-up rich girl, though she'd been neither. The art students and rockers had sneered at her as if though one day she might provide them inspiration for their work, they wouldn't be seen dead with her. The "nerds" worshipped but never dared approach her, conscious of their appearance and the stigma long-associated with the intelligent. Among them had wandered the painfully demure Muriel Hynes, but only for one semester. By the next, she'd already been interred in Oak Grove Cemetery after slashing her wrists in the bathtub. She'd been dead for over four hours before her father kicked in the door and found her.

Claire looked down at her own wrists, at the angry red lines carved into the flesh, and thought of Muriel, of the picture hanging in the hall at school. The girl in the portrait was smiling, but only just, as close to an imitation of the Mona Lisa as Claire had ever seen. In that moment, forever frozen in time, it seemed as if Muriel had been privy to knowledge that the Goths, for all their posturing and claims to the contrary, didn't know: *Living is hard; Death is easy. And there are no answers on either side.*

The night of Muriel's funeral, Claire had booted up her computer, logged on to the Internet and checked her old email folder until she found what she was looking for. It was the one and only communication she'd ever had from the dead girl. Eight weeks before her suicide, the girl had written to Claire with one odd simple message: "I like ur hair." Confused, Claire hadn't written back, but that night, as she reread those four words in an attempt to derive some greater meaning from them, some hidden significance that might help her understand why Muriel had taken her life, she wished she had. And then a strange and not entirely pleasant thought had occurred to her as she looked from the message to the girl's email address.

What if I answer now?

And even more unsettling: *What if she replies?*

The uneasiness these thoughts summoned had been enough to make her shut down the computer in a hurry.

Now, looking at the picture of Daniel, and the number scrawled on that small piece of paper—*Call Me!*—it came to her again.

What if I called?
What if he answered?

She struggled to remember what had become of Daniel's cell phone during the attack. Panic had blinded her, of course. She'd only been aware of the impossibility of what was happening, sure, right up until Katy was stabbed, that it had all been some kind of sick joke. She did not recall seeing Daniel reach into his pocket for his phone, and later, did not see their attackers take it.

But she'd heard it ringing.

In her prison, as the strength tried to leave her, consciousness flickering like a candle flame in a draft, she'd been pulled back into the cold horror of her circumstances by the distant sound of a computer circuit's attempt to replicate Mozart's "Symphony Number 9"—the familiar sound of Daniel's phone as someone tried to call him. Then his agonized scream had drowned it out.

Claire peeled the protective plastic away from the page of the photo album, and gently removed the yellow slip of paper. She held it in her trembling hands for a moment, then looked at the photograph of her dead boyfriend.

I loved you, she said. *Did you love me?*

She had only memories from which to draw an answer, but even they betrayed her, for Daniel had never told her he'd loved her, and so she would never know.

Unless she asked.

She turned her head.

The phone, girly pink like the rest of the room, sat on her nightstand, silent.

Don't be silly, she cautioned herself. *This is madness. It won't do anything but aggravate the pain.* She smiled grimly at that. She could not imagine a pain worse than this, no suffering worse than that of the sole survivor.

She pushed the photo album aside, eased herself across the bed, and picked up the phone, then set the number beside it, under the tasseled pink lampshade.

Her heart began to race.

What am I doing?

Carefully, breath held, she dialed.

The digits, registering as dull beeps in her ear.

Silence. The faint hum of the connection racing through space, running through wires. Then silence again. Time seemed to stretch interminably.

Stop now while you still——

A crackle, a click...

Then the connection was made.

Claire's stomach contracted. She thought she was going to be sick. Bile filled her mouth as panic seized her.

Stop this. Stop this now, oh Jesus what am I doing?

Beep beep. Silence.

Beep beep. Silence.

She imagined the sound of Mozart, playing his music with none of the beauty or fervor or passion it had been written to convey.

She imagined hearing it out there in the night, a thousand miles away and yet still audible, carried to her by her desperate need to hear it, to know her boyfriend was alive and would answer at any moment.

Beep beep. Silence.

Then Kara at the door, gently easing it open, her look of concern quickly turning to curiosity as she stepped inside.

"Claire?"

No. Go away.

Beep beep. Silence.

"Claire? Who are you calling?"

"No one. I'll..."

Kara approached her, slowly, but urgently.

It will ring out, Claire knew. *I'll hear his voice on the message service and it will kill me.*

But what she heard was: Beep beep. *Click.*

She felt every hair on her body rise, began to tremble uncontrollably.

Kara: "What's wrong?"

From the phone, silence, but it was not dead, not empty.

Someone had answered.

Someone was listening.

NINETEEN

Despite the fact that he was in his late fifties and had recently buried his only daughter, the man who answered the door was well dressed and healthy looking. He wore a light blue shirt with the top button unfastened, and a pair of dark pants, the creases sharp above a freshly polished pair of shoes. His dark hair had been recently barbered, and was streaked with gray, which made him look distinguished rather than old.

"Yes?" he asked.

"Mr. Kaplan?"

A curt nod. "Who are you?" He looked slightly annoyed as he appraised the man on his stoop, as if Finch had pulled him away from an important business meeting or a football game.

"My name is Thomas Finch."

"Finch?"

"Daniel's brother."

Anyone who believed the theory that death forged a bond between those left to grieve had obviously never met John Kaplan. With a sigh he stepped back into the hall. "I suppose you want to come in?"

"I won't take up too much of your time," Finch said and entered the house.

Everything about the Kaplans spoke of money: from the gleaming silver Mercedes in the driveway and Tudor house set at the end of a long winding flower-bordered drive, itself a half-mile from the main road, to the sprawling yards, which looked vigilantly maintained, as if Kaplan feared his competitors would take the first trace of overgrowth as a sign of weakness. And then of course, there was John Kaplan himself. As he led him through a short, oak-paneled hallway with polished floors, Finch detected an air of intolerance about the man, as if he reserved his interest only for people who could benefit him or his bank account. He wondered if what he had come to say might change that, but then for a man supposed to be grieving, Kaplan looked awfully composed.

The hall ended and opened out into a large foyer stuffed to bursting with vegetation. Planters hung on chains hung from the vaulted ceiling, spidery green legs trailing down to meet the explosion of growth from what looked like a variety of wild and frenzied shrubs anchored in a huge rectangular marble tomb. Tall thin plants with glossy spade-shaped leaves and bamboo sticks lashed to their stems stood guard in the corners, struggling upward to where a segmented glass window threw squares of light against the wall.

Kaplan didn't spare the jungle a glance as he turned left into another narrow hall. Finch followed close behind.

"Take a seat," John said, as they entered a small but impressive lounge. In here sat a brown leather armchair, positioned at a right angle to a matching leather couch, as if the Kaplan's interior decorator had aspirations of becoming a psychiatrist, or specialized in decorating for them. Sports and hunting magazines sat in a tidy pile atop a glass coffee table. The walls were lined with oak bookshelves, but Finch didn't bother to scan the titles. He wasn't much of a reader, and doubted anything he'd see there would be of interest.

"You'll have a drink," Kaplan said, and although it sounded more like a statement of fact than a request, Finch nodded and took a seat on the couch. The cushions yielded beneath him with a soft hiss. The lounge smelled faintly of cigar smoke.

"Scotch?"

"That'd be great, thanks."

As Kaplan poured the drink from a crystal decanter into two smoked glass tumblers, Finch wondered how rehearsed and tired this whole practice was for the guy. How many people interested or connected in some way to the murders had stopped by here to console, or seek comfort in a kindred spirit over the past couple of months? Finch envisioned Kaplan leading the latter kind to this room, perhaps with the intent to numb them enough with alcohol that they'd be left with the false impression that he had somehow eased their pain for a time.

Kaplan set Finch's drink down on the coffee table, then took a seat in the armchair. He sighed and took a sizable draw from his glass before studying his guest. "So, Mr. Finch. What can I do for you?"

Finch sat forward and clasped his hands. "I'm here to talk about what happened to the kids. To my brother, and your daughter, and their friends."

"Why?"

"Because we need to."

"I disagree."

"That so?"

"It is."

"Well if it's all the same—"

Kaplan sat back and crossed his legs. He held up his glass, examining its contents as if it was something he had never seen before. "Mr. Finch—"

"Thomas."

"All right, Thomas. It's not my intent to be rude—though you'd be far from the first person to leave this house with such an impression of me—but I'm a busy man. If you've come here to reminisce about how great our kids were and how they had such a good time together, and to tell me as if it's breaking news how goddamned awful it was what happened to them, I'm afraid all I can say is amen to it all and see you out. Does that seem cold?"

Finch set down his drink. "Until I can see my breath, I'll give you the benefit of the doubt."

Kaplan smiled tightly. "I have to meet with my attorney at noon, Thomas," he said, making the name sound like punctuation, "so the sooner you cut to the chase, the better your chance of a less terse reception."

"I'm here to tell you my plans, so you know what they are, and to hear what you think. Maybe even to get your blessing."

"Almost sounds like you're asking for my daughter's hand," Kaplan said. "But as you know, I'm all out of those. My wife will be coming on the market soon though, if you're interested."

That explains the attorney, Finch thought, his estimation of Kaplan dropping the longer he listened to the man speak. There was no emotion in his voice, none at all. Even the words he chose—*I'm all out of those*—suggested a man who either wasn't too torn up about his daughter's death, or wasn't yet fully aware of it, his mind protected from the horror by an impenetrable wall of shock. But *no*, Finch decided. This didn't look like shock. The man appeared fully in control, and eerily calm.

"I'm sorry to hear that," Finch said.

"Don't be," Kaplan replied with a dismissive wave of his hand. "This has made an addict out of her. If she's not popping Valium, she's out fucking the gardener. This has been a long time coming. At least something good came of Katy's death."

Finch frowned, embarrassed by the man's candor, and quickly scooped up his drink.

"See your breath yet?" Kaplan asked, amused.

Finch ignored him.

"My wife and I haven't loved each other in over ten years. In all that time she stayed with me for my money, fully aware that if we divorced she'd stand to get very rich very quickly and have her freedom on top of it. I stayed with her for Katy. But now Katy's gone, and I can afford to lose millions."

"Why?"

"Are you married?"

"No."

"Then you don't yet know what it's like to have the person you swore to love until the end of your days become your enemy overnight, to watch them with other men as they plot to destroy you. In my line of work, you expect to come up against predators and backstabbers every single day. But you expect to leave it there when you come home. Instead, it becomes everything. You get paranoid and you seek out the only thing you've got left. For me, that was my Katy. She resisted every effort Linda made to corrupt her. She stayed loyal to me, and I loved her for that."

He leaned forward and put down his drink. "Now she's gone, so what else is there to lose? Money? I can afford to lose it if it means getting that bitch out of my life. The only reason to keep this pretense, this *sham*, going is dead and buried."

"And what about you?"

He seemed surprised by the question, but considered it. After a moment he sighed. When he sat back again, the cuffs of his pants rode up a little and Finch noticed something odd. Despite the man's apparently flawless dress and perfectly manicured appearance, his socks didn't match. It seemed significant somehow, as if he was being shown the man's true nature, a glimpse behind the facade at the frightened and slowly crumbling creature that cowered behind the armor.

"I'll do what I always do," Kaplan replied. "Persevere."

Finch imagined this man at night, alone and weeping, his eyes bloodshot from a cocktail of barbiturates and alcohol as he looked down at a picture of his daughter. Even when he'd professed his love for Katy, his voice had retained the same lack of emotion that seemed to characterize him, but Finch was no longer so sure that's who he really was. The other parents he'd met had all displayed the expected pallor and vulnerability that death leaves in its wake, and he had recognized it as an accurate reflection of his own, but though Kaplan stood out in his apparent callousness and calm, Finch guessed that, even though it might take a year, or ten years, sooner or later the grief would claim him, if it hadn't already. And the longer he looked, the more he saw in Kaplan's eyes the defiance, the struggle to remain standing as currents of suffering tried to sweep his legs out from under him.

"So, what's your plan?" he asked Finch, after a moment of contemplating something beyond the arched window at the far side of the room.

Finch drained his glass. "I'm not letting it go," he said. "What they did to the kids. I'm not letting it die."

"Is that so?"

"It is."
"What are you going to do?"
Finch told him.

* * *

Afterward, Kaplan did not offer to see him out, so Finch left him sitting in a chair that suddenly seemed bigger, as if it had gorged itself on the man's restrained emotions, and made his way out. Before he exited the lounge, however, Kaplan mumbled something.

Finch hesitated at the doorway and looked back at him. "What?"

"I said you let me know if you need anything." Then he added, "My vampire bride hasn't drained me yet. I still have money."

Finch nodded. *And no amount of it is going to buy you back what you've lost*, he thought, but said, "Thank you," and left.

As he sat into his car, his cell phone chirped, startling him. He hated the goddamn things and had successfully avoided them all his life, but had realized the need to have one almost as soon as he'd spoken to Beau about the plan. With a sigh, he removed his hand from the car keys, reached into his inside pocket and grabbed the phone, fully expecting to see Beau's name and number displayed on the small rectangular LCD screen as he flipped it open.

But it wasn't Beau calling, and Finch felt himself go numb, a not entirely unpleasant tingling capering through him as he studied with feverish interest and a modicum of disbelief the name that flashed on the display.

Gray letters against glowing green.

He told himself to be calm, *just be cool hoss*, and pressed the small round button to answer the call.

"Hey you," he said, immediately wincing at how forced the casual tone had sounded.

"What the hell do you think you're doing?" Kara asked.

"What do you mean?"

"You know goddamn well what I mean. I saw you outside our house the other day. Are you stalking me or something?"

"Don't be ridiculous."

"Then what were you doing there?"

Excuses were appallingly slow to present themselves, so he opted for the truth. "I wanted to see Claire."

"Why?"

"To see what they'd done to her. To see how she looked."

"Who are *they*?"

"The men who did this to her."

Her sigh sounded like thunder in his ear. "There is no *they*, Finch. The *man* who did this to her is dead and buried. Don't you dare try to make us believe anything different."

"Who said I was going to?"

She laughed dryly. "Your door-to-door conspiracy meetings. Ted Craddick was here last night and we heard all about your little crusade."

Finch nodded to himself. He was not at all put out by this, had expected it in fact, and welcomed the word spreading among the families as a means of giving everyone a heads up, so his visits would not come as a cold hard slap across the face when they already had enough to worry about. He hadn't relished the thought of dispelling the illusion the police had given them, but so far they had greeted the revelation with grim resignation rather than rage. Though they were of course eager to see the true culprits held responsible for the murders, the fact remained that their children were still gone, and no amount of justice would ever return them. There were no hysterics, only silent assent at what he had proposed, or as in Kaplan's case, offers of financing.

It would work as long as no one decided the police needed to be let in on things. This was his concern now. That Kara had no love for him was painfully obvious, so she might have no bones about calling the cops to thwart him if it meant shielding her sister from further trauma. If nothing else, he had to appeal to the woman he'd known and hoped was still there beneath the hard shell she'd developed in the years since leaving him.

"Listen to me," he said. "You're not a fool. We both know that. And I'm no fool either, so don't pretend Claire hasn't talked to you about what happened to her down there. As soon as she was able she told the Sheriff they'd blamed the wrong man, that the doctor tried to *help* her get away from a bunch of lunatics. They didn't listen to her. I guess they were afraid after all their bluster and mutual glad-handing they'd look like morons. I mean, they'd managed to pin a bunch of unsolved murders on a guy who wasn't in a position to object, right? They took the easy route, and with no one left alive to corroborate her story, they just baby-talked Claire until she was out of their way. What about forensics? Did you see any reports? Me neither. The cops say anything about DNA extracted from the scene, or Claire's body? No. Someone did a thorough job of tidying things up. Case closed and the circle-jerk goes on. "

Kara was silent, which he took as a positive sign, but quickly continued just to be safe.

"A friend of mine is an investigator, sort of, and he did some digging for me. We found reports of people going missing down in Elkwood and the surrounding area going back twenty, thirty years. That was the mistake the police made. In their statements to the media they played up the part about Doctor Wellman going crazy and cutting people to bits because his wife died a sad and painful death."

"So?"

"So his wife died in '92. If he wigged out and went postal after her death, who snatched all those people for the twenty-odd years *before* that?"

"That was just a theory," Kara said. "Who's to say he wasn't dabbling in a little psychotic surgery from the moment he got his degree? You said he couldn't speak for himself now that he's dead, and you're right. He can't protest his innocence, but he can't confess his guilt either. So for all you know, maybe they did get the right man. Maybe that town has been harboring The Demon Barber of Fleet Street for thirty years. We don't know, and you sure as hell don't either."

"Wrong."

"Oh?"

"What did Claire tell you?"

"Nothing."

"Bullshit."

"How the hell do you know? Were you there?"

"No. I wasn't. But someone else was."

She fell silent, but he could hear her breathing. Then she said, "Who?"

"There was a kid. The one who brought Claire to the hospital. He took off as soon as the orderlies tried to talk to him. I called them, got a description, then called the Sheriff down in Elkwood. The kid's name is Pete Lowell. His father died the same night all this went down. Suicide apparently, and it happened shortly after he sent his boy off to Wellman's. So explain to me why a father would send his son off to the town lunatic and then kill himself."

He could hear the shrug in her voice. "Guilt? Maybe he wanted to kill them both but didn't have the heart to pull the trigger on his boy, so sent him to—"

"C'mon, Kara," he interrupted. "You don't buy that shit, do you? If you're going to kill yourself and you want your kid to die too, are you telling me that instead of giving him sleeping pills or something quick and quiet, you send him off to be tortured and chopped to pieces by a homicidal maniac? You're reaching and you know it."

"Reach—" She scoffed. "Reaching for *what*, Finch? This is a closed case. You can spin all the theories you want and it won't change what happened down there."

He frowned. "What are you saying?"

"I'm saying *it doesn't matter.*"

He had his mouth open, ready to tell her what he thought of that, especially coming from someone whose sibling had survived, but she continued as if aware of how he would take what she'd said.

"It doesn't matter because what happened *happened*. Claire was raped and beaten and damn near killed. She won't ever be the same girl she was before. You lost Danny, and I can't tell you how sorry I am about that. I loved him; you know I did. But he's *gone*, Finch. He's gone and you have to let this go. It doesn't matter if that doctor did this to them, or some bunch of carnival freaks. Nothing will change the fact that it happened, and now it's over."

Now it's over. Abruptly, Finch realized he didn't know who he was talking to, didn't recognize this woman as anyone he had ever known. He had fully expected a change from the *If You're Going To Hell, I'm Ridin' Shotgun* girl he'd loved, *still* loved, but this...this was like talking to a stranger.

"Tell me what Claire said," he told her, his voice flat, and cold.

"No."

"I have a right to know."

"She hasn't told me anything."

"You're lying. Kara, I—"

"I don't want you coming by here again, Finch. I mean it. If I see your car outside or your face at our door, I'll call the cops and let them in on your little game plan, understand?"

He said nothing for a moment, felt the anger colonize him. He reached up a hand and grabbed the steering wheel until his knuckles were white as bone.

"Look...just listen to me, okay? I need your help with this, if only to let me see her, just to talk, that's all, just to—"

"Stay away from here. I'm sorry about Danny, you have to believe that. But nothing can come of this but more hurt and grief and we can't take any more of that. We can't, Finch, so don't bring it down on us."

"The Merrill family," he said, as he let his gaze rove over the austere facade of the Kaplan house, and dropped his hand to the keys.

"Goodbye, Finch."

"That's their name. Merrill. That's who did this to Claire, and Danny, and Katy, and Stu. That's who—"

A drone in his ear told him she'd hung up.

"—hurt us," he finished, then snapped the phone shut so hard it sounded like a bone breaking.

Teeth clenched, he started the car.

TWENTY

Despite what the boy had said earlier, after talking long into the night, Louise convinced him to stay. The later it got, the less tolerant Wayne seemed to grow. Aware that she had yet to tell him about getting fired from her job, she advised him to go to bed with a promise to follow soon after. Then she cleared the coffee table of their cups and trash and dragged it to the far wall, exposing the stained narrow space of carpet between the sofa and the TV.

All the while, Pete stared at her.

Louise sighed. "I know you're hurtin'," she told him. "But I'm not sure this is such a good idea. Do you know how dangerous this is? You're just a boy. And what if you're wrong and it really was the doctor? You might just end up hurtin' innocent folk."

"It weren't the doctor," he replied. "It weren't. That much I know for sure."

She shook her head. "Why not just go to the police? Tell them to talk to the girl. Surely if you're right, she can tell them what she knows and back you up."

"I'm guessin' she don't remember much, not after what they did to her. I'm guessin' her mind didn't let her see all of what happened, so she'd be protected, like when you have a real bad dream but soon's you wake up it starts goin' away until you can't remember it no more?"

Louise nodded, and smoothed a hand over the cushions. She felt helpless, as if of a sudden she was being given a chance to do something right but for the life of her couldn't figure out how to make it happen. All she did know was that she could not let this child go through with what he had in mind. If it turned out he was right, then he would almost certainly get himself hurt, or worse. As bad as it had been to have to live with the guilt of abandoning him, she would not survive long knowing she had let him go to his death. But what could she do?

"I'm goin' to get you some blankets. I'll be right back."

He nodded, and lowered his gaze.

He was not going to stay here just because she begged him to, of that she was certain. He owed her nothing, not after what she'd done to him. So what were the alternatives? She could alert the police, tell them what the boy had told her. But then they'd want to see him, talk to him, find out what he knew. They might take him in and try to control what became of him. Courts might become involved, the social services people. Sure, he was of age, but his slow development might be the trump card the courts used to ensure Louise was not granted guardianship. And if not that, then they would use her unstable past and unreliable present against her. She had no job, no prospects, no way of taking care of him.

So no, the police were out.

Take him to see the girl?

What would that achieve? Fueling his murderous and quite possibly misguided fantasies could only lead to disaster in the long run. And who was to say the girl wouldn't react negatively, even violently, to his presence? If she had succeeded even a little in creating some small semblance of a life for herself after the incident, in fabricating a new world from denial and necessity, wouldn't Pete's visit cause that to come crashing down around her?

She entered the bedroom. Wayne was already asleep, or was pretending to be as he sometimes did when he didn't want to talk. He was lying on his back, one arm draped over his face, his mouth open slightly. Quietly, she reached down and gathered up the thick woolen blanket on the floor at the foot of the bed, then returned to the living room.

"I saw them once," Pete said, before she had the bedroom door fully shut behind her.

"What?"

"The people who done this. I saw them once, but thought it was a dream."

She came to him and sat on the edge of the armchair, one arm around his shoulders, the blanket on her lap.

"There was a tall man," he said. "Mean lookin'. And a boy, 'bout the same age as I was back then. They was in our house, in my Pa's room. The mean lookin' man was tellin' my father he'd do best to stay outta their business. He was holdin' a big blade. Looked like a lawnmower blade, I think. I always figured I'd dreamed it, but the way Pa was that night before he died...I knew I'd seen him look like that before but couldn't remember when. It came to me though. He was real afraid of those people, and I ain't hardly never seen him scared of nothin' or no one."

Louise nodded, then stood and set the blanket down upon the cushions. "You better get some sleep now, and rest yourself," she said. "We'll try to figure out what to do tomorrow, all right?"

He didn't answer, just scooted forward off the couch and dropped to his knees on the cushions.

"If you need anythin' in the night, you come get me, you hear? I'm just in that room back there."

He nodded, and set about unrolling the blanket.

After a moment spent searching for some words of comfort to offer him, Louise gave up. "Good night," she told him and headed for her bedroom. She had one handle on the door when Pete said, "You gonna come with me to see the girl?"

"I thought you didn't want my help," she said.

"Not with what's gotta be done later. I don't want you nowhere near that. But I need to find the girl. She told me the street, but I ain't sure I can find it on my own."

She looked at him for a moment, at the vulnerability peering out at her from behind a mask of hurt and smoldering anger, and she nodded.

"I'll help you. However I can."

Satisfied, and still wearing his jacket, he wriggled down under the blanket. "Good night then."

"Good night."

With one last lingering look at the boy, she turned off the light.

* * *

A sound jerked him from sleep. For a moment, in the dark with only the pale glow from a streetlight filtered through the snow and the grimy window across from him, Pete was unsure where he was. The shapes that rose around him as his eyes adjusted were unfamiliar ones, and for a moment fear rippled through him. Gradually, he remembered and allowed a long slow breath of relief to escape him. He relaxed, but only a little. These days, tension seemed to have made taut ropes of his muscles and resting only eased the discomfort they caused him for a short time.

He shivered.

It was freezing outside, and though the apartment was warm and he was still dressed, a chill threaded through him.

At last he sat up, and rubbed his eyes, then squinted into the dark until he made out the faint outline of the TV. Atop it, the time on the VCR read 4:30 in glowing green numerals. Pete got to his feet and kicked his shoes free of the blankets, which, though warm, had felt scratchy on the exposed skin of his hands. He grabbed one of the cushions, replacing it on the sofa before dropping heavily onto it.

I shouldn't't've come here.

Since stepping off the bus at the station, he'd felt out of place. Part of it was the fact that he could count on one hand the amount of times he'd been in a big city, but mostly it was because he felt alone, and isolated, as if no matter where he went or with whom, he would still feel as if he journeyed by himself. The death of his father had awoken terrible, frightening feelings in him that frequently debilitated him and left him weeping. He had no mother. He had no father. The farm was gone. Death had cut him loose and set him adrift in an alien world that had never seemed more threatening. Every shadow, every face, every street was a potential threat, and Pete felt in constant danger.

And there was the anger, the awful consuming hatred whenever he tried to picture the face of the man who he'd seen standing in his father's bedroom that night, or when he felt the phantom touch of the child who'd stood by his side, smiling. And though it had taken him some time, he'd finally understood why his father had been afraid, and why Pete had sensed hesitation in him the day they'd picked up the girl. Pa had known what he was calling down upon them by helping Claire, but he'd done it anyway. In Pete's book, that made his Pa a hero, and from what he'd gleaned from comic books and TV shows over the years, the death of heroes was always celebrated, and avenged.

Pete had never wanted to be a hero, only happy. For a long time, and due in no part to his father, and Louise in the brief time in which she had been content to be his mother, he'd managed the latter quite well. He'd wanted for nothing, though he hadn't wanted much. He'd worked and he'd played, and though his future had always been a latent concern, he'd always figured he could cross that bridge when he came to it.

But now someone had shoved him over that bridge and burned it down behind him, taking everything he knew along with it, and forcing him to confront an uncertain future. He was alone, his father murdered, a hero dead. And then there was the girl, who'd been hurt too, left barely alive and lucky to escape. Who knew how many others had had their lives destroyed by these evil men?

They'll hurt you, maybe even kill you too, he told himself when the fear and doubt overwhelmed him. *And no one will ever know.* But he learned to counter this with steely determination and whatever courage he could draw up from the dark well of pain inside him. *I have to set things right. And if I die, then all that means is I'll be with Pa again.* This was the simple truth and he embraced it. The people who had done these terrible things to Doc Wellman, his Pa, and the girl, needed to be punished. It was only fair. And he would go alone, for to take anyone with him, as comforting as the thought might seem, would only be putting them in danger, and he was unwilling to bear such a burden.

He looked again at the clock. Only a minute had passed. He wondered when Louise would wake, or if he should leave and come back later when she was likely to be up and ready to face the day.

On the street outside, a dog barked.

It was followed by low murmuring.

The dog barked a second time, then yelped.

Pete rose and went to the window, wiped away the cloud of his own breath and peered down.

There were three men in the street, all of them dressed the same. They were talking animatedly, but keeping their voices low so they would not wake the tenants in the buildings around them.

He strained to hear what they were saying, but they were being too quiet.

He returned to the sofa and sat, his head turned toward the window.

Claire's face swam to the surface of his thoughts, and he felt his nerves twitch. He hoped more than anything she didn't hate him for leaving her alone at the hospital, and made a note to tell her that he wouldn't have, if he hadn't been frightened by the amount of people suddenly rushing toward him at once, all speaking at the same time, the look in their eyes serious, demanding answers. He'd fled, and hadn't made it a whole mile down the road before he'd regretted it.

There was still time to set things right. That's why he was here. There would be ample opportunity to explain himself to her in person. The thought made him smile. He imagined her as he'd seen her on the news—scarred and bruised but cleaner and healthier looking than she'd been in Elkwood. Her eye was still gone though, and he ached at the thought of how much pain it must have caused her, both in having it torn out, and waking to find it gone. The picture he'd seen had shown her looking exhausted, the lids of her missing eye stitched together with black thread so that it looked as if she might only have been in a serious fight. Her hair had been combed, her lips colored a little. The sight of her had made his heart beat faster.

Down in the street, there came the rumble of a car engine, the slight squeak of brakes. One of the men raised his voice, but his words were no clearer. He sounded annoyed.

Though Pete had long abandoned the idea that Claire would fall madly in love with him just because he'd had a hand in rescuing her, he hoped more than anything she would be glad to see him. He wondered what she would say when he told her that he was going back to Elkwood to punish the men who had done such horrible things to her. Would she think him a hero, or a crazy fool? Would she try and stop him? *It's too dangerous*, she might say, and he would have no words to argue, because it was true.

The men down there might hurt him. They might kill him. These things he knew, and it saddened him to think that all he might find back in Elkwood was failure. His father would go unavenged, and he would never see Claire again. And then of course, there was Louise, who he had never dared believe he would find, and yet here he was now, sitting on her sofa while she slept in the other room.

He worried that she might try to stop him, that she might lie to him and lure him to the police station where she would tell them what he was planning to do and they would throw him in jail to prevent it. This sudden concern was so strong he almost leapt to his feet and bolted. But then he thought of the cold, and of the men in the street, and stayed where he was.

A car door slammed shut.

Someone cursed loudly.

Pete sighed, suddenly feeling more alone and more frightened than he'd ever been. Tears leaked from his eyes as he pictured his father as he had last seen him. Fear in his eyes. The terror. The desperation. Why had he left him alone? Why hadn't he *known* there was something terribly wrong and stayed to help his Pa deal with the men?

Because you're none too clever, he heard his father say. *And you never was.*

In truth, he had known something was wrong, but the fear of his father if he disobeyed him had been greater, and so he'd taken the truck and headed out to Wellman's. But it wasn't only that and he knew it. He'd wanted to see the girl so bad it had muddied his instincts, made him reluctant to stay with the old man.

And now his father was dead.

Behind him, the bedroom door opened. He turned and saw in the doorway the vague shape of the man who lived here with his second mother. His eyes were dark hollows in the gloom. For a moment he lingered there, watching Pete, then slowly eased out into the room, pulling the door almost shut, but not quite. Then he quietly crossed the room, stopping by the sofa where Pete sat looking up at him.

"What you doin' up?" Wayne whispered.

"Somethin' woke me," Pete whispered back.

Wayne glanced toward the window, nodded pointedly.

"Those men out there?"

Pete shrugged. "Maybe."

"Well, you just forget all about them, now, you hear me?"

There was a hard edge to his voice that Pete didn't like, so he nodded. He knew it was wrong to judge a man he hardly knew, but he couldn't help it. 'Wayne' had driven the car that had spirited his mother out of his life all those years ago and the pain that came with that memory made it impossible to think of the man as anything other than mean. And now the tone of his voice—conspiratorial, vaguely threatening—only added to Pete's disdain for him.

"I'm just goin' for a walk is all. To get some air."

Again, Pete nodded.

"If Louise wakes up, you tell her I couldn't sleep and went down to the All-Night store for cigarettes." He rose, but continued to stare at him. "I'll be back soon."

Curiosity, as it had so often in his life, got the better of Pete and he asked, though he knew he shouldn't, "Where are you really goin'?"

"That ain't none of your business, boy."

Wayne watched him for a moment longer, but then the voices from the street drifted up as if summoning him and he sighed and headed for the door. "Remember what I said," he told Pete, and exited the apartment.

As Wayne's footsteps echoed in the corridor outside, Pete turned his head toward the window and listened to the voices from down below.

TWENTY-ONE

Distant thunder rumbled on the horizon as Papa-in-Gray stared at the wall. Before him was a chipped mug full of some kind of murky brown liquid he had as yet failed to identify, but it smelled like toilet water. He shoved it away from him and stared at the wall. There was little to see there but cobwebs and flaking paint. Jeremiah Krall hadn't bothered decorating the place, though he'd been living here for years. Every surface was coated with a thick layer of dust. A stone fireplace held nothing but a shroud of spider webs speckled with small brown egg sacs. Broken wood littered the place, as if rather than venture into the surrounding woods for firewood, Krall had smashed up his furniture, sparing only one rickety table and two wobbly chairs for comfort. He was a capable hunter, and hunted often, and yet the cabin remained utterly devoid of trophies, skins, or prize animal heads. His living room was just that, a room for living in, nothing more. Still, Papa wished there was something other than the stained surface of the table and that crumbling wall to focus on, because while they might be *living* in this room, he had come to talk about death, and one he feared Krall was not going to take too well.

He looked down at his fingers, at the faint maroon stains on his skin. It seemed he always had blood on his hands no matter how hard or how often he washed them. He wanted to believe it was a sign from God—stigmata of a sort—that he was doing His work, and doing it well. This would have encouraged Papa, though he secretly wished for more than some ambiguous rusty stains on his skin as acknowledgment of his commitment, reassurance perhaps, however slight, that a life spent worshipping and serving God hadn't been in vain, and that in the end, the Men of the World would not be victorious.

"Gimme strength," he whispered to the room.

As a child, he had questioned the existence of God, reasoning that the beauty of the world was not proof enough, that there had to be something else, something more. Something a child could look to for solace, and hope, for in his world there was little beauty, even less when his mother took the old belt to him for daring to doubt their Lord. She would punish him, and then order him to pray for forgiveness. Over time, he learned to view his fervent whisperings in the dark as penance he should not have to give for simply expressing his curiosity, and learned to resent the god for whom they were intended.

Then, one night, everything changed.

He was not yet eleven years old, but he had learned to stop questioning, his doubt a secret rebellion against the mother who had forced him to associate faith with pain. But not believing did not reduce the agony. His mother's big city boyfriend saw to that, and between them they rendered for the boy an adequate picture of Hell.

That night, early in the summer, as he lay in bed eyes screwed shut, tears streaming down his cheeks, the wounds from the belt raw and sore and burning but not nearly as much as the sharp thrusting of the grunting, drunken man atop him, something happened. A particularly vicious tearing sent red pain shooting through him. He gasped, convulsed in the bed and opened his eyes.

There was light, and within it he glimpsed angels, redolent in shimmering muslin robes that did not bind their wings, allowing them to beat at the air, cooling him. Their hair seemed made of frost, eyes a liquid blue, and in them he saw the answer to the questions his mother had refused to answer. Abruptly, adrift on a sea of pain that had carried him to the shores of epiphany, he knew why she had not sated his curiosity. She had been afraid of the power that might be bestowed upon him if God deemed him worthy.

She feared wrath.

The pain ebbed away, became a dull throbbing that kept time with his rapidly beating heart, and he felt a longing for the light as it faded, retreated into the walls.

But what he had seen had been enough.

In that room, bathed in sweat not his own, the stench of alcohol suffocating him, his mother's boyfriend hissing curses down upon his prone form, he had found God, or rather, God had found him, and bestowed upon him a great gift, a gift he quickly used.

To the man's surprise, the boy had risen up from the bed of his torment, a crude homemade hunting knife gripped tightly in his hand, fire in his soul. He remembered the days spent making that knife, but could not recall secreting it beneath his mattress. Not that it mattered, for though they had appeared to leave him, the angels still sang in his ear, advising him to do what needed to be done before it was too late.

"You git yer ass back down in that bed," the man had commanded, and slapped him hard across the face.

Kill him, cried the angels, and the boy obeyed, earning his freedom with just a few short slashes aimed at the man's face, neck and crotch. And when it was done, he had wept, but not for the depraved big city man, and not for his mother, who had rushed into the room—lured by sounds very different from those she'd grown accustomed to ignoring—and straight into his waiting blade. No. They were headed for Hades where they belonged.

He was weeping with joy.

God had answered.

God had saved him, and as he packed up his things and headed out into the night, the stars became His eyes, the wind His whisper, and he finally saw in the world the beauty he had refused to believe was there. He had been reborn, as all wayward souls must, or die screaming.

But as he sat at the rickety table staring at stains that might only be rust, or dirt ingrained in his skin, he realized that ever since the girl had escaped them, the same doubt that had corrupted his youth had begun to creep back in again, dulling the light that burned in his heart. In the years since his rebirth, he had lived off the land as God intended, and taught his kin to do the same. Theirs had been a humble life, modest and meek.

And every step of the way, they were challenged, if not by those corrupted souls seeking to destroy them, then by God himself, who made the crops go bad, tainted the water, and sent ferocious winds to tear down their home. Papa had chosen to interpret these things as punishment for something they had done of which they were not yet aware, the slight missteps that made a man deviate from the chosen path without him being aware he was doing so. Perhaps it was the cussing, his fondness for a tipple, or the things he liked to do with Momma-In-Bed on those fine summer evenings when the children were playing in the woods. Maybe they were getting lazy and not being vigilant or efficient enough in their hunting. He didn't know, but stepped up his efforts accordingly. He was harder on the kids, and though he was affectionate with Momma, he stopped laying with her. Instead he sat with her and talked, or read from the Bible. Every morning at sunup, the family congregated in her room and they prayed until noon, then again before bed. He told the children they would no longer wait for strangers to come wandering onto their property. They would expand the hunt, culling sinners from the roads and the land beyond.

For a time, it seemed his efforts were appreciated.

Then his daughter, his own flesh and blood had turned against him, and he had been forced against his will to offer her as a sacrifice to placate a God he worshipped but feared greatly. He had wept for her passing, but greater was his terror at the power the Men of the World had to project their disease into one of his own. Afterward, they did not eat her, for her flesh was corrupt.

From then on, the children were made to bathe in scalding hot holy water, then scrubbed mercilessly with steel wool before bed. The diseases that ran rampant in the outside world could be sent to them on the air, he told them, for when sick people breathe, the corruption travels. If one of their own died, they would eat them to preserve and absorb their strengths, as Papa had been taught by the old man he had met and befriended on a logging trail during his adolescent travels. The man had taken him to a cabin in the Appalachians, where he died, but not before imparting his wisdom to the impressionable boy. *Eat the flesh and drink the marrow*, he'd said, *If'n you want to know all I know.*

The children learned, as he had learned, to look upon the Men of the World, the coyotes, as emissaries from Hell who poisoned everything they touched. He had taught them that the very earth such creatures walked upon could turn black underfoot. He supervised their prayers, and often their slumber, periodically checking to see if they were touching themselves or each other. If they did so, even in their sleep, he would haul them from bed and beat them severely, punctuating the blows with quotations from the bible, so they would understand what they had done, and why the punishment was necessary.

For a year, he withdrew his focus from the outside world and all its dangers to his own house and the potential for evil that hung like a cloud around his kin. Punishment became pain. Transgressions were paid for in flesh. It was the only way. The children grew to fear him as much as he feared God.

And though he had never admitted it aloud, not even to Momma, he feared Luke, who he had caught in congress with his sister. How much of the poison had she transferred to her brother?

At night, in the quiet, he sought Momma's counsel. She was his sole source of comfort in a world that seemed determined to destroy them all. She listened to his concerns, her manner eternally light despite the ever-increasing weight of her flesh, and the first obvious signs that her docility had not made her immune from God's wrath. She was stricken with aches in her joints, stabbing pains in her chest (which Papa feared might be God's way of reminding him of the night he had found his faith), and lethargy. Then came the sores, the rashes, and the angry welts across her back, so much like the wounds from a belt.

"This is what becomes of us if we lie still for too long," she told him. "I guess God's tryin' to make us see that we better not get too content with things. We gotta keep pushin' 'till we're as close to His grace as we can get short of bein' by his side."

He'd considered that for a moment, then leaned forward until his lips were pressed against her ear, and "What if I can't?" he'd whispered, as softly as he could, even though he knew there could be no secrets from the Almighty.

Momma closed her eyes and shook her head. "Givin' up's a sin in itself when you've been blessed with His light," she said. "Now pray with me and forget your weaknesses before you're made to pay for 'em."

But pay for them he had. His daughter was dead, a sinner had escaped them, and Luke had been poisoned. The rest of them had been forced to move, to seek out a man Papa despised in the hope that he would offer them sanctuary.

* * *

An hour passed before the front door swung wide and Jeremiah Krall stomped into the cabin. His enormous gut strained against his tattered plaid logging shirt, the sleeves rolled up to his elbows, revealing meaty forearms dark with coarse hair. Dirt and blood stained his faded jeans. His large boots were untied and left muddy prints on the floor.

Papa rose from his seat and nodded in greeting.

In the dim light from the room's bare bulb, Krall appraised him as he might a snake, and spat tobacco juice on the floor. His eyes were the color of old bark, and glared from a small clearing in the frenzy of wild dark brown hair that smothered his skull and face.

When they'd pulled up earlier, Krall had been leaving. He'd scarcely acknowledged them, but nodded at the cabin, which Papa took as an indication that he should wait. Now he hoped he hadn't misinterpreted the signal.

"What's in your truck?" Krall asked, and unslung a burlap sack from his shoulder. The sack was cinched at the neck with dirty cord. It made a dull thump, suggesting weight, as it hit the floor. Blood pooled around the bottom.

Papa started to speak, but Krall interrupted him.

"Got your goddamn kids sittin' out there lookin' like sledge-hammered sows. Big tarp in the back looks like you got somethin' wrapped up. You bring me a present?"

Again, Papa started to speak, but this time he forced himself to wait. Blurting out that Krall's only remaining connection to the world was dead might not be the best introduction. Not when he considered where he was. The cabin stood in the shadow of Hood Mountain, at least a half a day's ride to the nearest town. It was remote, and that suited Krall, especially after killing with his bare hands three men who had jokingly called him a fibber when he claimed to have killed a buck that was roughly the same size as himself. As bold as Krall was known to be, the murders alone might not have inspired him to self-imposed exile, but finding out one of the men he'd killed was the brother of a Sheriff did.

"We need a place to hole up for a while," Papa said, and regained his seat, figuring that if he appeared relaxed, Krall might do the same.

He didn't.

"This is my place," he said coldly. "You got your own damn house. Go stay there."

Papa knew Krall was not a stupid man, and that he was only being obtuse simply to make what Papa had to say all the more difficult.

"We can't," Papa told him. "There's been some trouble."

"Kinda trouble?"

"We caught some kids in our woods. Wanted to teach 'em a lesson. They kilt my boy Matt."

It was hard to see if the news affected Krall any, given that only his eyes and the bridge of his nose were visible beneath his unkempt hair and above the undergrowth of his beard, but Papa doubted it.

"Which one's he?" Krall asked, sounding disinterested.

It was not a question that required an answer, rather Krall's way of ensuring Papa knew he was not welcome, no matter who he had lost.

"You still goin' on with all that God work?" he asked then. "Preachin' and huntin' up people you think's sinners?"

"I still believe, yes," Papa answered, but felt the color rise slightly as he recalled what he had been thinking only a few moments before. "Our work is needed now more than ev—"

Krall raised a massive hand. "Don't you go preachin' to me now. God ain't here or anywheres around me, and I ain't one for any of that bible-thumpin' bullshit."

"It's not—"

"Why'd you come here?"

Papa felt flustered. He had rehearsed what he was going to say and how he intended to deliver it, but realized he should have known from the few conversations he'd had with Krall in the past, that the exchange would go entirely Krall's way. He would hear what he wanted to hear, and that was all there was to it, and if he decided Papa and the boys needed to go, then they'd go. No one ever argued with Krall and came out the better of it.

"I told you," he said. "We had some trouble."

"I got plenty trouble of my own without you bringin' more."

"They won't come lookin' for us here."

"Who's they?"

"Coyotes. They killed my boy, and turned another one against me."

Teeth appeared in the dark tangle of beard as Krall smiled. "Weren't them turned your boy against you, I reckon."

"What does that mean?"

"Means you a goddamn hypocrite, and a loon. And that ain't the first time I've told you that neither, so quit lookin' surprised. You was standin' in my woodshed the day I told my sister the same thing. Told her she were makin' a mistake runnin' off with the likes of you. Saw it on your face every time you turned up, knew you'd be nothin' but trouble, and here you are tellin' me you lost your boys on account've someone else." He shook his head. "You ain't no man," he said. "You ain't nothin'. Way I see it, no God in his right mind'd have anythin' to do with you."

The frustration was gone in an instant. Papa grit his teeth. In a fight, he'd die at this man's hands, but at that moment he felt his temper flaring, heating his skin from the inside out until he was sure it made the air shimmer between them. He wasn't accustomed to being insulted, but then, there were a lot of things happening lately he wasn't accustomed to, none of them good. Mama-In-Bed had whispered that it meant the end was coming, the end of times, if only theirs, but to Papa that meant the same thing. He lived for his kin, except when they got themselves poisoned and turned against him. Then the coyotes could tear them asunder for all he cared. Otherwise, he was prepared to kill, and die for them until God reached down and plucked them up to face His judgment, and when that happened, Papa knew they'd be celebrated as angels for the work they'd done on a world gone to hell.

In years past he might have attempted to convert Krall to his way of thinking, to guide him in painstakingly slow steps into the light. But there was no salvation for a man so full of hate and loathing. Krall was ignorant, stuck in exile but closer than most to the eyes of God and yet he forever stood with his back to Him. Such disdain spoke volumes, and Papa decided the only thing left to do was tell the man the other reason he'd come, and see what happened next.

He watched as Krall scooped up the burlap sack and jerked open the tie.

"The tarp you seen before you came in," Papa said.

Krall did not look up as he spoke. Instead he frowned and yanked a skinned fox out of the bag by its hind legs. Drops of blood speckled the floor. "What is it if ain't a present?"

Papa exhaled slowly, his body tense. "Your sister," he said.

TWENTY-TWO

He didn't know how long he'd been listening to the men in the street. Occasionally he was able to make out their words, but not enough for him to be able to figure out what could be so important that they would need to gather down there in the cold at this time of night. But although the subject remained a mystery to him, the tone did not. Someone among them was angry, and when Pete finally tired of listening and returned to his mattress of cushions on the floor, that anger culminated in a gunshot that rattled the windows and startled a cry out of him.

Immediately he was on his feet and back at the window but his frightened breath occluded his view. Nevertheless he got the impression of scattering bodies as the car once more rumbled to life. The echo of the shot had not yet faded before he heard the bedroom door open behind him.

"Wayne, that you?"

Pete turned and saw Louise standing in the doorway of her room, the light from the streetlamps showing the concern etched on her face.

"No," he told her. "It's me."

"Pete. Did you hear that shot? Where's Wayne?"

He nodded. "He told me to tell you he went for cigarettes."

She brushed past him and hurried to the window. Despite his curiosity, he stayed where he was, watching as she blocked out the light and rubbed the ghosts of his breath from the glass.

"There's someone down there," she said, a note of panic making her voice high and tremulous. "I think someone's been shot."

Pete stood dumb, waiting for whatever was to happen next. Louise turned and looked at him, wringing her hands together. In her haste she hadn't tied the robe properly, and now it slid open. Though she was now backlit by the window and therefore all but cloaked in shadow, Pete averted his eyes anyway.

"When did he leave?"

"I dunno," he told her. "Maybe an hour ago. Your robe's come opened."

She seemed to take a minute to register this, then cursed and when next he looked, she'd cinched it tight around herself and was rushing toward him. "I want you to call 911. There's a phone in the bedroom. Can you do that for me?"

He nodded, because he was knew he was supposed to, but he had never had to call 911 before and wasn't entirely sure what it might entail beyond dialing the numbers.

"Tell them someone's been shot at 663 Harrison Avenue. Can you remember that?"

He watched her dig her feet into slippers. "Yes."

"Good. Give me your coat."

"My coat?"

"Yes, I need it. *Quickly*."

"You ain't goin' down there, are you?"

"Pete..."

He did as she asked and handed it over.

"You want me to come with you?"

"No." Shrugging on his jacket, she hurried to the door. "Stay here," she said without looking back, then jerked open the door of the apartment.

A shadow stepped in front of her, blocking her path, but she was still looking back at Pete and hadn't yet noticed.

The boy froze, felt a word of warning rush up his throat but it died before it hit the air, drowned out by Louise's scream as the man pushed his way into the apartment and slammed the door shut behind him.

"Please...don't..." Louise said, her voice brittle with panic.

"Shut your goddamn mouth," the man said, and as Pete's eyes adjusted, he could see that his initial assumption that it was Wayne he was looking at, perhaps angry because of something the men down in the street had said to him, was wrong. This man was shorter, thinner, and his voice higher in pitch than Wayne's had been. Also, though Pete hadn't studied Wayne too closely, he was sure he hadn't had a gun.

"Red," Louise said, cinching her robe even tighter and hugging herself. "Wayne ain't here."

Red looked furtively around the darkened apartment, as if following the path of an agitated bird. "I know he ain't," he said tersely. "Your boy's down there in the street with a big hole in his chest."

Louise said nothing, but started to shake her head.

Pete stood rooted to the spot with fear. He was unable to register what he'd just heard. Wayne, the man who had taken his mother away from him had gone out to buy cigarettes, or to talk to those men, and now he was lying down there shot? He couldn't quite understand how or why that had happened, and wasn't entirely sure how he felt about it if it was true. His attention was fixed on the man with the gun, and Louise, who looked terrified.

"The fuck's this?" the gunman said, jerking the weapon in Pete's direction.

Louise didn't answer.

"The fuck're you?" he asked again, looking at Pete.

"I...Louise is my second Mom."

"*Day*um," said Red, and raised the hand holding the gun to chuckle into his wrist before leveling it at Pete. "You think you're some kind of hero? You thinkin' about messin' my shit up in here?"

Pete shook his head. "No, sir."

Red smiled, his teeth gleaming a dull metallic color in the gloom. "That's right. Yes *sir*. You don't fuck with me, we all be cool, geddit?"

"Why are you doin' this?" Louise asked between sobs. Her head was lowered. "Why are you here?"

Red turned his attention back to her. "Take a seat. You and the kid. Sit down on that sofa and get comfortable. Wayne's got somethin' I need. Once I get it, I'll be on my way, and then you can go back to playin' house with my little homeboy here."

Louise didn't move.

"Hey babe?" Red said, leaning in close.

Slowly she raised her head to look at him.

"Do what I fuckin' *tell* you to do," he said, and in a flash, his hand was in her hair. He pulled hard and sent her sprawling across the arm of the couch. Instinctively, Pete made to move forward, whether to help her or tackle the man who had hurt her, he wasn't sure. His insides were on fire, his whole body quaking with the need to do *something*. And that something was fueled by anger at what he had just seen.

"Don't hurt her," he told Red. "Don't you put your hands on her again."

Red smiled and raised his hands. "Easy there, Shaft. Just helpin' her out is all. She don't hear too good. You know how bitches are. All mouth."

"Don't touch her," Pete said again. "She ain't done nothin' to you."

"Not yet," Red said, and began to move toward where Pete still stood fists clenched by his sides, trembling. "But who knows where the night might lead."

As the man approached him, Pete tensed himself for the same pain he had managed to forgive when it came from the fists of his father, and was surprised when the man veered away and stopped before the television set.

"Let's see what's on," Red said, and took a step back. Pete's eyes fell to the man's gun, which was now close enough for him to grab if he wanted

149

to. But as if sensing his intention, the man looked over his shoulder at him. "Go help your Momma, kid, or I'll put so many holes in you you'll look like a salt shaker."

Pete did as he was told. He sat down on the couch and watched as the man reared back and launched a kick at the TV screen. It toppled from its stand but did not shatter. Red kicked it again, harder this time, and the glass exploded under his heel with a dull *whump*. Blue sparks sizzled and hissed. A thin wreath of smoke rose from the exposed hole in the front of the TV.

From his pocket, Red produced a small pen-sized object, thumbed it and a thin ray of light pierced the smoke. Despite his fear and anger, Pete was curious. He'd never seen such a small flashlight before, and immediately felt the urge to ask the man to let him see it. An urge he quickly repressed. Instead, he put his hand on Louise's back as she straightened and sat on the arm of the couch. She was sniffling and rubbing her nose. He wanted to tell her it was going to be all right, that any minute now the man would leave them alone, but he wasn't sure that was true, and didn't want to lie. So he said nothing, and watched as the man fished something out of the guts of the TV.

"All right," Red said appreciatively, and quickly pocketed the item, which had looked to Pete like a small pouch of some kind. Then once more, the man's attention turned to them.

"See, now that wasn't such a big deal, right?" Red asked as he approached them, stepping over Pete's long legs to get to Louise. "Hey," he said, and she raised her head to look at him. Her mascara had run, making her eyes seem hollow and empty.

"Wayne told me you said he was lazy. That made him feel real bad, you know." He smiled, revealing the lie in his words. "So he came to me, and I hooked the brother up. He made some good money." He patted his pocket. "Trouble with that piece of shit was he was greedy, and the boys he workin' for don't tolerate that, know what I'm sayin?"

"He was your cousin," Louise said.

Red shrugged. "Yeah, but shit, I didn't cap 'im. I ain't that cold, Louise."

"So what now? You just goin' to walk outta here after what you've done. You just goin' to leave us here to talk to the cops?" Her voice, though unsteady, was rising, as anger told hold. "Or are you gonna do what the other thugs told you to do and kill us both?"

Red stared at her for a moment, then glanced at Pete. "Get your ass up for a sec." He waggled the gun and Pete rose from the couch and moved back toward the shattered TV, which was still trailing smoke. Red sat in his place and put his hand on Louise's knee. Instantly, she snatched it and shoved it away. In response, he shoved the muzzle of the gun up under her chin, forcing her head back. Louise bared her teeth, the muscles in her neck visible even in the feeble light. Again, instinct propelled Pete toward them, but Red spoke without looking at him. "Lot easier for me to pull this trigger than it will be for you to try to fight me, kid."

Pete stopped, agonized by helplessness.

* * *

Louise grunted against the strain, her eyes fixed on Pete. *Stay where you are. Do as he says and we'll be fine.* But nothing was going to be fine. She knew it, and she knew Pete knew it. Here, in this cold dank apartment in a frozen city she hated, she was going to die, along with the boy who'd escaped his own misery to find her.

Still holding the gun under her chin, Red brought his other hand up and slipped it inside her robe. She flinched. His hands were cold, his skin rough. She closed her eyes. "Stop," she pleaded, weakly. The urge to strike out at him was great, but she knew she would not get very far before he pulled the trigger and ended her life.

"Told you I ain't gonna hurt you," Red said as he massaged her breast. "But today, maybe tomorrow, someone you don't know's probably gonna stop by and do what I ain't got it in me to do, know what I'm sayin'? Wayne was a fuck-up, honey. Real loser. He made enemies faster than most folks make spit. Made a whole lot of people out there mad as hell. Tonight they took care of one problem. You, and I guess the boy now, are another one. Talk to the cops all you like, is what I'm sayin' here. Won't make no difference."

He checked over his shoulder, to be sure Pete wasn't up to anything, and satisfied that he wasn't, cocked the hammer on the gun. "Don't," she whispered.

Where are the police? she thought, panicked. *The gunshot was like thunder. Why aren't they comin'?* She couldn't even hear them in the distance. Her heart sank further as it occurred to her that maybe they lived in one of those places the police preferred to ignore.

Red's attention on her body increased. "That no-good son of a bitch didn't deserve a fine hunny like you," he said. "Soon's he brought you up here and showed you to me, I told him he'd make more money if he put you on the streets. But he was the jealous type, as I'm sure you know." He slid his hand down her chest, parting her robe with his thumb.

"Please don't."

"He didn't want nobody havin' his woman," Red continued. "Which don't make no sense considerin' he liked to brag about whuppin' you. Man didn't know how to treat a lady. But I do."

His hand slid down over her stomach and lower, but Louise kept her knees pressed tightly together. It was no use. Red's insistence came with the threat of death if she denied him. She winced as his rough fingers dug between them.

"Red, stop...I don't want the boy to see this. He's been through enough."

"Shit," Red replied. "We've all been through enough, ain't we?" he said with a grin as he slipped his fingers inside her, turned his head and smiled at Pete, who Louise realized was suddenly standing very close behind him, his face lost in shadow.

Red grunted. "Now what the f—?"

Abruptly, Louise realized the boy's intent and immediately grabbed Red's hand, jerking the gun away from beneath her chin. It went off, deafening her and blowing a hole in the wall by the door as the light from the muzzle filled the room, just long enough for her to see Pete drive a shard of the broken TV screen into Red's eye.

TWENTY-THREE

Finch couldn't remember the last time he'd been so drunk. If not for the alley wall, he knew he'd be on his face right now, perhaps singing into a puddle or laughing at some half-remembered joke. Very carefully he let himself slide down until he was on his haunches, his back pressed against the red brick wall of Rita's Bar. A light breeze played with his hair, and crept down the back of his neck into his jacket. He shivered, momentarily thankful for the numbing effects of alcohol.

The buildings around the cobblestone alley were too tall for him to be able to see if there was a moon tonight. Not that he cared. The moon was for romantics, and even if he'd been one in his younger days, he'd long forgotten how to be one now. He turned his head and looked to the mouth of the alley, where Beau, who had remained perfectly sober thanks to a night spent sipping orange juice, was holding open the door of a taxi as a tall black woman touched his cheek and smiled the kind of smile Finch had only ever known once in his life and now could scarcely recall. It made him feel suddenly isolated and terribly alone, and he wished Beau would either hurry up and say his goodbyes to the woman—Georgia, her name was—or else jump in the cab with her and take off, so Finch at least would know the score.

A moment later, her feet lost in a writhing red-tinged river of exhaust fumes, Georgia kissed Beau long and hard, then vanished into the darkness inside the cab. Beau stood for a moment, hands in his pockets, and watched as it pulled away. Then he turned and started back up the alley toward Finch.

"You still with me?" he called out.

"Barely."

"Well, don't quit on me just yet. We got things to discuss."

Finch knew he was right, but at that moment he found himself wishing that his friend had accompanied the woman home. He didn't want to think anymore. Didn't want to talk anymore. He just wanted to sleep. At home. In the alley. Wherever. He was tired of thinking. Tired of feeling as if his head was going to explode from all the anger inside it, and the sorrow. The sorrow was worse because it came unbidden, and unlike the anger, which demanded action, pain, a release of any kind, sorrow asked nothing but for him to just be still while it spread through him like a cancer and drained his resolve, his will to do anything but sleep and feel sorry for himself.

"Hey." Beau nudged him with his foot, and Finch looked up, startled. Without knowing it, he'd started to doze off, and now, like stop-motion animation, his friend had somehow moved from the alley entrance and materialized right in front of him.

"Jesus," Finch said and rubbed a hand over his face. "What a lightweight, huh?"

"We ain't kids anymore, man."

"No shit. Too bad, too. I had a lot of fun as a kid."

"Most folks do until they get saddled with responsibility."

Beau plucked two beer crates from beside the dumpster to their right, and set them down—one for himself, one for Finch. Glad to take the pressure off his aching knees, Finch nodded his thanks and lowered himself onto the crate, one hand against the wall to steady himself.

"Man, you're in bad shape," Beau said, laughing.

"You mean because of the beer, or otherwise?"

Beau joined him, their shoulders touching. "The beer," he replied. "Not that I don't think you ain't messed up enough without it."

Finch had to narrow his eyes to dissuade double vision. He hated being this drunk, and had only allowed himself to reach this point because of the euphoria it had promised, and which, for a brief spell, had delivered. Now though, he was sad, angry, and more than a little miserable, every speck of those feelings directed inward despite the availability of much better, more reasonable targets.

"I'm going to kill them, Beau," he said, nodding slowly. "Every fucking one of them. And I don't care what happens because of it. They had no right to do what they did."

Beau sighed. "No, they didn't. But if you're hell-bent on lookin' for fairness, you're on the wrong damn planet."

Finch squinted at him. "The fuck's that mean? I know what the world's like. Doesn't make a goddamn bit of difference. Look at the World Trade Center. Thing comes down, the whole nation gets mad and demands justice. The President sends us in to kick the shit out of them. Now all of a sudden people are complaining about his choices, and no one's demanding anything anymore other than that he wise the hell up."

"What's your point?"

"Point is, I've never seen a bigger tragedy than 9/11, and yet everybody not directly related to the victims seemed to get over it real quick."

Beau shrugged. "It's the nature of people, I guess. We're designed to grieve and mourn, and do what we can to move on."

Finch scowled. "Yeah? Well, not me."

"Not you," Beau echoed. He sounded resigned.

"Let me ask you something," Finch said, straightening so he could appraise him. "If those terrorists hadn't used planes...if instead they'd sat in their cars a few blocks away...say a dozen of them, and used remote detonators to set bombs off to bring those buildings down..."

"Yeah?"

"And after it was done...people discovered those guys sitting in their cars congratulating each other."

Beau said nothing, waited for him to continue.

Finch did. "What do you think would have happened?"

"What do you mean?"

"Aw c'mon," Finch said, throwing his hands up in disgust. "You know *exactly* what I mean. There wouldn't be a cop within a thousand miles would raise an eyebrow over what would happen to those terrorists. Those fuckers would have been torn asunder by the people who found them, torn to goddamn *ribbons* like those poor bastards in Somalia last year, and not a judge in the whole country would make them accountable for it."

"I don't know about that, man."

"Sure you do."

"Okay, so say I do. Where are you goin' with this?"

"A man catches someone attacking his wife. How does he react?"

"Gets pissed."

"Yeah, he gets pissed, even if the attacker is twice his size and built like a tank, and even if he knows it will mean his death. Hell, if you were married, had kids, and found out someone was sleeping with your wife, or messing with your kids, you'd want to beat the living shit out of that guy, right?"

"Right."

"And if those terrorists had been caught, instead of doing the kamikaze thing, the people there would have murdered them without a second thought. And why? Because they were *there* when it happened. They saw their world being violated, threatened, plundered in a day and age when we're supposed to be safe, when everybody is supposed to be your friend and those who aren't are too far away to be a danger. But if those enemies *hurt* you, *threaten* you, shatter your world and you *see* them do it with your own two eyes, or you can reach out and *touch* them, tell me, Beau, that you wouldn't do what instinct told you to do before weighing up the consequences."

He was out of breath, and incensed, the blood rushing through him, warming him against the cold. A dull ache throbbed in his temple.

After a moment, Beau sat back. "Yeah," he said.

Finch looked at him. "Yeah?"

"Yeah. I'd tear 'em to pieces, along with anyone who tried to stop me, probably."

"Then why, knowing what those guys did to Danny, are you trying to keep me from doing what needs to be done?"

It took Beau a long time to reply, but when he did, he looked squarely at Finch. "Because you're my friend."

Despite his inebriation, Finch was surprised. Not by the sentiment, but by the fact that Beau, a characteristically stoic man, had said it out loud. It moved him, perhaps a little more than it might have because he was drunk, but nevertheless he appreciated it.

"All the more reason for you to be behind me on this then."

"I am behind you on it. You know that. I told you—"

"I know what you told me," Finch interrupted. "And I know what you said, but I want you behind me one-hundred percent. Not because you know I think it's the right thing to do, but because you agree with me."

Beau looked annoyed. "So you want me to validate what you're doin', is that it? You want me to tell you I think murderin' a bunch of people and maybe gettin' yourself killed or sent to prison for the rest of your life is a spectacular idea I can't wait to be a part of?"

Finch smiled grimly. "Something like that, but without the sarcasm."

"Can't do it," Beau told him. "And if you really believed in what you aim to do, you wouldn't *need* my approval, or care what I think."

"Yeah, well...I do."

"Why?"

Finch smiled. "Because you're my friend."

"Asshole. You read those printouts I put in the folder with the other stuff?"

"Sure. Veterans suffering from PTSD."

"And?"

"And they came home, didn't get the help they needed and went apeshit, shot a bunch of people before killing themselves. Is there a moral there I'm missing?"

"It fucks you up. War. Chews you up and spits you out. It's one of the few places where you're given free reign to act like a psychopath and then one day you're standin' on your lawn, maybe pickin' up the mornin' paper and suddenly you find yourself back there, lookin' at the world through crosshairs. And you either run screamin' for help you probably won't get because there's a mighty long queue, or go get your gun so you can keep fightin'."

"Jesus...you need your own talk show, man. Seriously."

Beau ran his palms over his bald head and sighed heavily. "I'll go, all right? That's as good as I'm givin' you. I got your back. Whatever you need. But I'm not holdin' your hand down there and I'm not going to be your goddamn cheerleader."

Finch pursed his lips and nodded. "Too bad. You'd look good in the outfit."

Beau rose. "No wonder half my brothers are on crack. Bet it makes it easier to listen to crazy white guys."

There was silence then, but for the late night sound of slow traffic sizzling through the wet streets, water running down a drain, distant laughter as revelers headed home, the far-off drone of a plane delivering bodies eager for a night of sleep without turbulence. Beau stood there staring at the mouth of the alley, as if trying to decide whether or not it was time to leave. Instead, he turned, looked at Finch, and folded his arms.

"How are you goin' to do it?"

"We need guns," Finch said flatly.

"Covered. My uncle Leroy has a gun shop over in Powell. He'll give us whatever we need, as long as we don't tell him we're goin' on a huntin' trip and then ask for a bazooka, and as long as we got the money. He ain't big on family discounts."

"Katy Kaplan's father is going to cover the expenses."

"Nice, how d'you swing that?"

"He offered. I'm guessing he's the kind of guy who approves of my idea but prefers to stay well clear of the war zone."

"So he's a politician?"

Finch smiled. "We're gonna need maps. And we're going to need to know everything that happened from the moment the kids stepped foot in Elkwood until the time Claire was found. We need to talk to the Sheriff down there."

"The Sheriff? Why? You think he's goin' to help?"

"We're not going to give him a choice. Someone down there did a good job covering things up so the trail would lead away from the killers and right to Wellman's door. Tell me how a Sheriff can live a few miles from a bunch of murdering lunatics for years and not know anything about it."

Beau thought about this. "Maybe they threatened him."

"Yeah, probably. But if you're living in fear for your life in a town with a bunch of maniacs, you don't stick around. You move, and then you tell people all you know."

"So you think this guy's a rotten apple."

"That, or a coward. But we need him. And Claire. I want to know all she knows. The more information we have about who, or what we're going up against, the better prepared we can be."

"What makes you think she'll tell you anythin'? You know what it's like to walk through Hell. It isn't somethin' you enjoy talkin' about, right?"

"Like I said, when someone you love has been killed, there's a whole lot of rage. And she loved Danny. She'll want justice as much as I do."

"And if she doesn't?"

"Worst case scenario, we work with what the Sheriff gives us."

"Assuming he'll talk."

Finch gave him a dark look. "Beau, you're not hearing me. I said we're not going to give him a choice."

Beau began to pace. "So when we leavin'?"

"Friday night."

Beau stopped. "*This* Friday?"

"Yeah. We got two days to get our shit together."

"Why so soon?"

Finch looked annoyed. "It isn't *soon*, man. It's been eleven goddamn weeks. As it stands it'll be a miracle if that family hasn't already pulled up stakes and moved on. If they have, our job is going to be a whole lot harder. We need to do this now before they vanish off the face of the earth forever."

TWENTY-FOUR

"I once beat a man until he cried like a baby just for looking at my sister the wrong way," Jeremiah Krall said. "What makes you think I won't chop your goddamn head off for deliverin' her to me dead?"

Papa shook his head. "Because it ain't my doin', that's why. I can understand what you must be feelin' right now: hurt, anger, sadness, but you're quarrel ain't with me. Outsiders done this, and if what Momma said before she died has any truth to it, then it won't be long before they send folks to try to get us. I figure you might appreciate bein' here to see their murderin' faces when they do."

They were standing at the back of the battered truck they had bought from Lawrence Hall, the old mechanic back in Elkwood. Stricken by fear at the sight of Papa-In-Gray limping into his garage, he'd sold the vehicle for a song and eschewed the paperwork in an effort to be clear of him quicker. But from the start, the truck hadn't run right. It didn't much favor steep inclines and spluttered a lot, but it was better than nothing, and they'd only needed it to get them as far as Radner County, and Krall's place. Once they got settled, assuming Krall allowed them to stay, they could seek out a replacement and dispose of Hall's junker.

In the bed of the truck was an enormous dirty white tarp they had once used to drag bodies from one shed to another and to cover logs in winter. It was raised up enough to obscure the small window at the back of the truck's cab, but Papa sensed the three boys watching.

"What happened to her?" Krall asked. There had been no discernible change in his tone since he'd first stepped foot into the cabin. Even the news of his sister's death hadn't appeared to rattle him, but Papa guessed he should be glad of that. Another man might have used his grief as an excuse to kill the messenger.

"Heart, I reckon. She's had problems for a while."

"You *reckon*?"

"We didn't have no time to get her seen to, and there weren't much sense in it. She was gone, and we needed to be quick about leavin'."

The tarp moved. Papa saw it and was not surprised, but he saw Krall frown and look around, as if expecting to find the wind had risen suddenly. It hadn't, and he drew his gaze back to the truck.

The tarp moved again, rising in the middle as if the body underneath was struggling to get up.

"Now what the hell is this?" Krall said, and despite his apparent fearlessness, moved back a step. "You sure she's dead?"

Papa nodded a single time. "I'm sure."

This time something seemed to punch at the tarp from underneath. Rainwater that had puddled in the folds ran down the material.

"If'n you let varmints get at her, 'ol man, you ain't drawin' another breath," Krall told Papa. Now that the initial surprise had abated, the man's gruff tone had returned, though it was laced with a note of confusion.

Without a word, but not without effort, Papa grabbed the edge of the truck bed and hauled himself up. Krall watched impassively as the old man began to untie the cords that were restraining the now pulsating corpse. Rain made the sound of fingernails drumming against the material as Papa hunkered down with a wince—his leg had been bothering him since the night Luke had clipped him with the fender of the truck, and it was not showing any signs of getting better—and grabbed the upper hem of the tarp. He paused, both for effect, and to look up at the boys. Aaron, Isaac and Joshua had their faces pressed against the cab window, their features misted by their breath against the glass. He offered them a faint smile. All the way here Aaron had chatted excitedly to his silent brothers about the unveiling Papa had promised them once they reached Krall's cabin, and now Papa was keeping that promise.

The old man glanced over his shoulder at Krall, who stood in the rain looking as fierce as always, but now he looked curious too.

"I'm sorry for your loss," Papa told him. "And mine too. But it's times like these we got to think about rebirth, about the good that can come from tragedy. Momma-In-Bed asked me to make her a promise and to let you know it was her wish."

He began to unroll the tarp. Maggots spilled out onto the truck bed. Noxious fumes rose from the corpulent remains, but they did not bother Papa. To him it was a sweet perfume and one he would miss once they put his wife in the ground. He took a moment to whisper a short prayer over the body, then rose and tugged the covering away from her. Underneath, she was naked, the enormous mounds of skin a bluish gray.

"Goddamn maggots," Krall said in disgust and waved a hand. "It's them that's makin' her move."

Papa looked at him serenely. "No," he said. "It isn't." With a nod he indicated the thick black stitching that ran from the base of Momma's throat to her groin. Some of the stitches had ripped. Krall stepped up onto the bed to get a better look, though there was scarcely room, and the truck was in danger of flipping over backward under his weight. He stooped forward a little and shook his head, then looked coldly at Papa.

"You said you didn't bring her to a doctor."

"Correct."

"So who cut her opened?"

"We did. At her request."

"The hell for?" Krall was outraged.

Suddenly Momma's midsection lurched upward, pushed from within, sending maggots tumbling, and he took another involuntary step back. The truck rocked on its wheels.

Papa reached into his coat and produced from within a pocketknife, the edge well maintained and razor-sharp. "Momma died from fear, Jeremiah," he said. "She knew our world was comin' to an end, and couldn't bear the thought of us bein' claimed. They already poisoned our baby girl, and then Luke. She loved that boy and wanted to take him back. To give him another chance." He smiled. "So that's what we done."

He bent low, stuck the blade between two of the stitches, and began to saw at them. The pressure from within the corpse subsided. It took only a moment for the thread to snap, the flesh to gape, and when it did Krall joined him in looking down.

"Jesus Christ Almighty," Krall whispered in horror.

"Rebirth," Papa said simply, as both men stared down at the fingers slowly wriggling out from inside Momma-In-Bed's corpse.

TWENTY-FIVE

"What are you doing up?" Kara asked. "It's late."

Claire shrugged, and fingered the cell phone on the kitchen table, setting it spinning. She watched the slow revolutions until it came to a stop, then did it again. "Couldn't sleep."

"Well, you should try. I have some pills."

"I don't need pills. I'm sick of pills."

Kara, dressed in a pair of red silk pajamas, came around the table and sat down opposite her sister. Claire's eye was swollen from crying, the lid puffy, and there were dark bags beneath both sockets. Her hair, always so lustrous, was lank and tousled. Kara didn't imagine she herself looked any better. She had slept a little, but not much. Worry for her sister, and the memory of her conversation with Finch had kept her awake.

She looked around the kitchen, quiet but for the sound of Claire playing with the phone. It seemed odd seeing the room like this. Ordinarily such a hodge-podge of activity, for both girls and their mother loved—or had loved, at least—to cook, in the early morning hours, it seemed abandoned despite their presence, the sun not yet risen to give it the cheery glow they were used to seeing. The clock on the microwave told her dawn was still an hour or so away.

"We should make breakfast for Mom," Kara suggested. "It'll be nice."

"I don't feel up to it," Claire said. She continued to stare at the phone until Kara felt compelled to do the same. Earlier, she had walked in on her sister and found her on the phone, her dead boyfriend's number on the nightstand, and had quickly deduced what she was up to. Saddened, and more than a little frightened, she had attempted to talk some sense into Claire, then watched as her sister went rigid with shock as she hung up the phone, dropped it on the floor and began to sob into her hands. *There was someone on the line*, she'd said, and though Kara had no doubt Claire had imagined it, it still broke her heart to see her sister this way.

She's broken, she thought. *And I don't know how to fix her.*

Maybe Finch does, another part of her suggested, but she quickly overruled it. Finch was handling his grief the way he had handled every other trial in his life, the way he had handled *her*—with anger. Whatever he did, short of therapy, would solve nothing. All she could do now was protect her sister from his obsession.

"Maybe I'll make us something," she said, to get away from the same incessant badgering of her thoughts that had denied her a good night's sleep. "Maybe a ham and cheese omelet? Some onions, peppers..."

"I'm not hungry," Claire said.

Since she'd joined her, Claire had yet to make eye contact. She was so fixated on that damn cell phone, Kara had to resist the urge to snatch it away from her.

"Somebody answered," her sister said now, surprising her, as if they'd both been tuned in to the same mental frequency.

"What?"

"Somebody answered when I called Daniel's phone."

Kara exhaled slowly. "I know you think—"

Claire continued as if she hadn't heard. "Somebody answered. Whoever it was didn't say anything. They just listened."

The strength of the sincerity in her voice, coupled with the eerie look of intense concentration sent a shiver through Kara. "Honey..."

"I wonder if it was enough."

"Enough? For what?"

And now Claire did look up. Her eyes were free of tears, of sleep, and startlingly clear. "Enough to trace the signal," she said.

* * *

She didn't expect Kara to believe her, and didn't care. She loved her sister, but her presence here, now, while Claire was lost in her thoughts, meant that she was good only as a sounding board for her own. And it had worked. She knew from the movies that signals could be traced when someone made a *call* from a cell phone, but not if the phone being answered was traceable. But she was determined to find out. There was little sense in sharing this idea with Kara; she had done so only to hear it spoken aloud, and it still sounded reasonable. The killers had Daniel's phone. Tonight they had answered it. If she could get that information to someone who would believe her, someone who could use that information, then it might make all the difference.

She looked at her sister.

"I don't..." Kara said, looking helpless, frustrated.

"I've changed my mind. Let's make the omelet," Claire said, to deny Kara another chance to make her doubt herself. Relief washed over her sister's face and she reached over and squeezed Claire's hand. Claire forced a smile to placate her further, but behind her eyes she was remembering what Ted Craddick had said earlier. *Has Danny's brother been to see you? He's calling on all the parents, and he mentioned wanting to see you too.*

She studied the name displayed in black against the cell phone's glowing green LCD background:

T. FINCH

* * *

Red was still alive, and wailing like a child with a cut knee, though of course his injuries were a lot worse than that. He was on his back on the floor, rolling over and back. Louise stood by the couch, a trembling hand to her mouth, alternating horrified glances from the writhing form of Red to Pete, who watched her, eyes wide, his whole body shaking violently.

Get it together, she told herself, but for most of her life, that secret, inner voice had tried to guide her and she had seldom heeded its advice. *Don't go with Wayne,* it had said, *or believe for one second what he's promisin' you. You're smarter than that. Don't leave the boy. Don't leave Jack, the only man who didn't hit you and never would for one who probably will.* Again and again, she had refused to listen to reason, opting instead for spontaneity and gut instinct to lead her to greener pastures and ultimately, the fulfillment of ambitions she'd harbored since childhood. And not a single one of those gambles had paid off. Now, she intended to pay attention, and to do what good sense was telling her.

"Pete," she said. "We've got to get out of here."

He simply stared dumbly at her.

Quickly, she stepped around the fallen man. The end of the shard jutted from his ruined eye, his hands weaving around it as if desperate to pull it out but afraid what might happen if he did. Occasionally the heel of one palm would bump the shard and he would convulse and cry out. His right cheek was drenched in blood.

"Pete," she said, louder now as she came to him. He continued to stare at her. The boy had saved them both from certain death. For now. But he was young, and the guilt and horror of what he'd just done to another human being would no doubt override all others. All he would see was that shard, slicing through a man's eyeball, over and over again.

She clamped her hands on his shoulder and brought her face close to his. "Thank you," she told him. "Thank you for helpin' me. He would have hurt us both before he was through. You know that, don't you?"

He didn't answer.

"Look...I know you feel bad, but we've got to get out of here. We've got to run, and I can't do that on my own. I'm gonna need your help. Are you with me, Pete?"

Expressionless now, his eyes on hers, lips parted slightly, she feared she might have lost him again, this time to himself and not as a casualty of her selfishness, though both incidences were, at the back of it all, her fault. Had she not left him in the first place, he wouldn't have had to track her down, and wouldn't have—

Stop it, she chided herself. *Just stop. This is gettin' you nowhere. You start thinkin' about blame and in a few minutes both of you are goin' to be walkin' out of here in handcuffs because you lost the will to move.*

"Shit." She struggled against tears. "Will you do this with me? Will you do this for your Momma?"

At that, a small light reentered his eyes. He blinked but his expression remained the same.

"He was goin' to rape me, Pete. You had to stop him. And now we gotta get goin' or they'll throw us both in jail."

He wouldn't, or couldn't speak.

With rising urgency, Louise noted the faintest strains of red peering through the buildings beyond her window like blood in the cracks between tiles. They were out of time.

On the floor, Red was muttering curses. "Fuggin'....*kill* youuu....they'll...."

"C'mon," Louise said, and clumsily guided Pete toward the door, shielding him with her body as best she could from the sight of the wounded man. At the apartment door, she put her hand to his cheek. "I want you to wait for me outside."

He looked at her.

"I want you to wait outside," she repeated. "Don't talk to no one. Don't go nowhere. I'm just goin' to be a few minutes. Gotta get dressed, okay?"

She didn't wait for a response, doubted he had one, so she opened the door and gently pushed him over the threshold. A quick check showed no one in the hall. Satisfied, she stepped back into the apartment, leaving him alone. "Wait," she told him, with a look of pleading, and closed the door behind her.

* * *

"Fuggin...bitch...My *eye*...." Red moaned. He was up on one elbow, struggling to get up. Louise watched him from the door, her hummingbird heart threatening to stall under the weight of panic.

You can't leave him like this. You know that.

Red dug his heels into the carpet and after a moment, managed to get to his knees. He swallowed, and glared at her, the ruined eye only adding to the malevolence. "Gonna kill you," he said hoarsely. "Wasn't gonna, but now..." He sneered, blood trickling over his lips, streaking his cheeks. Breath rattled from his lungs.

"I'm sorry," Louise said, and meant it. This was not part of any plan. No one had promised her this. It had happened all on its own, and now it would have to continue.

"Bitch," Red said, swaying slightly.

Louise took a deep breath and in three short strides was across the room and standing before him. She saw him tense to strike her despite the extent of his injuries, but he never had the chance. She was crouching down and in his face, one hand grabbing a handful of his hair and yanking his head back before he could even draw back a fist. Then, eyes narrowed so she might be spared the full extent of her actions when the memory of them came back to haunt her, opened her free hand and drove her palm against the shard, slicing her own skin and forcing the thick glass into Red's brain.

He was dead in an instant, his remaining eye wide in surprise as he fell awkwardly back on his legs. As his lungs expelled a breath meant for a scream, or a plea he had not lived to deliver, she reached into his coat pocket and withdrew the pouch Red had retrieved from the guts of the destroyed television. It felt heavy in her hand, and when she opened it and angled it toward the light, she saw what was inside and her own breath left her.

Diamonds.

Swallowing back the terror, she hurried into the bathroom, quickly washed the gash on her hand and bandaged it, then moved to the bedroom where she tugged on whatever clothes she could find, and checked her face in the closet mirror for blood, or any evidence of what had happened here tonight. Satisfied that she did not look too conspicuous, she hurried out to join Pete.

Diamonds, she thought, stunned by the implications of everything that had just transpired in her roach-ridden fleapit of an apartment. But there would be time to think later, if they weren't apprehended before they even reached the front door of the building. In the forefront of her mind for now, was the fear that Pete had already fled, that his own turmoil had propelled him away from her and she would never find him. His guilt might lead him directly to the police.

But he was there, waiting where she'd left him, and she couldn't restrain a heavy sigh of relief.

She led him out of the apartment into the cold street, where she was stunned to see that though there was plenty of blood on the pavement amid the stubbed out cigarette butts and beer bottles, there was no body. The grief too, would come later, she knew, but was now glad that there was nothing to see here, nothing to distract her from what she planned to do.

As she hailed a cab and waited for it to slow, Pete finally spoke.

"Where we goin'?" he asked quietly.

Bolstered by this small sign that he was returning to himself, she brushed a hand against his cheek and summoned a smile.

"Home," she told him.

* * *

Finch's alarm clock showed 8:55 a.m. He sat up, groaning at the immediate assault of pain in his skull, and rubbed his eyes. The phone had dragged him from sleep without consideration for the amount of alcohol he had put away mere hours before, and he was not pleased with the interruption.

Grumbling, he blinked a few times and reached across the bed to the phone and snatched it up, muscles aching.

"What?" he snapped into the receiver.

The voice that came back at him did not alleviate his suffering, but it chased away all thought of sleep.

"Finch?"

He smiled, despite the shock. "Claire?"

"Hi."

"Where are you?" he asked. Her voice was low, as if fearing she might be overheard.

"Out in the yard. Told them I was going for some air. I'm stuck behind a goddamn bush right now in my pajamas."

"Well, I'm glad you called."

"Me too. I wasn't sure what to do."

"About what?"

"Ted Craddick told me you're visiting all the families."

"Trying to at least," he admitted.

"Why?"

"To talk about what happened."

"Is that all?"

"No. No, it's not all. I told them what I planned to do."

"And what are you planning to do?"

"I'm going back down there, Claire. To Elkwood."

"Why?" The tone of her voice told him she already knew, and just wanted to hear him say it.

"To stop the men who did this from ever doing it again."

"How do you know it was them and not the doctor? Everybody else seems to think he did it."

"Did he?"

"No," Claire said. "No, he helped get me out of there. I'd be dead if not for him."

She was silent for a moment, and when she spoke again, there was no emotion in her voice. "I can't stay long. I'll try to call back later if I can. We need to find some way to meet."

"You're a grown woman, Claire. They can't keep you a prisoner in that house."

"Yeah. Tell *them* that." Her sigh rumbled over the phone. "When are you going?"

"Friday."

"Okay."

"Why did you call, Claire?"

"Because I can help you. I think I have a way of finding out where they are."

Finch experienced something akin to a jolt of nervous excitement in his guts. Since making his decision to go after the killers, he had dreaded the notion that maybe he would get there and they'd have vanished underground, or hidden themselves away in a place not found on any map. The chance that someone in Elkwood would know where the Merrill family had gone was a slim one. Getting them to tell him even if they did know would be even harder. But it was all he had. That, and whatever Claire was willing to share. But now she was offering him more than he had dared expect.

"How about tonight?" he asked.

"Sure, but how?"

"I'll call you. You can tell them it's Ted Craddick, and that he wants to see you to reminisce about his boy. If they object, throw a fit. Accuse them of smothering you with their attention. Say you're old enough to make your own decisions. Call your sister a bitch or something."

"You would say that."

He smiled. "Head for Ted's house. I'll be parked outside."

"Okay. But I gotta go now. Kara's calling me."

"Sure. I'll call later."

She was gone. Finch stared at the phone in his hand for a long time before hanging it up. Though his hangover was severe, it almost didn't matter. He was elated. As he headed for the shower, he felt that same nervous excitement course through him like adrenaline, diluted by the slightest undercurrent of fear.

In the bathroom he paused before the mirror and studied his wan, unshaven face. His eyes were like ice chips anchored in place by dark red threads.

We're coming for you.

He was readying himself for war against a foe he'd never seen, in a place he'd never been.

It would not be the first time.

TWENTY-SIX

Kara lit a cigarette and through the smoke and the rain-speckled windshield, watched her sister cross the street, her progress slowing as she scanned the other cars parked alongside the curb for the occupied one. Finch was parked somewhere among them, Kara knew, so Claire was unlikely to look down the row of vehicles far enough to spot her. She watched, fiery anger demanding she put a stop to this immediately, before any further damage was done. But for the moment, she resisted and dragged deeply on her cigarette—a habit she had managed to keep secret from her mother for ten years until the night they'd brought Claire home. Even then, it had been her mother lighting up first that had triggered her confession.

"I didn't know you smoked," she admitted to her mother, aghast. Her mother had shrugged. "Didn't know you did either." And they'd smiled weakly and lit up. It had helped eased the tension that had existed between them ever since the night her father had died and Kara, in an inexplicable and uncharacteristic moment of frightening rage, had struck her mother, when it was clear the woman wanted nothing more than to join her husband in death. They hadn't exactly been friends since, and her mother's contention that what had happened to Claire in Alabama was their fault, the result of not being caring or vigilant enough with her, hadn't helped. Throughout their vigils, sitting in antiseptic-smelling waiting rooms, corridors, and starkly furnished hotel rooms waiting to see how much the ordeal had affected Claire, Kara had had to listen silently to her mother's allocation of blame, the self-flagellation, the expressions of guilt, and it had almost driven her out of her mind. *We should have known*, her mother had said, though of course there had been no way of knowing. *I felt it in my gut. I just knew something had happened to her. A mother knows.* Kara had recognized this last for what it was—misremembered maternal instinct fabricated to perpetuate the self-punishment her mother seemed to need, so she'd ignored it and gritted her teeth and tried not to be infected by it.

For Kara's part, she'd been sick with worry for Claire, but as strained as her relationship with her mother had been, her relationship with Claire had—and still was, she supposed—even more fragile. And for this, she did blame herself. After their father died, their mother had lost something of herself, had grown distant and stayed in that gloomy place which rendered every smile false, every kind word forced. With every passing year, it seemed as if her only goal was to find a state of consciousness that would allow her to get closer to the husband she'd lost, until her body felt compelled to follow. It wasn't fair, but it was fact, and so Kara had, without being aware she was doing so, adopted the role as guardian to Claire.

I tried, she told herself as she rolled down the window a crack to let the smoke out. Five cars ahead, Claire smiled slightly, tucked a lock of her hair behind her ear, and opened a car door, then slid inside and shut it behind her. The cars parked between them blocked Kara's view of the vehicle, but it didn't matter. She knew who her sister was meeting here.

That bastard. Again the anger tugged at her, tried to force her hand to the door, but she stayed where she was. *Not yet.* The longer she thought about it, however, the more uncertainty gained a foothold in her mind. Why was she here? To protect Claire from Finch? It didn't seem to make a whole lot of sense now that she studied her motives more closely. Finch wouldn't harm Claire, and what harm there was to be done, had been done over two months ago in that backwoods town. Claire had survived a nightmare that had claimed her friends. She was alive, if not altogether recovered, but that would come with time. Why then, was she sitting here, overwhelmed by the urge to rip Claire from the car and smash Finch's face in for luring her out to meet him? It was too late to protect Claire. The damage had been done, and the measure of compensation didn't exist that could ever again make her feel safe. So again: Why was she here? The answer when it came, was simple, and heavy with truth.

She was here to keep her from Finch.

He might not hurt her, but nor was he a presence she wanted in her sister's life. She had taken that one for the team, thank you very much, and there was no valid reason why he should have contact with anyone she cared about ever again. The man she had once, and foolishly, loved with all her heart, had almost destroyed her so driven was he by the compulsion to destroy himself. For him, happiness was an elusive thing, a concept infrequently understood and mistrusted when it came. He had told her stories of his past that had made her skin crawl—the abusive father, the bullying at school, the shyness he had eventually managed to cast off during his unsteady journey through puberty, the hunting trips with his father in later life which had invariably ended in arguments, and in one case, a mutual threat of murder, the alcoholism, the drugs, the fistfights. She had not been surprised when he'd accepted the call to war. He was not a happy man, nor was he even remotely patriotic. Finch was his own country, the government unstable, the population volatile. Often during their six month relationship, she had seen glimpses of the man she wished he could be, the man she suspected Finch himself wished he could be, but they were transient and towards the end, vanished altogether, leaving only the anger and the cruelty behind. She would never deny that a part of her still loved him, but it was a small part, a speck on the great wide-open plain of her hatred. He had hurt her, and he would keep going until he had hurt everyone around him.

And she would not let him do that to Claire.

* * *

"I'm glad you came," Finch said. "Wasn't sure the jailbreak would work."

In the passenger seat, Claire smiled. There were slight wrinkles around her mouth that did not belong on the face of someone so young, but Finch knew that no matter how old it might say she was on her I.D., what those men had done to her had shoved her headlong into adulthood. They had taken her innocence, her friends, her spirit, and left her as good as dead, for he had known Claire before the trip, had often kidded around with her while he waited for Kara outside the house, and he saw now that the light that had always danced in her eyes had gone out. Had been snuffed out. Her once lustrous blonde hair was now jet black and greasy, as if she'd dipped it in oil—a clear indication of her prevalent mood. Or perhaps it was meant to compliment the black pirate-style patch she wore to hide the scarring from where they had gouged out her eye. Either way, she did not look herself, did not look familiar to him.

"Kara was in the shower," Claire told him, looking down at her hands, absently rubbing the smooth pink nubs where two of the fingers on her left hand should have been. "So I left a note. My mother was...my mother. I'm not sure it even registered that I was leaving."

Finch thought of his own mother, at home, watching game shows and alternating between cursing the world and weeping while she reached down beside her rocking chair for one of the many vials of pills that stood like attentive soldiers around the runners.

"Everything's going to be all right," he told her, because she appeared as if she was waiting for him to say it. He draped his arm over her shoulder, gently, as he was not yet sure how she might react to a man's touch. She stiffened slightly, but did not move away, and when she looked up at him, he saw the pain in her face.

"You're going to kill them, right?" she asked, so matter-of-factly, she might have been asking a quarterback about an upcoming game.

He nodded. "That's the plan."

"Good." She went back to looking at her fingers. "I want to go with you."

"No."

She turned in the seat and glared at him. "What?"

"I said no."

"I don't care. I said I want to go, and you don't get to tell me I can't."

"Jesus, Claire...why would you *want* to go back? If what we uncovered is true, then these guys have been snatching people and murdering them for years. You might be the only person who ever lived to tell the tale."

"A tale nobody believed," she said flatly.

"I believed it. But that's beside the point. What I'm trying to say is that I can take care of this. I'm going to. There's no need for you to be there to see it. When it's over, I'll come see you, and we can talk. I'll tell you everything. But for now you need to stay here where you're safe."

She laughed, but there was no humor in it. "Safe? Here? Finch..." She gestured at the world outside the car. "Don't you get it? It doesn't matter where I go. Here, back there, France, the North Pole, it doesn't matter. I'll never be safe again. You could build a castle around me and seal it up and I'd still be what I am. And what I am is scared. What I'm *afraid* of..." Her voice broke, and she cleared her throat, then looked at him with fiery resolve. "What I'm afraid of isn't out *there*. It's in *here*," she said, tapping a forefinger against her temple. "And no matter where I run, it'll follow me, whether you kill those men or not."

"Why do you want to come if it won't change anything for you?"

"I'm alive and I shouldn't be," she said sadly. "And I don't know how long I'll be able to last with that voice telling me I should be with my friends, but in that time I'd like to see those men, and those *children*, understand what they did to us. To feel the pain and the fear they were so fucking *eager* to inflict on us. " Her eyes shimmered with tears. "I want to know they're dead. Maybe it will change things, maybe it won't, but I need to be there. I need to see the world put back on its axis, things put right, even if I don't belong in it anymore."

"Don't say that."

"It's true."

"You still have people, Claire."

"Who? You?"

"No. Your Mom, and Kara. You still have people who care about you and who'll protect you. The rest of us have been left with nothing."

She looked squarely at him. "Do you blame me?"

"What?"

"For what happened? Do you blame me?"

"Don't be ridiculous, of course not. You didn't make it happen."

"But does it make you mad that I lived and Danny didn't?"

He avoided her eyes for a moment. The truth was, in the beginning, he had been mad at her. He might even have hated her a little for being the sole survivor, questioned fate as to why she had been chosen above the others. But it had been a passing thing, the hate quickly redirected to the proper target, where it deepened, grew potent, became rage.

"I'll take that as a yes," she said to his silence and he quickly drew her close.

"No," he said. "I'm not mad that you survived. Not mad at you. I blame *them* because that's where the blame belongs."

Head resting against his shoulder, she asked, "Do you think it will go away when you've killed them? The pain?"

"No," he answered truthfully. "I don't think that'll ever go away. Not fully. Not after what you've gone through."

"I wasn't talking about me."

He smiled tightly, her hair tickling his chin. "I don't suppose it'll go away for either of us."

"Then why bother?"

"Because it's how it needs to be."

She pulled away from him, folded her arms. "So can I come?"

"No."

"Why?"

"I'm spoiled for reasons, Claire. Firstly, forget about those fucking lunatics down there for a minute. What do you think Kara will do if she finds out I've taken you back?"

"Who cares?"

"I care, and you will too because she'll have the cops on our asses so fast we won't even see their lights before I'm in jail and you're back under house arrest. Christ, you know as well as I do that Kara wouldn't stand for it. She'd make my life a living hell."

Though she shook her head, Finch could see in her face that she knew he was right. "Plus," he went on, "You've been through enough bad shit. You don't need to be put back in harm's way after escaping it once just to see *more* bad shit."

She fell silent, almost sulking, but he understood her feelings. They were the same as his own. Behind all the pain in Claire's face, he recognized the fear, the grief, and the kind of stark, utter hatred that could only be sated by vengeance.

"Did you bring your phone?"

Quietly, she nodded, and slid it out of her jeans pocket, then handed it over. Finch inspected the cell phone. A slim, silver Nokia. Nothing much different from the kind of phones most of the kids were carrying around these days. "Keep it," she said.

"I don't need it. Just the number. I have a friend who will know if we can use it to trace the signal to whoever answered it, or at least to *where* they were when they answered it. Danny's phone needs to be on, I guess, for us to have any hope of tracking it. If it isn't…" He shrugged.

"You didn't need to see me for that. I called you. You already have my number."

"I wanted to see you." When she said nothing, he nudged her shoulder. "Hey."

"What?"

"I'm sorry, all right? I know why you need this. And I can't stop you going alone. You just can't come with me."

A moment more of silence, then she cracked the door and stepped out of the car. She had grown so thin since Alabama he could see her shoulder blades pressing like incipient wings against the thin blue plastic of her raincoat. "Then who needs you," she said and slammed it shut before he could say anything further.

In the rearview, he watched her—a nineteen-year-old girl once pretty and vibrant, now bitter and prematurely aged—as she walked back to where he knew her sister was waiting.

TWENTY-SEVEN

"Hello Miss Daltry, and isn't it a fine morning?" the pawnbroker said cheerfully, his pudgy face molded around a large thick-lipped smile. Louise resisted the urge to look over her shoulder at the urban snowscape framed by the grimy storefront window behind her. It was a horrible day in almost every conceivable way, and as a result she had little tolerance for people like Rag Truman, who felt compelled to find the upside of everything and would probably keep on smiling even if he looked down at himself and realized he was on fire.

She hurried to the counter—a glass cabinet marred by greasy fingerprints, within which gold and silver jewelry on black velvet cushions sat next to nickel-plated revolvers, an assortment of cell phones, lighters, hunting knives, men's ties and women's silk scarves. Behind Rag was a blue steel door with a card reader to the left. A small red light showed that it was securely locked. A faded sign read: PRIVATE. All around were high metal shelves, packed with treasures for the undiscerning eye. There was so much of it in the musty room, it made Louise claustrophobic, but she acknowledged that a lot of that might not be the size of pawn shop, rather the feeling that a net was rapidly being cinched tight around her.

"I have somethin' that might interest you," she told the pawnbroker.

"Do you indeed?" He leaned closer, his hands braced on the cabinet, large ring-studded fingers smudging the glass. Evidently all the fingerprints there were his own.

Louise nodded, put her hand in her coat pocket, and then hesitated. Since taking the life of the man in her apartment, it was as if her senses had been enhanced. Her hearing, in particular, seemed to have strained itself, so that now the slightest sounds, once innocuous, registered as potential threats. As she stood there, frozen, fingers pressed against the soft material of the pouch in her pocket, she could hear the whistling of Rag's breath through his nose, the moist click of his dentures as he poked at them with his tongue. And outside, on the street, every engine sounded menacing as cars carved channels in the slush. She expected sirens at any moment as the police came to take her in. The thought of them rushing at her, guns drawn, broke her paralysis. She withdrew the pouch from her pocket and tossed them onto the cabinet between Rag's hands.

"And what's this?" he asked, with a curious smile.

"Open it."

He did. She expected him to be shocked, to whistle his appreciation, or pale at the sight of the diamonds, but reminded herself that in all his years of business, he'd probably seen more remarkable things. There were no exclamations as he upended the pouch into his palm and peered nearsightedly at the gems. If anything he seemed largely unimpressed, perhaps a trait he had adopted to keep his customers from overestimating the worth of their "treasures."

"Interesting," he said, and, spreading the sparkling diamonds out on the back of the pouch, fished beneath the counter and produced a small black loupe, which he screwed against his eye until it appeared affixed to it. Then he plucked a diamond from the pile and brought it close to the lens.

Time seemed to stretch interminably. Beneath her coat and despite the cold, Louise was sweating, could feel it trickling from her armpits, running like spiders down between her breasts. The world outside the shop seemed to be holding its breath, counting the seconds until it could release a scream of sirens. Controlling her breathing was an effort as panic squeezed her lungs.

At length, Rag finished his inspection of each and every one of the gems laid out before him, and he looked no more impressed than he had when he'd first seen them. *Maybe they're fakes.* Louise felt her heart skip as she watched him carelessly tug the pouch out from under the diamonds, scattering them across the surface of the cabinet before picking them up one by one and putting them back into the bag.

"I won't ask where you came by these," he said calmly, and drew the drawstrings tight before placing the pouch down between them. "Because I already know."

How? Louise thought in desperation. *How could you know?*

"There's much talk on the street about a certain robbery at the LaSalle Bank over in Troy a few months back," he said, folding his arms. "The cops have already been here three times, inconveniencing me greatly." He smiled and a gold incisor gleamed. "You see, whomever you *acquired* these from would not, I suspect, have been foolish enough to try to pawn them. I imagine there would have been some kind of a deal between those who facilitated their removal from the LaSalle vault and someone with enough money to buy them without drawing undue attention to his or herself.

This," he said, with a dismissive gesture of his hand in the air above the pouch, "This would be the last place they'd try to offload them. Too many risks. They would have to be very desperate indeed to even attempt it."

"So you don't want them," Louise said, her attempt at a calm tone falling short. She reached for the pouch, but Rag beat her to it, drawing the small sack toward him and raising a hand, palm out to halt her.

"I didn't say that, exactly."

"Then what are you sayin'?"

He sighed dramatically. "If I purchased these from you, it would convert me from a humble pawnbroker to an accessory in the eyes of the authorities. My livelihood would be at stake. In short, I could lose everything just by helping you."

"So don't," she said, but made no move to retrieve the pouch. She simply glared at him, willing him to cut the crap and make his decision so she could be free to make her own.

Then she watched, incredulous as he picked up the pouch and slid them into the pocket of his soiled baggy slacks. "Here's what I'm going to do," he told her. "I'm going to hold onto these, for your sake. I'll give you two thousand dollars—call it a loan, or a late payment on that pretty ring you sold me when you first hit town—to help you on your way, and I'll turn these over to the police. I'll fabricate the description of the seller, of course, and make it a very good one. It should give you a considerable head start before they pick up your scent. What do you think?"

"I think you're a crook," she replied. "I think you don't have a goddamn notion of turnin' those gems over to the cops. You know you have me over a barrel, so you figure there ain't a goddamn thing I can do about it either, right?"

"I'm offended," he said, and clearly wasn't.

She stared at him for a long moment, watching the small smug smile play over his fat lips. She was not entirely surprised at this development, had known there was every chance he was going to rip her off, but with no money and a bag full of diamonds, he had been her only option. Her previous dealings with him—the first to pawn her grandmother's engagement ring; then later, a brooch her mother had given her—had left her less than satisfied, but with Wayne unemployed and nothing ahead of her at the time but a few interviews for waitress jobs that might come to nothing, she'd had little choice. Now, the avenues available to her were even more limited. But she was not going to stand here and watch what little hope she had left being crushed by a man who, despite his claims, was in all likelihood as shady and crooked as the thugs who provided him his merchandise. She found herself wondering how much of his stock had come with clear evidence of how they'd been acquired. *Probably pays less for bloodstained goods*, she thought, disgusted.

Resolute, "Let me tell you how this is goin' to go," she said, and withdrew from her other pocket the gun Wayne's cousin had used to keep her docile, and leveled it at him.

"Whoa now," he said, and yet there was still no change in expression, as if facing a gun was something he endured daily.

She cocked the hammer. Rag didn't blink.

"You're goin' to keep those diamonds," Louise said. "You're right about that part. I didn't come here to rob you, and you need to understand that. So they're yours. All I want is a fair price, that's all. I have a boy that needs help and I can't give it to him here, not with what's happened, and not without money. Now those gems ain't mine, but I figure after what I've been through today, maybe I deserve them. What I don't deserve—" she said, stepping closer, so that her hip was pressed against the edge of the counter, the barrel of the gun scant inches from the bare spot between Rag's tumultuous eyebrows, "—is to have everythin' go to hell because of some greedy son of a bitch."

Rag sighed, as he might have over any deal that was not going his way, and narrowed his eyes. "So what do you consider a fair price then?"

She took a moment to consider this. All the way here she'd told herself that ten grand would be a good start. Enough to get them away for a while until she could think things through. Without knowing how much the diamonds were worth, she saw it as a reasonable sum to hope for. Not anymore. Rag might have found it disturbing if she told him that instead of disheartening her, his stoicism toward the gems had persuaded her they were worth even more than she'd guessed.

"How much do you think they're worth?" she asked him. "And before you answer, keep in mind that I might already know. After all, I brought them to you, didn't I? So if you lie to me, I'll put a bullet in your skull."

She had no intention of pulling the trigger, of course, and hadn't even checked to see if it was loaded. Red had shot a hole in the apartment wall, but for all she knew that might have been his last bullet. The pawnbroker, however, didn't know that.

"Maybe a million. I'd have to take another look," he said.

"You don't need another look. You can fondle them as much as you like once I'm gone."

"Can you take that gun out of my face?"

"As soon as I have the money."

"How much money?"

The words barreled up her throat and were out of her before she had a chance to consider them. "Hundred thousand. Do whatever the hell you like with the stones after that, but that's what I want for them."

Finally, Rag's expression changed. He glowered at her, face flushed, blue-red veins visible under the bulbous flesh of his nose. "You're out of your fucking mind. What makes you think I have that kind of money lying around here, or that I'd give it to you even if I had?"

"I guess because when you're given the choice of makin' a fair trade or havin' your brains blown out, you take the easier route. Maybe I was wrong." Pulling on all the crime shows she'd ever seen in her lifetime, she tightened her grip on the gun, leaned forward and pressed the muzzle between the pawnbroker's eyes. Again, he defied expectation. Rather than pleading, or accepting the fate she'd promised him, he scowled, cursed at her and turned away. She watched, shaken by her own resolve, as he withdrew a slim white keycard from his back pocket and angrily jerked it down the slot in the reader by the metal door. The light on the display turned green. There came a short sharp electronic honk and Rag grabbed the door handle, about to yank it open. Louise stopped him.

"I'm comin' around," she said. "Leave the door open. You try anythin'..."

"Yeah," Rag said, half-turning. His eyes were glassy with anger. "I know how it goes."

He disappeared inside, Louise following close behind.

TWENTY-EIGHT

They buried Momma in stony earth on the summit of Hood Mountain. From where they stood, they could see the great dark bulk of the water treatment facility on the horizon. Between the plant and the mountain the land seemed sick, diseased, poisoned. The hue of the earth suggested it had been sustained by the blood of those who'd tried to farm it. Rough patches of overgrowth marked the boundaries of long-fallow fields. Here and there, small stands of trees, buckled by storm winds and infection in their roots, stood defeated and spiritless, their arms weak and hanging empty. The mountain had been sheared by mining, the east side oddly flat, almost smooth, veins of red hematite iron ore still threading its hide, adding to the impression of something living cut in half. Intermittent beds of shale and sandstone gave it a leprous hue.

At the foot of the mountain stood Krall's cabin, its chimney threading smoke. It was surrounded on three sides by thinned out groups of pine trees. To Papa-In-Gray, it was hardly protection enough from invasive forces, but the mountain at its back would help limit the avenues of approach for their attackers. If they were vigilant, and kept their eyes open, his family would survive. They would be ready.

Though the weather was warm, the wind carried a chill to them, and with it, the scent of rain. For Papa-In-Gray, it seemed fitting, as Momma had loved the rain, the sound of it a lullaby that carried her to sleep.

Gently, he removed his hat, and bowed his head. The boys flanked him, their postures equally reverent. Jeremiah Krall stood opposite, at the foot of the grave, staring at the earth as if were a brown pond from which his sister might surface at any moment. The horror that he had witnessed had changed him, though how much Papa could not yet tell. He still appeared a character roughly carved from hard rock, his eyes wintry, his disposition hostile, but something had shifted within him. He looked like a walking battlefield, upon which wars were raging to determine which emotions should preside over the landscape. He had said little since witnessing Luke's rebirth.

"Our Lord," Papa began, his voice loud enough to carry the words halfway down the mountain. "Gather your faithful servant to your breast and keep her safe. Accept her into Heaven, and your glory. Recognize within her the light you so generously instilled in her, and which she did not waste. Just as she come into the world, so does she leave it, with an unspoiled soul." He paused, and the boys murmured "Amen."

"Guide us, good Jesus," he continued, raising his face to the darkening sky. "Guide us in the ways in which we can strike the devil from your green earth and vanquish the defilers. Lend us your wrath so that we might turn the tide of corruption that even now laps at our shore. Give us the strength and the means so we can tear the skin from the sinners and cast them down into Hell."

"Amen," said the boys.

"We give you Momma, a good, proud, strong woman who loved you more'n anyone, and we will not weep. We give her to you so that you may in turn give us what we need to smite the Men of the World, the coyotes that sniff around our borders. We give our beloved wife, and mother, to you, so that you might make her a saint and return her to us as an angel who would instill in our veins the power we need to prevail. Hear us, our merciful God…Amen."

"Amen."

Papa lowered his gaze from the mercurial sky. *You were a pure soul*, he added in silence. *And I'll miss our talks, and your strength.* He looked up, and wiped a hand over his eyes. The breeze dried quickly the dampness beneath them, and for this he was grateful. "Jeremiah," he said. "Is there anythin' you wish to add?"

The big man returned his gaze, held it for a moment, then looked back down at the grave. He did not reply.

Papa watched him carefully, then turned to Aaron, who stood solemnly by his side. "Go down. I want you to get all our weapons together. Feed your brothers, and see to Luke. Clean him up. We'll need him. Then send Joshua up here to keep watch. Before it's dark, I want you all ready and waitin' for 'em to come."

"How do you know they're comin', Papa?"

He thought about this for a moment, then ruffled the boy's hair. "God sent an angel to whisper in my ear while I was sleepin'."

"How many do you think will come?"

"Enough. Now you best get movin' while the light's with us."

Aaron nodded, and set off down the mountain, herding the twins ahead of him. Papa waited until they were gone, then walked over to stand beside Krall.

"I know you're hurtin'," he told the big man. "And that's only right. But if you don't end up seein' where all this is supposed to lead you, all that pain's for nothin'."

Krall continued to stare down at the ground. His lips moved slightly, but the words were lost to the wind, if indeed he was making any sound at all.

Papa studied him for a few moments, then clamped a hand on his shoulder. "The coyotes are comin'," he said. "Just like Momma knew they would. They took her from you, and I'm sure she'd be proud to know you joined us in wipin' them off the earth."

Without another word, he turned his back and left Krall to his mourning. It would pass, Papa knew. And when it did, it would leave only the rage.

This at least, they could use.

* * *

"Get out of the car."

Finch sighed, and rolled up the window. Stubbing out his cigarette, he was not entirely surprised when his door opened without him touching it. He would not have been any more surprised if Kara had reached in and slapped him. But she didn't. Instead, she held the door and waited for him to step out into the rain before slamming it shut and poking a finger in his chest.

"What did I tell you? What did I *say*? Were you listening?"

He glanced back over his shoulder to her car, where inside, he saw the ghostly shape of Claire watching from behind the reflected sky. He turned back to Kara.

"I told her she couldn't come. And she isn't. At least, not with me."

Kara's eyes blazed. "That's not enough."

"What do you want me to do?"

"I want you to undo what's already done. She can't deal with this kind of shit. Now she thinks there's some kind of merit to your suicide mission. Thinks maybe if she tags along it'll help her make peace with being the only one to get out alive. She's vulnerable, and looking for somewhere to put the anger."

"So am I."

"Oh *fuck* you," Kara said, and this time he knew she was going to hit him. But he didn't move, and the strike didn't come. Inside she turned, cursed under her breath and walked a few steps, then turned.

"This is typical you."

He shrugged. "I don't know what to say to that."

"Say nothing. Go home. Check yourself into a mental hospital. Do something other than this."

"I can't."

She stepped close again, the fury making her face ugly. "No, you can't, can you, and the last thing you'd ever consider would be getting help. It's far easier for you to fuck up everybody else's lives."

Finch folded his arms. "Look, I'm sorry. I told you I wasn't letting this go. I tried to talk some sense into Claire but—"

"Talk sense into Claire?" Kara raged. "How could that happen when you don't have any sense yourself? Think your age and experience makes you wiser? Sorry, Finch, but you're still a kid, a goddamn brat with a temper and everybody has to pay for it but you. Finch the Almighty versus the World."

That annoyed him, and this time she couldn't hang up on him before he got to defend himself. "Hey, I've *already* paid for it, all right?" he countered. "I lost my brother. You got Claire back, so don't tell me what I should or shouldn't do, or what's wrong with the way that I feel because you haven't a fucking clue."

She smiled bitterly. "Danny. I know you loved him, Finch, but if it weren't Danny, it would be some other cause. Someone or something needs to be destroyed because God forbid you should look in instead of out for a change. Well," she said with a dismissive wave of her hand. "Do what you have to do, I guess. But sooner or later you're going to run out of mirrors to shoot at. Then what will you do?"

"Wow...watching *Oprah* again, are we?"

She shook her head. "I don't know who you are, Finch. Not sure I ever did. But I recognize this part of you, and I should. It's why I left you. That was something else you destroyed."

"This isn't about me, Kara."

"Really? You sure about that?"

"Yeah."

She nodded slowly, a grim smile on her lips. "I'm sure you believe it too." She stepped past him, headed for her car. "Stay the hell away from Claire," she said without looking back. "Or I'll call the cops. And don't think I won't if it means protecting her from you."

He opened his mouth to reply, but the glare she threw him before getting into the car dissuaded him, leaving him standing alone on the street. Only then did he find his voice.

"I'm not the bad guy," he said, and wondered who he was trying to convince.

After a moment, he pulled his cell phone from his pocket and dialed Beau's number. "Hey," he said, when Beau answered. "We're leaving."

"Now?"

"Now."

"Why?"

"I just spoke to Kara."

"And?"

"And I don't trust her not to put the kibosh on this whole gig just to piss me off."

"Savin' your life would piss you off?"

"You going to be ready to go, or what?"

"Give me an hour, okay? I'm standin' here with my uncle Leroy. Negotiatin' the acquisition of the *tools* we'll need."

"Remember, John Kaplan's footing the bill so don't feel obliged to be frugal."

"Got it."

"I'll pick you up at your place in an hour."

TWENTY-NINE

They were in the park.

Pete didn't know what had gone wrong, or when, but the world in which he moved now was not one he recognized, or liked very much. It seemed everyone he loved had died, or was hurt, or walking through the same nightmare as he was, as if mere contact with him was enough to drag them into the dark. He didn't want that for Louise, but it was already too late. In the time it had taken her to take care of her "private matter" at the pawnshop, it seemed she'd grown older. She looked sick, tired and old, and he knew it was his fault.

"You drive real good," she said now, easing herself down onto the park bench beside him. "I've seen it, I know. Sometimes I think your daddy taught you to drive before he taught you to walk."

The mention of his father pained him, and it seemed from her feeble smile that it pained her too. Pete wished she wouldn't mention his Pa. He wished she wouldn't mention anything but getting to the girl, so he could be sure what was coming next. So there was a set plan. Because something about her now didn't sit right with him. It made him uneasy, because he couldn't tell what it was. Had she called the police on him, or changed her mind about taking him to see the girl? She must have. Why else would she be talking about him driving?

"You can get yourself a car," she said. "In that lot over there. I know the guy runs it. But I wanted to talk to you first."

"What's to talk about?" he asked. "We should just go before the police find us. If they do, I ain't never gettin' to the girl, and those folks who hurt my Pa'll get away."

"I know that," she said, and winced as she took her hands in his. Light snow drifted down around them. She was shaking from the cold. Pete drew close, hoping the heat would be enough to warm them both. The park was empty but for the bare snow-laden branches of oak trees and narrow concrete paths rimed with frost.

He looked down at her fingers, her clothes. "You're bleedin'."

"No," she said. "It's not my blood."

"What did you do?"

"There's no time. You're gonna have to go soon," Louise told him. "It isn't safe around here anymore."

"You're comin' too," he reminded her, the fear already seizing his heart. He could tell by the look on her weary face what she was saying, but refused to believe it until the words took away the choice.

"No, I'm not."

"Why?"

"All you need to know is that I love you, and I would go with you if I could, but I can't. It's too late. Too much has happened, and I need to go where the road is takin' me. Unfortunately, it ain't the same road as yours."

"How do you know?"

"I just do. Trust me on this, okay? Have I ever lied to you?"

He shook his head.

"Okay. Then please just do this for me. I'll catch up with you in a few days' time if I can. And here," she said, withdrawing Red's gun from her pocket. "Take this. You might need it, but I sure hope you don't. Hasn't exactly brought us much luck, has it?"

He did as she requested, though the weight of the gun felt ugly and unnatural.

Sirens pierced the chill, icy air and she flinched, looked around. Quickly, she turned back to face him, her eyes wide and imploring. "Here," she said, digging into her coat pocket. Into his hand she stuffed a large wad of bills. Pete had never seen so much money in his life. "Take this, and get yourself a ride. Guy's name is Mike. He was a regular of mine when I worked in the Overrail. Tell him Louise sent you. Tell him your story. He'll believe you. You got an honest face. People like him...they recognize honesty, seein' as how they got so little of it themselves." She gave him a weak grin, and shivered.

Panicked, Pete grabbed her coat. "You left me before, 'member? Please...don't do it again. Come with me. I can't do this by myself. S'why I came to find you."

She hugged him lightly and stroked his hair. "We're outta time, Pete."

The sirens increased in volume, and over her shoulder Pete saw a cruiser swing into view at the far end of the street, lights flashing. "They're comin'." He felt Louise nod, then she pushed him away.

"Hurry, now, but don't run. You don't want to draw them on you, okay?"

"They'll follow me."

"No. They won't. The only two people around here who've seen you with me are dead. You won't be involved."

"Why can't you come with me? I don't understand."

"Because I didn't do things right. I never have, and like always, I gotta face the music now."

"No, you don't. Come with me. We can—"

"If I go, they'll come after me and dog me for the rest of my days. I don't want that, for either of us. If I stay, they won't bother with you. There'll be no reason to."

Tears in his eyes, "Please come..." he said, one last time, but knew it would change nothing. The pain in her eyes hadn't been there the first time she'd left him. It was there now and he knew it was because this time it was for good. He would never see her again, and the thought almost crippled him. But the police car was close enough now that he could hear its tires sizzling through the slush, so he bent low, kissed her, and without another word, crossed the street. As he walked, he looked down at his fingers, at the smudges of blood on the tips. It reminded him of the night they'd found Claire. He had held his hands out to the rain to cleanse them, and afterward it had made him feel bad, as if he'd washed a part of her away. Though it was snowing now and he could simply reach down into the slush to clean them, he closed his hands instead. This blood he wanted to keep for as long as he could because although Louise had said she'd never lied to him, he knew now in his heart that she had, just this once, and only to protect him from the hurt.

It's not my blood.

As he started to turn the corner into the car lot, he cast a final glance back at her, and saw that she was rocking slightly.

In his head, he heard her singing him to sleep.

* * *

Despite what she had told the boy, Louise did not believe she had ever found her road. She had only found the end of the one she had stumbled blindly along her whole life. The wrong one. It saddened her to think of so many squandered chances and wasted possibilities. She could have been something, had always known she was *meant* to be something and had tried her damndest to show the world what she was made of. But in the end, she realized she would not be spoken of in the same breath as Aretha Franklin, Ella Fitzgerald, or Joyce Brant, because none of them had been thieves and murderers. Her singing voice would not be remembered, only the violence, the death, and her frantic attempts to set a boy on the road that might turn out to be his own eventual end, simply because he'd asked her to. It was all he wanted and she had agreed, partly out of guilt, and partly because she'd wanted him to follow his goal to its finish, no matter how misguided a goal it might prove to be.

She began to hum, a sweet melancholy tune that had been with her since her mother had sung it to her as a child. The name seemed so important now, but the fog in her mind obscured it. As her vision grew dim, she raised her head, and wondered if the snow had grown heavier, or if her time was almost at an end. The cold was gradually giving way to warmth, and that at least was good. It allowed her to be calm and focused in whatever time she had left.

She heard the squeak of brakes and the whoop-whoop stutter of the siren as the police car pulled up alongside her. More wails rose in the streets and alleys, a thousand echoes like dogs howling at night. Doors cracked open. Holsters were unclipped, guns drawn. She did not acknowledge those sounds, or the voices that barked at her, filling her ears with commands. She was dying, and had no use for them.

"Ma'am, I'm gonna have to ask you to stand, real slow."

Louise smiled, and opened her coat.

Momentary silence, then someone said: "Get the medic. *Now*."

She shook her head. *Too late*.

Steam rose from the slash in her stomach where the pawnbroker had dug his boxcutter into her. The sudden shock of it had made her muscles tense, including the one in her trigger finger, and she'd left Rag with a bullet in his shoulder. The pain had made even the simplest of tasks seem monumentally difficult, and she feared grabbing fistfuls of money and padding the wound would deny her the time she needed to get back to Pete and set him on his way. She should have died quickly—the wound would not stop bleeding—but she'd refused. She had left the boy once before. She would not do it again. Not until she'd seen him off.

It seemed only right.

She laughed at that, but it was short and made her double over with pain. Nothing in her life had been right, and it had culminated in the sheer wrongness of the past few hours. She had killed two men, and lost the one she'd been betting on to free her. And her son, a boy who was not her blood, but shared her heart, she had sent away, to fight for all that remained.

"There's a gun in her pocket," a man said gruffly.

Arms grabbed her, stopping her from sliding to the frozen ground as her heels failed to find purchase on the slick concrete. But still the mirth leaked out in airless chuckles, trailing from her in clouds that swept around the hard faces of the men, diffusing them, making them unreal.

"Take it easy. She's hurt bad."

Maybe, she thought, *this was my road. Maybe it was all I was supposed to do. Ain't that a kick in the head?*

She didn't know, and was too tired to think about it any longer.

"Can you stand, Ma'am?"

Tired of trying to keep myself together.

All that was left were the colors.

The gray.

Tired of trying to hold myself in.

The white.

"She's passing out."

The red.

Then nothing.

PART THREE

THIRTY

Elkwood, Alabama
October 2nd, 2004

"Sheriff McKindrey?"

McKindrey jumped, and put a hand to his chest, though the only thing he was likely to suffer today was heartburn after the burritos and refried beans he'd put away not an hour before. Still, the jolt had been enough to remind him that three beers combined with the soft chuckling of the water in the creek had made him drowsy, and persuaded him there was no need to be on his guard. Hell, even if a catfish nibbled on the bait currently floating around out there on the end of his line, he wasn't going to be fussed, and the slight chill to the breeze hadn't been enough to penetrate his languor. To him, the act of fishing was simply that: an act. The peace and quiet, the ambience, and of course, the beer, were the real draw. He was seldom bothered by anyone down here, but just as he'd been about to doze off and let the folding chair accept his weight, he'd heard feet crunching upon the dry earth of the bank, and then the voice.

He scratched his head and wondered how it was that a Podunk next-to-dead town like Elkwood always managed to have something somewhere that needed attending to, usually when he was in no mood to do anything other than get drunk.

Annoyed, he sat up in the chair, felt it wobble beneath him and stamped his feet down on the grass to stabilize himself. It wouldn't do to end up flat on his ass in front of someone who might have urgent business. He craned his neck around and squinted at his visitor.

Quickly, he rose.

"Yes?"

Strangers meant trouble. In all his time in Elkwood, he had yet to see one that wasn't. Even if they themselves weren't the source of it, it wasn't long finding them. And when that happened, McKindrey ended up with stress headaches and high blood pressure, which frequently left him short of breath and sweating like a hog in a heat wave, though Doc Wellman had liked to pin those symptoms on his excess weight. Whatever the culprit, he grew sensitive to sound and his bowels got a mind of their own whenever he found himself forced to weather the scrutiny and interminable questions from severe looking troopers, investigators and officials, all of whom looked at him like he was some dumb yokel who liked to sit around all day chewing chaw and diddling his sister. True, he supposed he wasn't as well-educated as some of the suits who showed up to throw names like Quantico at him—which McKindrey thought sounded like a college for grease monkeys—but nor was he a fool. He'd had his share of learning, and abided by the belief that most of what he'd kept and valued in the way of education he'd come by out in the world, not sitting in a snug chair listening to some professor waffling on about numbers and theories. But he never said as much to the stern-faced men with their square, clean-shaven jaws, funeral suits, and slick-backed hair. They thought him a buffoon and that suited him just fine. Better that than to have them suspect he knew more than he was telling.

The man standing on the bank appraising him did not look like any official he'd ever seen, and he wanted to believe that was a good thing. But the expression on the guy's face told him that might be a premature assumption.

"Catch anythin'?" the black man asked. He was tall—very tall; the Sheriff put him at about six-six—and well built. His head was shaved bare, and he wore sunglasses that reflected McKindrey's perplexed face back at him. He was dressed in blue jeans, a black belt with a silver buckle, and a white shirt, open at the collar. He was smiling, but it didn't put McKindrey at ease.

"Nothin' I want," McKindrey said flatly. "Help you with somethin'?" While he waited for an answer, he mentally reviewed the proximity of his weapon, which he'd taken to removing before he sat down so the weight of it didn't make the holster chafe his thigh.

"I hope so."

"How'd you find me?"

"Lady at your office said you'd be down here." He grinned. "She sure was nice. Pretty too."

McKindrey made a note to reprimand Stella as soon as he got back, assuming the man wasn't here to rob or kill him, in which case he wouldn't be getting back at all, at least not in one piece. That Stella was his wife didn't make a lick of difference. If anything it meant she should be even more cautious about who she sent after him.

Making his impatience clear, he said: "So, what is it you need?"

"Answers."

"'Bout what?"

"About a family that lived around here up until a few months back."

McKindrey remembered where he'd left the gun, and now that he knew what the black man wanted, it suddenly became very important that he retrieve it. He could see it resting on the ground next to his cooler twelve feet or so away, its barrel on the rim of his hat, the handle in the grass.

"Which family would that be?" he asked.

"I think we both know the answer to that," the man told him. "What you might not know is what's goin' to happen to your cracker ass if you try to pick up that gun over there."

McKindrey did not immediately look away from the gun. Instead he took his time until he had formulated what he felt was an adequate response to the insult he'd just been dealt. Hooking his thumbs into his gun belt, he smiled tightly. "I know you, son?"

"Doubt it. My name's Beau, though, just so we can officially say we're acquainted."

McKindrey reckoned it sounded like a faggot's name.

"Well, *Beau*," he said. "Why don't you give me one good reason why I shouldn't drag your black ass to jail for insultin' an officer of the peace?"

Without hesitation, the man nodded. "I'll give you two."

McKindrey felt himself tense as the man reached behind his back and produced a handgun, which he held up for the Sheriff to see as he cocked it. "This is one," Beau said, then nodded at something over McKindrey's shoulder, something the Sheriff realized much too late was the sound of more footsteps, coming at him fast. He cursed.

"That's two," the black man said, and McKindrey turned. He had the impression of a pale-face looming in his vision before something struck him hard between the eyes and he went down into the darkness.

* * *

He awoke with a groan and almost immediately two things dawned on him:

First, his nose was broken and throbbing like a teenager's pecker at the prom. He tasted blood on his lips. The tops of his cheeks were stiff and unyielding when he tried to gauge the extent of the damage by grimacing.

Secondly, he was no longer at the creek. The absence of sound was his first clue. The smell and the gloom confirmed it. Slaughterhouses had a similar odor, like shit and rotting carcasses. Automatically he tried to wrinkle his nose but the flare of pain stopped him and he spat a wad of blood and phlegm that landed with a smacking sound on the stone floor between his feet. He blinked to coerce his vision into cooperating, and a moment later, the room in which he sat with his hands bound behind him and his feet tied to the legs of the chair came into focus.

A kitchen, dirty and abandoned, the windows caked with dust, the floor littered with trash, broken dishes, and mouse droppings.

The kitchen of the Merrill place. He had never been inside the house before, but the procedures he'd been required to follow had occasionally brought him out this way, and more than once he'd peered in through the grimy glass to see if anyone was inside. Even when the Merrills had lived here, it hadn't been any tidier than it was now. Hygiene had never been a priority for that clan.

"What am I doin' here?" he croaked, every word scraping its way out of his raw throat.

A few feet away, the black man—Beau—leaned against the kitchen table eating a bag of Doritos. His gun rested on the table. Standing directly opposite McKindrey was the man he assumed had struck him.

"Nice of you to join us, Sheriff," he said.

This one was white, his hair coarse and dark above brilliant blue eyes that were almost manic. He was unshaven, a few days' worth of stubble framing thin lips in a gaunt, narrow face. He wore a wrinkled black T-shirt and jeans.

"Who are you people?" McKindrey asked, and spat again, the bitter expression on his face intended to let them know the action was only partly out of necessity.

"This is Finch," Beau said around a mouthful of chips.

"That don't answer my question," McKindrey said. "But I hope you boys know the shit you're wadin' into by doin' this."

Finch appeared to be mulling this over, then he shrugged. "Not a whole lot I'd imagine, considering the way things tend to get forgotten, or breezed over in this town. People vanish all the time in your jurisdiction, don't they? So why would you assume anyone will miss you?"

"I got a wife," he told them. "Couple of hours and she'll have the state police out lookin' for me."

"You think?"

McKindrey nodded. "If I was you, I'd cut me loose and get goin' before you bring more trouble down on yourselves."

"We'll take that under advisement," said Finch, and stepped close to the Sheriff. "First I have a few questions. I suggest you answer them quickly and truthfully or your wife won't recognize you even if you do make it home, you understand?" While he spoke, he cocked his gun and aimed it at the floor, squinting through the sight. "Because unfortunately for you, we can't leave without some information, and my gut tells me you have it. So..." He dry-fired the gun, then retrieved a magazine from the table. "The sooner you tell us what we want to know, the sooner you'll get out of here." He slammed the clip home and leveled it at the Sheriff. "But for every question you don't answer, I'm going to shoot you somewhere that will hurt unlike anything you've ever felt before, but it won't kill you. And Beau here makes a killer tourniquet. I could cut off your head and I bet he'd be able to keep you alive long enough to answer our questions."

"Don't know about that," Beau said and upended the Doritos bag. Rust-colored crumbs filled his palm.

Finch smiled at him. It faded when he looked back at McKindrey. "So what's it to be? Are you gonna be a hard ass and make us get tough with you or what?"

"You boys are fools," McKindrey replied with a sour grin. "You think this is the way to get someone to cooperate? Y'all can go fuck yourselves way I see it."

In two steps Finch was up close and shoving his palm against McKindrey's broken nose. The agony was unbearable and the Sheriff writhed against it, the ropes digging into his hands as he clenched his teeth to keep the scream behind them. Unconsciousness loomed and was denied as Finch slapped him across the face, once, twice, and then a third time. "Listen to me you redneck fuck," he said, "You pass out and when you wake up there'll be pieces of you missing, got it?"

McKindrey took a moment to swallow the pain, to steel himself, though it was an enormous undertaking. "Go to hell," he said when he finally found his voice.

Finch shot him in the left foot. The bang was like a wrecking ball through the kitchen. McKindrey screamed.

"Fuck," Beau said, rubbing crumbs from the legs of his jeans. The Doritos bag was lying on the floor by his feet. "Warn me when you're gonna do that shit, all right?"

"How about now?" Finch asked, glaring at the Sheriff. "You sensing the rhythm we have going here?"

"Okay, okay," McKindrey told him, shutting his eyes as blood filled his boot. "Shit..." He was awash in sweat. "What do you want to know?"

"The Merrills," Finch said. "I want to know all *you* know about them. Who they are, where they went, and lastly, how they've managed to turn this town into the Bermuda Triangle without anyone taking them to task for it."

"I don't know," McKindrey said, spitting blood onto his shirt. He jumped at a sudden hiss, but it was only the black man, who had twisted the cap off a bottle of Orange Crush. Beau smiled at him as he took a sip.

"Wrong answer," Finch told him, and stepped back, gun aimed at the man's right foot this time. He cocked the hammer.

"No," said the Sheriff. "Wait. What I meant was I don't know everythin' you're askin'."

Finch didn't lower the gun. He waited.

McKindrey went on.

"They run this town, not me. That's the first thing you gotta understand. They run it because they own it. However it were done, whoever they kilt to get it, they own more than sixty-five percent of the land around here, mostly unpopulated, old farms, woods, that kind of thing. But even if they didn't, people here have learned to coexist with 'em best they can. They stay out of anywhere's got the Merrill name on the deed. No one interferes with their business, and they don't interfere with ours. You probably seen what happens when that changes."

Finch nodded. "Wellman and the farmer."

"They've been around long enough to know better. Should've just stayed out of it."

"And let a girl die."

McKindrey knew he had to be careful. He did not yet know what connection this man had with the girl that had escaped the Merrills. "That was unfortunate," he said.

"What was?" Finch asked. "What they did to her, or that she survived?"

The Sheriff shook his head. "Elkwood's nowhere. Six minutes away from not bein' on no goddamn map no more. Nobody cares what happens here, 'cept those few who come lookin' for all that rustic rural bullshit. World's changin', ain't no place left that's got the feel of the old times to it. So sometimes folks come to Elkwood, lookin' for God only knows what. But that ain't what they find, and ain't no one gonna hunt 'em off. If'n you lived here, you'd understand. Fear can be a great governor."

"You saying Elkwood's a town full of cowards?"

McKindrey glared at him. "I'm sayin' it's a town full of scared folk, folk who feel bad for what happens here but ain't about to get kilt for doin' the right thing."

Finch smiled bitterly. "And your role is—what? Chief chickenshit?"

"I handle whatever I can. Whatever's in my power to handle. That's the job I were given and that's the job I do. Folks here feel safe because of me. They know nothin' gonna happen to them as long as they mind their business."

"So you do nothing, in other words."

McKindrey felt the strength ebbing from him, despite the awareness that he might need it if an advantage presented itself. He was exhausted and in a great deal of pain. "I don't know what you want me to say."

"I want you to tell me why you never called someone up in the dead of night who maybe wasn't such a spineless weasel and told them to get an army together to eradicate the Merrills. State police, FBI, whoever. There were always options. Why didn't you take them?"

"That dog don't hunt. Anyone who ever tried to go up against them ended up in the dirt," McKindrey told him. "They're vicious people, Mr. Finch. They'll stop at nothin', and there's no one they won't kill in the name of their God."

This gave the man pause, and a curious look passed over Finch's face. After a moment he asked, "Who is their God?"

McKindrey shrugged. "Same one as ours."

"Where do we find them?"

"I don't know."

Finch uncocked the gun, walked to the table and set it down beside his friend. Any relief the Sheriff might have experienced as a result of this development abated when the man picked up a hunting knife.

"Do you know what they did to the girl?" he asked.

"Yes," McKindrey admitted.

"Good. Then you might want to reconsider your answer. We've already taken your toes, just like the Merrills did to Claire. And in keeping with their methods, your fingers are next. Then your eye." He looked at his friend. Beau drained the bottle of orange crush, smacked his lips and handed it to him. Finch held it up and looked pointedly at the empty bottle as he spoke.

"They also raped her, Sheriff."

McKindrey felt cold in the pit of his stomach. He had no doubt that they would do all the things they'd threatened to do if he didn't give them what they want. So he started talking.

"The Mother," he said. "She got a brother or a nephew or somethin' livin' in Radner County. I don't know who he is, or whether he's as crazy as the rest of 'em, but he lives about twenty miles north of the chemical waste plant in Cottonwood. There's nothin' out there but dead land, a few abandoned homes. Can't say for sure that's where they went, but it's the only one of their kin I know about, and that's the God's honest."

Finch and his friend exchanged a look. Beau nodded.

"You've been a great help, Sheriff," said Finch.

They started to move, holstering weapons and sheathing knives. McKindrey waited until it was absolutely clear that they were not going to untie him before he started yelling.

"You sonsabitches! Let me go!"

The men had been heading for the door. Now they stopped. Beau muttered something in his friend's ear, then looked at McKindrey. "Nice knowin' you," he said and left, the door clattering shut behind him.

Finch lingered at the door.

"Untie me, I done told you all I know," McKindrey said.

Finch shook his head. "We'll get you on the way back," he said with a grin, and went outside.

In disbelief, McKindrey waited for the sound of their return, certain they were only making him sweat it for a few minutes more. But then came the unmistakable sound of their car starting up and then pulling away.

"You ain't comin' back, you hear me?" he screamed. "Mess with them and you ain't never comin' back!"

THIRTY-ONE

Papa-In-Gray looked up and smiled as Krall entered the cabin. "Join us in prayer, Jeremiah."

They were gathered around the table, waiting for him.

Krall looked from face to face. Disgusted, he turned without a word and stalked back outside, slamming the door behind him.

"We have to be patient," Papa explained, and reached out, palms turned upward, inviting them to join hands. All but Luke obeyed, preoccupied as he was by something over the door only he could see. His mouth was open, his face vacant. Aaron had washed him, but hadn't expended too much effort on it, as he was not entirely convinced that Luke would not turn on them again. He had yet to see proof that there had been any change at all. As a result, there were still smudges of blood on the boy's face and neck, and flecks of flesh tangled in his hair. Aaron roughly grabbed his hand and a moment later, Isaac, on the other side of Luke, did the same.

"Your uncle's grievin'," Papa continued, "And we know what that can do, no matter how strong your faith. Ain't we grievin' ourselves? But we know how to use that for the good, how to turn it into fuel in our fight against the coyotes. Poor Jeremiah has no faith, not yet, so he don't even have God to hate."

"So he hates us instead," Aaron said sourly. Grieving or not, Aaron didn't much like Uncle Krall. He'd never met the man before, and wasn't too impressed now that he had. For one, he was not a man of faith, and Aaron had watched his expressions as Papa told them what had to be done, and why. Up until he'd seen Momma, he'd shown contempt, whether for Papa or his beliefs Aaron didn't know, but in his mind they amounted to the same thing. Papa was a vessel for the Almighty, which made Krall's disdain akin to blasphemy. His sudden interest in Luke was troubling, as if Luke's poison might be spreading, infecting him too.

"He only has himself," Papa said. "He'll come around."

"What if he don't?"

"It'll come," said Papa. "Soon as the outsiders set foot on his land and try to claim him, he'll find his faith."

Aaron sighed and glanced at Luke, who was still staring vapidly at nothing. "I think Luke's gone slow," he said, "He ain't talked since we took him outta Momma."

"What you're seein' in your brother now," Papa said, addressing them all, "is the effect of the poison when it's been purged. It leaves you empty, hurts your mind. Like your uncle, Luke's return will take time, but return he shall, and he'll be stronger than us all."

Aaron remained doubtful. Papa seemed certain that Luke's rebirth would cure the poison. The twins wanted to believe it. But they hadn't been the ones to find Momma-In-Bed that night after Luke tried to kill their father. Whatever a medical man would say was the cause of death would be wrong. Fear and heartbreak had taken her from them. Fear of the coyotes that were gathering in the woods, biding their time, drawn by the scent of panic. She would have sensed them out there, knowing long before they went to try and track down the girl that it was already too late, that the end was coming. And maybe, as Luke was turning on them all, angels had come to her and told her what had happened at the Wellman place, what her favorite son had tried to do.

She'd died alone, and screaming.

Aaron had found her with her face paralyzed by terror, her dead eyes bulging from their sockets, her long tongue blue and limp against her flaccid chin. The stink in the room had been terrible, worse than it had ever been while she'd lived, forcing him to try to open the window for the first time in years. But it was stuck firm; some kind of greasy brown sludge had hardened in the gaps, and in the end he was forced to take off his shirt, wrap it around his hand and shatter the glass.

As he'd set about cleaning the waste that had flooded from her as her bodily functions quit working, he thought of what his brother had done to Papa, to them all. He recalled Papa's bravery. Or perhaps it had been the same misguided belief in his son's faith that he was showing now that had made him stand his ground as Luke tried to run him down. Either way, he had shot Luke in the throat, causing him to jerk the wheel to the right and away from Papa, clipping him with the fender and cracking his knee. Once the full extent of his brother's corruption had been made clear, Aaron had found himself disappointed to realize the bullet had only grazed Luke's throat.

It would have been better if it had killed him.

Papa squeezed his and Joshua's hands in his own. "Now," he said. "A final prayer before the war."

Aaron waited until their heads were bowed before he glanced again at Luke. He leaned over so that his lips were touching his brother's ear. "If'n you ain't better," he whispered. "I'll do to you what I done to that whore sister of ours."

"Aaron," Pa chastised and yanked on his hand.

"Yes, Pa."

They began to pray, and when next Aaron looked, he saw that Luke was no longer staring at the wall, but at him, his eyes empty and soulless.

* * *

Almost four hours after leaving Louise to die on the park bench, Pete arrived on Redwood Lane, a long tree-lined street wet from the recent rain. He had missed the turnoff the elderly man he'd approached for directions had told him to look for, and had ended up going almost three miles too far before turning around and going back.

Now he was on the street, but wasn't sure which of the many houses was Claire's. He rolled down the window admitting the smell of smoke and damp earth, the breeze winding through the boughs of fire-colored leaves to bring him the scent of autumn. After almost an hour spent driving the half-mile length of Redwood Lane hoping to catch a glimpse of her in one of the yards, or on the street, or perhaps as a pale ghost through one of the large windows at the front of many of the expensive looking houses, he conceded and pulled the truck up a short gravel driveway. The house was painted sky blue with rusty red trim, the lawn neatly clipped. As he got out and walked up the drive, an old man wearing a brown wool sweater and dark brown slacks opened the front door and peered warily out at him.

"Hi," Pete said, and stopped in his tracks.

The old man stepped out, continued to stare, but nodded. "Evening."

"My name's Pete Lowell."

The man said nothing.

Pete continued. "I'm lookin' for Claire Lambert."

A look of distaste passed over the man's face, but he shut the door behind him and walked slowly toward Pete. "The Lamberts? What do you want with them?"

"I'm a friend."

"That's what everyone says who wants to bother them."

"I don't want to bother 'em, honest. I'm a friend of Claire's. I'm from Alabama. From Elkwood, where the bad stuff happened to her. I brought her to the hospital, helped her get home."

The breeze swept around the old man as he stopped close to Pete and appraised him. He smelled to Pete like pipe smoke and sardines. "You did, huh?"

Pete nodded. "She told me come see her. So I'm here, but I don't know which house is hers."

The old man nodded thoughtfully, and nibbled on his lower lip as if weighing the wisdom of telling the boy anything. Then he released a breath that somehow diminished his size, and nodded pointedly to his right. "Missed it by about two houses. That's it over there. The white one with the SUV parked out front."

Pete felt relief flood his senses. He had begun to fear he would never find Claire's house, and had no intention of knocking on every door in the neighborhood until he did. Sooner or later it would make someone even more suspicious than the old man appeared to be, and they might call the police on him.

"Thank you," Pete said, and smiled. "I've come a long way to see her."

"You're welcome," the man said, and turned to go back inside. Then he stopped, and looked over his shoulder. "But if you're who you say you are you know that they've been through Hell. No telling if you'll be welcome or not. Could be they won't appreciate the reminder." He raised his eyebrows. "Something worth thinking about is all."

Pete watched the old man disappear inside his house. He didn't need to consider what the old man had said. He had thought about it a hundred times over the past few weeks, and had come to the same conclusion. Claire might not want to see him at all. She might greet his presence on her doorstep with hostility. But it was a chance he would have to take, because he had promised he would come see her, and in all his life, he had never reneged on a promise. He wasn't about to start now.

He headed to the truck, slid behind the wheel, and started the engine, noticing as he did so the curtain move in the picture window of the old man's house.

* * *

Kara straightened her blouse, checked her makeup in the hallway mirror and grabbed her keys from the kitchen table, where Claire was sitting eating messy spoonfuls of chocolate ice cream and staring at her.

"Can I trust you not to go running off playing Rambo with that maniac Finch while I'm gone?"

"Nope," Claire said and grinned, her teeth brown. "But you needn't worry. I'm sure he didn't hang around waiting for you to fuck up his plans.

In fact, knowing him, he's already down there now, causing all kinds of trouble."

"Don't use that language with me, Claire. Please." There was little vehemence in her tone. She was tired, and though she loved her sister, playing the role of nurturing guardian had proved exhausting and required from her levels of patience she hadn't known she possessed. Ever since they had come home from the hospital and their mother had retreated into herself rather than face the task of caring for a damaged daughter, Kara had been forced to step up to the plate. She was tired, cranky, and today was her first day back to work. She had too much to worry about. Any more and her head was likely to explode from the stress of it all. She knew leaving Claire alone was not the wisest idea, and that it would not be at all surprising if she stole the SUV and headed off after Finch. But she didn't think that would happen. The idea had excited her sister for a time, for one dangerous moment when the opportunity had been handed to her to see Finch's warped sense of justice play out firsthand. But that moment had passed. Claire was right. Finch would already be gone, and God help him. But her sister was here, and Kara had come to realize that she could not stand watch over her forever, nor was it fair to impose such restrictions. A little leeway might mend the broken bridge of trust between them. Maybe sometime soon, counseling would expedite that process.

One thing at a time, she told herself.

The time she had taken off to care for Claire had ended an hour ago. Her boss at the manufacturing company she handled the accounting for would not be thrilled at her tardiness. Of course, he wouldn't say anything, given the circumstances, but Kara herself loathed being late for anything.

"I have to go," she said, exasperated and stuffed her wallet into her purse. "How do I look?"

"Flustered," Claire said, without looking at her.

"I'll be home at nine." She leaned over so her face was almost level with her sister's. "Please be here. Mom needs you."

"Mom needs to lay off the Vicodin."

Kara sighed and headed for the door. Hand on the doorknob, she turned and looked back into the kitchen. Claire was licking the spoon.

"A friend of mine from the police will be cruising by every now and then. Just to keep an eye on things."

Claire lowered the spoon. She had a goatee of chocolate, which she fingered as she watched her sister open the door. Kara could tell that whatever she was going to say was not going to be pleasant, so she decided not to wait to hear it. She stepped outside and closed the door behind her.

* * *

The woman who stepped from the house was not Claire, but her sudden appearance had shaken him, and almost propelled him back to the truck. But he told himself to be calm, despite the feeling that the blood in his veins had been replaced with water, his bones turned to jelly. It had been a long hard road to get here, but he was here, and if he ran, he knew he'd regret it for the rest of his days.

The woman stepped off the porch and stopped abruptly as she saw him. Pete clutched his hands to keep them from shaking. The woman was pretty, but severe-looking, as if she spent so much of her time frowning that the lines had permanently etched themselves onto her face. She wore that frown now as she looked him up and down. Her expression was not that much different from her elderly neighbor's. It was as if the houses had been invaded not so long ago, leaving the residents with a fear of strangers.

"Who are you?" she asked, one hand straying to her purse.

"Pete Lowell," he said quickly, in case it was a gun she was reaching for.

"What can I do for you Pete Lowell?" She did not sound welcoming. Rather, her tone made him feel as if he had a limited amount of words with which to explain his reason for being here before something bad happened.

"I...I came to see Claire."

"I'm afraid that's impossible."

"Oh," he said, crestfallen.

"She's not seeing anyone. We recently had an incident that has left her—"

Pete nodded. "I know. I were there."

The cautious look on the woman's face deepened to outright suspicion, perhaps even fear, and from her purse, she produced a slim black cylinder with a red trigger.

"You were there?"

"Yes Ma'am. I drove her away from Elkwood. Took her to the hospital."

He thought she might have relaxed a little at that, but couldn't be sure. His mind raced, caught between advising him to flee while he still could and standing his ground until he made the woman understand.

"You're Pete," the woman said, her tone unchanged.

"Yes Ma'am."

"She mentioned you. Quite a bit."

That pleased Pete immensely, and it must have shown on his face, because this time the woman did relax, her shoulders dropping a little, the frown a little less severe. She did not, however, put the small cylinder back into her purse. Instead she lightly thumbed the trigger while she stared at him.

"I don't think it's a good idea for you to see her," she said. "But you should know she's grateful to you. We all are. You're a hero, Pete. If not for you..." She trailed off and shook her head. "Maybe in a few months we can arrange a visit, but now...now's not a great time. I'm sure you understand."

He nodded, but he didn't understand. Didn't want to understand. He was so close. Claire might be just beyond that door, maybe even listening to the woman telling him he couldn't see her. Maybe any minute now she would come running out to greet him and everything would be okay. "I'm sorry," he told the woman. "But I've come a real long way today. Had to get here on my own, but that's all right. I just want to see Claire, just for a little bit. I don't even have to come in. Even if she just comes to the window. That'd be fine too. But I'd like to see her, see how she's doin', maybe talk to her for a little bit. If it helps any, I know she don't like to sing." He smiled at the memory of Claire's words. "I don't neither."

Finally, the woman dropped the black cylinder back into her purse, slung it over her shoulder and walked to meet him. She returned his smile, but it didn't reach her eyes, and Pete felt his hope drop another notch.

"Pete..." the woman said. "You're a sweet boy, but you being here now, today, it isn't the best idea. Claire's trying to forget what happened to her down there. I'm sure you can appreciate that. But even though you're a hero and you saved her, you're still part of that memory." She sighed and put a hand on his shoulder. "Seeing you might hurt rather than heal her. It might bring back everything she's trying so hard to forget."

When he didn't move, or give her any indication that he saw the logic in her words, she walked toward him, her hand still on his shoulder, and steered him around until he was facing the truck and walking at her behest. "I promise you," she said, "When things improve and she's up to seeing you, we'll arrange something. Can you leave your contact information?"

When he looked blankly at her, she said, "Somewhere we can reach you."

He shook his head. "Ain't nowhere to reach me. They burned down my house, and my second Momma's gone too."

The woman's frown returned, carving a deep groove between her eyes that could hold a dime. "Where do you live then?"

He shrugged. "Don't know yet."

At that moment, the sound of the front door opening made them both turn. Pete felt his heart swell, his throat tightening. For one confusing moment he worried he might wet his pants.

"Claire," the woman said. "Go back inside."

Pete stepped away from the woman. She'd been blocking his view of the door, but now he could see the frail figure who was standing in the doorway. Every fear and hope he'd entertained since that night in Elkwood when he had put her back onto the road from which she'd strayed came together in a vortex that threatened to suck him into itself and grind him up. His trembling intensified. He swallowed. Couldn't move.

"Claire..." the woman began, but slumped and sighed heavily. "Goddamn it, I can't *do* this now." Then she walked past him, and a moment later, Pete dimly registered the sound of a car's engine as she drove away.

Still he stood rooted to the spot as Claire, barely recognizable with her dark hair and the equally dark eyepatch, stepped out into the light. "Pete?" she said, her voice little more than a whisper.

He nodded, felt a thousand words cram into his throat, strangling him.

Claire's face split into a wide smile. "You came."

The colors of the world seemed brighter in that moment, as if God had, without anyone noticing, touched them up just for this occasion. And still Pete couldn't speak. All he could do was nod dumbly.

A moment later, the need for speech was negated as Claire hurried toward him, her gait strange and uneven. She stopped before him, her smile wavering as she wept.

Pete willed himself to speak.

"I promised," he said, and almost cried out with the fright as she dove into his arms.

THIRTY-TWO

They crossed the line into Radner County at dusk. To Finch it was as if whoever was responsible for the distribution of bucolic beauty had run out of materials to work with and left everything beyond the county line stand as an advertisement for desolation. The road narrowed and quickly disintegrated, pummeled over the years by heavy machinery, logging trucks, perhaps, or semis carrying toxic materials to and from the chemical waste facility that even now appeared as an unsightly block of shadow and a tall thin chimney at the far end of acres of fenced-off land. No one had bothered to repair the road, no more than they had felt compelled to repair the fields the treatment facility had contaminated. The air here seemed denser, the sky a curious shade of purple and red, the horizon tinged with emerald green, as if foretelling of tornadoes. Finch thought such a noxious place appropriate for the quarry they were hunting, a natural miasma to which the corrupt would gravitate.

"You do realize there's every chance McKindrey was bullshittin' us, right?"

Finch nodded. "Of course, but if he was, you can't help but feel respect for a guy who would get his nose smashed and toes shot off and then lie to you."

"Not sure respect is the word I'd use."

"Your friend Niles get back to you?" Finch asked, referring to the communications officer Beau had known in the Gulf and whom they had relied upon to track the signal from Claire's cell phone to Danny's. "Yeah, and that's why I'm not too confident about McKindrey's tip."

"It didn't come from down here?"

"Nope. If we were trying to track the signal in a city, it would have been a hell of a trick to get it, but out in the sticks there aren't as many cell phone users, so fewer towers, which made our boy's job easier. But Niles was able to triangulate the signal to within a ten mile radius, and Elkwood was sitting smack dab in the middle of it."

Finch shrugged. "All that means is Danny's cell phone is still in their house, or somewhere nearby. We didn't exactly turn the place upside down. It doesn't mean the Merrills themselves are still there."

"Hope you're right."

While they drove, neither of them commented on the thick, ugly atmosphere that surrounded the car. Dark, stagnant pools resisted the caress of current or breeze and lay still beneath skins of yellow foam. They saw few animals other than an occasional coon or possum lying on its side on the road. Vultures circled overhead, seeking carrion a little more tantalizing, a little less rotten. On all sides of the road, stretched countless miles of boggy, swampy land, all of it seeming to emanate from the plant, a large sandy-colored building fronted by a tall white chimney which coughed billowing black clouds into the sky while ugly liquid vomited forth into a putrid lake from culverts at its base. The many windows in the building's face were made of reflective glass, as if the laborers within felt more secure in their deeds if they went unseen. A chain link fence sealed off the perimeter. Behind the closed gate at the entrance stood a booth with the same reflective glass as the building's windows. It was impossible to tell if it was manned.

A place of death, Finch thought, and was struck by the sudden, alarming notion that it might well be the place where he himself would die. It was a notion he resisted with everything in him.

He recalled something Beau had said when it became clear they had left the bustling cities far behind them, the nature-burnt leaves falling away to be replaced by spindly-limbed, skeletal trees, the air darker and less pure: "Know what's funny?" he'd said, out of the blue. "You keep mentionin' 9/11 and the World Trade Center, comparin' this to that. Mostly I haven't agreed with you, thought you were gettin' carried away with yourself, to tell the truth, but you got me thinkin' about it now."

"And?" Finch had asked, wondering if his friend had finally come around to his way of thinking. It didn't take long to realize he hadn't.

"And I think those chickenshits flew planes into those towers and killed themselves because they knew they'd never beat us on our own soil. Like you said, if they'da been on the ground, we'd have messed their shit up. So they stuck to the sky where we couldn't touch them. What they *did* though was set a trap, make the whole damn country so mad the president wouldn't have no choice but to send our troops over *there*, into *their* crib, where the bad guys'd have the advantage. It was a trap, and we fell for it."

"What's your point?"

"My point is, bro, that you and I are doin' the same goddamn thing. Walkin' into a place we don't know, to fight an enemy we know even less. And the advantage is all theirs."

"It would be," Finch told him. "If they were expecting us, and if we weren't armed."

"You puttin' too much faith in that shit, man. Way too much. Our boys had plenty of guns in 'Nam too, but they didn't know where to point 'em. Didn't know the enemy could burrow like moles and have 'em killed before they could get a shot off. Always gonna be a strike against you if you ain't familiar with where you're fightin'."

As long as he'd known him, Beau had liked to debate about matters of war, and apply his extensive knowledge of it to current events, military-related, or not. His clinically clean apartment was crowded with bookshelves, each one packed full of volumes about various historical conflicts. Ordinarily, listening to Beau ruminate about the Viet Cong, or Napoleon's folly, or Custer's ego, didn't bother him, but it did now, because he had yet to compare their present situation to any battles in which the good guys had emerged victorious.

"This shouldn't be a revelation to you, man," he'd said. "You've been out of your element before. We both have."

He was talking about the Gulf, a subject Finch preferred to avoid as much as possible. Unfortunately, given his love for such topics, Beau had no such reservations, but at least he had the tact not to mention the events at Sadr al-Qanat, events which had left Finch, for the first time in his life, contemplating suicide.

Still, in times of despair, when he kept his eyes shut for too long, he saw the woman in the black abaya—the traditional Islamic cloak—hustling toward him, arms held out, imploring. Her expression was one of pleading, of resignation, and of fear, for around her waist she wore an explosives belt. Finch had called a warning, not because he had seen the belt—which he hadn't, that would come later—but because she wasn't supposed to approach the soldiers. The previous weeks had seen a number of his comrades blown to pieces by seemingly innocuous locals, and they were now on their guard. Frequently he repainted the woman's expression, gave it a devilish aspect, a demonic leer, but in reality there had been no such thing. Only fear, incubating beneath a veil of grim acceptance.

He'd punctuated his third warning with a gunshot, and watched as a fine red mist emerged from the back of the woman's head. She was dead before she hit the ground, and later he had sat in his tent weeping and trembling, and ultimately tried to replicate what he had done to the woman, this time to himself.

Beau had walked in at that moment, a bottle of hooch in his hand, a wide smile on his face that had not lasted long.

"The fuck you doin', man?" he'd asked, though surely the fact that Finch had a gun in his mouth had made it obvious.

Beau had talked him down that night, his "we were put here to do things that ain't always pretty" speech penetrating the caul of misery and terror that had, without him sensing it, overwhelmed Finch. Beau had war stories of his own, tales of men and women murdered in the name of war. Few of them were pretty, but all, Beau contended, had been absolutely necessary.

"I see her every time I blink," he told Beau. "She's haunting me. Her eyes haunt me. I see them gleaming from the shadows, and I can't make it stop. I see her from the corner of my eye, sitting in the dark."

"Bury it," Beau had told him. "Stick it in a box and study it later. It's the only thing you can do."

Finch had, but the crawling sensation, the darkness inside had never left him. It felt like a parasite, feeding off the negative energy, and every time he was called upon to kill, it grew bigger, until it had its hooks in his mind, forcing him to question what kind of creature he was and what kind of future might possibly exist for such a thing. Before, he'd thought the enemy an almost mystical thing, an entity whose very nature meant they would not look remotely human, would be faceless, and therefore easy to destroy.

The eyes of the woman had changed his mind.

And then he'd been called upon to kill again and again, and despite what he'd been told, he had remembered every one of the faces, every glint in the eyes of those who'd fallen before his gun.

Why then, had he thought this would be any different?

"You scared six shades of shit out of that Sheriff," Beau said. "Me too, by the time you were done."

Scared myself too, Finch thought. Everything he'd done to the Sheriff had been governed by the same automatic impulse that had driven him in Iraq after the death of the woman, the knowledge that—as Beau had said—though it would not always be pretty he was fighting for more than his own survival. They'd needed McKindrey's knowledge to have any hope of seeing the operation through and he had switched on a dangerous part of himself to ensure they got what they came for. But perhaps "switched on" wasn't the right way of saying it because it suggested control, and that was something he most certainly did not have over the more frightening aspects of his character. Often, it came unbidden.

Tonight, he knew it would come again.

He looked out the windshield at the dark shadow of a mountain a few miles ahead of them. In the fading light, it looked crimson, alien, something from a Martian landscape.

"Hood Mountain, I assume" Beau said and unfolded a map, his finger tracing a line from Columbus all the way down to Alabama and further, to where a thin thread turned away from highway and entered a geographically barren area.

He looked at Finch. "Looks like we found 'em."

* * *

When he stepped inside and Claire had the door shut behind him, her demeanor changed completely. Gone was the weak weepy girl who had hugged him, kissed him right on the lips, and sobbed her delight at the sight of him outside. Now her face was serious, her eyes intense as she shoved him aside, moved to the small narrow window beside the front door and peeked out. After a moment, she let the curtain fall and offered him an apologetic smile.

"Sorry about that. I wanted to make sure she was gone."

"Who?"

"My sister. The woman you met. Her name is Kara."

"She seemed nice," he lied.

"Yeah, she usually does. Then you get to know her."

She turned and walked ahead of him to the kitchen. Helplessly he stood, awaiting instructions on what to do next. The abrupt change in her manner confused him, and now he wasn't so sure she really was all that glad to see him.

In the kitchen doorway, she turned. "C'mon."

He followed. "I'm glad to see you," he said, with an uncertain smile.

She had moved to the sink and was filling a glass with water from the faucet. She nodded, tossed back a pair of white pills and noisily drained the glass. Afterward she closed her eyes and sighed.

Pete still stood at the threshold to the room, feeling awkward.

"Why did you come?" she asked him in a coarse tone.

"I said I would, 'member?"

"Not really."

Pete's smile faded. He wondered what had happened between the driveway and the house to bring such a sudden change upon her. "The night I drove you to the hospital," he explained. "We was talkin' about singin'."

"I don't like to sing," she said.

Encouraged, Pete stepped further into the room. "That's right! You said that, then you told me come see you soon's you was better."

"Then you're early," she said.

He wasn't sure what that meant, and so said nothing, just watched as she set the glass down and turned, leaning against the edge of the sink, her arms folded as she appraised him. "Pete."

"Yes Ma'am?"

"*Why* did you come?"

"I said I would. I promised."

"You already told me that. I want to know why else you came."

"To see how you was. To see if you was all right."

"And?"

"What?"

"And how am I? How do I look?"

"Tired, I guess," he said truthfully. "And different."

"Different how?"

"Your hair," he said. "And the patch."

Absently, she fingered a lock of her dyed hair. "Do you like them?"

"I dunno," he said. "I like the patch I guess. Makes you look like a pirate."

She gave him a slight smile. "You want something to drink?"

"That'd be nice."

"What do you want?"

"Coke's fine, or hot chocolate."

"Haven't got hot chocolate." She jerked open the refrigerator hard enough to send some of the myriad magnets on the door flying. Wide-eyed, Pete followed their trajectory, then looked back to Claire.

"Are you mad at me for comin'?"

"Nope," she said and withdrew a liter of Coke from the fridge. "I'm glad you're here."

Only slightly relieved, he said, "Okay."

"Because," she continued, unscrewing the cap from the bottle, "You're going to drive me to Elkwood."

She slammed the bottle down on the table, and didn't offer him a glass.

"Drink fast," she said.

THIRTY-THREE

Thunder grumbled over the city. Kara parked the car and looked out at the drab gray building in which she worked. The clock on the dashboard told her she was already an hour and fifteen minutes late, but she couldn't care less. Her mind raced with thoughts about the boy who'd showed up at their door. He'd wanted to see Claire, and it was clear by her sister's reaction that the visit had been a welcome one, eliciting more emotion from her than Kara had seen in months. So, though she'd been against the idea, maybe it would work out to be a positive thing in the end.

You don't really buy that, do you?

She couldn't help but grin at her own pessimism, but it was true. She *didn't* buy it. The kid's connection to the events that had chewed Claire up and spit her out would only justify her dwelling on them for another while, and that was counter-productive to their cause.

Cause. What cause? she asked herself. Naturally she wanted Claire to recover, and soon. But how much of that was for Claire's benefit, and not her own? How much of it was simply a selfish desire to be as free of her sister and all her emotional baggage as Claire wanted to be of her? Kara felt cruel even thinking it, but no reassuring mental voice hurried to debate the theory.

Kara had a life. Granted, not much of one, and even Claire couldn't be blamed for the worst of its deficiencies, but the idea of being her sister's keeper forever made her chest tighten. It couldn't happen. It wasn't fair to either of them. And what good was she really doing anyway? Trying to curb her sister's self-destructive impulses of late seemed to be having the opposite effect. Claire appeared to be waiting for the opportunity, the right moment before she took that final step over the precipice into the abyss where the demons she had escaped would welcome her back and rend her asunder.

Kara had just lit a cigarette. Now she froze, smoke streaming out around the filter, and thought of the boy. More specifically, she thought of his truck.

She's waiting for an opportunity.

Their mother was at the doctor's office.

Kara was here.

You just gave her one.

"Damn it." As if by some miracle he might sense it, Kara cast a brief apologetic glance up at her boss's window on the fifth floor, then started the engine and reversed out of the parking lot fast enough to force the driver of an oncoming car to jam on his brakes and slam on the horn.

Tires screeching, she headed home.

* * *

She estimated she'd been gone from the house less than forty minutes, but it could have been a day for all the difference it made.

After only a few minutes, she quit searching the house. The silence that had greeted her should have been enough to confirm what she already suspected. The boy's truck was gone. So was the boy, and with him, Claire.

"Shit," Kara growled, struggling to keep the panic out of her voice because to hear it only worsened the fear that was trying to paralyze her. *Calm down*, she commanded herself. *They could be gone anywhere.*

But they weren't, and she knew it.

Quickly, she made her way into the kitchen, and picked up the phone. She had already dialed 911 when she spotted the single piece of notepaper on the kitchen table. She did not hang up, but reached out and snatched up the page, reading as the call went through.

Dear Kara, it said. *You know where I'm going. What you don't know, and probably wouldn't understand even if I broke it down for you, is why I'm going there. Pete, in his simple way, does. Together we're going to do this because we have to. There's no other way. I'm guessing you're gonna call the police on us. That would be you all over. But do me a favor. Give it a few hours. Give us a head start. If you don't, I promise you we'll find a way around it. We're young, not stupid. So do this for me. You've been trying to help, and I appreciate it even if you're a pain in the ass 90% of the time. Now's your chance to really do something for me. You never know. This might have a happy ending. Love, Claire.*

Kara shook her head and crumpled up the note. The breath had evaporated from her lungs. She stared in shock around the kitchen.

I did this, she thought. *This is my fault.*

Already she saw what it would do to her mother.

She pictured them standing over Claire's grave, the sky cold and gray, rain speckling the polished oak of the coffin.

"911. What is your emergency?" said a voice in her ear.

She's going to die down there, and I let it happen.

"Hello?" said the dispatcher.

"I'm sorry," Kara said into the phone and ran a trembling hand through her hair. "I need the police."

* * *

Joshua was tired, and cold. Night was coming and the soft breeze had gathered strength, become a sharp chill wind that scoured the peak of the mountain, blowing red dust in his face.

He kept moving to keep the worst of the cold at bay, his eyes continuously scanning the flat plains that stretched out around the mountain. It was getting harder to see anything out there, and he didn't think whoever was coming would be dumb enough to have their lights on, so it seemed silly that he was up here at all. The thought took hold until it began to let suspicion creep in. What if Papa had posted him as lookout just to keep him out of the way? What if he was slowly beginning to wonder if all his children might be turning against him like Luke and Susanna had? He'd been a baby when his sister had been killed so didn't remember a whole lot about it, but from what Aaron told him, she hadn't gone quietly and so the end, for her, had been messy. Joshua wished he'd been there though because he couldn't imagine it being any different from the other people they'd killed and yet when Aaron spoke of murdering their sister, the gleam that entered his eyes told him it had been very special indeed. Perhaps she had been so corrupted she had changed, revealed her true hellish form before he'd stilled her heart. He'd never know because his brother only spoke about it when the mood came upon him, and never answered questions about it. But it didn't matter. She'd been poisoned and Papa had ordered her death. Luke had been poisoned too, and Joshua couldn't imagine what it must have felt like to spend so much time wrapped up in Momma's dead body. He shuddered at the thought of it, but knew if offered a choice between what Papa had done to Luke and what Aaron had done to Susanna, the former would be the obvious choice. Luke had been granted mercy, the chance at rebirth only because he'd been Momma's favorite. They all knew that. But Joshua was nobody's favorite and so he didn't much like the idea that he'd only been given the job of lookout because his usefulness to the clan was in question.

He stamped his feet and wondered if it would be wise to desert his post, just for a little while, long enough to find Papa and swear an oath that he hadn't been poisoned, that he would serve God until He chose to pluck him from the earth and make him an angel.

He shook his head and frowned, deeply troubled by the direction his thoughts had taken. He was *sure* he hadn't given Papa cause to doubt his devotion, but now the worry nagged at him.

Then a sound stopped his pacing and his thoughts at the same time.

He was facing out over the west side of the mountain, where a thin ribbon of dirt road threaded through the trees and twisted itself around for miles before coiling around the chemical waste facility and out into the world. From here the road was little more than a pale snake in the gloom, but from somewhere, he was sure he'd heard the distant drone of an engine. Such a thing might have gone unnoticed in a place where traffic was expected, and normal. But this was not such a place and so it registered immediately. For what seemed like hours Joshua stood frozen, ears strained, his heart thumping slowly in his chest.

Then, out there in the growing dark, a muted light pulsed briefly and was gone so fast Joshua wasn't sure he'd seen it at all. It had been as if a giant hand had passed in front of a lantern. He waited another few moments, breath held, the cold forgotten, eyes struggling to bring whatever was out there into focus, but it didn't come again. The trees were thick at the borders of the clearing, so it was possible he'd imagined it, that it had been little more than the effect of staring too long into the dark. But he didn't think so, and if he was wrong and ignored it, they might all pay with their lives.

Joshua allowed himself a smile, and turned to run down the rough path to the cabin. The urge to shriek the news was hard to restrain, but he was wiser than that and kept his mouth shut. It wouldn't take long before he could tell Papa what the old man had been waiting to hear.

He'd been right.

The angels hadn't misled him.

The coyotes had come.

But then he found the way obstructed by what seemed to be darkness itself and felt his muscles tense, a startled cry forming at the base of his throat as, in one fluid move, the man reached down to Joshua's belt and disarmed him, brandishing the handmade knife before shoving the boy to the ground.

Joshua struggled to keep his balance, his arms pinwheeling, feet digging into the ground. Luck was not with him, and he went down hard, his back thudding against the rocks, knocking the wind from him.

"Stay down, kid, and this'll go a lot easier for you," a voice commanded.

Breathless, Joshua rolled over onto his side. *Only one*, he thought. *There ain't but one voice.* Bolstered, he reached out, making it seem to his attacker that he was simply trying to find purchase in the uneven terrain. His hand found a rock, heavy and sharp.

The darkness swooped down on him as if to vomit its poison into him, or breathe the foul air from its lungs into Joshua's own, and he struck out, swinging his arm out, the sharp edge of the sandstone rock aimed at where he judged the side of the man's head to be. At the last second, a vice locked on his arm, halting the arc, and dismayed, the boy felt the rock slip from his grip and fall.

He opened his mouth to scream a warning.

The man straddled him, forcing the air out of him again, and pinning his arms to the ground.

He wheezed, struggled against the man's weight, sucked in a breath.

"Don't," his adversary told him.

The breath caught. Joshua tried to scream.

The man punched him in the mouth.

It felt as if the attacker had picked up the rock and rammed it into his face, and for a moment Joshua saw stars, felt teeth come loose and lodge in his throat. He coughed. His lungs burned. He tasted blood. His lips stung. And still he struggled, thrashing beneath the man who was sitting on his legs, kneeling on his wrists, his monstrous face barely visible in the dark, as if they were one and the same.

No, he thought, panicked. *This can't happen. He'll corrupt me. He's too close. Papa will—*

Abruptly, the pressure left one of his arms as the man tore something with his teeth. In a moment of startling horror such as he had never in his life felt before, Joshua feared it was his flesh. It made a zipping sound as it came away from bone. But no, he knew the sounds of a flaying, and it never sounded like this. Most likely it was tape to bind him or keep him quiet. A second thought followed quickly on the heels of the relief: His arm was free.

He clenched his fist, dug the other hand into the stony earth and with all his strength, bucked his hips in an attempt to knock the man off balance. Success. The pressure vanished from his second arm as the man wobbled atop him. In one swift move, Joshua brought his left hand up and threw a fistful of stones and dirt in the man's face. With the other, he punched wildly, hoping to connect, but the blow glanced off the man's cheek. Adrenaline enhanced Joshua's efforts and he planted his palms on the ground, using them to lever his body out from under his assailant.

"Stop," the man said, but his words only made Joshua's struggles more frenzied. He flailed his fists, and the man caught one of them, squeezing until Joshua feared the bones were going to snap like kindling. It didn't deter him. He swung the other, his legs still pinned, an animal-like grunting low in his throat.

The man's free hand shot forward and Joshua saw the silvery sheen of a roll of duct tape before it crashed into his nose. He reeled back, his fist suddenly free, and the attacker's hands clamped around his throat, jerking him back and slamming him to the ground.

Dazed, Joshua wondered if it might be better to just concede defeat rather than return to Papa poisoned. The attack would seem like nothing if his father decided he needed to be cleansed. But instinct prevailed and he willed his head to clear, to enable him to see the man he was bound to rend asunder with his bare hands, as he had been taught. But his head wasn't clearing because the man was leaning into him, increasing the pressure around his throat, refusing him the air he needed and forcing the blood to thunder inside his head.

Possum, he thought suddenly, and looked up at the man whose face was pure night, as featureless as the dark side of the moon. Possum. It was a trick. And he used it now.

His face contorted. He began to cry as much as he could without the air required to power it.

For a moment the man's grip did not loosen or the pressure ease, but he could tell by the stiffening of his body that he was affected.

"God...*help*...*me*..." Joshua croaked, gagging as the tears trickled down the sides of his face into the dirt. "For...give me..."

As he wept, Joshua recalled the instances in which he'd lain on the road or on the forest floor sobbing while at the same time listening to the approach of strangers, their voices high with concern—"Son, are you all right? You hurt?"—only to find themselves surrounded while Joshua stood and brushed himself off, his hand moving to the knife tucked in his belt.

The knife.

If only he could remember what the man had done with his knife after taking it from him.

His attacker's grip was slackening. Joshua scarcely dared believe it. Now, though drawing breath was still hard and burned his throat, it was progress, the first step toward turning the tables on the coyote.

The knife.

The man had stuffed it in his belt. He was almost certain. Joshua let his eyes drift down, imagined he could see the pale handle. He intensified his sobbing. "Please...I'm *sorry*..." and miraculously one of the man's hands moved away from his throat. One remained, but the grip was loosening, merely holding him down and no longer strangling him. Once again, Joshua's eyes found the spot where he imagined, *knew*, the knife to be. There was nothing keeping his hands pinned this time, and gradually, in excruciatingly slow movements, he allowed them to creep toward the man's belt.

"*Sorry*..." he whimpered, fingers like spiders creeping down his own legs toward his attacker's thighs.

Then the man's arm came back around, and though there was insufficient light to see what the black shape in his hand was, there was no mistaking the sound of a hammer being cocked.

"I am too," the coyote said.

* * *

The gunshot echoing about the valley was as good as a declaration of war, and Aaron flinched. In battle he imagined it would have been the signal for troops to start charging, but nothing so dramatic would happen here. Holding his position, he slowly turned his head away from the trunk of the pine tree. In the woods around the clearing, the darkness was thickest and that suited him, but he knew better than to make any sudden movements. The sound of a twig breaking or a sharp breath could be enough to bring about his doom. His eyes strayed to the source of the shot, where he saw a tall shadow, visible only as a darker shade of night against the backdrop of the stars, rising for one brief moment before vanishing down the other side of the mountain.

They got Joshua, Aaron thought, fire in his chest that made him want to tear strips of bark from the tree with his nails and scream aloud his plans for the Men of the World. But instead he did nothing, and this was well advised, for not thirty feet away stood one of *them*, hunkered down in the tall grass just inside the protective circle of the trees, a gun in his hand, a pair of binoculars held to his eyes. It was torture resisting the urge to run at him like one of the old Indian warriors Momma-In-Bed had liked to tell him about, but he knew well the folly of such a rash move. The coyote would cut him down before he made it clear of the trees. So he waited, as still as the trees, and watched.

Soon the man would move, and when he did, Aaron would be ready.

THIRTY-FOUR

Pete stared out at the night, afraid to look at Claire for too long in case she snapped at him as she had already done more than once during the long drive. The journey had taken them nine hours, but it felt like an eternity, each one of those miles chipping away another part of the illusion he had held in his head for so long about the girl he thought he loved. He was at a loss to understand what had happened to her. Had she been like this since the hospital, or had she reserved her hostility only for him? If so, he couldn't imagine what he had done to deserve it.

"Slow down," she told him, and immediately he eased his foot off the gas.

Outside, there was nothing but endless fields to see, but Pete knew them better than he knew anyplace in the world. He had driven these roads a thousand times, and suspected the reason Claire wanted to stop now was because she recognized it too.

Surreptitiously, he watched her. She had rolled the window down and was leaning out, her hair blowing crazily around her face. The night breeze was cold around her, and Pete shivered.

She looked back at him. "Stop," she said and he did.

"This is where Pa and me found you," he said quietly.

"Yeah, I know." She opened the door and stepped out. He waited for his cue to follow, but it didn't come. Instead she just stood staring at the barbed wire that separated the field of cotton from the road. At length, she turned. "Do you have a flashlight?"

He nodded slowly. For Claire, he knew it was a simple request, but the small slim object, no bigger than a pencil, that he slid free of his jeans pocket came with a story she hadn't given him the opportunity to share.

He had driven a shard of glass into the eye of its previous owner, and couldn't remember taking it before he and Louise had left the apartment, but as soon as he'd sat down on the park bench, he'd felt it digging into his thigh and realized that at some point, despite the circumstances, his curiosity had gotten the better of him.

Afraid Claire might be able to read the story from the lines of guilt on his face the longer he withheld it, he gave it to her and looked away, studying the road, where his father had made a decision to save a life and end his own.

Maybe it was a mistake, Pete thought, and was startled by the venom that accompanied it. Then he decided that it was justified. Saving Claire had cost Pa his life and turned Pete's upside-down, and for what? He glanced back at the girl, who was now leaning on the barbed wire, lowering it so she could climb over. He knew he should help, but staying where he was made him feel better. She was not the girl they'd rescued. Not the girl Pa and Doc Wellman, even Louise, had been willing to die for. She was a stranger, and perhaps *he* was the fool at the back of it all. Who was to say this wasn't the real Claire? He hadn't known her before the men tried to kill her and yet he'd invested his hope and his weak heart in her before they'd ever exchanged a word. Why should he be surprised that she was like all the other girls he'd fallen for over the years? He'd first seen her as a battered broken thing and his empathy had quickly become desire. She would wake, he'd believed, and she would need him.

But it was clear now that she needed no one. He suspected if he hadn't agreed to take her to Elkwood with him, she'd have hurt him and taken the truck herself.

Well, you got her here, he told himself. *Nothin' to stop you drivin' away now. She looks well enough to fight if she runs into trouble.*

But that wasn't true, and though he was angry, he made no move toward the keys, just slumped over the wheel, his hands resting atop it, eyes watching the road for lights or any sign that trouble was bearing down on them.

The simple elemental fact of it was that no matter how cold or dismissive she was, she was all he had left in the world, and he still loved her. Had to. If he gave up on her, the loneliness would crush him.

* * *

The cotton whispered against Claire's legs, the thorny twigs on which they seemed merely suspended scratching the material of her jeans as she stood motionless, surveying the field for a glimpse of what she knew was there. When it failed to resolve itself from the dark, she began to walk, the flashlight in hand but not yet switched on. For now, she preferred to rely on her memories of this place to lead her. The ground was uneven beneath the cotton, making traversing it treacherous, and the last thing she needed was to fall and twist an ankle, so she carefully made her way along them. A bird rose from the field and took off, flying low. Night creatures scurried away from the unwelcome intrusion of her feet.

At last, she stopped, out of breath from the exertion, damp with sweat despite the chill. It had been a long time since she had pushed herself, or in truth, tried exercise of any kind, and it proved only how out of shape and unhealthy she was. But that didn't matter. She looked ahead and up, at the spindly branches of a tree so large it blocked out the stars, and turned on the flashlight.

A twisted, bone white trunk rose before her, its surface gnarled and ancient and rotten in places where industrious insects had attended to it. Some of the roots were above ground, tangled together in a chaotic jumble that seemed to Claire to symbolize confusion and anguish, their inability to find the earth from which they wished to draw nourishment, prevented from doing so by nothing more sinister than their own brethren.

She raised the flashlight, aimed the beam upward.

Shadows fled. An explosion of limbs radiated out from the tapering trunk, the branches themselves seemingly heavy enough to force the tree to bend toward her, like a Victorian woman bowing beneath her umbrella, or a jellyfish pushing upward, the weight of the sea forcing its tentacles down and around itself.

Tentatively, she reached out to touch the trunk, almost expecting to feel an electrical charge or a rush of memory as she did so. But when her fingers brushed the dried wood, she felt nothing. Whatever the tree had represented on the day she had stood bloodied and bruised staring at it, eluded her now.

With a sigh, she reached into the pocket of her jeans and retrieved a small penknife, then slowly, painfully got down on her knees and dug the point of the blade into the bark. It sounded hollow, as if she were carving into the last layer of its protective skin before the elements and the insects ground it to dust, erasing it from existence forever.

In the trunk, she etched out:

K.K.
D.F.
S.C.

And underneath:

WE WERE HERE

Then she stood and studied her dead friends' initials, each one filled with shadow thicker than oil as the breeze made the branches tremble, the wood creaking as the tree swayed.

She turned her back on it, felt as hollow as the tree and wished she could recall why it had meant so much to her. For one fleeting moment it had seemed like the only thing in the world to her, a savior.

I was out of my mind, she thought. *In shock.*

The breeze grew stronger.

She stopped.

All around her flecks of cotton rose from the field like fireflies, caught in the beam of her flashlight as it carved a channel in the dark. Her hair fluttered around her face, her senses filled with the smell of earth and smoke, and without knowing why, she smiled as the million specks of cotton rose ever upward like souls released to the Heavens to join the stars. It was over in a moment, and to anyone else, it might have seemed a perfectly ordinary thing, something visible on any day of the week.

But to Claire, the significance she'd sought from the tree was there in the cotton, and with it, came the answer to the riddle of what she'd thought she'd seen in the field that day.

There is something else, she thought. *Something afterward. Life ends and something follows.* In all her years, she had never been asked about her faith, nor had her family ever assumed a denomination. If forced, however, they would have claimed agnosticism as the closest representation. But with that lack of faith came a great fear of death. Without proof of an afterlife, they were intimately aware of their mortality and the limitations of it. The passing of her father and what Claire had endured here eleven weeks ago only reinforced that fear. *Nothing follows*, they'd thought. *You die and you turn to dust.*

Standing naked and wounded on the road outside this field, she had known she was going to die. Not of old age, not of some unforeseen event waiting to claim her in a few decades time, but right there and then, bleed to death from wounds inflicted on her by maniacs. The terror had been as potent as the pain and she had looked to the tree, looked to anything that could, to her shocked mind, be compared to a figure of salvation. And she had seen her mother. The tree had held out its arms, beckoning to her, promising a reprieve from the pain in its maternal embrace, and she had tried, wept as the barbed-wire kept her at bay like the restrictions imposed on her by her own lack of faith.

She began to walk. *There is something afterward*, she repeated in her head. *Katy, Daniel and Stu are somewhere else, at peace.* It was not yet a conviction, and barring proof of some kind beyond what she had seen here tonight, she doubted she would ever fully believe it. But it was a start, a step forward from pessimism. All that remained was for her to find the same succor.

* * *

"What the hell did you do?" Stella asked her husband, daubing the cuts around his broken nose with antiseptic that made him feel as if she were applying it with a heated needle.

"Already told you," McKindrey said. "I weren't catchin' nothin' down at the creek so I headed up to the far side where the river's wider. Tried to climb up that steep edge where those Pike boys got themselves drowned few summer's back, and I fell. Did a real job on my foot."

"How come you ain't scratched no place else? That place is full of thorn bushes and stickers."

McKindrey shook his head, irritated. Not only was Stella being a pain in the ass with her questions, but she was also blocking his view of the TV, so he couldn't even have that as a distraction. She had bandaged up his foot so heavily he couldn't fit his boot over it, so instead he'd had her wrap strips of an old shirt around it. It would do for a while and at least he wouldn't have to be stuck in the house listening to her for God knows how long. He took a long draw of whiskey, felt it numb him and fill his nose with fumes that took the edge off the pain. He was mad as hell, but had reined it in for now. Wouldn't do to be trying to explain to Stella why he was filled with murderous rage over his own stupidity.

"Oh, damn it to hell anyway," Stella said now and backed away from him as if afraid he was going to hit her.

He took another sip of whiskey, winced and looked at her. "What's the matter?"

"You got a call while you was out."

"So?"

"It were the state police guy from Mason City. Marshall Todd."

"What did he want?"

"Said he got a call from the sister of that poor girl got herself in trouble down here few months back."

With great effort, McKindrey sat up, his bandaged foot resting on an old ottoman. "And?"

"And she told him the girl's on her way back down here. Should already be here as a matter of fact if she's comin' at all. Asked if you'd keep an eye out, and bring her in if you can. They'll have someone here in the mornin' to help you out. But I can call him and let him know—"

He raised a hand. "No. I'll take care of it." And thought, *It's gettin' to be a good time to retire from this shit.*

"How you gonna drive with that foot?"
"Very goddamn carefully," he said.

THIRTY-FIVE

It seemed grimly ironic to Finch that Beau, after practically interrogating him about his willingness to kill children, had been the one to do it first. He watched his friend reach the foot of the mountain, saw through the night vision binoculars the eerie green shape of him raising a hand in the air and signaling that he was going to proceed toward the house. It was also Finch's cue to head for the tree line and approach from the left side of the valley so they would be coming at the cabin in a pincer movement.

"Last chance," Beau had said. "If you want to turn back, now's the time to say it."

"No," Finch told him, without pause for thought.

"That kid looked to be about twelve."

"So what?"

"So are you gonna be able to shoot him if he draws down on you?"

"Beau, he might be a kid, but he's also a killer. They kill indiscriminately. We're going to do the same."

"If you're sure."

"I am, and if you're in this with me, you need to be sure too or you're the one needs to turn back."

"Don't worry about me."

Up ahead, the cabin looked abandoned. Oddly, at some point a poor attempt had been made to put a slate roof atop it. Now most of the slates were gone. There was one window in the front, but the dirty yellow curtains were drawn, denying them a peek inside. Feeble light showed through cracks in the wooden door.

Finch was surprised that the shot hadn't drawn the family out of the cabin, or from wherever they were hiding. He'd fully expected to see dark shadows springing up and screaming, armed with axes or knives as they charged at Beau, intent on taking him down for killing one of their kin.

But there was no sign of anyone, and now even Beau had disappeared.

Reminding himself that time was not a luxury he could afford to squander, he kept low and darted to the left, toward the thick crowd of pines, his eyes flitting from one imagined shape to the next, waiting for one of them to break free and come at him. But he made it into the thick of them unchallenged, and paused to catch his breath, the Glock raised in front of him, his body pressed against the trunk of a pine sticky with sap. His breathing sounded like a bellows, and he imagined at any second someone would hear it and come find him. His heart pounded so hard in his chest his whole body vibrated. *Let them come*, he thought. He shut his mouth, drew short breaths through his nose, felt his limbs quiver with adrenaline. He estimated the distance to the cabin was less than a hundred yards from where he stood, but it would take him longer as he would have to approach it slowly, and with as little noise as possible. The darkness in the field had been nothing compared to the cloying, impenetrable blackness in the woods. He told himself that such poor visibility worked both for and against him. On the one hand, he couldn't see a damn thing, but then it was unlikely anyone else could either, and he at least had the NV binoculars so he could watch them from a distance if it came to it. It didn't, however, help at close quarters, and he cursed himself for not instructing Beau to buy night vision goggles. It was an oversight he feared they would pay for. Spotting the child on the mountain had been sheer luck. If he'd stayed down, they'd have missed him, but just as Finch was scanning the peak, he rose, and Beau was off and running.

Too late now, he thought, and said a silent prayer that the luck that had reduced the number of their enemies by one would hold out for a little while longer.

Counting to three in his head, he steeled himself.

Stepped out from behind the tree.

And his legs were torn from under him. He went down fast and hard, twigs and pine needles puncturing his skin, the hand holding the gun bruised by something unyielding beneath the leaves, the other pinned beneath him. Struggling to find his breath, he desperately tried to turn, knowing he would not be able to see his attacker, but willing to take the chance that the shot would find its target.

The darkness changed.

Someone hurried away.

Quickly sitting up and scooting back, Finch leveled the weapon at the unmoving dark, waited a heartbeat, his finger tensing on the trigger...

...And felt a punch in his left shoulder. At first he assumed he'd been struck by a fist, or someone's boot, but when he raised his free hand to probe the area, he found a long smooth object protruding from just below his collarbone. Raging pain followed and he winced, aware he did not have the time to spend assessing the damage, but unable to stop himself. The smooth aluminum-like shaft ended in hard feathers. *An arrow*. Someone had shot an arrow into him, and despite the pain, his skin prickled, every nerve waiting to protest the invasion of another one into his flesh. Abruptly, he felt surrounded, imagined bows being drawn taut, arrow-points aimed at his throat, his heart, his face, and dove behind the nearest trunk, drawing his knees up and pulling at the arrow. It budged only slightly and the pain that came as a result was enough to force him to trap a scream behind his teeth.

"*Shit.*"

He heard footsteps. Whoever had shot him had apparently decided that the time for stealth was over and was now coming back to finish him off.

Finch grabbed the arrow again and yanked on it. His palms were slippery with sweat and slid harmlessly off the shaft, but not without causing him pain. His vision whirled. He closed his eyes. Grabbed the hem of his T-shirt and brought it up, using it to improve his grip as he grabbed the arrow one last time and pulled with all the strength he had in him. With excruciating slowness, it began to slide free. Trembling, he had barely managed to clear the arrow of the wound when the footsteps registered to his right—too close—and he sensed the presence of someone rounding the tree.

Panicked, slick with blood, Finch dropped the arrow, quickly brought the gun around and loosed off a shot as soon as he detected the presence beside him. The flash from the muzzle blinded him, left the impression of a pale, hollow-eyed face contorted with fury floating before him and then it was gone, the darkness flooding back in, thicker than before. The absence of even a grunt of pain discouraged Finch and he quickly fired again. The bullet whined as it struck the tree opposite. Bark flew.

A low hum in his ear made Finch turn and duck, but it was not another arrow bound for his skull, only a mosquito drawn by the blood.

Heart palpitating madly, he frantically searched the night for the shape he'd seen, the malevolent presence that had just a split-second before been right there in front of him. The roaring of his own blood in his ears had deafened him to the man's retreat, if indeed that's what he'd done and was not instead standing on the other side of the same tree Finch was using for protection. He moved, peering around the trunk, his wounded arm hanging uselessly at his side. His left hand felt swollen with blood to the point of bursting. Even as he flexed his fingers and tightened his grip on the Glock, he heard a whistle and ducked back an instant before an arrow sheared through the bark next to his head and impaled the earth by his feet. Finch glanced at it, aware how close he had just come to having his skull ventilated. Then he noticed something. He could see the shaft of the arrow clearly. It was gleaming, reflecting burgeoning silver light. Almost afraid to hope, he raised his head.

Free of the dark clouds, the moon shone through the thick canopies, limning the branches with silver, and turning the forest floor into a patchwork of light and shadow. Moths rose from the carpet of needles and mounds of deadfall, summoned by the celestial glow. Flies became silver lures calling to larger prey. Finch risked a glance around the tree, ready to withdraw at the sound of another arrow being nocked, and glimpsed a figure ducking behind a trunk not twenty feet away.

A moment later, he heard a voice. "You ain't walkin' out of here, coyote. More of us than there are've you. Might as well just step right on out and get it over with."

Finch got to his feet, ensuring the tree was still shielding his body as he rose and extended his arm close to the trunk, aiming his gun in the direction of the voice.

They now shared the advantage the moon bestowed on them. If either of them moved, the other would see, so for now it was stalemate.

But stalemate wasted time.

Finch aimed a shot at the tree, hoping to see the man flinch, or better yet expose enough of himself to give him a clean shot. It didn't happen. His arm like a lead weight hanging from his shoulder, Finch pressed his back to the tree, aware that Beau was out there somewhere, in the cabin most likely, alone or worse, surrounded. The fact that no shot had come from that direction in the last few minutes worried him. But he couldn't move. There was nowhere to go. The man with the bow and arrow was blocking the route back to the vehicle and out of the clearing. If he headed out into the tall grass where there was no cover, he was as good as dead. That left moving toward the cabin and deeper into the trees as his only option and this too would expose him. He realized his relief at the moonlight had been premature. In darkness, he'd have had a better chance of making his way unseen.

He closed his eyes, and abruptly saw an image of his mother, sitting in her chair watching the news and seeing his face on the screen, the phone ringing incessantly but going ignored as she popped her pills and wept into her vodka. Or maybe she would see the story and feel nothing, secure in the oblivion she had sought out after Danny's death. At that moment he envied that oblivion, thought that perhaps he should have taken a cue from her and found his own instead of seeking an end to the burning hatred that seethed within him for everything. A fire that could never be extinguished as long as he was alive but perhaps could have been tempered and controlled by drugs and alcohol. *Too much time spent among the dead instead of the living...*

An arrow slammed into the tree, startling him.

"Come on out," the other man called. "Ain't no sense in hidin'."

Finch took a breath, held it, and released it slowly. His upper body felt strangely numb, as if the cold from the arrow that had been embedded in his flesh was spreading.

There was only one way this was going to end. Any minute now more of them might show up and he'd be surrounded, or dead with an arrow through his heart before he even heard them coming.

He stepped out, gun pointed at the tree, and started—

—shooting into daylight.

The ground shifted beneath his feet and he almost went down, a hot gust of air blowing into his face, carrying with it grains of sand to blind him. He blinked and the action took far too long, the gap between darkness and light taking forever. He slowed his pace, looked up in confusion at the searing watery orb of the sun. It seemed very close, the burning eye of a god inspecting him. He was aware that there were other men with him, aware that he was far too hot, wearing far too much clothing for the heat, when someone cried out his name and on impulse he raised his rifle—rifle?—and leveled it at the woman kneeling on the ground before him. Finch's eyes widened; sweat trickled down between his shoulder blades. His knees were shaking. The eyes of the woman in the black abaya were impossibly large as she rose up, the pupils huge and ringed with gold like solar eclipses as she reached out with one quivering, bloodstained hand. Tears carved tracks in the dirt on her cheeks, her face contorted with grief and still she was coming, still she was rushing him and Finch shouted a warning only he could hear because it was inside his head, not meant for her but for himself—stop, oh GodJesus please stop—and now her other hand was falling, falling—no don't no please—to her belt. Except, of course, there was no belt, no explosives, only her hand gripping the material to raise it above her feet to keep her from tripping as she ran, ran, ran to ask him in words he would never understand but would forever read in those eyes that were the whole world, why he had shot her baby boy.

Finch pulled the trigger. The woman's head snapped back. The breeze spirited away the blood. She crumpled, fell backward. The silence roared. He lowered his gun. "You all right, man?" someone asked. He didn't answer, and they didn't wait for one. People were screaming, running away. His eyes moved to the boy, bleeding from the throat but dead, flies crossing the frozen lakes of his eyes. He'd thrown a rock, just a rock, but it had caught Finch by surprise and his rifle had replied. He could feel a burning now where that rock had hit him, a blazing hole in the center of his chest as he jerked abruptly.

Daylight faded.
The moonlight returned.
Finch tasted fresh blood.

"Gotcha," said the boy.

THIRTY-SIX

"They ain't here," Pete said. "Ain't nobody here."

Claire ignored him, but knew he was right. Had she expected anything different? Finch had told her the Merrill clan would have moved, so why then was she surprised to find the place abandoned? There were no lights on in the house that squatted crookedly in the dark before her, the weeds weaving sinuously around its base like snakes caught under its weight. Nearby, Spanish moss hung from the palsied limbs of a silver birch, veiling the roof. The sheds, so terribly familiar to her, were empty, the doors hanging open, as if to invite her inside, back into the heart of the nightmare she had come here to put to rest.

She headed toward them.

"Wait," said Pete.

She didn't, kept walking until she was at the mouth of one of the sheds, the same one in which she had been tied to a wooden post, raped and tortured, the same one in which she had taken the life of a man, driven by panic and rage and self-preservation. And how shocked would the world be to know that killing that rotten fuck haunted her more than outliving her friends? But it was true. He'd deserved to die, had forced her to take his life, and yet the guilt that haunted her every waking moment was not alleviated by that truth. The realization of what she'd done, when it dawned on her in the days that followed, stunned her, shoved her over the edge of a precipice into a dark place where even the specters of those she'd lost could not reach her.

She stepped inside.

It smelled like dirt, sweat, and human waste.

The moonlight cast her shadow on the floor, a frail twisted thing trapped in an oblong of cold blue light.

She flicked on the flashlight.

Chains hung from the roof like roots in a subterranean cave. They clinked together in the breeze, the rusted hooks clamped to their tails appearing to move toward her, but she was not afraid. There was no further pain to be drawn from her by those hooks or anything else.

A shelf lined one end of the room. Atop it were canisters full of nails, and Mason jars with some kind of amber liquid inside. Next to these was a jelly jar filled with different kinds of feathers. Claire recognized the iridescent plumage of a bluejay, and maybe the tail feathers of a cardinal. The jars were book-ended by an identical pair of small, cheap looking plastic statues depicting Jesus in prayer, His lifeless blue eyes turned upward as if He was in the throes of death, his shadow reaching up from his skull to claw at the ceiling. A speckling of red paint or old blood colored the right cheek of the statue on the left. There were a few old suitcases and a garish-colored leather purse tossed on the dirt floor. Various work tools hung from nails on the wall. Here was an old two-handed saw with some of its teeth missing. Here, hoes of all sizes pinned to the wall by their throats. There, a row of sickles, some of them missing the upper part of the blade. A single sheet of bloodstained plastic was bunched in the corner beneath a three-legged chair that had been propped against the wall.

By her left shoulder was the stake, a rough-cut oaken log that had been wedged between floor and ceiling. The wood was stained in places with all that remained of the dead. Claire shook her head and reached out a hand. Again, she anticipated flashes of memory on contact with the stake, an assault of visions reminding her that once it had been her body pressed against the wood, her blood and sweat permeating its surface, her fear saturating it. But there was nothing, only the feel of rough bark against her fingertips. It was just a hunk of wood. Lifeless.

Behind it, the six-foot high cord of wood, stacked unevenly against the wall, long shards poking out here and there, intended to make the prisoner even more uncomfortable as they prodded into their flesh.

"Claire," Pete said, from outside.

"What?" she muttered, her eyes drawn to the floor where once she had watched a man's lifeblood soak into the dirt. There was nothing there now but old boot prints.

She had asked Pete to bring her here, knowing full well she wouldn't find the Merrill family. They were long gone, and even now Finch and his friend were tracking them. Perhaps they would succeed in exterminating her tormentors, perhaps not. But such a vigil no longer seemed so pressing, or urgent.

They were alone here, tourists at the site of an atrocity, and it evoked little feeling from her.

"Claire," Pete said again, and when she turned to look, the beam of her flashlight showed his brown eyes filled with alarm. "Someone's comin'."

Claire stepped outside and killed the flashlight.

Pete turned, looking toward the road.

She joined him.

A car was meandering its way toward them, flashers blinking red and blue, but soundlessly, shadows dancing in circles around the dark bulk of the vehicle.

A cop.

Claire shook her head. *Goddamn you, Kara.*

She looked from Pete to the brooding house behind him, then began to make her way toward it.

"*Wait*," said Pete. "What are you doin'?"

"Stall him for me," she called back, and broke into a trot. "I need to find something."

The cruiser crested the hill, pinning Pete in its headlights.

Claire disappeared into the house.

* * *

With a sigh that sounded almost like relief, Finch dropped to his knees. He felt little pain other than the dull burning ache in the center of his chest from the second arrow the man—or rather *boy*, as he saw now—had shot into him.

"Ain't feelin' much yet," said the figure standing before him. He could see that the boy was no more than eighteen or nineteen, but tall, his face in the moonglow possessed of a ferocity that was startling. Rarely, even in war, had Finch been afforded such a glimpse of concentrated malevolence. The boy was breathing hard, the adrenaline making his limbs jerk and twitch, his hands trembling as he held the bow up, an arrow nocked, the string drawn back, waiting to deliver the fatal shot. "Reckon if I let you you'll start feelin' somethin' soon though," the boy continued. "Papa had us put some stuff from the doctor's house on our arrows. Said it makes your mind go funny, numbs you fer a while, makes you no more dangerous than a stunned possum. We even tried it on Luke, and he ain't lifted a finger since."

Finch was dying. He could feel it, the heat in his chest unable to compete with the rapidly encroaching waves of cold. His mouth was dry, his throat raw with the struggle to draw air.

"Maybe I'll just wait and see if it wears off," said the boy. "So maybe you can feel what I do to you next. But you might as well toss that gun now, as you ain't got no more use for it."

Finch lowered his head, icy sweat dripping down his face. He had almost forgotten that the gun was still in his hand. Now he looked at it, moved it so the moonlight glanced off the barrel, and slowly brought it up.

"I'm warnin' you."

"Shut up," Finch hissed, and raised the gun.

We're not doing this your way, he vowed, as he swiveled the barrel toward the boy even as the third arrow was released and cleaved the air between them.

He pulled the trigger. Light flared. The boy staggered back, darkness blossoming in his shoulder.

A split-second before the arrow found him, Finch saw another shadow detach itself from the trees behind the boy. He might have cheered, might have cried to realize that it was his friend come to save him. But the chance for salvation for men of their kind was long gone, and would never be found here, or anywhere else.

* * *

Stunned, Aaron fell backward, his momentum halted by what he assumed was a tree until it moved, large hands grabbing fistfuls of his hair and jerking him off his feet. He fell, the gunshot wound burning in his shoulder.

"You son of a *bitch*," his assailant cursed, and then was upon him like a ravenous animal, punching him in the face, ramming his meaty knuckles into the flesh, cracking bone. Aaron did not struggle. He simply lay there, enduring the battering, one hand silently and slowly straying to his belt and the knife nestled there, the handle hard against his exposed belly.

"Where are the rest of them?" the man asked and abruptly rose, dragging Aaron to his feet. The boy let the strength leave him so that the man was burdened with his weight and would have to struggle to keep his own balance. "I said where the fuck *are* they?" Spittle flew from his lips and Aaron had to restrain a cry as it found his eyes. *He's poisoned me*, he thought desperately. *His venom's in me. Oh Jesus...*

Driven by fear of a kind previously unknown to him, he grabbed the knife and swung it up and out in a short arc. His attacker moved away, but not quickly enough. The blade slashed his chest, and he grunted in pain. Aaron did not wait for him to recover. He moved in low and fast, dodging the man's fists, and jammed the blade up to the hilt in his belly and kept it there even as those large hands found the sides of his face like a lover about to impart a secret, and squeezed.

Aaron moaned.

"Fucker," the man said, and began to turn Aaron's face away from him. The boy tried to jerk the knife upward but his hand no longer felt under his command, refusing to obey his instructions to keep traveling up until the coyote was split wide open. Agony seared his throat as his neck muscles began to protest the angle at which his head was being forced to turn. His vision wobbled, dimmed.

"Stop," he whimpered, his voice sounding muffled and very far away.

The man merely grunted, his trembling hands clamped like a vice against the sides of the boy's head.

"*Stop*," Aaron said once more as his muscles became ropes of fire, bones cracked and split, and he was suddenly facing in the opposite direction, all feeling gone but for a momentary incredible starburst of pain that buzzed through his brain before the lights went out.

* * *

On the bank of a sluggishly moving river almost a half-mile to the north of Krall's cabin, Papa-In-Gray knelt down in the reeds, joined his hands and prayed. Beside him, thrumming with anxiety, stood Isaac, who had come to deliver the word that Aaron and Joshua had fallen to the Men of the World, but not, he'd said with obvious pride, without taking their attackers with them.

When Papa was done with his requests that his boys be sainted, and fairly recognized in the Kingdom of Heaven, he rose with a grimace of pain and put a hand on the boy's shoulder. "We move on," he said. "No place they've touched can be used again. They'll have turned this place to poison, and it will spread." He shook his head in sadness. "Your brothers were brave," he said, gazing down into Isaac's eyes, in which he saw no grief, only anger and impatience. "As were you. But we must take our mission elsewhere." He sighed, and crossed his arms. "Where is Luke?"

Isaac shrugged.

"Did they take him?"

The boy shook his head.

"If he's alive, he'll find us. Your Uncle Krall knows where we'll be, assuming that fool has come to his senses and ain't so much raw meat scattered by the coyotes."

Together they walked the bank, following the moon, until they found a spot where the river was shallow and hardly moving at all, a tangle of broken branches and other detritus forming a natural dam, so that the water was only a few feet deep. As quietly as they could, they waded across the freezing water, both of them keeping a vigilant watch on the trees ahead, as well as those behind. Isaac had said two men had fallen, but there might yet be more of them, and if they let themselves relax without being sure, it could be the end of them. Every shadow was a coyote in hiding, every snap of a twig a footfall, every rustle one of them shifting their weight in preparation for ambush.

They reached the riverbank on the opposite side, and gingerly ascended through the reeds and cattails. Isaac's breath was a low steady hiss, and Papa knew he was eager to have his taste of war with the Men of the World, that he envied the glorious deaths of his brothers. They had fought the fight of angels, felling the demons that had come to corrupt their hearts and souls, and it must have been a magnificent sight to behold. But he would get his chance sooner or later, because on the heels of the coyotes would come others seeking vengeance, seeking an end to Papa and his kind.

Papa was tired. As he paused a moment to catch his breath, his knee aching, he looked up at the stars above, their glow lessened by the great light of the moon, and felt a pang of sadness at all he had lost. Matthew, Joshua and Aaron were gone, murdered by the Men of the World, and Mama-In-Bed too, killed by her fear of them, and from the heartbreak at seeing Luke contaminated. Luke's own allegiances remained to be seen, though Papa had faith. He had no choice. Alone he was defenseless against the awesome forces which existed to oppose him, and Isaac was young, an efficient killer but naïve, and not strong enough to be of much use if their nemeses came again. He needed Luke now to stand with him.

Isaac radiated impatience, his dark eyes twinkling in the gloom, and Papa nodded, waved a hand for him to proceed into the dark woods ahead. He watched as the young boy, limbs rigid with tension, hurried into the trees. After a moment, he followed, stowing that sadness, for it was not an emotion that could be used. It was a weakness, and for as long as he'd walked the earth, it had been a flaw easily exploited. He had encouraged his boys to shun it and they had learned to do so. That it should come back now, after all this time, unsettled him, tempted him to question the wisdom of proceeding any further.

No, he decided, angry at himself. *We must.*

He had doubted before and God had punished him.

He would not doubt again.

Teeth clenched, he ignored the nagging pain in his leg and willed himself forward into the woods.

THIRTY-SEVEN

The cruiser crept so close that Pete thought for a moment it was going to run him down. With great effort he stood his ground and the vehicle halted, the headlights on either side of him, the grille almost touching his knees. Dust swept out from under the tires, momentarily blinding him. He swallowed, and wiped a hand over his face. He was hungry, tired and dirty, in need of a bath, and he was afraid, though it felt odd to be afraid of Sheriff McKindrey, who had always been decent to him and had treated him with sympathy and kindness once it had been revealed what had happened to his Pa. But back then, Pete hadn't been on the run, had done nothing to give the police reason to track him down. They sure had a reason now, and more than one.

For a moment, after the car stopped, nothing happened. The engine made the sound of a clock ticking away the seconds as it cooled. The lights were still on, so Pete could only see the vague shape of the man inside the vehicle. It unnerved him further, made him think of running and to hell with the consequences. But he was not alone, and to run would put more than himself at risk. Claire needed him, as she had needed him from the moment he'd first set eyes on her, and nothing she would ever say or do would convince him he was wrong. She was hurt, angry, confused. He knew that now, and realized he should have recognized it before, having felt those same exact emotions in the days after his father's death.

He loved her, and so would do as she had asked.

The cruiser door opened and above the lights, Pete saw McKindrey wince and lean on the door for a moment as he put his hat on and tugged the brim down so that it cast a shadow over his eyes. A wide white bandage was taped over his nose and deep bruises ringed his eyes.

"Pete," he said by way of acknowledgment.

"Hi Sheriff," Pete said.

McKindrey rested his elbows on the door and looked around. "What brings you all the way out here? Last I heard, you'd split town."

"I come back," Pete told him. "Wanted to see if I could find whoever hurt my Pa."

McKindrey nodded his understanding. "But we got the man did that, son."

"No."

"No?"

Pete shook his head. "Weren't that doctor did this. He were a decent man. He wouldn'ta hurted no one. He tried to help."

"That so?"

"Sure is."

"They say he was out of his mind. Went crazy after his wife passed."

"People say whatever they like. I knew him. Saw him that night and he looked fine to me."

McKindrey nodded at the house behind Pete. "So what was it you was plannin' to do if you found them out here?"

Pete shrugged. It was an easy question to answer because he hadn't really known from the moment he'd set his sights on the Merrills what he'd hoped to achieve if he ever found himself face to face with them. He wanted them all dead, that was for sure, but it wasn't likely he'd ever be able to do that on his own, and now, they weren't even here and he was probably going to end up in jail just for thinking about it. "Dunno," he said.

"Well," McKindrey said, finally moving away from the car door and shutting it behind him. He moved only a foot or so before he grimaced and leaned against the hood. "Shit."

"You all right?"

"Yep. Busted myself up pretty good down by the creek."

"Sorry to hear that."

McKindrey nodded. "My own damn fault. I gotta learn to keep my eyes open." He folded his arms. "Pete...you know you shouldn't be out here."

"Yes sir."

"And you know I told you I'd find out all I could about what happened to your daddy and try to put this whole thing to rest, didn't I?"

"Yes sir."

"Well, you should've listened to me. Have I ever lied to you?"

"No sir."

"Right. Then why do you want to go causin' trouble for me?"

"I didn't think about it, to tell the truth. I just wanted to come back here and try to teach these people a lesson. They shouldn't be let to kill people like they do, Sheriff."

McKindrey's gaze was hard. "Well now, that's a mighty big accusation to be puttin' on folks unless you've got proof of some kind. Do you?"

Pete thought about this, was about to admit that he hadn't any proof other than the memory of waking up to find the Merrill family in his house that night years ago, when he remembered Claire.

"I reckon I do," he said, and smiled. "The girl who escaped 'em is with me. She knows the doctor didn't do nothin'. She knows who did."

McKindrey nodded, as if he knew all along that Pete wasn't alone. "Where's she at?"

"Inside," Pete replied. "But she wants to be let alone for a while. I reckon she's tryin' to find whatever's left of her friends' belongin's."

"Trespassin's what she's doin', Pete," McKindrey said, but to the boy's relief, didn't make a move. "Now I been sent out here to get her by her sister, who wants her home. She's been through enough without makin' it worse for herself and worryin' everybody else."

"We didn't want to make it worse," Pete told him. "We just had to come back. Couldn't just let things die the way they did. Nobody knows the truth and I reckon they need to know. And I figure Claire's come back to close the door on some of that bad stuff. I guess once we're done, you probably won't never see her again."

"That would suit me," McKindrey said. "Goddamn town has enough trouble without folks who was lucky enough to get free of it comin' back to stir up more." He glanced briefly down at his foot, which was wrapped in bandages and shreds of an old shirt, and shook his head. "Now you know I'm real sorry about what happened to your Pa, but you've gotta accept the fact that he weren't a happy man. He took his own life, son, and that's the truth of it right there. Whatever happened with those kids and that doctor, or whoever done it to them, it doesn't involve you and you shouldn't be stuck in the middle of it."

"But Claire said—"

McKindrey raised a hand. "It don't concern me what Claire said. Whatever happened to her messed her up real bad and I reckon, between you and me, that she probably ain't been right since. Probably convinced herself that some family she saw passin' by her on the road were the ones that did this to her. It happens, you know. Mind has a funny way of makin' up for lost memory. Happened to my own stepbrother Willard. He went out harvestin' corn, got drunk and fell over, hit his head on a rock. Swore up and down it was the scarecrow had thumped him upside the head. Still believes it too."

"It ain't like that, Sheriff."

The Sheriff frowned. "How the hell do you know what it is or ain't, son? Were you there when whatever happened to that girl happened?"

"No," Pete admitted.

"So how do you know who done what?"

"She told me."

"Don't matter what she told you if her mind's half-gone now does it?"

Pete shrugged.

"Hell boy, if I told you a bear chewed on my foot would you believe it?"

"I guess so."

"Why?"

"Because...you're the Sheriff."

"And you figure I wouldn't lie to you."

"Sure."

"You believe everythin' that girl tells you because maybe you got your eye on her, am I right?"

Pete felt his cheeks grow warm. "I dunno."

"Yeah," McKindrey said with a grin. "That's it all right. She could tell you the sky's green and the grass's blue and you'd believe it if you thought she were gonna let you into that sweet pink paradise of hers."

"What does that mean?"

"Never mind. It don't matter. What does matter, son, is somethin' you may not be aware of."

"What?"

"Her sister thinks you kidnapped Claire."

Pete's mouth dropped open. "No...She asked me to take her here, I swear it!"

McKindrey hushed him. "I believe you. I do. But a whole lotta folks won't, and the longer you stay down here foolin' around, the deeper the shit you're in's gonna get."

"I wouldn't kidnap no one."

"Course you wouldn't, but folks'll suspect you're sweet on that girl, and they'll know she ain't right in the head, so they'll reckon you told her to come down here so you could have her to yourself."

"That ain't how it is."

"But that's what they'll say. They'll ask themselves why a rich white Northern gal like that would come all the way down here with a poor young buck like you, and they'll come up with all sorts of awful notions. Then *you'll* be the bad guy."

"Claire'll—"

McKindrey limped away from the car and put his hands on the boy's shoulders. Like a lame dog, he kept his wounded foot slightly raised. "Listen," he said in a quiet voice. "Claire won't do shit for you when you need it. You need to forget about her before she hangs you out to dry. See, the folks who done this to her are long gone, way out of her reach, so she needs to punish someone. That's why she's here. She can't stand the fact that no one's gonna swing for what they did to her, so she'll maybe lead you inside that house, let you fuck her, then she'll cry rape and claim you tried to kill her just like you did before."

Alarmed, Pete shook his head. "Sheriff...I took *care* of her. I drove her to the hospital."

"Sure you did. And she'll say you did it out of guilt for what you did to her after killin' her friends and havin' your way with her. She'll say she was confused, thought someone else did it, but when she saw you at her house it all came back to her. Then she'll say you dragged her into your truck and brought her back here." He shook his head in sadness. "And who's gonna say otherwise? Wellman might have backed you up, but he's dead. Your Pa too. Who else is gonna prove what you say is the truth?"

No, Pete told himself. *You don't know Claire. She wouldn't do that to me.* But as he had already realized earlier, though he had committed himself to the task of protecting her, at the back of it all, he *didn't* know her at all, and hadn't liked what he seen since arriving at her house. She was cold, and weren't cold people capable of the kinds of things McKindrey was suggesting now? Nevertheless it seemed impossible that he could be so completely wrong about someone. But why would McKindrey lie?

His head hurt from the strain of trying to make sense of it. He was torn between the desire to stay and look after Claire, all in the hope that she would show her appreciation for his efforts, and heeding the Sheriff's advice to avoid the kind of nightmare the man had detailed for him as the most likely reward for his loyalty.

"What do I do?" he asked.

McKindrey nodded as if Pete had answered a math problem correctly. "You get goin'," he said. "They're only interested in the girl, not you, unless you give them reason to be. Head back into town and wait for me in my office. Stella's there, she'll make you a nice cup of somethin'."

"What are you goin' to do?"

The Sheriff sighed and put his hands on his hips. "Talk to her, I expect. See if I can get her to come with me without makin' things hard. We need to get her back to her people."

"Why can't I wait and get a ride from you?"

"Because I don't want you around if she decides to make up another one of her stories. Least if you're with Stella, she can vouch for you, you know?"

Pete shook his head.

"She can say you were there and not here," McKindrey explained.

"You ain't gonna hurt her, are you?"

"No," McKindrey told him. "Not even a little bit."

* * *

Breath trapped in her throat, a hand over her nose to keep the foul stench away, Claire stood by the grime-encrusted window, listening. She hadn't been able to make out what the Sheriff had said to Pete, but whatever it was, it proved enough to convince him that he was better off leaving her. She watched, incredulous, as the boy cast one final longing glance back at the house and started down the path toward the road, and the truck. McKindrey, looking like every hillbilly sheriff she'd ever seen on TV, stood with his hat tipped back away from his forehead, fists clenched on his hips, monitoring the boy's progress. All he was short was some chaw. She could clearly imagine him leaning over and spitting a great gob of tobacco juice into the dirt.

She didn't know the Sheriff, but now she was alone with him and he could only be here for one reason: to take her back home. She did not wait for him to turn and start toward the house. Instead, she quickly moved away from the window, her eyes watering at the smell of death that seemed to seep through her skin to get at her. In the small beam from the flashlight, she could see what looked like an ornate bed, the cast iron rusted and stained. The filthy mattress in the middle had sunken so low into the frame it was almost folded in two, springs and wires poking out here and there and coated with what looked like dried skin and coarse dark hair. Opposite the bed was a haphazard mound of clothes of every conceivable kind: T-shirts, shorts, underwear, jackets, hats, raincoats, shoes, socks. Fighting the urge to gag, she reached down and began to feel her way through the clothes.

What are you doing? This is insane!

She had thought all along that she had come here to confront her attackers, the murderers of her friends. But they weren't here and yet she wasn't leaving. Even with the means of her departure stalking toward the house, she was still ransacking through old clothing, looking for...

Looking for—what?

For them, she realized. *For their clothes, for things that belonged to them and were never meant to belong to anyone else. Things that still carry their blood, the scent of their sweat, their perfume, cologne. Their private things. The things that were pieces of them. The things I need to take with me so I won't dare forget.*

With her tears came a desperate, frantic search through the last few items heaped on the floor. She found wallets, purses, a soiled wig, a toothbrush, a pocket mirror and some makeup, but nothing she recognized as anything her friends had once owned.

She fell to her knees, removed her hand from her mouth.

The noxious smell invaded her. She gagged, reached for something, anything with which to cover her mouth. Dug a hand into her pocket. And found the phone.

What if he answered? The memory of that night came back to her and she tore the phone free of her pocket, hit the menu button and raised it up in front of her face. The green glow aided her in locating Danny's number. *The phone was here*, she thought. *He was here. I want it back. I want* him *back.*

Sobbing, hands trembling so hard she feared she might not be able to keep the phone from slipping from her grip and smashing against the floor, she dialed the number.

Time spun away from her, the bilious stench forgotten, the bedsprings groaning for a moment as if a ghost had rested its weight there to watch her. Startled, she looked up.

His phone should be dead by now. Or turned off. But even the promise of his recorded voice thrilled her. A little piece of him she could always keep. The only part of her he'd given her.

The call went through.

Danny's phone began to ring.

It was here. Afraid to believe, she slowly rose, and lowered her phone, obviating the distraction so she could use both ears to guide her toward the sound.

She stepped out of the room into a narrow corridor carpeted by dust and debris. She turned her head, closed her eyes and listened.

The phone was not in the house.

The sheds then, maybe.

She stepped back into the room she had just left and peered out through the window, straining to see through the grime. Annoyed, she scrubbed a rough circle clear with her sleeve. Looked out again. Scanned the yard, but saw nothing, not even the Sheriff.

Then finally, she located the source of the sound.

Her heart skipped a beat.

Cold filled her.

Danny's phone was out there, ringing, and now she could see it too. It was on its back, display facing up, the violet glow granting an eerie luminescence to the inside of the Sheriff's car.

THIRTY-EIGHT

"Hell of a way to go," Beau said as he lowered himself to the ground, one bloody hand pressed against his belly.

Finch was breathing, but only just. Every inhalation felt like he was drawing boiling water into his lungs; every exhalation felt like waves of ice. He couldn't move, and didn't try. The mere idea of it made him want to throw up.

Beau sat back against the tree. "Kids," he said. "Who'd have believed it."

"You would," Finch said hoarsely, and tried to smile. He was on his back, the ground cold beneath him. The shaft of the final arrow protruded from his stomach. Blood ran freely. "You could probably have told me how this was going to go right down to the last detail."

Beau said nothing, and for a moment Finch assumed he had died, but then he spoke softly. "I could, but it wasn't what you wanted to hear."

Finch's smile faded.

"Was it?" Beau asked.

"No."

"You find what you were lookin' for down here?"

"I think it found me."

"Deep," Beau said and chuckled. It quickly turned to a fit of coughing. "Shit...Any time you'd like to call 911 is fine by me. I'm not dyin' here or nothin'. Unless you want me to do the honors."

"What do you want me to say?"

"Start with: We're dyin'. They'll probably take the ball and run with it after that."

"Then what?"

"Then wh—? Shit, now I get why people in movies tell dyin' folks not to talk. They talk shit is why. They'll send someone to patch us up."

"So we'll be in full health in prison. Two dead kids lying out here, Beau."

Beau started to respond, then thought better of it.

"I'm sorry," Finch said. "I fucked this all right to hell."

"It was pretty much the only way it could go, right?"

"Guess so. But I'm sorry for bringing you down here."

"Hey," Beau told him. "You don't owe me no apologies. I knew what I was doin'."

"*I* didn't," Finch said and smiled.

"Yeah, no shit. So now what?"

"I think," Finch told him. "I'm just going to lay real still and rest for a while."

Beau shifted and moaned in pain. "You always was a lazy sonofabitch. I'm gonna try and get my ass to that cabin. Maybe they got a first aid kit or somethin' so I can sew my stuffin' back in. Hell, maybe they even got a phone."

They hadn't seen any telephone poles on the way in, but Finch didn't bother pointing that out. Beau already knew, but talking and thinking was better than dying any day of the week.

"Maybe they've got a mini-bar," he continued. "And a Jacuzzi. Hell, I bet these boys got their own game room. Didn't see any, but that don't mean they ain't there."

"Turntables and a karaoke machine," Finch added.

"Yeah, and a waterbed, with pink cushions and silk sheets."

Finch laughed despite the pain. "Heart-shaped."

Beau snorted. It looked like it hurt. "Barry White on Dolby surround."

Though the pain was unbearable, Finch couldn't stem the mirth that rippled through him. "I can't feel my legs."

"Why would you want to?" Beau asked. "They're not much to look at."

"Aw shit," Finch said, and his voice cracked. "We failed, man."

"We thinned the herd," Beau told him. "It's all we've ever done. Tried to reduce the threat, just like in the desert. Certain things just are, you know. Bad things. And nothin' will ever stop them. Even if we'd wiped these fuckers off the planet, there are a million others just like them out there, preyin' on people whenever the mood takes them. We weren't gonna make a difference down here, Finch. No matter what we did."

"It might have made a difference to us."

"To you," Beau said. "Not me. This was never my fight. It's like that friend you have when you're in high school whose younger brother gets jumped. The friend organizes a lynch mob and without a second thought you agree to go kick the livin' shit out of a bunch of strangers. You do it because it's important to *someone*, and because maybe the violence appeals to you on some level you prefer to keep hidden, even from yourself."

"That why you're here?"

"I'm here because I'm the cheerful type."

"The hell does that mean?"

"Means everythin' *about* me's bullshit. A front. I saw what you did in the desert, and I fed you…some speech about it being par for the course in wartime. Well, that may be so but it don't make it right. And I wasn't lecturin' you. I was tryin' to make myself…believe it."

With great effort, Finch turned his head to look at him. Pine needles pricked his cheek. Beau's eyes were closed.

"What did you do over there?"

Beau might have shrugged, or it might have been the shadows around him deepening as the moon slid behind a cloud. "Tried to stay alive. Same as everyone else."

"You know what's funny?"

"Do tell."

"For as long as I can remember I've been pissed off. Only time it got even a little better was when I was with Kara. And still, I pushed her away, let some of that anger rub off on her. Then she broke up with me and I accused her of being cold."

"That's not funny," Beau said. "Gotta work on your comic timin'."

"Yeah."

"I'm bleedin' like a stuck pig," Beau told him. "If I'm gonna get us help, I'd better get my ass up."

Finch pondered this, and when next he spoke, to tell Beau that for a guy in a hurry, he sure wasn't getting very far, he didn't receive an answer, only the insects in the brush and the birds high in the trees. He listened to them for what seemed like eternity, before he let his eyes drift shut. Peace washed over him, alien and new and he embraced it.

Kara's face materialized in the dark. He thought about calling her, but realized he didn't have the breath left to power the words, and maybe that was for the best. He had nothing to tell her that she didn't already know.

* * *

Claire considered hiding, or running, or seeking a back exit, but indecision kept her rooted to the spot. She stood in the room with the monstrous bed, her back to the window, watching as the Sheriff stepped into the hall and made his way toward her. Opposite the window was a door leading outside and she could easily have taken this route while the Sheriff was looking for her, but a chain had been looped around the simple bolt, and a rusted padlock hung from the links. She had already tested it, and it had opened barely enough for her to get her arm through.

"There you are, Missy," the Sheriff said cheerfully. So cheerfully in fact, that she was struck with sudden doubt. Maybe he found the phone on the road, or at Pete's house, or the Doctor's place? There were any number of ways in which he could have come by it, so why had she immediately assumed the most malevolent one? Still, she refused to let herself relax too much. The last time she'd seen that phone, it had been in Danny's shirt pocket. Now Danny was dead, and the phone was in a Sheriff's car when there was no reason for him to have it. He should have returned it to Danny's mother. And what about the call? The sense she'd had of someone listening?

Hidden behind her back was a length of wire she had snapped off the bed. It was coiled, but ended in a kinked, three-inch piece that would serve as an adequate weapon with which to buy her time, if it became necessary for her to do so.

The Sheriff was limping, she noted. This too might give her an advantage if it came to a chase. The gun in his holster, however, kept the odds firmly in his favor, and abruptly, she wished Pete hadn't abandoned her. Not that she blamed him. She had hardly given him a reason to stay.

"My name's Sheriff McKindrey. I assume you're Claire?"

"You assume right."

McKindrey continued to pick his way along the debris-filled hallway, occasionally glancing with distaste at something on the floor. The flickering cruiser lights made his shadow large and jittery on the hallway wall.

"Your sister sent me to fetch you," he told her. "She's awful worried."

"I'll bet she is."

Back in the car, Danny's phone stopped ringing as she snapped her own cell phone shut and slid it into her pocket.

"Why do you have my boyfriend's phone?" she asked him as he cleared the hall and with visible relief, stepped into the gloomy room.

"What?"

"My boyfriend. The people who lived here killed him. I was looking for his phone so I called it. It rang in your car."

"Of course it did," McKindrey said, with a wide smile, which showed a slight gap between his front teeth. "Papa-In-Gray gave it to me."

Claire frowned. "Who?"

"Papa-In-Gray." He nodded his understanding. "Of course, you probably don't even know their names."

Claire felt her chest tighten. "Names?"

"The names of the people who hurt you and killed your friends." He stepped closer, but it took work, as he gingerly set the bandaged foot down to gauge how much it was going to hurt to put his weight on it. "Papa-In-Gray's the daddy. Momma-In-Bed's the Momma," he said, indicating the bed. "She's dead now, good riddance to the 'ol bitch. Gave me more than a few nightmares. And of course you met the kids, Isaac and Joshua and Aaron. Matt's the one you killed. Luke's the oldest. They've had a bit of trouble with him. Said he's got notions. Seems more like good sense to me."

"So you know what they did?"

"Of course. Papa gave me your wallets and jewelry and phones and such after it was all done."

Claire couldn't believe what she was hearing. "Why?"

"Call it a tip for keepin' my big 'ol mouth shut." He grinned. "Hell, the one question folks keep puttin' to me is why I stick around here when there ain't nothin' to stick around for. Usually I just shrug and say 'everyplace needs the law' but that's bullshit. Truth is, and this is between you and me, I stay for the watches, rings, billfolds, gold teeth, radios, all of which is pretty easy to offload if you know who's buyin'. But the best money comes from cars. Oh yeah. They give me a bunch of those. I send them to my stepbrother Willard in Arkansas. He's a bit slow, you understand, but he can move a vehicle in record time. I give him a percentage and enjoy the rest. Makes workin' here quite a treat when you know all those goddamn suits are lookin' at you like you ain't got nothin' when in fact you could buy and sell 'em if you was of a mind to. Been buildin' up quite a nest egg, and while I hadn't figured on retirin' for another few years yet, you getting' away has forced me to rethink things. Kinda annoyed about that to tell the truth, but I know it ain't your fault."

"Jesus Christ…they *kill* people," Claire said, backing further into the room.

"Exactly. *They* kill people. I don't."

"But you're gonna kill me."

McKindrey stopped in the middle of the room. He looked genuinely offended. "Look here, Missy. I ain't never killed nobody and I don't aim to neither." He brightened as he took another small step in her direction. "Take a look at this…" He rolled up his sleeve and held out his right wrist. "What do you make of that?"

It was Stu's wristwatch, a Rolex his father bought him for his graduation. Claire clearly recalled him showing it off, turning the back of it up to the light so they could read the inscription on the back: *To my boy. There's no stopping you now, kiddo. Love Dad.*

"That isn't yours," she said, choked with sorrow.

"Hell, the owner don't need it. Better on my wrist here than in a hole or stuck on some dusty shelf somewhere."

"You have no right to do this."

"Probably, but that's the way the world turns, ain't it? No such thing as fair anymore. But hell, you're actin' like I did the killin' myself and I ain't no killer," he said around a smile. "I'm a collector."

Claire moved back until she was pressed against the wall, her shirt stuck to her skin with sweat. Dust rained down around her, turned to fireflies in the beam from her flashlight. "You're a fucking psycho, just like the rest of them. You might as well be the one cutting people up."

McKindrey raised his hands in a gesture of placation. "Look, all I'm goin' to do is take you for a ride that's all."

"A ride where?"

"Into Mason City, to the state police. They'll make sure you get home."

"You expect me to believe that you're going to hand me over to the police after just telling me you've been profiting from the murders of all these people over the years?"

McKindrey shrugged, his smile wide.

"If you touch me," Claire said. "I'll kill you."

"Oh c'mon, Missy. I'm the one with the gun." As he spoke he unclipped his holster, pulled out his weapon and drew back the hammer. "Now it's been an unpleasant enough day for me already. Don't make it worse. My foot's killin' me, my nose feels like it's full of fire ants, and all I want is to get home and get drunk, all right? So you'll be doin' me a nice favor if you just come along."

There was less than six feet between them.

She didn't move.

He leveled the gun at her.

"I'm not going anywhere with you."

"Well, if you don't, someone else's just gonna come by and be a lot less pleasant about it."

"Like your friends, those killing fucks you're working for?"

"Honey," he said sweetly, and closed the distance between them. "I'm done talkin'. Now you're gonna move, and that's all there is to it."

"What did they do with them?"

"With who?"

"My friends."

"You know that well as I do. Scattered 'em around the doctor's place."

"What did they do with the *rest* of them?"

McKindrey sighed. "Buried 'em."

"Where?"

"Different places. Some parts here, some in the woods, some out in that field with the dead tree."

That gave Claire pause and for the briefest of moments she experienced a blissful absence of any kind of feeling at all. Sound itself seemed muted, the room blurring as an image of the field with the wisps of cotton floating upward in the breeze superimposed itself over the present.

Everything isn't dead, she thought then. *Only gone.*

THIRTY-NINE

Finch was dead.

Beau knew it as soon as he woke and put a hand on his friend's shoulder. The man's skin was icy cold to the touch, and a search for a pulse yielded nothing. Beau shook his head and expelled a ragged breath. He had let Finch down, though of course Finch would never have seen it that way. To a man like that, culpability would always be directed inward and everything that happened in his life would be a result of his own failings. Finch had existed to suffer, driven by a burning rage he had never understood, a cold engine that drove him toward his own inexorable death without ever revealing its motives. It was like this for some people, but not for Beau, though he considered himself equally directionless. Born into a poor but nurturing family, he had depended on his instincts to survive on the cruel streets, and his fists had seen him through. He was a walking cliché—kid born in the ghetto made strong by necessary violence, and yet he shared none of the characteristics of his brothers, who walked with an attitude, their shoulders low, eyes frosty and darting from face to face as if searching for one that required punishment. Anger had never been a driving force in Beau's life, only sorrow, but the origin of that sorrow was as much a mystery as Finch's rage. It had felt as if he were grieving for people who had died long before he'd come into the world, and had found himself forever unfulfilled, as if he'd been born without some vital component necessary for total happiness. He'd drifted, seeking people more emotionally deficient than himself, for in them he found a kinship. The shared unhappiness did not cancel either out, but neither did it exacerbate it, and this was how he lived. In Finch he found a carnival mirror, a distorted reflection of himself that bound him to the man.

It had led him here, to the dark and the cold, with a gash in his stomach that was bleeding profusely and playing with his consciousness.

Beside him, Finch had found peace, and for a moment Beau envied him so much that his eyes started to close, and he quickly shook his head, braced a hand on the ground and raised himself up. He cried out and stopped, but did not abandon the progress he'd made. With one hand clamped over his belly, he drew his legs beneath him, relying on their strength to help him up, and they did. He stood, shoulder pressed to the tree, gasping, his knees trembling, the front of his jeans soaked with blood. Beau was weak from blood loss, but he was not yet dead, and that was something. He took a moment to steady himself and looked down at Finch, who was little more than a long shadow with a pale smudge for a face. Beau made a silent promise that he would do everything he could to make sure Finch wasn't left here to rot or be picked apart by animals, even if it meant burying him himself. "No man left behind" was the motto for fallen soldiers on the battlefield, but Beau wasn't sure he'd ever really understood it. What lay at his feet was no longer anyone he knew. Whatever happened next would hardly bother Finch. He was gone. Only the body remained. *Desecration*, he thought. *We leave no one behind to be desecrated by the enemy*. Still, he wondered why it made such a difference to anyone. It was the soul and the spirit people mourned, not the body, so why should it matter what became of it?

He realized such musings were simply a way to stall, to avoid moving when he knew it was going to be agony to do so. It was also a means of trying to disseminate the guilt he already felt at the thought of leaving Finch here alone. But if he didn't, he too would die.

He pushed himself away from the tree and stumbled through the woods toward the cabin. He had been mistaken about the agony, he realized. There was no agony in his belly. It was utter torture.

The moonlight faded, and for one panicked moment, Beau thought it was unconsciousness coming to claim him and he stopped, leaned against a tree until the light silvered the woods once more. Breath pluming in the air before him, he focused on the murky yellow light from the cabin window up ahead and hurried on, the blood sticky between his fingers.

Keep goin', he told himself. *Not far. Get there and you can sit and figure out what happens next. But keep movin'.*

The light in the cabin window was a beacon, drawing his wounded form toward it. In his waistband, the gun, cold against his skin. In his pocket, the reassuring weight of his cell phone. He prayed there was a signal. There was only one call worth making now and he would do it even if his injury conspired to leave him dead on the forest floor. One call, and perhaps everything they'd done wouldn't have been in vain after all.

Keep m...

He was within hailing distance of the cabin when the world abruptly swept up and away and nausea gripped him.

The darkness came again.

This time it was not the moon.

* * *

Despite his injury, McKindrey's approach had up until this moment been confident, as if he knew without a doubt how this was going to play out. But now, with Claire backed up against the wall, he stopped and licked his lips. In the light through the windows, she could see perspiration beading his sallow skin. He did not look nervous, but wary, the gun pointed at her chest. His eyebrows were knitted, as if he'd suddenly forgotten the finer points of hostage taking.

"Just take 'er easy now," he mumbled, as if advising himself.

With no room to move, her hand bent behind her, Claire felt the wire she'd taken from the bedsprings poking her between the shoulder blades. She told herself to relax, that panic would get her nowhere, but then realized that was a lie. Stark panic had freed her the first time she'd found herself a captive in this charnel house. But would it do so again? And even if it did, did she really want to give herself over to such impulses a second time when she was still haunted by the guilt of the first?

"Don't do this," she said. "If you let me go, I won't say anything."

"Why not?" McKindrey asked.

There was no response to that. She shook her head dumbly.

"I would think it'd be the first thing you'd do, mad as you are at me."

"I'm not mad at you," Claire lied. "I'm mad that my friends are gone and I can't bring them back."

"But I had a hand in that."

"Not the worst one."

He smiled unevenly, appraised her anew, but the gun was steady in his hand. "You're a clever girl. I'm real sorry you're stuck in this, though I expect you won't believe that."

She closed her eye. "If you are sorry, then you might as well do me a favor and end it." The wisdom of the request eluded her, but whatever had motivated it, it suddenly felt absolutely right. With it came a calm similar to the one she had felt when McKindrey had mentioned the field with the dead tree. An end was coming, and though she did not know the form it would ultimately take, she welcomed the peace it promised.

"End it how?"

"Pull the trigger," she told him. "You've helped put a whole lot of people in their graves. Might as well help one more."

In the darkness, she relied only on her senses and the small voice that drifted up from somewhere deep inside her that whispered, *There's no way out except his way. You fight and even if you escape him all you'll ever do is fight. Why not end it right here, right now? What do you even have that's worth fighting for?*

She heard the raspy sound of his breathing.

The jingle of the keys on his belt.

The creak of leather.

But the sound she expected, feared, hoped for...didn't come.

She looked.

He was still standing there, still staring at her, the cruiser lights flickering behind him, the headlights painting one side of his face, the other mired in shadow. Frustrated, she asked, "What are you waiting for? You have me. I'm giving you what you want."

He nodded once. "So I see. Why?"

The void dissolved. Anger and the anguish that had plagued her since the day she'd fled this place coalesced inside her, surged upward on the crest of a red tide that made her whole body tremble.

"What difference does it make? You suddenly give a shit? Pull the fucking trigger, you hick bastard."

The uncertainty that had come over him did not evaporate under the brunt of her insult. Instead he stiffened, seemed to consider what she'd said and then looked down at the gun. To her disbelief, he gave a rueful shake of his head. "Real sorry for what they done to you. Better dead than be left—"

Before she knew she was going to do it, she rushed him, expecting the surprise of it to make his trigger finger spasm and send a bolt of hot fire into her chest, but instead he staggered backward, away from her, his mouth open in a dark circle. His wounded foot betrayed him and he stumbled, fell heavily to the left and landed on his side. Claire was on him. He quickly brought the gun up, even as she brought the wire down like a tribal Indian spearing a fish.

An odd roar accompanied the downward arc of the wire and the upward swing of the gun. The light through the windows changed, brightened, became the sun on a new morning though it was far too early.

As a cry of primeval rage burst from Claire's mouth, the wire found its target, piercing the side of Sheriff McKindrey's throat, his eyes widening in surprise. Dark blood spurted from the wound. Cursing, one hand flying to his neck, he pulled the trigger but the gun was now aimed upward and though the shot deafened her, the bullet plowed harmlessly into the ceiling.

Dust and splinters rained down.

Claire withdrew the wire and stabbed again. All she could hear now was a distant rumble and a low whistle in her ears, which worsened as McKindrey scrambled, his feet scrabbling against the bare wood as she straddled him, the wire held overhead in a two-hand grip. He flailed at her, the cold metal barrel of the gun smashing into her right temple once and again. She persisted despite the nauseating tilt of the world through her good eye, gouging his arms, his face, his chest with the rusted wire. She smelled old death and decay, new blood and sudden fear. It inspired her, and she doubled her assault on the man who was three times her weight and twice her height, empowered by rage to keep him down. Panic did not fuel her. There was no name for the impulse that pounded through her now.

McKindrey bucked. She held on, her free hand planted on his chest, the other incessantly perforating his bulk with the wire. He cried out as she punctured his jaw, punched his broken nose.

Then the wall and windows seemed to detonate as the light exploded into the room and they were enveloped in a storm of flying wood and glimmering glass.

* * *

Beau came to on a hard flat surface. Immediately he realized that he was no longer in the woods.

He was also bare-chested.

And he was not alone.

Instinctively he reached out a hand for his gun, driven by the unreasonable hope that whoever had brought him here had left it close by. Unsurprisingly, his trembling fingers found nothing but air.

Sudden scalding pain in his belly made him roar and ram his knuckles into his mouth, biting down to keep from chewing on his tongue, and he raised his head to identify the source of the agony through the tears in his eyes. He blinked furiously, struggling to clear his vision, but already he knew what he would see. The pain could not suffocate the dread that came at the thought of it.

They had him.

Leaning over Beau, who was lying on what he now realized was the kitchen table he'd seen earlier on his inspection of the cabin, was a giant, blocking out the strained light from a naked bulb, which reduced him to a wild-haired silhouette.

"Aw *God*," Beau moaned as another round of fierce pain blasted through him from his wound. He convulsed, began to scream and did not stop, even when the man's large hand covered his mouth and he tasted blood and dirt.

FORTY

Claire lay on her stomach and waited.

She felt weight on her feet and wondered if she'd lost them, or at the very least broken them and tangled the nerves. But there was no pain, only heat. Beneath her face, the surface of the floor was rough like sandpaper, but she didn't move. Wasn't sure she was able. Any moment now McKindrey might rise up, shake off his discomfort and pump her body full of bullets. Even if he had been short on reasons to hurt her before, which he hadn't, she'd given him ample motive to hurt her now. She had attacked him like an animal, and though she did not mourn the passing of that peculiar, frightening impulse, nor did she regret it. It had served its purpose and again, though the dangerous resignation with which she was growing grimly familiar had swept her up in its calming embrace, she had fought for her life. The absence of reasons for it to continue had not been enough to drain whatever resolve existed in that untouchable, unseen reservoir inside her.

"Claire?"

She did not raise her head. Gradually, small campfires of pain registered across the dark landscape of her body. Cuts, lacerations, bruises. She didn't care. *Superficial*, the doctors would say, just as they had said at the hospital in Mason City and she had sneered at them. Nothing about what had been done to her had been superficial. Every incision they'd made with their dirty blades had branded her with the memory of the faces and intent of those who'd made them.

"Claire?"

She opened her eye. The room was filled with fog. The air was thick with dust. Nearby, through the haze she glimpsed an empty shoe. McKindrey's. A few feet away, a foot without a sock, the leg bent over the cast iron frame of the overturned bed. Three rivulets of blood ran down the ankle. Dark against pale.

Hands found her and she flinched, felt new pain erupt but dismissed it. She squinted up at the lithe shadow bent over her, thought for a moment she saw the sun behind it as she lay on the road in the heat of the day, but it lasted only a moment.

"Pete?" she asked, then coughed.

He knelt down next to her. "McKindrey's dead. Looks like he busted his neck. You all right?"

"I'm alive," she told him. "That's a start."

He helped her turn over and put a hand on her back as she sat up. She dabbed at blood on her face, probed a tender spot at the side of her skull and winced.

"I'm sorry," Pete said.

"You've nothing to be sorry for," she said, and blinked. Took in the chaos in the room. The wall with the padlocked door was gone, only splintered beams hanging like crooked teeth in a gaping mouth, the tongue a vehicle with its front end parked inside the room atop a mound of rubble, one light glaring up at the far wall, the other shattered on impact. The fender was gone, the hood buckled so she couldn't see the windshield. After taking out the wall, the car had plowed through the room, striking McKindrey. How it had missed Claire, who had been sitting astride him when the car had come through, was a mystery. Or maybe not. She recalled, in those now surreal and hazy seconds before the car plowed through the wall, McKindrey's hands on her chest, crushing her breasts, forcing her away. Perhaps it had only been self-defense. Perhaps he had simply been trying to get her off him so he could scamper out of the way himself. She didn't know, and never would, and thus found it easy to reject the repulsive notion that he had, in the final moments of his life, tried to save her.

"I was almost gone," Pete said as he assisted her in standing. Her ankle hurt and there was a nasty gash in her right thigh, but she thought of these as nothing more than reminders that she was not dead.

"I know."

"He lied to me," he continued. "Told me all sorts of awful things, none of 'em true." He guided her around the rubble, one hand braced on the buckled hood. "I believed him."

"You didn't have a reason not to."

He nodded, but looked troubled as she wrapped an arm around his shoulders for support. "I know, but I would've left if it hadn't come to me what he said. He kept sayin' the Doc kilt your friends, but before I left, he said 'the *folks* who done this to her are long gone.' Didn't realize it then because I guess I ain't too quick, but soon as I sat in the truck and thought it over, I knew he was lyin' and he said he ain't never lied to me. But he did, and I had to come back."

"It's all right, Pete," she said as they emerged into the cool night air. Above them, the stars shone bright and clear. Claire took a deep draw of the crisp air and felt it catch in her throat as the dust rolled around in her lungs. She coughed violently, then wiped her mouth and sighed. "Thank you for coming back."

He shrugged.

"I mean it, Pete. Thank you for saving me." She reached out a hand and touched his face, felt a slight peppering of stubble. "Again," she added, and smiled.

He started to say something then, but she drew him close, slowly, mindful of the pain in every joint, and kissed him softly on the lips. When it was over, he said nothing, though he seemed desperate to find the words. She didn't wait. Instead she leaned against him and let him put his arm around her this time.

"We need to burn it down," she said.

* * *

"Hush now, else they'll hear you," the giant advised him, and at first Beau assumed that meant anyone who might come to his rescue—*Shut up, or you'll doom your friends too*—but then he looked down at himself and realized the agony had come as a result of whiskey that had been splashed over the wound. Confused, he withheld further complaint until the man stomped off and returned a few moments later with an old-looking needle in one huge hand, a fistful of catgut in the other.

"What are you doin'?" Beau asked him.

"Puttin' your stuffin' back in," the giant said in a low gravelly voice. He pulled a chair up to the table and sat, then gently threaded the fishing line through the eye of the needle, which was as big as a pencil. He started to bend down close to the wound, eyes narrowed as if he was poor-sighted, but then stopped and glanced askance at Beau, the point of the needle raised. "'Less you prefer it hangin' out?"

Convinced now that he was delirious and imagining it all, Beau shook his head. "Naw. You go right ahead, as long as you're not fixin' to tie the wrong parts together."

The giant frowned, as if he didn't understand what that was supposed to mean, and went about his work, carefully easing the needle through Beau's flesh.

"*Shiiiit.*" Beau bared his teeth, clenched his fists, but the pain, though it was severe, didn't last long. In what seemed like minutes, the worst of it was over, and this time when the wound was soaked with alcohol, Beau felt the burning, but considerably less agony. Afterward, he lay in silence for a long time, watching as the man lumbered about the cabin looking ill at ease, like a man unsure what to do next. Beau wanted to think of him as his savior, but other than the rudimentary stitch-job and the fact that he was still alive when he'd given the giant ample opportunity to kill him, it was too much of a stretch for the moment. He was, after all, still in enemy territory.

"Why'd you do this?" he asked, wondering if perhaps he'd been fixed just so he'd be in better shape when they tortured him.

For a long time, the man didn't answer. Then he stalked across the room, grabbed the whiskey bottle from the table and shoved it at Beau, who took it with a half-hearted nod of gratitude and, eyes never leaving the giant's face, drank deeply.

"You ain't never done nothin' to me," the man said.

Beau waited, the whiskey burning a path straight through him, hewing a route to the pain. When it was clear that was as much of an explanation as he was going to get, he asked, "They won't like that you did this, you know."

The man sat, easing his great frame into a chair that seemed unlikely to be able to hold him. It creaked loudly as he settled himself and put a hand out for the bottle. Beau gave it to him.

"I don't much care for 'em," he said, and took a draw from the bottle. "Never did. They kilt my sister. She were all I had left in the world. But she didn't never listen to me when I tried to tell her what she were gettin' into, and now she's dead. All because of them crazies. 'Sides, I ain't scairt of 'em, and after tonight, I don't reckon I'll be hearin' from 'em again."

"I'm sorry about your sister," Beau said, because it seemed, for now, about the only appropriate thing to say. They made an odd tableau, the two of them—a wounded black man lying on a table, overseen by a wild-haired giant. But gradually, Beau felt the tension and anxiety ebb from him. If it turned out to be a trap, there wasn't a whole lot he could do about it anyway, so he figured it was best to just see where things went and hope for the best.

For the next ten minutes, they shared the bottle in silence. Though feeling a little better, Beau was exhausted. His eyes were drifting shut again when the screech of the chair legs against the floor jarred him back to alertness. In panic, he looked furtively around the room, half-expecting to find that the giant was standing there with a knife or a hatchet or a rifle getting ready to finish him off. But the man had simply pulled his chair closer to the table and was looking intently at Beau.

"I killed a buck one time that was damn near big as myself," he said.

Beau stared back at him for a long time. Then he raised his eyebrows. "That's one big motherfuckin' deer, man. Venison for a year."

Krall nodded, and the faintest trace of a smile began to creep through the undergrowth of his beard.

FORTY-ONE

Standing in the flameless epicenter of an inferno as the buildings burned around her, Claire heard the cell phone chirp over the splintering crack of the Merrill House caving in on itself. During the melee inside the room with the sagging bed, the phone's display had cracked and now showed nothing but inky blotches against the gray screen, veined with milky fissures. She couldn't see the caller I.D, but answered and held the phone to her ear.

"Hello?"

"Claire?"

"Who's this?"

"My name's Beau. I'm...I was a friend of Finch's."

"Was? Is he...?"

"Yeah. They got him. But he went down fightin'. Took out a couple of 'em on the way too."

Tears welled in Claire's eyes. Pete approached and stopped before her, head tilted questioningly. She swallowed and tried to offer him a smile. "Are they dead?"

"Yes," Beau told her. "They're all dead. It's over."

The tears came freely, sobs pummeling her chest as she shut the phone and let Pete embrace her.

It's over.

The acrid smell of the smoke and the heat from the flames soon forced them out of the ring of fire, toward the road, where the truck was waiting.

* * *

As quietly as the woods would allow, Isaac led Papa-In-Gray through the night. The moon was high in the sky and Papa frequently raised his face to it, as if it was nothing short of God's light, drawing them to their destiny. The need for a sign was great within him now that he had lost so many of his kin, but he resisted the urge to beg. Once they were clear of the killing ground, clear of their hunters, he would have endless time to disseminate the events that had set them running. Was this truly what God had intended for them? That his children should be sacrificed? He shook his head, forcing away the questions. The pain in his knee was making it difficult to walk and he slowed, watching as Isaac pulled ahead.

It weren't ever supposed to be this hard.

"Son," he said, breathlessly, and the boy stopped, glanced back. "We should rest up some." With great effort, he sat himself down on a rough moss-covered rock that protruded from the forest floor like a boil.

The look on Isaac's face made it clear he did not think this was wise, but he acquiesced, pacing restlessly and jerking his head toward the small clearing they could see through the pine trees ahead. His knife was out and while he stalked, he jabbed at the air and twisted the blade, his young face bejeweled with sweat.

He senses the injustice of it too, Papa thought. *The failure. He ain't satisfied to leave this unfinished.* Nor was Papa, but their options were limited. Without knowing the extent of the threat, only a fool would go back. McKindrey had told them there were only two men on their trail, but who knew how many were elsewhere, waiting for the call to arms? That the Sheriff hadn't seen them did not mean they were not there. It was best to err on the side of caution. There was time. In the coming days, months, however long it took, they would regroup, and plan a strategy. Over time, they would rebuild their ranks. He would find a woman, spiritually vacant, awaiting his love and his knowledge, awaiting God, and she would have sons and daughters he could lead. They would rise again. And perhaps in their new town, the local law would be just as sympathetic to their cause as McKindrey had been. Such minions were hard to find, and McKindrey had proven invaluable. The call Papa had made to him from a payphone on their way here had confirmed that the Men of the World were on their way, allowing them the time to prepare. It had also allowed Papa to perpetuate the belief that he held congress with the angels, bolstering his children's faith in him. With a smile, he nodded and turned to Isaac, who might be sated, however briefly, by Papa's new resolve.

The boy was no longer pacing. Now he was standing still and facing the clearing, his body rigid, the hand holding the knife trembling violently.

"Isaac," Papa whispered, slowly rising from the rock. "What is it?"

Isaac was silent, but something held him in thrall.

Papa limped toward him. "What do you hear?"

Since Papa had taken the child's tongue for some violation he could hardly recall, the boy had not spoken except for cluttered mumbles, and even these were rare. He employed them now however as his stump of a tongue tried to tell Papa something.

As he came abreast of him, Isaac reached out a finger, pointing in the direction of the clearing. Then, he turned his body sideways, which Papa knew was done to make himself less of a target, just as he had taught all his children. Despite not seeing or hearing whatever had alarmed the boy, he started to do the same himself, at the same time reaching into the lining of his coat for Doctor Wellman's gun.

"It's all right," he whispered. "We'll get 'em."

A swishing sound reached their ears, and instinctively, Papa stepped back, dropping to a crouch that made his leg feel as if the jaws of a bear trap had snapped shut on it. Grimacing, he scanned the trees ahead. The moonlight revealed nothing, but the strange swishing sound continued.

Isaac started to head for the clearing, the twigs snapping underfoot, his urgency forcing him to betray his location.

For whoever was watching them, it was enough.

A rope sailed out into the dark toward them, the end coiled into a noose that moved through the air like a bubble, the loop wobbling.

"Isaac," Papa yelled, and the boy raised his head, then his arms, hands splayed as the noose came down and was jerked tight, the rope cinching around the boy's wrists instead of his neck.

Papa rose and hobbled toward Isaac. "No!"

The boy was jerked off his feet so fast and hard his head snapped back and his legs kicked straight out behind him as he was pulled with impossible speed into the trees.

Cursing, Papa was momentarily paralyzed by indecision. Follow and try to save the boy, or seek cover? It was a trap, he knew. Going after Isaac was just what the coyotes wanted. They would draw him in among them where he would be outnumbered and they would kill him.

From the trees, a muffled moan.

"Isaac," he whispered.

He had to hide.

He heard a dull thumping sound that changed as he listened, became wet, like someone smacking a rubber glove against a fencepost. Slowly, Papa began to back away, stopping when the sound did. He removed the gun from his coat and readied it, his ears attuned to the slightest of movements from the trees.

The cessation of that sound told him that Isaac was lost. He was alone now, except for Krall and Luke, neither of whom had been seen since the coyotes showed up. For all Papa knew, they might have fallen.

He had to get away from here. The corrupted were encroaching on him from every side. He could sense them now, thought that he could even see them as fleeting shadows between the trees. And he could smell them, the musky putrid scent of poisoned flesh. It was growing stronger and now he turned full circle, catching faint glimpses of their burning ember eyes watching him in amusement from wherever the dark was deepest.

He had to get away, but there was nowhere to go.

"Papa," a voice said, and startled, he spun, aiming the gun at the trees. A shadow detached from the phalanx of pines. "It's me."

"Luke?"

"Yes."

Papa did not lower the gun. "Where's your brother?"

"They're dead, Papa. All of 'em. The coyotes got 'em. Isaac too. I was hidin' up there on the far side of the clearin', waitin' for you. I saw 'em take him. But I got the son of a bitch. He's trussed up in there, ready for you."

Papa didn't move. He wanted to believe what Luke was saying, but the history between them suggested the enemy he should be fearing was not a coyote at all, but his own son, who should have been reborn, but had resisted, as he had resisted Papa all his young life.

"You lyin' to me boy?" he said, as he thumbed back the hammer and pointed the gun at Luke.

"Why would I lie?"

"'Cuz you've changed. Bein' inside your Momma changed you, but I suspect not the way we all wanted, not the way *she* wanted."

"I'm changed all right," Luke told him and stepped back into the trees. "I seen the light."

"Well," Papa said, licking his lips. "That's good, ain't it?"

"I reckon it is. I'm just mad I didn't see it sooner."

"They did this to us, Luke. This is all *their* doin', and there's only us left standin' to stop it."

"The corruption," Luke said. "The poison."

"That's right."

"Thing is," said Luke. "The light I seen told me somethin' different."

"Oh?" *Come out you little shit*, Papa thought. *Face me like the man I taught you to be.*

"Yeah. Angels told me you're the poison, and always have been. Said you used God as an excuse to hurt people, includin' your own kin."

Papa sneered. "Then it weren't angels you was hearin' boy."

Quiet settled in the woods. Papa listened, eyes narrowed, trying to discern Luke's form from the dark, but he could no longer make him out.

Of course, Papa himself had taught the boys how to make use of the night. He'd taught them well. Too well.

"Why don't you come out here and we can talk face to face? There ain't no cause for you to be lurkin' around in the dark. I'm your father. Whatever you need to discuss with me, we can discuss it right here in the open. I won't hurt you."

Nothing.

"Luke, I know you got questions, and I know you ain't yourself. But like it or not, I'm all you got left, and you're all I got. Time for both of us to make a clean break, son."

Leaves rustled as something scurried over them, but there was nothing to suggest he wasn't alone.

Breathing fast, he scanned the trees.

"*Son?*" Luke said suddenly, coldly, close to Papa's ear, and with a startled grunt, the old man turned. He had time only to register that Luke was holding a machete before it was buried in his shoulder, all but severing the arm holding the gun. His hand spasmed. The gun fell to the ground, and he staggered back screaming as Luke, bearing a face far too malevolent to ever be that of a mere devil, yanked the long blade free with a spurt of blood. The world dimmed and Papa clenched his teeth, animal panic paralyzing him. "Stop Luke...stop...for God's sake..." He raised his good hand, palm out. "Please, just... *listen*..."

With a short swing, Luke severed the hand. It tumbled into the leaves.

Papa screamed a second time, a hoarse guttural sound of horror and disbelief, the echo of it caught and sent back by the trees and the hills beyond. He dropped to his knees, unable to cradle the severed limb due to the unimaginable agony in the other.

"Stop it," he told Luke. "Listen...you have to stop. They...they poisoned you—"

"*You* poisoned me," Luke said tonelessly.

"No. No, there's only us. Only us, Luke," Papa babbled. "Me and you. Ain't too late. Not yet it ain't. Only *us*, Luke."

He looked up, tears streaming down his face.

Luke, bare-chested and blood-spattered, stood with his body lit by the moonlight, his face a patchwork of shadow. He was breathing calmly, his eyes like black ice.

"There ain't no us no more," he said, drawing back the machete like a baseball player aiming for a home run. "Only me."

The swing took Papa's head clean off at the shoulders.

For a moment, the old man's body stayed kneeling, the neck spurting blood upward like an offering to whatever God might thirst for such corrupted wine, then it dropped heavily to the ground.

Afterward, Luke tossed the machete into the brush and set about making a fire, being careful to ring the shallow pit he'd dug with stones to avoid burning down the woods. Then he stripped the old man's body naked, cut off the genitals and cooked them over the fire.

Under the stars, the eyes of his father still watching, the dead face given the impression of life by the flames, Luke sat alone, lost in thought.

He ate in silence.

FORTY-TWO

"I guess I gotta go," Pete said, looking longingly at the house in which Claire had said she expected a minor kind of Hell was awaiting her in the form of Kara's histrionics. Although he didn't say it, Pete would have considered such a greeting a fine one if it meant there was a house and people in it who loved him enough to care what became of him. Back in Elkwood, there was nothing but questions and the memory of violence he wasn't sure he'd been given the right to commit, if a right indeed even existed for such terrible acts. On the surface he'd done what he'd had to do to protect Claire, just as he had blinded a stranger to protect Louise, but when it came time for judgment, whether by man or by God, would those reasons be enough to save him?

"You don't have to," Claire said. Since leaving Elkwood, she had not let go of his hand, and he cherished the contact, the feel of her skin warm against his own. He knew he would wed her right then and there if he thought for one second she'd agree to it, but it was a preposterous idea. He could hope until the stars burned out and it wouldn't change the fact that they were two people from completely different worlds. For a time they'd walked the same road, but ultimately they were bound for different poles. It saddened him to think of leaving her, but staying would only mean more hurt.

"I do," he told her, meeting her watery gaze. "I don't belong here and I reckon over the next few weeks you're gonna have your hands full all over again." He sighed heavily. "Me too, I expect."

Around the truck the sky was vermilion, the clouds bruised violet. Morning birds awoke and began the opening strains of their day's symphony. The world was waking. To Pete, it signaled the end of their shared nightmare, but also the end of their association. He knew they would promise to stay in touch, but wouldn't as time forced them to grow back into their own routines.

"You did nothing wrong," Claire said, the sentence dropping in pitch as she glanced toward the house. Pete followed her gaze and noticed that a light had come on. "You were there for me."

"We're friends," Pete said with a shrug, wishing he had the courage to say more. *We're friends and that's all we'll ever be, but I love you, Claire. And right now, you're all I got in the world.*

"That sounds so simple," Claire replied. "And wrong."

With another wary glance at the house, she leaned over, cupped a hand behind his head and drew him close. During the drive here, he had rationalized the kiss at the Merrill House as one of relief or gratitude, particularly considering the iciness she had shown him prior to that moment, but there was no mistaking the motive behind the kiss she gave him now. It was soft and wet, and prolonged. As soon as she broke contact, she quickly initiated it again, her tongue briefly touching his own until he felt like he'd been electrocuted.

Finally she drew away. "We will see each other again," she said, and smiled. Then her face darkened. "Shit," and she opened the door and got out. He started to say something but instead watched as she hurried into the street. Her sister, Kara, was doing the same, coming from the opposite direction, dressed in a robe, her hair tousled, face grim, eyes dark with anger. Pete's hand moved to the keys, waiting for the moment when he would know without question that it was time for him to get moving.

The women met in the street and immediately began to argue, Kara's eyes roving over her sister, registering every cut and bruise as she gesticulated madly. Claire had her hands in her hair and was shaking her head with a pained expression. Then they stopped, and Kara looked directly at Pete.

He glanced away. The look had been his cue, and yet he couldn't turn the keys. His fingers gripped them tightly, his eyes on the road, his heart pounding, but he couldn't start the engine. He didn't want to, aware that as soon as he did, he would not just be leaving a quiet street in the rearview.

A tap on the glass made him jump. He looked and was surprised, and more than a little dismayed to see Claire's sister looking in at him. He cleared his throat, watched as she made a circular motion with her index finger.

He rolled down the window, the word *Sorry* already on his tongue.

"You got a call," she said, and that made him swallow the word. It had been the last thing he'd expected to hear.

"A call?"

Kara ran a hand through her hair. She looked tired. Dark bags hung under eyes made shallow with worry. "Yeah. A cop in Detroit."

Pete swallowed, felt himself stiffen with panic. "What...?" he started to say, then shook his head.

"They said they want to talk to you."

"About what?"

"About a woman up there. Louise something."

The mention of her name made him ache inside. In all that had happened, his mind had not been able to entertain more than one sorrow at a time, but he realized now, in the days ahead, he would have nothing but time to ponder them.

"She's dead," he said. "She got hurt."

Kara frowned at him. "She's not dead."

He gaped at her, sure he hadn't heard her correctly. "What?"

"She's in the hospital, but she's not dead. She asked for you. Told the cop you were her only living kin, so they want you to come up. Wanted you to know she got hurt, but apparently that's not news to you."

Stunned, he smiled at her and shook his head.

Kara did not look like she shared his joy. "Seems like trouble just draws you to it, doesn't it?"

"Thank you," he told her with genuine warmth. She could stick her arms in and throttle him, or curse him to high Heaven and it wouldn't make a damn bit of difference now because Louise was *alive*. He was almost afraid to believe it. "Thank you, Ma'am," he said again and glanced at Claire, who'd been listening. She was smiling at him, a light in her eyes anyone else might have said was simply a reflection of the sun as it crept over the horizon, but he knew better.

ABOUT THE AUTHOR

Born and raised in Dungarvan, Ireland, Kealan Patrick Burke is the Bram Stoker Award-winning author of five novels (*Master of the Moors*, *Currency of Souls*, *Kin*, *The Living*, and *Nemesis: The Death of Timmy Quinn*), over a hundred short stories, three collections (*Ravenous Ghosts*, *The Number 121 to Pennsylvania & Others*, and *Theater Macabre*), and editor of four acclaimed anthologies (*Taverns of the Dead*, *Quietly Now: A Tribute to Charles L. Grant*, *Brimstone Turnpike*, and *Tales from the Gorezone*, proceeds from which were donated to children's charity PROTECT.)

Kealan has worked as a waiter, a drama teacher, a mapmaker, a security guard, an assembly-line worker at Apple Computers, a salesman (for a day), a bartender, landscape gardener, vocalist in a grunge band, and, most recently, a fraud investigator. He also played the male lead in *Slime City Massacre*, director Gregory Lamberson's sequel to his cult B-movie classic *Slime City*, alongside scream queens Debbie Rochon and Brooke Lewis.

When not writing, Kealan designs covers for print and digital books through his company Elderlemon Design (elderlemondesign.com). To date he has designed covers for books by Richard Laymon, Brian Keene, Scott Nicholson, Bentley Little, William Schoell, and Hugh Howey, to name a few.

In what little free time remains, Kealan is a voracious reader, movie buff, videogamer (Xbox), and road-trip enthusiast.

Visit him on the web at www.kealanpatrickburke.com.

Printed in Great Britain
by Amazon